Daughter of Wind and Moonlight

K. S. Gerlt

Special thanks to mom and all of my dear friends for your love and support.

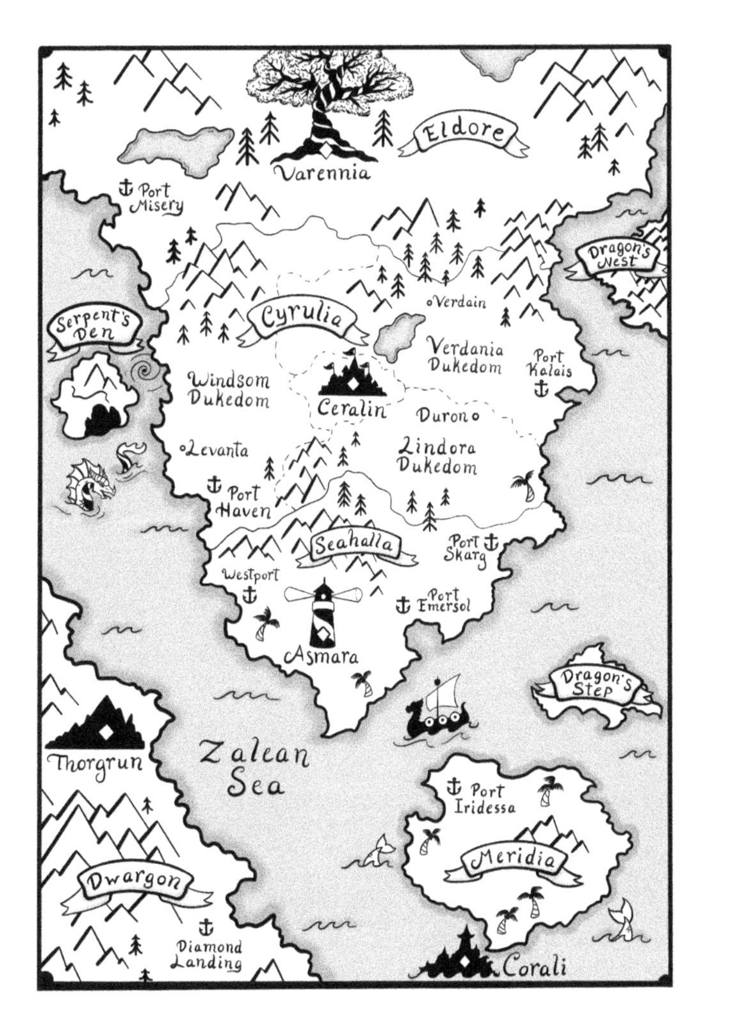

Varennia
Eldore
Port Misery
Dragon's Nest
Serpent's Den
Cyrulia
Verdain
Verdania Dukedom
Port Kalais
Windsom Dukedom
Ceralin
Duron
Lindora Dukedom
Levanta
Port Haven
Seahalla
Port Skarg
Westport
Port Emersol
Asmara
Dragon's Step
Thorgrun
Zalean Sea
Port Iridessa
Meridia
Dwargon
Diamond Landing
Corali

Prologue

Another day, another fight.

Today my opponent was an elven warrior, her twin daggers flashing in the flickering torch light. The disgusting mud beneath my feet, a mixture of dirt, sweat and blood, made it difficult to dodge her whirling blades, but I was used to that.

Unfortunately for her, I was well versed in how to defeat an opponent wielding twin blades. The memory of the friend who had taught me that rose unbidden in my mind, along with an accompanying pang of grief and regret. But I pushed it down, burying it deep in my mind, in the place where all my happy memories were laid to rest.

I felt a sting across my cheek as one of the elf's daggers flashed by my head, my blood the price of my moment of distraction.

I growled at her smirk, tightening my grip on my own twin daggers. If that was how she wanted this fight to go, I was more than willing to oblige her. I darted in close, steel ringing on steel as our blades clashed. I dropped into a crouch, sweeping her legs out from beneath her.

She landed on her back with a soft *oof*, as the air left her lungs. Before she could recover, I pinned her arms to the mud with my knees, my blades resting against the scarred skin of her neck, just above her black collar.

The crowd went wild as the announcer called my victory. The downed elf glared angrily at me, her hatred stemming from the knowledge that her loss had just cost her tonight's dinner. But I stayed where I was for an extra few seconds, forcing the elf to remain in her submissive posture.

I wanted her to remember this moment the next time she thought to taunt me.

After another few moments, I got to my feet and sheathed my daggers in one fluid motion. I glanced half-heartedly at the crowd of masked spectators, the dark shadows in the eye holes of the masks making them seem far more monstrous than any of the opponents I was forced to face.

When I had first arrived here, I had desperately searched through the crowd of masked faces every chance I got, hoping against hope that I would see a pair of familiar blue eyes. Even a hint of sympathy would have eased my mind.

But all I saw today was glittering gold and silver, mouths turned up in greedy smiles or down in annoyance. Those who frowned should have known better than to bet against *me*.

But they would learn.

They would all learn.

I turned away, only the barest whisper of disappointment in my heart. I had a feeling that I wouldn't be looking for a familiar face much longer.

It was more than I could take.

More than I could bear.

As I exited through the tarnished bars of the pit's cage, I lightly bumped shoulders with the werepanther as she went to take my place in the ring for the next match. The barest hint of a smile touched her mouth, an expression echoed on my own features.

We silently wished each other luck in our own hidden language. After what had happened to my last friend in this place, I hadn't wanted to give away another piece of myself that I could never get back.

But the werepanther had been here far longer than I, and knew to keep a careful balance between her wins and losses. If it was her, I didn't have cause to worry, so long as we could avoid facing each other in a death match. So far, we'd been lucky, as I'd kept my win streak higher than hers to avoid that very scenario.

But the future was a silly, fickle mistress. And she took pleasure in dealing the final blow, once you thought you could sink no lower.

As the next match was announced and the crowd began to cheer and holler once more, I slunk into the shadows. My eyes swept over them for what I knew to be the final time, the embers of the hope I'd kept alive through it all finally going dark.

After tonight, I would not be looking for hope in that crowd.

Not one of those monsters knew sympathy.

And no one was coming to save me.

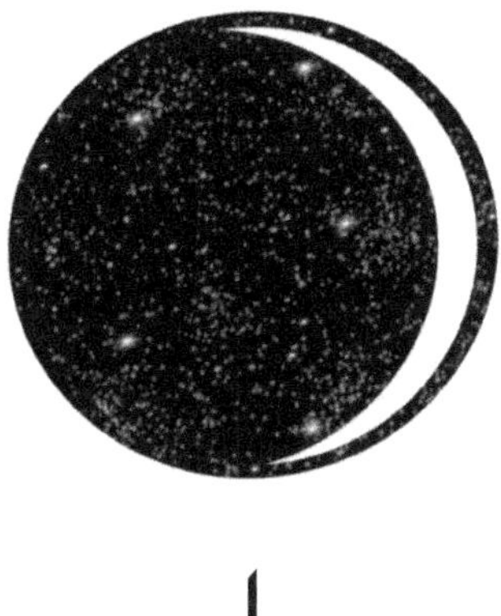

1

"Here's the next batch of dough," Aly grunted as she unceremoniously dumped the sticky mound onto the countertop in front of me.

Aly's new official title was Head Pâtissière, and she had taken to her pastry-making duties with gusto. Her warm brown eyes shimmered with delight as we baked, despite the smears of flour on her face and hands. Not that I was one to talk, considering I'd managed to get flour and frosting *in my hair*, of all places.

"Thanks Aly," I said warmly, a smile tugging at my lips.

She nodded and went back to frosting the cinnamon buns that were still cooling, leaving me with my thoughts and the task in front of me. She was so perceptive that way—she could tell when I needed some time to work through my thoughts.

I got to work kneading the dough as Aly began humming a cheerful little tune, the luscious aroma of baking rolls mixing with the sweet scent of the icing. Somehow, it seemed like the only thing in my life that hadn't changed drastically was making—and eating—cinnamon rolls.

Two and a half weeks had flown by since I narrowly escaped marriage to the now deceased son of Duke Lindora, as well as death by his hand. It was only thanks to Fenn that I was still alive at all—though the cost of my life had been steep.

My humanity.

I hadn't had the nerve to try and get close to my horse, Atlas, since that day. Though a little thrill ran through me at the thought that I actually owned a horse—finally! Ever since I was little, my dream was to one day own my own horse ranch, and I'd been working towards that dream little by little, day by day, at the Rangers' ranch just outside of my hometown, Verdain. Just a couple more years, and I would have owned my favorite horse, Soren.

But when Lester Lindora had waddled into my life, that future had gone up in smoke. Literally. The madman had actually burned down the Rangers' ranch after he imprisoned them in order to blackmail me into submission. I had been devastated to learn from Chris, my childhood friend, that Lester had slaughtered my dear Soren, and either taken or sold the rest of the horses. At least I knew Soren had gone to a better place—the dream-like ranch I saw as I lay dying.

I sobered at that thought. Fenn had also arranged for a proper funeral and burial of what remained of his parents and little brother on the grounds of the Verdania's family cemetery. It had been a marvelously dreary affair—all of the nobles, and even the emperor himself, had attended. The ceremony was incredibly difficult for Fenn. I held his hand through the whole thing, rubbing calming circles on the back of his hand, despite the crescents his nails left on my skin. I think laying his red rose on top of their coffin was the hardest moment for him. Even my eyes misted over.

But we'd managed to get through it all, somehow. At least now Fenn had some closure, and a place to visit his parents and little brother. He and I had spent an afternoon planting a red rosebush behind the elegantly carved headstone ourselves. Come springtime, there would be a dusting of rose petals there, next year and every year after.

Now finished with kneading the dough, I began cutting it into long strips, laying each one aside. Next, I generously sprinkled cinnamon on the strips before rolling each one up and placing them on a baking sheet. Fenn and I didn't exactly have to worry about running out of ingredients anymore, thanks to the stolen funds the Lindoras had returned to Fenn.

A large portion of that money was being used to restore the Verdania estate to its former glory, as well as re-establish the road connecting the castle to the town of Verdain. Without constant magical maintenance, the forest would grow over anything in its way.

A smaller chunk of the funds Fenn was saving to fund our upcoming search—and hopefully rescue—mission. In a last-ditch effort to save his skin, Lester had revealed that after he'd finished "playing" with Fenn's sister, he'd sold her as a slave to the highest bidder. He'd died before we could get any more details out of him, but at least now Fenn had a whisper of hope that his sister was alive, somewhere.

For the time being, we were waiting for Baldie—otherwise known as Dorent, a shadow assassin of the dark guild Keir—to turn up with some new leads for us. Dorent could dig up just about anything—for the right price, that is. Fortunately, gold was no longer an obstacle.

Besides, Fenn had been absolutely buried under a mountain of paperwork since the moment we'd returned. Turns out being the acting duke actually just entailed piles of paperwork and decision-making, instead of simply attending social events. Well, at least when it came to Fenn anyways. I think he felt bad about leaving the people in his territory to fend for themselves for so long after his parents were killed, and was trying to fill the void they had left behind.

Alone.

I clenched my fists compulsively.

If only I could help him, lessen his workload. I could read and write, and do some basic arithmetic, but that was about the extent of my knowledge. And that wasn't nearly enough to make any kind of significant dent in the paperwork pile, let alone help him make strategic decisions about revitalizing trade routes that had become prey to bandits, managing the finances of the castle, or organizing diplomatic meetings and relations with the kingdom on Verdania's northern border, Eldore.

The sharp clang of metal hitting metal made me wince, startling me out of my somber thoughts. Aly was pulling the puffed-up cinnamon rolls out of the oven and depositing them on the cooling rack, which was the noise I'd heard. I still wasn't used to my newly-enhanced hearing, and noises I'd heard hundreds of times before now threw me off with their sharpness. Fenn had assured me that I'd get used to it eventually during the training sessions he still managed to make time for everyday. I could practically hear him pacing, the grass crunching under his boots...

I glanced at the clock by the oven, surprised at how late it had gotten. The first rays of dawn were already filtering through the beveled glass windows. I cursed under my breath. I was late!

"I've got to get to training! Fenn is going to kill me," I groaned, annoyed with myself for losing track of time. *Again.*

"Have fun rolling around in the dirt with the Duke of Good Looks!" Aly teased good-naturedly, glancing in my direction.

"By the way, I think you've kneaded that one well enough, Serena," she stated as she looked pointedly at my right hand, which was still clenched in a fist.

I gasped when I glanced down to see the sticky remains of the cinnamon bun I'd been forming when I zoned out. Hurriedly, I scraped the dough off my palm and popped it into my mouth. My cheeks flamed, whether from her teasing or the mangled pastry, I wasn't quite sure. Maybe both.

"Sow-wry," I mumbled sheepishly around the sugary dough as I scrambled to wash my hands and take my apron off at the same time.

"Now we have an odd number," Aly scolded, her eyebrows pinching together. But there was laughter in her eyes, and a rueful smile on her face, so I grinned back at her.

"Let's make it even then!" I exclaimed as I grabbed one of the still warm, iced buns from the latest batch as I ran out the door.

Aly's laughter rang out behind me as I dashed out of the kitchens and darted past the rose garden and white gazebo where I'd first met Fenn—well, human Fenn, anyways. Rounding the newly trimmed hedges, the scent of freshly-cut grass and flowers invading my nose, I nearly ran into Chris, my quick reflexes saving him from having a cinnamon bun squashed into his shirt.

"Serena!" he exclaimed, surprise and delight flitting across his features.

"Hi Chris," I said a little too breathlessly.

His warm brown eyes flicked over my messy hair, noting the spots of flour that had managed to find a way around my apron and the pink still staining my cheeks, and deepened into pools of molten chocolate.

I glanced down, confused by the heat in his gaze. I'd seen his eyes take on that molten hue plenty of times before, like when he'd pulled a stray piece of hay out of my hair when we were working in the stables, and when I'd laughed at his silly jokes during dinner with the Rangers. Before I'd met Fenn, I hadn't thought anything of it, but now...

My eyes fell on the pastry still clutched in my hands, and I abruptly lifted it up, holding the treat out to him.

"Here, this is for you," I said quickly.

"Thanks, Serena," he said a little huskily.

His warm, calloused hands brushed mine as he took the cinnamon bun, lingering a little longer than necessary. I quickly drew my hands back, hiding them behind my back.

"It's fresh out of the oven. I've been baking with Aly today. Oh, and you don't have to worry about it being too sweet—Aly won't let me dump the entire bag of sugar into the frosting," I rambled. I really needed to go find Fenn.

"I'm sure it could never be as sweet as you," Chris murmured, his eyes dropping to my lips.

I swallowed nervously, his gaze tracking the motion.

"Think of it as a gift for doing such a good job looking after Atlas for me," I said quickly, scrambling for a topic that felt safe.

"He misses you, you know," Chris said seriously. "We both do."

I smiled stiffly, the motion not quite feeling right on my face.

"I know. I mean, I do too. I just...need a little more time to heal," I said softly, my eyes shifting to look over Chris' shoulder as the lie left my lips.

"You can always still visit him, even if you're not ready to ride yet," Chris said gently. "Have most of your injuries healed now?"

I glanced at his face, relaxing a fraction at the genuine concern in his now normal-looking eyes.

"You're right," I said, smiling for real this time. "I'm doing much better now, and I'll come to the barn for a visit. Soon."

"I'm going to hold you to that," Chris said jovially, gesturing with the cinnamon bun in a mock salute.

"I have to get going, but I'll see you later," I said as I stepped around Chris.

"See you later," Chris replied, the same way he always used to whenever I went home after a day of working on the ranch with him.

Except this time, I felt his eyes lingering on my back long after I rounded another corner and was hidden from his sight.

2

I couldn't help the smile that bloomed on my face as I spotted Fenn waiting for me in what had become our training spot. He wore his usual breeches, soft leather boots and a simple linen shirt, though he'd started actually combing his hair these days, now that he had so many meetings to attend.

And he was indeed pacing back and forth across the grass.

"Fenn!" I called out to him as I jogged over.

His pacing stilled as he stopped to look in my direction. Butterflies took flight in my core as our eyes met, though they settled down at the frown creasing his face.

"I'm so sorry I'm late," I gushed as I reached him, trying not to sound too winded. "Though I'm surprised you didn't hear me coming," I added, tilting my head in question.

"I have too much on my mind," Fenn snapped, his eyes flashing. "I would have brought some work to do if I'd known you were going to be this late."

I flinched at his tone, surprised.

"I really am sorry Fenn. I know how busy you are. It won't happen again," I stated evenly, dropping my gaze and reining in the urge to snap back from the sting his words caused. "I made some fresh cinnamon buns with Aly and simply lost track of time. I was hoping you and I could enjoy them together this afternoon, if you have a few minutes to spare."

I glanced up at Fenn as I said that last part, noting how his gaze softened, the brittle blue returning to that shade of calm blue waters I loved so much. He ran a hand through his hair, sighing.

"That sounds great. You know I love anything you make. And I'm sorry for snapping," he said ruefully. "I just—I wasn't ready for all of this—this responsibility and pressure."

"It's all right, I understand. Please tell me if there's anything at all I can help you with," I offered sincerely, taking his hands in mine.

Fenn smiled down at me, interlacing our fingers.

"I will," he said warmly. "Seeing you already does wonders for me."

He leaned his forehead against mine, creating a secret space for our breath to mingle. The world finally quieted, the distant murmur of voices and hammering of wood fading into obscurity. There was only the two of us in this moment.

I breathed in, his sunshine and pinewood scent dancing on the tip of my tongue, flooding my senses. I closed my eyes, tilting my face ever so slightly upwards. Wordlessly, Fenn captured my lips with his own, kissing me so gently and sweetly that even a freshly baked cinnamon bun couldn't compare.

He pulled back as he ran his fingers through my ruby hair, his eyes deepening into azure pools.

"What's this?" he laughed as he brought his hand up to his nose, sniffing at the frosting on his fingers.

I blushed as he licked his fingers, embarrassed but strangely happy at the same time.

"I told you I was baking," I mumbled through the grin on my face. "What do you think of the frosting?"

"It's sweet," he said with a smile. "Not as sweet as you, though."

At that point, I think my face must have matched the color of my hair.

"Come on, let's get to training," I laughed, turning and pulling Fenn behind me.

If Fenn noticed my clumsy attempt to change the subject, he didn't mention it. Though my newly enhanced hearing picked up on his low chuckle.

Once we got to the starting point for our warm-up run, Fenn was—mostly—all business.

"Let's go for three laps today," he instructed. "I think your stamina should be at the point where you can handle that distance now."

I bit my lip, but nodded. This reminded me of the time I'd raced Fenn around the estate, him on foot and me on Atlas. Fenn had won, much to my surprise. On my own two feet, I'd barely been able to sprint one lap without getting winded.

Well, before the change, at least.

We started off running, Fenn leading the way in front of me, making sure not to drift too far ahead. We both took in the sights and smells of the castle waking up. The late risers were just scurrying out of their beds and to their work areas, only to be scolded by their department heads. The scent of fire drifted on the air as the chefs began preparing breakfast. I smiled, imagining Head Pâtissière Aly cutting off any complaints about the early hour with a quick, "You call *this* early?" The distinct sound of whinnying and then munching reached my ears as the stablehands—including Chris—filled the horses' troughs with grain and hay. I felt the urge to go and run my fingers through Atlas' silky mane, and pet the soft muzzles of the other horses that had been reclaimed from Lester's stables. But I resisted, partly because my changed scent might frighten the horses, and partly because of who I knew would be there.

Our run flew by in no time, and I was not even breathing heavily. Even the added weight of the dagger I always kept strapped to my thigh had barely slowed me down. The approving nod Fenn directed my way sent warm tingles through me.

"Next up, conditioning and hand-to-hand combat," Fenn said.

"Race you there?" I challenged playfully.

Before Fenn could respond, I took off across the grass, aiming for our sparring ring that was situated between the rose garden and the stables, behind the estate. I heard surprised laughter behind me, followed by the sound of Fenn's boots flying across the grass, quickly closing the distance.

"You'll have to go faster than that," Fenn teased as he came up next to me.

In lieu of a reply, I put on another burst of speed and our training grounds rapidly drew closer. Just as I was about to set foot on the dirt, I half-turned to say, "That fast enough for you?" with a triumphant grin on my face. But then Fenn blurred past me onto the dirt, cocky grin firmly in place.

"Never slow down until you've reached the goal," Fenn teased gently.

I sighed dramatically, walking over to him slowly.

"You and your sayings can eat my foot," I complained with an exasperated smile.

"Don't tempt me," Fenn growled playfully, a mischievous spark in his eyes.

My ears grew warm, but not from the run.

"Pft. You wicked carnivore! C'mon, quit teasing me and start teaching me already," I told him.

"Fine, fine," Fenn said, gesturing for me to take up my fighting stance.

I did so, and we went through a quick review of the proper forms, Fenn's warm hands gently correcting the posture of each stance until I had it correct. Next, we moved on to some light, patterned sparring. But when I went to throw a punch, I underestimated my speed, and instead of my fist stopping just shy of Fenn's blocking arm, I accidentally made contact.

"Ugh, not again! Sorry Fenn, I didn't hurt you, right?" I asked as I stepped back.

Fenn grinned at me. "It would take much more than that to hurt me."

I smiled at him, but then scowled and looked down. "I had this down before. Why can't I manage to do any of the moves properly?"

"You have to be patient with yourself. It will take some time before you get used to the changes that come with being a werewolf," Fenn said gently. "Before, when you were human, you knew what your limits were, and what you were capable of. You discovered what those limits were over time, by pushing yourself."

I nodded.

Fenn thought for a moment, then continued.

"Now, those limits have been pushed farther back. Where before, you would have hit a wall, now there's nothing there but empty space. I know that must be unsettling for you. But it's the exact same process as before; push yourself to find out where your new limits lie and what your body is now capable of. Once you have, regulating how much speed or strength you need to use will become second nature to you again."

"How long will that take?" I asked with a sigh.

"That all depends on you. But based on the fact that we haven't had another *Incident*, I would say you're making great progress," Fenn finished with a little smile.

I groaned at the mention of The Incident.

"That was so embarrassing," I grumbled.

My very first training session after I'd woken up as a werewolf, after speeding through my old conditioning exercises without breaking a sweat, I'd tried practicing with my throwing knives on a red target that was just a little further away than usual. Long story short, my aim was off, and my newfound strength had propelled my little knife straight through the sculpted lion statue nearby, which had been a solid fifty feet behind my target.

Fenn had stared at the crumbled ruin where the statue used to be and promptly said, "Remind me not to get on your bad side." At my horrified look, he'd laughed, but then tried valiantly to say with a straight face, "I never liked that one much anyways." He'd waved off my apologies, saying that he was planning on remodeling that particular sculpture when the repairmen arrived, anyways.

I couldn't help glancing over at the sculpture guiltily. I could see a couple of men who were in the process of removing the rest of the rubble to make room for a new sculpture. I felt bad for adding to their already full workload. I was curious about what kind of statue would take the old one's place, but I hadn't yet worked up the nerve to ask Fenn about it.

Fenn caught me looking and smirked.

"You're never going to let me live that one down, are you?" I asked ruefully.

"Not in this lifetime," he said cheerfully.

"Just you wait until *I* have something to tease *you* about!" I threatened half-heartedly, shaking my finger at him.

"Like that'll happen," Fenn scoffed. "But if you insist, maybe I should make the replacement statue a monument to you and call it 'The Incident.' I can just see it now!"

"You wouldn't dare!" I gasped dramatically, delicately putting a hand over my heart in mock outrage.

"Oh, wouldn't I?" he asked, lifting one eyebrow.

For a second, we both just stared at each other. Then we burst out laughing at our own ridiculousness.

"Thanks, Fenn," I said with a smile.

"Feeling better now?" he asked with such a tender look in his eyes that I wanted to melt.

I nodded, not trusting my voice at that moment.

Fenn glanced at the angle of the sun, which was now well above the treetops.

"What do you say we get a little more practice in before I have to get back to work?" he asked.

"Sure!" I said, happy for any extra free time he had to give me.

The butler who had once worked for Fenn's parents, and whom Fenn had recently located and re-hired, Harold, found us furiously playing a game of tag a short while later. Fenn said that playing games like this would help me with figuring out where my new limits were even better than simply doing strengthening exercises, or even patterned sparring.

Either way, I certainly found it more fun. The only problem was, that meant time flew by much faster too.

"Your Grace, it's almost time for your first meeting of the day, with the builders!" Harold called out from a safe distance.

I looked over at Harold, noting how the morning sunlight bounced off of his bald crown. The poor man was suffering from a receding hairline, which seemed rather ironic given his name. He always seemed to keep a handkerchief on his person, and was constantly dabbing at the ever-increasing expanse of his forehead.

My moment of distraction nearly cost me. I managed to dodge just in time, as Fenn's hand whipped a hair's breadth away from my shoulder.

"Ha!" I shouted as I moved out of the way. I wobbled for a second, trying to regain my balance.

Fenn pounced, lightly pushing me backwards so that I fell into his arms.

"I see you've fallen for me," he teased, blue eyes finding mine.

I grinned up at him, too comfortable where I was to be mad about losing the game. Again.

"What's not to love?" I answered without thinking. My cheeks flamed when I realized what I'd said. I vaguely remembered telling Fenn I loved him as I was fading, and although he seemed happy to kiss me and tease me, he hadn't actually said the words back. Of course, I had no intention of pushing—he'd just buried his family, for crying out loud—but I couldn't help the slight twinge of unease.

Fenn's eyes dropped to my lips, and he kissed me a little more demandingly this time. I wrapped my arms around his neck, pushing any doubts to the back of my mind, and kissed him back, running my fingers through his short, pitch black hair.

"A-hem!" Harold cleared his throat loudly.

We reluctantly separated, Fenn setting me on my feet. I looked down self-consciously, embarrassed about having an audience.

"Yes, Harold?" Fenn sighed.

"The meeting, Your Grace," Harold stated stiffly, pulling out his pocket watch, "started five minutes ago."

Fenn swore, scrubbing a hand through his hair.

"Looks like I'm running late now too," he said, glancing affectionately at me.

"Just tell them they can pillage a batch or two of cinnamon buns, and I'm sure they'll forgive you," I said sweetly.

Fenn chuckled. "Good plan. I've got to go, but you can keep practicing if you want."

He interlaced our fingers and brought the back of my hand to his lips, pressing a light kiss to it. A warm tingle lingered there even after I'd let my hand fall back to my side.

I nodded as he and Harold started walking back towards the estate.

"Don't forget about tea this afternoon!" I called to Fenn's retreating back.

"I would never," he assured me with a little wave.

3

"Lady Serena, are you almost done in there? If we don't start getting you ready soon, you'll be late for tea," Sophia warned.

I jolted fully awake, some of the now lukewarm bath water sloshing over the sides of the clawfoot tub. I was so comfortable that I must have dozed off.

"I'll be right out!" I called.

Although most noble ladies expected their personal attendants to bathe them, I had been extremely uncomfortable with the idea. I'd insisted I could bathe myself, thank you very much, and that had been the end of that. However, I gladly accepted the appointment of Lily and Sophia as my personal maids. I could definitely use their help when it came to styling.

I hastily climbed out of the tub, trying not to spill more water for someone else to clean up, dried myself off with a fluffy towel, and threw on the luxuriously soft robe Fenn had given me. After wrapping my long hair up in the towel on top of my head, I exited the bathroom into my new room.

Sophia and Lily looked up from what they were doing. Lily tried desperately not to laugh, but ended up making a funny little wheezing noise instead. Sophia came over to me, armed and dangerous.

I gave Lily my best stink eye expression, and she was suddenly very busy arranging the dress she'd selected for me.

"I'll do her hair while you finish up with the dress," Sophia instructed Lily as she led me over to the vanity and set her weapons—I mean, the combs and brushes—down with a sharp *clack*.

"What was so funny?" I asked Sophia, raising one eyebrow.

"You missed a strand," she informed me, pointing to my updo in the mirror.

I laughed aloud when I saw the strand of long red hair seemingly sprouting out of the towel at an impossible angle. I sighed, rubbing my hands over my face, and peeked at Sophia from between my fingers.

"So it seems. How bad is it?" I grimaced.

Sophia pursed her lips, critically examining my hair as she unwound the towel. My hair fell to my back in one big, wet clump.

"Well, it's certainly very tangled. But," she said, glancing at the clock, "I think I can manage. Any special styling requests today?"

"Just something simple," I suggested.

"I'll do my best," Sophia assured me, arming herself once again with her weapon of choice—a fine-toothed comb.

I tried not to wince.

An hour of excruciating detangling later, I stood in front of the floor-length mirror, admiring the results of my personal attendants' hard work. The long, flowing dress I wore whispered against my skin as I moved, the pastel florals reminding me of springtime. The bodice was trimmed with crystals that sparkled when I moved, and the sleeves fluttered about my shoulders like gossamer fairy wings.

My hair hung down my back in gentle waves, with two sections pulled back and tied with a jeweled hairpin. Two more sections framed my face, and an elegant emerald necklace glimmered at my throat. I touched it reverently, my fingertips gliding over the smooth facets of the gemstones.

I looked like a princess.

I felt like an impostor.

Just a handful of months ago, I was sleeping on straw, wearing clothes covered in hand-sewn patches, and mucking out horse stalls. Now here I stood, wearing an outfit whose cost likely would have fed and clothed myself and my mother for *years.*

I loved Fenn, and I was grateful for the nice things he insisted on giving me. But I couldn't help but feel...uneasy. Like at any moment, Fenn would suddenly change his mind, and I'd go back to living in the little cottage by the woods. And he'd continue on as the new Duke Verdania, forgetting all about me.

"Lady Serena?" Sophia asked, concern tinging her voice. "Is something wrong?"

I shook my head to clear it of such silly thoughts. Fenn cared about me, and that was all that mattered. Even if the worst happened, I swore I would never end up like my mother, alone and bitter. That oath was etched into my soul.

Pasting a smile on my face, I turned to Sophia and Lily, who were waiting by the door.

"No, everything is fine. You both outdid yourselves today. Thank you," I said with genuine warmth.

Sophia looked relieved, and both she and Lily dropped into a curtsy and murmured, "Our pleasure, Milady."

"I will see you when I get back," I informed them. I had just enough time to walk to the tearoom, so I would arrive perfectly on time.

Both nodded.

Just as I stepped out the door, I half-turned and said, "Oh, and there may still be a few cinnamon buns in the kitchen; I would hurry though, before Aly and Wendy eat them all!"

I winked cheekily at them, happy to see their big smiles. With that, I strode through the hallways, noting how the freshly-polished wooden floors now gleamed in the afternoon sunlight. Even the decorative suits of armor were now dust-free and sparkling.

As I made my way to the tearoom, memories rose unbidden in my mind. Of the torturous walks to Lester's tearoom, dread coiled in the pit of my stomach like a serpent. Of the relief I'd felt on the walks away from Lester's tearoom, when even my own skin felt like it had become covered in filth.

My hand automatically rose to my throat, searching for my silver crescent moon pendant and Vulclaria feather, but finding only emeralds and gold. I panicked for a moment before remembering that my moon necklace was safely stored in my room, since I could no longer touch it without being burned. The lack of its comforting weight made it feel like I was missing a part of myself. But at least I'd tied my downy Vulclaria feather to the hilt of my dagger, which I kept strapped to my thigh at all times. Well, except when I was bathing. Then I kept it within arm's reach.

I gave myself a mental shake. Having tea with Fenn was *nothing* like teatime with Lester. I could handle it. And I could enjoy it. No, I *would* enjoy it! Besides, taking tea "properly" achieved two things at once; first, it meant I could spend more time with Fenn. Second, it ensured that bad rumors about Fenn would not start circulating among the nobility of the Cyrulian Empire, who would have looked down upon a duke licking frosting off of his fingers, in the kitchens, with some random girl he picked up in the forest.

I sighed. And here I'd thought the aristocrats could make their own rules.

I slowed as I approached the closed doors to the tearoom. A little thrill of anticipation ran through me. I glanced down self-consciously. I wondered what Fenn would think, and my face grew warm.

Before I could psych myself out any more, I opened one of the gilded doors and slipped inside, eagerly scanning the room. Large windows looked out over the gardens, letting indirect sunbeams light the space with a warm, cozy ambiance. Beautiful oil paintings of flowers and peaceful landscapes lined the walls, which featured elegant wainscoting.

In the center of the room stood a small, round table, which was laden with teacups, trays filled with cinnamon buns and other fine pastries Aly had whipped up this morning, and a three-tiered stand, which contained artfully arranged macaron cookies in every color and flavor imaginable.

Placed on either side of the table was a cushioned chair, each covered in fine floral embroidery and gilded thread. These had likely been in Fenn's family for quite some time, considering that the Verdania family crest was carved into the backs of the chairs.

Both chairs, however, were empty.

I felt a little touch of disappointment, but quickly brushed it aside. After all, I had been a little late to our training session this morning. I supposed it was Fenn's turn to be late to something and even the score.

While I waited, I tried not to look at the enticing array of sweets spread out before me. I was determined to do the polite thing and wait for Fenn, so that we could enjoy the pastries together. I'm sure each one was the epitome of mouth-watering perfection, so I'd have to remember to give my compliments to Aly. And maybe I could save some for Sophia, Lily, and Wendy, just in case Aly didn't have any extras.

I glanced at the ornate clock on the wall. It felt like time had slowed down, invisible weight preventing the gilded hands from moving.

Fenn was fifteen minutes late.

Twenty.

I looked out the window, watching the birds flit amongst the newly manicured hedges and bushes, each singing its own unique song. I even spotted a little brown lizard, sunning itself on a rock.

Thirty.

Forty.

The ticking of the clock pounded in my ears, the sound reverberating in my skull. I could hear the scratching of a mouse in the walls, searching for crumbs. The murmur of the servants in the hall, the metallic clanging of pots and pans in the kitchens.

Fifty.

Sixty.

With nothing to focus on, nothing to distract me, the cacophony of the castle pressed down on my eardrums, getting louder and louder. I started breathing too fast, the rasping of my breath only making things worse. The sweet aroma of the pastries flooded my senses, choking me and turning rancid in my lungs, making bile rise in my throat.

I squeezed my eyes shut, clenching my teeth and my fists in an effort to calm down. But it just got worse, the talking and the breathing and the cleaning and my heart beating too fast, too loud. And then—quiet, and pain. I winced, opening my eyes to look down at my hands. The noises had receded to the background, replaced by the throbbing in my hands and gums.

Slowly, I uncurled my shaking fists. My nails had punctured the skin on my palms, leaving angry red crescents. I looked at my nails, and was alarmed to see wickedly pointed claws where my nails should be.

I gasped, somehow terrified and excited at the same time. I lifted my hands right in front of my face and examined my claws, marveling at their length before realizing they were still growing longer and wider.

My gums gave a pronounced throb, and I carefully felt around my teeth with the pads of my fingers, trying desperately not to scratch myself. I touched my canines and realized they were growing longer and sharper.

Suddenly I noticed that my shoes were now pinching my feet. Quickly I kicked them off, horrified to see claws rapidly replacing my toenails.

I felt way too warm and itchy. My blood felt like it was heating up, preparing to boil. I felt panic rising up my throat—I couldn't think, couldn't breathe.

I wasn't ready for this!

I had to think—hadn't Fenn mentioned something about how it had been challenging for him to stay calm and maintain human form when he'd had to speak with Lester's parents a while ago?

That must be the answer—I needed to calm down.

My skin rippled with goosebumps, a prickling, itching sensation sweeping over me, as if fur was about to sprout all over me.

I closed my eyes, covered my ears, and put my head between my knees. I erased every thought from my mind, and focused on breathing in deeply, and then slowly exhaling.

Over.

And over

And over.

When my mind was empty and my heart had stopped racing, I slowly sat up and opened my eyes. Cautiously, I peeked at my fingertips.

I felt a huge wave of relief when I saw my normal, clawless fingers in front of me. I felt my gums, examined my toes and my skin. All normal.

I sighed, leaning back in the chair. Even the cuts on my palms were almost gone. Now only thin pink lines remained.

Slowly, I put my shoes back on and wiped the blood off my hands with one of the linen napkins that was still beautifully folded on the table.

Glancing at the clock, I realized it was now two hours past when Fenn had agreed to meet me for tea.

I walked to the wall and pulled the rope that was meant to summon servants via the bell attached to its other end in a different room, hoping someone would appear. After a few minutes, an unfamiliar maid appeared, and I asked her to send the butler to me.

At least ten minutes later, Harold appeared, looking rather irritated.

"How can I be of assistance?" he asked, hands clasped behind him.

I noted the complete lack of respect, not only in his words but also in his tone of voice. I also realized his near-constant habit of clutching his handkerchief and dabbing at his shining chrome seemed to be exclusively active when Fenn was present.

Duly noted.

But after what I'd just gone through, I wasn't feeling quite as...eager to please as I usually did. In fact, I felt downright indignant. After all, where had this oh-so-important and proper man been when Fenn's family was attacked? Where had he been in the time since? Fenn may have been happy to see a familiar face, but I had my doubts. I narrowed my eyes at his haughty gaze. I let the silence stretch uncomfortably long.

Harold shifted awkwardly. His moldy scent took on an undertone of unease.

"Lady Serena?" he finally asked, shifting from foot to foot. He dropped his gaze submissively.

I grinned toothily at him, oddly satisfied with the display. But then I realized what I was thinking and felt a little shaken. *What was wrong with me?*

"Will Fenn be joining me for tea anytime soon?" I collected myself enough to ask.

"I'm afraid he has been extremely busy today," Harold sniffed, but quickly added, "My Lady," at my look.

A sinking feeling went through me. Really, what had I been expecting, anyways? Days filled with nothing but sweets and Fenn? He was a duke. He had responsibilities to take care of now. And I...here I was, sitting alone in a room for two hours. Useless.

"Harold, please take this to Fenn, so he may keep his strength up while seeing to his duties this afternoon," I instructed the butler as I filled a plate with two cinnamon buns and an assortment of small pastries and macaron cookies.

He looked rather surprised when I handed the plate to him, as if a lowly commoner such as myself should be incapable of a considerate act. If I wanted to be taken seriously, I needed to look and sound more like Fenn did when giving instructions.

"And have the rest of this packed up and distributed amongst the staff," I continued, my mind already racing ahead of me. "I will take a plate to my assistants myself. Please inform Fenn—" I paused, trying to keep my emotions out of my voice, "Please inform His Grace that should he have a spare moment, I will await his call."

"Yes, Lady Serena," Harold replied, an emotion I couldn't quite name flitting across his wrinkled features before disappearing, before he mumbled something. "Just like her."

"Just like who?" I asked, my sharp hearing making out the quiet words.

"Ah, pardon me, My Lady. You just...reminded me of my daughter for a moment." He looked surprised that I had heard him correctly.

"Oh, is she around my age? Does she live in Verdain?" I hadn't been aware that Harold had a family, and I was surprised that she didn't live here with him, like most of the servants' families did.

"She would have been a few years older than you, had she lived." Anger furrowed his brow, his haunted eyes staring through me and into a memory only he could see.

"I'm...terribly sorry to hear that," I stammered. "Though I will take it as high praise that I reminded you of her."

"Of course, Lady Serena," he responded stiffly, his features smoothing back into a placid expression. Despite his words, it felt like perhaps his statement had not quite been a compliment after all. The look in his eyes unnerved me, though I couldn't quite say why.

I quickly threw together another plate, piling it high with the sweets I knew Sophia, Lily, and Wendy would like. I'm sure Aly had had her fill long before the pastries ever reached this table.

"You may be dismissed," I said softly, not bothering to turn and look at him.

Harold stood still for a moment before he turned and left the way he'd come without another word.

Once I'd heard his footsteps fade down the hallway, I let my shoulders droop with an accompanying sigh.

After spending a few moments with my forearms braced against the table, eyes closed and breathing deeply, I straightened, grabbed the plate and walked to the door.

Before I stepped out, I squared my shoulders and took a deep, calming breath. I still felt a little queasy, and the pastries under my nose weren't helping. Normally, I would have been ecstatic to have so many expensive treats in my hands, but I could barely even look at them now. I had a feeling that even one bite would taste like ash in my mouth.

Schooling my features into a mask of nonchalance and trying to put the butler's odd behavior out of my mind, I opened the door, careful not to spill any of the sweets onto the newly polished floors. I strode purposefully back to my chambers, heedless of the whispers and pitying looks of those I passed.

I arrived at my rooms a short eternity later. Sophia and Lily were both working on adjusting the hem on one of my new dresses, but they looked up when I walked in. Two pairs of eyes took in my expression and then honed in on the plate in my hands.

"How did it go?" Lily asked tentatively.

She and Sophia set their work aside to come over to me.

"It didn't," I said curtly. "Fenn has other matters to attend to, and I'm tired of sitting alone. But I brought these for you to have. Could you also send some to Wendy?"

"Of course, Milady," Lily said as she took the plate from me and set it on a table. "Thank you for thinking of us."

"I'm sorry to hear the timing didn't work out," Sophia said quietly. "Would you like to continue your reading practice this afternoon?"

I paused, considering it, before shaking my head.

"I think I'll spend some time in the stables," I said slowly. "I need some fresh air. Would you help me change into some riding breeches?"

"Yes, right away," Sophia said, gesturing for Lily to go and fetch my riding gear. "Let's put away the hair pin and the necklace for now."

"Could you pull my hair into a low ponytail for me?" I asked, settling into the vanity chair with a sigh. "It doesn't need to look nice."

"As you wish, milady," Sophia acquiesced, her long, delicate fingers gently tugging my hair out of its carefully woven style and tying it at the nape of my neck with a simple ribbon.

After I changed into my white linen shirt and brown breeches, I pulled on my leather riding boots. I reattached my dagger to my thigh, running my fingers through the soft Vulclaria feather as I did.

"Thanks," I told Lily and Sophia. "Enjoy the pastries while I'm gone."

The pair curtsied as I exited my rooms once again.

I practically flew out of the main estate and headed straight for the stables, not even pausing to greet the repairmen. I needed to feel like *me* again.

Not the victim of Lord Lester.

Not the guest of Duke Fenrys.

Not a werewolf.

Just a girl with red hair who loved horses.

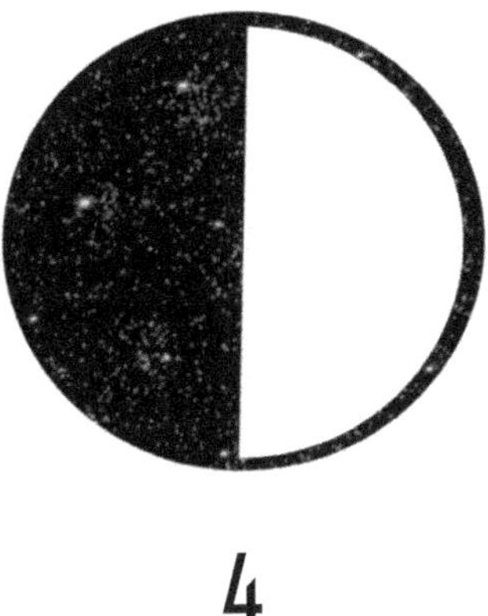

4

Setting foot inside the stables felt like coming home. I breathed in deeply, savoring the scents of leather, hay, and horses. The comforting sounds of the horses munching on hay, softly whickering, and stamping their hooves filled me with nostalgia. A feeling of warmth enveloped me as I slowly walked along beside the row of stalls. The bottom half of each door was closed, but the top half was open so that stablehands could check on the horses, and the horses could poke their heads over the door and check on the stablehands.

I glanced around a little nervously, searching for a familiar shade of sunny blonde hair. But the only other person in the stable was a young boy with brown hair, who was busy wheeling a wheelbarrow full of manure out towards the gardens.

Some of the horses that I passed pricked their ears forward at my approach, a couple flicking their ears back and forth uncertainly. I murmured a few quiet words to them, and that seemed to convince them that I meant no harm.

A few snorted at me in recognition. They were the Quarter Horses I'd helped take care of on the Rangers' ranch. I went over to them, tentatively reaching out a hand to stroke each velvety muzzle. They huffed a bit at my changed scent, but that didn't seem to bother them for long. Or stop them from nosing my hand, searching for carrots or treats.

"Next time," I promised, giving each horse a final, loving pat before I moved on to look for Atlas.

I soon found his name plate, and cautiously peered into his stall.

"Atlas?" I called softly.

I felt a touch of unease. Surely Atlas wouldn't be afraid of me now, would he? The other horses had known me longer, but I'd spent quite a bit of time with Atlas too.

Then Atlas poked his head over the stall door, hay sticking out of his mouth. I approached slowly, just to be safe, and held out my hand for him to sniff. He did, and then surprised me by pushing his nose under my hand, clearly asking for some petting.

A weight I hadn't known I'd been carrying seemed to lift from my shoulders, and I smiled in relief. I gently stroked his soft nose, delighting in the sensation of my fingers running over his silky coat.

"There's a good boy," I murmured, my eyes examining him from head to toe.

Clearly, someone had been taking very good care of him. His dark coat gleamed in the low light, and his silky mane and tail looked like they were tangle-free. He'd certainly been eating well, and his stall was as tidy as could be expected, given Atlas' tendency to move the bedding around to his liking.

"Fancy a trail ride today boy?" I asked quietly. "I promise this time will actually be relaxing—no more running for our lives."

His ears pricked forward eagerly.

"I'll take that as a definite maybe," I said with a smile.

I grabbed the rope halter that was hanging from a hook by his name plate and let myself into his stall. Atlas backed up to give me enough room to enter comfortably and lowered his head so I could slip the halter on. I paused to let him grab another mouthful of hay from the nearly-depleted pile before leading him out of his stall and to the spacious cross-ties.

I clipped the two ropes to either side of his halter and took my time giving him a thorough grooming with the neatly organized brushes that lay in their wooden box.

After giving Atlas a few loving pats on the neck, I turned and walked into the tack room. I scanned the rows of saddles, looking for the one I always used on Atlas. My eyes finally landed on it, ridiculous tassels and all. The style suited Atlas, even if it seemed a little flashy to me. Besides, it was super comfortable.

I took a few more steps into the dim interior and absently grabbed Atlas' saddle pad from the top of the pile. I noted disinterestedly that someone had left their cowboy hat next to the saddle pads.

"Hey, I was using that there blanket," a sleepy voice protested.

I jumped back, barely suppressing a shriek as I dropped the saddle pad and blindly reached for my dagger. The figure sat up, the hat that had been covering his face falling into his lap. I had almost fully unsheathed my weapon before I realized who I was looking at.

With an exasperated sigh, I resheathed my dagger, the whisper of metal ending in a solid *thunk* as the hilt connected with the top of the sheath. My heart rate slowly returned to normal, and now that I wasn't doing my best to completely block out the scents and sounds around me, I could indeed pick up on the sound of a heartbeat besides my own, accompanied by his warm scent of leather and hay.

"Chris!" I whisper-yelled, placing a hand over my heart, "You scared the living daylights out of me! What are you doing here?!"

"Well, I do work here, you know," Chris quipped as he stretched, his biceps pulling taut at the motion.

"Yes, I am aware," I said sarcastically, rolling my eyes at him. "I *meant*, why are you sleeping in the tack room in the middle of the afternoon?"

"Because I've already done everything that needed doing, and normally," he explained, glancing at me coyly, "no one comes to bother me this time of day."

"Well," I said, slightly amused, but trying not to show it, "I suppose that makes sense."

"It works out perfectly, doesn't it?" Chris said, a self-satisfied smile on his face.

"It does so long as I don't tell your mother about this little arrangement," I stated matter-of-factly with a straight face.

Chris' face actually paled a bit. He sat up straighter.

"You wouldn't dare," he said, his eyes narrowing in mock anger.

I tapped a finger on my chin, pretending to think about it.

"I suppose," I started, enjoying Chris' reaction, "I might be persuaded to keep this little incident just between us, if..."

"If what?" Chris asked, leaning forward, eyes glued to my face.

"If...you go on trail rides with me whenever I ask," I announced with a triumphant little grin.

Chris laughed out loud and slapped his knee. I pouted, a little put out by his reaction.

Catching sight of my expression, he reined himself in, wiping at the corner of his eye.

"I agree to your condition," he said with a mostly straight face. But then he cracked a grin and said, "You know I would have said yes to you anyways, without the blackmail."

"I know," I said with an answering smile of my own. "But teasing you is just too much fun to pass up."

"You can tease me anytime," Chris said a little huskily.

Choosing to ignore that comment, I bent down to retrieve the saddle pad I'd dropped earlier.

"I was actually coming in here to get Atlas' saddle to go on a trail ride right now. Want to come?" I asked, keeping my tone light.

"Absolutely," Chris said.

He scrambled to his feet, hastily popped his hat back on his head, and went to go get his horse ready.

I leaned forward in the saddle as Atlas flew over a fallen tree trunk, exhilaration swirling through me. When we landed, I directed Atlas to one side of the little clearing, giving him a pat on the neck for a job well done.

Then we both turned and watched as Chris and his bay horse sailed over the downed tree next, a grin lighting up his face.

"I'm so glad we found this clearing!" I said. "Let's come here every time we go for a trail ride."

"Don't have to tell me twice," Chris replied good-naturedly.

"One more time before we continue on?" I asked.

"Sounds like a plan."

Grinning, I lined Atlas up in front of our make-shift jump and urged him into a canter. I kept a light tension on the reins, estimating how many strides we had to go until we got to the log. When the last stride ended just a couple of feet from the jump, I pushed my hands and the reins up his neck and leaned forward as Atlas launched up and over. I loved this split second of weightlessness, when the whole world seemed to go still, if only for a moment. As Atlas' front hooves hit the earth once more, I leaned back in the saddle, bringing my hands back to their usual position in front of me.

After a few more strides I brought Atlas to a stop near the little path we'd forged through the undergrowth, giving him another love pat. I waited until Chris had also cleared the jump and had pulled up behind me before I turned Atlas onto the nearly invisible trail. We'd both learned the hard way that one horse starting to leave without the second horse would cause the second one to panic and disregard its rider in its desperation not to be left behind. Horses lived in herds for a reason; a lone horse was a dead horse.

Humans didn't seem too different in that respect. Loneliness wasn't fun no matter the species. I gave myself a mental shake, irritated at the direction my thoughts had taken.

"So, how is your family doing, Chris?" I asked, half-turning in the saddle to look back at him.

"They're all doing as well as can be expected," Chris replied after a brief pause.

A pang of guilt hit me, and it must have shown in my expression, since Chris hurried to say, "What happened wasn't your fault Serena. And they know that, same as I do."

"But if I hadn't attracted his attention, if I hadn't run away that night, then Lester never would have burned down your ranch, or thrown all of you into his dungeons," I whispered, my eyes misting. "And Soren would still be alive."

Chris urged his horse up next to mine now that the trail had widened up.

"Serena, it's not like you asked for any of this to happen," Chris sighed, running a hand through his hair. "You didn't seek out that bastard or ask him to marry you. He was rotten to the core long before you and I were even born."

His words reminded me of what Fenn had told me not long after we met, and the thought made my trembling lips form the ghost of a smile.

Seeing my tiny smile, Chris continued, "I think I would have been more disappointed if you'd gone along with his demands. Besides, knowing his personality, even if you had done as he wanted, he probably would have still taken anyone you cared about, just so he would have the leverage to keep you in line."

That made me pause. The truth of those words hit home, and I shuddered involuntarily. Lester had always needed to be in complete control of everything—and everyone—around him.

"You might be right," I murmured.

"Of course I'm right," Chris quipped confidently. "I'm always right."

That made me smile for real.

"So...your parents and your little brother don't...hate me, right?" I asked, my voice only wavering a little bit.

"Of course not! Sure, times were tough for a little while," Chris reassured me, a dark shadow passing across his features for a moment, as if the mere memory of his time with Lester brought phantom pain. "But you were able to get everyone Lester had taken out of there. And from what I heard of what happened, you weren't exactly having a picnic either."

"I was horrified to see how many people he'd imprisoned for no good reason," I added, remembering all the dirtied and bloodied faces that had emerged so fearfully into the light of day once more. The emperor himself had organized aid for those poor people.

"And as...great as Duke Verdania is, I don't think he would have offered to both rebuild my family's ranch complete with the horses that were taken *and* employ my entire family without some serious persuasion from a certain redhead," Chris said tentatively, casting a sly look in my direction.

I felt my ears grow warm.

"Fenn's been doing his best to help everyone who was affected by Lester's actions," I defended.

Chris raised an eyebrow.

"Though I may have asked Fenn to help you out a little more than he was originally planning," I conceded. "But I knew your parents had always wanted to travel around Cyrulia and visit Seahalla, and it just so happened that Fenn wanted to find some of the horses that Lester had sold off or lost in bets. It seemed like the perfect solution to have the Rangers make a family trip out of finding those horses for Fenn."

"It was just what they needed," Chris agreed. "The letter they sent detailed all the fun they were having. I don't think my brother will ever stop talking about it once they get back."

"You could have gone with them, you know," I said, peeking at Chris from the corner of my eye.

"I could have," he said slowly. "But then who would have kept an eye on the horses? Not that little guy, Tom."

"You mean that stableboy I saw earlier, mucking out stalls?" I asked. "He seemed to be doing a pretty decent job."

"Please, you haven't seen him try to tack up a horse. Somehow, he managed to put the halter on upside down and the saddle on backwards!" Chris complained.

"Did he really?" I asked, laughing at the picture of that scene in my head.

"*Yes!* And the girth was so loose, whomever had tried to get on would have ended up sliding off the other side of the horse!" Chris continued, animatedly gesturing for emphasis.

"As hilarious as that would be to watch, I'm glad you stuck around," I told Chris with a chuckle.

"Me too," he said, glancing at me sideways. "Besides, I would have missed you too much."

"It is nice having a familiar face around," I said slowly, trying to pick my words carefully. I'm not sure I liked where this conversation was headed.

"Have you been to Moonglen yet?" I asked quickly, before Chris could say anything else.

"Moonglen? Where's that?" Chris asked, furrowing his brow.

"It's what I've decided to call this beautiful little glen I found the first time I entered the Forgotten Forest," I told him. "Though we should probably call the forest something else now, since it's not-so-forgotten anymore."

"The Not-So-Forgotten Forest. I like it," Chris joked.

I laughed at his antics, happy to be on safe ground once more.

"The Not-So-Forgotten Forest it is," I announced. "Anyways, you'll love Moonglen, and it's a great place to water the horses. If we go that way—"

I looked further down the trail we were on, the sight of a huge, gnarled tree triggering memories of one of my desperate runs through the forest, the sounds of baying hunting dogs and angry men echoing behind me, my breath rasping in my throat, Atlas' sides slick with sweat—

"Serena?" Chris asked uncertainly when I didn't continue.

"W-what? Oh, right," I stuttered, trying to calm my suddenly racing heart. I glanced down at my hands, only to notice the claws that were now changing back into my normal nails. If I'd been alone...

Atlas pranced under me, pawing at the ground. Laughing nervously, I glanced at Chris, hoping he hadn't noticed anything unusual. I hadn't exactly mentioned my recent...change to Chris. He didn't seem to be aware of what Fenn had done to save me. Either way, talking about this with Chris would make it too...real. I knew I couldn't avoid the subject forever, but for now...I just wanted things to be normal, the way they used to be.

"Moonglen is just a bit further up this path and to the left," I got out, trying to keep my tone light and even. "And I think Atlas still has some energy to burn. Let's canter a bit on the way!"

Without waiting for a response, I gathered the reins and gently squeezed Atlas' sides until he broke into a nice, easy lope. I let the wind in my face lift my thoughts along with my hair, letting them dance and swirl without a care in the world. As we passed by spots among the trees that haunted my dreams, I let the memories they conjured pass through me like the ghosts they were, and left them behind.

The rhythmic sound of our horses' hooves pounding into the soft loam underfoot soothed my soul. I breathed in the refreshing scent of the pine trees around us, and became vaguely aware of the tranquil murmuring of a brook nearby.

All too quickly we neared Moonglen, and I reluctantly slowed Atlas to a trot, and then a walk. I heard Chris do the same behind me, and we walked in comfortable silence as the horses' breathing and heart rates slowly returned to normal.

Atlas seemed a tad out of breath, so I resolved to come and ride him more frequently. That way he would regain his stamina and I wouldn't have to worry about him getting bored.

"We're here," I alerted Chris as I ducked under a low-hanging branch and entered the clearing. "Watch out for that branch!"

I heard muffled cursing behind me, and stifled a laugh. Chris never had been particularly good at listening, had he?

Moonglen looked just as I remembered. Lush grasses and moonflowers surrounded the tranquil pond, and a pair of rabbits dashed away at our approach. Though the sun was only just starting to set, a few fireflies were already winking in and out of existence around the pond, adding their twinkling light to the deepening shadows.

"Wow," I heard Chris breathe behind me as he drank in the sight.

When we got to the center of the glen, I dismounted, and led Atlas over to the pond so he could have a drink. Chris followed my example, and I even noticed he was doing his best to step on as few moonflowers as possible like I was. I appreciated his thoughtfulness.

"So, what do you think?" I asked him curiously.

"This place is beautiful," he replied as he continued to scan our surroundings.

"Isn't it?" I sighed, watching the reflection of the winking lights on the rippling surface of the pond.

"It's the perfect place for a picnic—or a date," he added suggestively.

I looked up, startled. This time, I was at a loss for words. Atlas raised his head too, water dripping from his muzzle.

"Chris, I—" I started, but snapped my head towards the rustling undergrowth on the other side of the pond as the scent of pine and sunshine tickled my senses.

A serious sense of deja-vu hit me as I spotted the icy-blue eyes staring at me from across the water. Seconds later, Fenn emerged from the shadows, his shirt clinging to his chiseled torso. He quickly made his way over to us, and I couldn't help but notice the tense set of his shoulders.

"Serena," Fenn practically growled, "what are you doing here—without a guard?"

Worry and some other emotion I couldn't name flickered across his features as he scanned me for injuries. Taken aback by his tone, I didn't respond right away. It wasn't as if I'd come alone. Besides, no one was sending hunting dogs and mercenaries after me anymore.

"I'm...riding, Fenn," I answered slowly, my brows pinching in confusion.

"I would never let anything happen to her, Your Grace," Chris said reassuringly, stepping forward.

Fenn finally tore his gaze away from mine.

"I would like to have a word with Serena, if you wouldn't mind. You may be dismissed, Ranger. I'm sure you have work to get done," Fenn ground out, clenching his jaw.

Chris faltered, anger and uncertainty furrowing his brow. Just as he opened his mouth, I quickly stepped in.

"Thanks for coming with me today, Chris. I feel much better now. I'll see you at the stables another time," I told him. "You can get back by retracing our steps down the trail."

Chris closed his mouth, clearly trying to decide what to do. I gave him a reassuring smile, and that seemed to help.

"Fine. I'll be waiting for you, Serena. Your Grace," he nodded tersely at Fenn and I winced internally, hoping Fenn would let that bit of rudeness pass.

Chris mounted his horse and headed back the way we'd come, his tense posture speaking louder than words. We waited in silence until the sound of hoofbeats faded. I braced myself.

"When you weren't in the tearoom, and I couldn't find you anywhere, I thought—I thought," Fenn said, a slight tremor going through him.

I softened my expression, realizing Fenn must have thought I'd gotten myself into trouble again.

"I'm safe, and I'm not going anywhere, Fenn," I sighed, taking his hand with my free one and lacing our fingers together. My touch seemed to calm him, and he visibly relaxed.

"You shouldn't be alone in the forest with *him*," Fenn spat, glaring daggers in the direction Chris had gone.

I bristled, and I said a little more irritably than I meant to, "*He* is my childhood friend. His family took me in when I was too afraid to return to my own mother. I don't appreciate the way you just treated him, Fenn."

Fenn looked down, frowning.

"Why weren't you in the tearoom? When I arrived, I could smell blood. It was faint, but I know it was yours," he rumbled. "I panicked."

"Didn't Harold give you my message?" I asked quietly.

Fenn looked up sharply, his eyes narrowing.

"Message?" he asked.

I silently cursed Harold and his scheming. Clearly he was trying to make me look bad. I wouldn't make the mistake of trusting him to do his job a second time.

"When I left, I told Harold to give the pastries to the staff, to send the plate I put together to you, and to inform you that I would wait for you to call for me when you were done with whatever you were working on. But I needed to get some fresh air, so I went to see Atlas," I began.

"Harold never mentioned anything," Fenn puzzled. "But why didn't—"

"Fenn, I waited there for you for over two hours," I said quietly. "But after a while, all the constant sounds and smells started...getting to me. It was just too much. I felt trapped in that tiny little room, and it reminded me...it reminded me of all those times when I had to take tea with Lester. I started feeling really hot, and I started to...to change."

Fenn stiffened, his eyes searching my face. Understanding and regret slowly dawned in his eyes.

"I was terrified. I was alone. And the blood...that was from my nails...my claws...they—" I shuddered, unable to continue.

Fenn wordlessly pulled me into him, his strong arms encircling me, like a wall that would protect me from the world. I melted into him, closing my eyes and letting my head rest against his firm chest. His steady heartbeat filled my ears, and a feeling of safety settled into my bones.

"I'm sorry I wasn't there for you today," he said gruffly into my hair. "Next time, I will be."

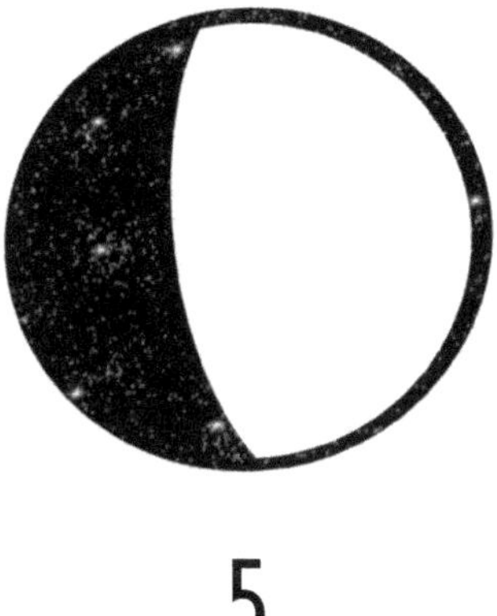

5

The next day dawned bright and warm. The birds sang their tribute to the sun, and the estate slowly came to life. Breakfast was prepared, the horses fed, and the repair work was resumed.

Probably.

I wouldn't really know whether that actually happened, or if a massive army of small garden gnomes had invaded like a tidal wave. Why? Because I was too busy trying to convince myself to continue my planking exercise instead of collapsing on the ground.

Sweat beaded on my brow, and I'd lost count long ago of when my arms had started to shake from the strain. And here I'd thought everything would be so easy now that I was a werewolf.

"Good, we can stop here," Fenn said as he rolled out of his own planking position and back onto his feet.

"Finally!" I panted, unceremoniously flopping onto the grass, all dignity forgotten. "How long that time?"

"That was a good fifteen minute plank. We'll be working our way up to a thirty minute plank, so we're halfway there," he informed me with a devilish smirk.

I glared at him, unamused. Fenn wasn't even breathing hard.

"If I didn't know any better, I'd say you were trying to wear me out on purpose," I grumbled, rolling onto my back and sitting up.

"T-that's ridiculous," Fenn quickly stammered, averting his eyes.

I narrowed my eyes in suspicion, an idea tickling the back of my mind. Well, two ideas.

"Fenn, you wouldn't happen to be tiring me out on purpose, either so I don't have any energy left to accidentally shift or go out riding, are you?" I asked, focusing closely on the sound of his heartbeat.

"Well..." Fenn mumbled. He ran a hand through his ebony hair, making my fingers itch to do the same. "I mean...maybe?"

I stared at him for a second, dumbfounded. His heart rate stayed steady, so he must be telling the truth.

"I'm not sure whether to be touched or annoyed," I finally responded truthfully.

"Both are fine," Fenn said a little sheepishly. "How about I make it up to you?"

"How would you do that?" I asked curiously.

"Special training," Fenn suggested mischievously.

My eyebrows shot up. With Fenn, I could never be certain if his idea of "fun" or "special" was the same as mine.

"What did you have in mind?" I asked cautiously.

Fenn pulled out a strip of black cloth, a lopsided grin on his face.

"How do you feel about practicing with your throwing knives...blindfolded?" he asked.

"Will you be tied to one of those rotating targets, or will you just be running around for me to hit?" I quipped with my own wicked little smile.

It took him a second to understand what I meant, but when he did, his face noticeably paled.

"Now wait just a minute, that's not what I—" he stammered nervously.

"I'm joking," I said, watching him visibly relax. "Mostly."

He laughed with me and offered his hand. I took it, and let him haul me to my feet. But even when I was standing, he didn't let go, his hand encasing mine with warmth.

"I already have some targets set up, far, far away from anything breakable," he joked, surreptitiously glancing at the shattered statue from *The Incident*. So maybe he wasn't joking after all.

"All right," I said, pink rising in my cheeks, whether from that little reminder of *The Incident* or the feel of my hand in his, I wasn't quite sure. Perhaps both.

The trek over to our practice clearing was shorter than I would have liked. Too soon, Fenn slipped his hand out of mine in order to finish setting up. He handed me the harness with the knives on it, and I quickly strapped it around my hips. Fenn had set up three circular wooden targets with painted rings on them, all at different distances.

Fenn came to stand right behind me as he gently settled the cloth over my eyes. His breath tickled my neck as he tied the blindfold, sending shivers down my spine.

Once the knot was in place, he set his hands on my shoulders and guided me a few feet from where I'd been standing, so I couldn't rely on my memory of where the targets were set up.

"Now," he breathed in my ear, "I want you to focus on your sense of hearing and smell for this exercise. Block out everything but the sounds you are looking for. Pinpoint each target by the noises they make and the scents they give off. The wind can help you locate them."

Fenn stepped back to give me some space, the sudden absence of his warmth almost making me shiver. I gave myself a mental shake, trying to refocus. If Fenn thought I could do this, then I would, even if it sounded kind of ridiculous.

Even though the blindfold did a pretty good job, I closed my eyes and took a deep breath, tasting the air on my tongue. The slight breeze was blowing towards me from the general direction of the targets. I blocked out Fenn's scent of pine as best I could. I could smell the lush grasses underfoot, the rich scent of the living soil. The breeze told of bacon that had just come out of the frying pan, and the dust being disturbed by the maids. Sifting through all of the various scents was trickier than I thought it would be.

Inhaling deeply, I filtered out the fainter scents, trying to narrow in on the strongest, and therefore closest, ones. I could distinguish between the different types of trees around us, but there—the scent of deadwood, overlaid with the slightly acrid tang of paint. Each of the three targets smelled slightly different, and the scent was stronger or weaker depending on how close it was.

I turned my head towards the closest one, focusing on my hearing next. I understood what Fenn had meant about the wind helping with scent, but how would that help with sound? I heard him move behind me, his boots crunching on the grass. I cocked my head, listening to the sounds in front of me. I could hear the leaves of nearby trees rustling in the wind, the sounds of birds singing, their feathers whistling as they flew through the air.

And then I noticed the faint noise of wood creaking as the wind pushed against a target before flowing around it to continue its endless journey. With scent and sound combined, I think I had a pretty good idea of where the targets were.

Unsheathing my first knife, I readied it, picturing in my mind the path it would take to its target. I drew back my arm and then whipped it forward, the knife slicing through the air—and landing with a soft *thump* in the grass. I frowned, confused.

"Don't forget to account for the increased distance and the wind altering the knife's path," Fenn reminded me from behind.

"Right," I muttered, berating myself for forgetting such important details.

I tried again, and this time I heard the satisfying *thunk* of the knife's blade sinking into wood.

"Better. Now the rest of them," Fenn instructed.

One by one, I sent each of my ten knives flying into the targets. I only missed one more of my shots, the first time I aimed for the farthest target. When I was out of knives, I slipped the blindfold off so I could see how I'd done.

Eight of my knives were embedded in the targets, though only one, the knife in the closest target, had landed in the bullseye.

"That was really good for your first try," Fenn said as he came to stand beside me, arms crossed over his chest.

I beamed at the note of pride in his voice.

"Thanks," I said shyly, happy I'd figured out how to better use my senses.

Fenn walked to the targets and collected the knives, handing them to me one at a time so I could return them to their individual sheaths.

"Fancy another go at it?" Fenn challenged.

"Naturally," I replied, silently offering him the blindfold.

He raised an eyebrow but took it nonetheless, repeating the process of placing it over my eyes and leading me around a bit to confuse my senses.

I smiled and got to work pinpointing the targets, my first knife at the ready.

After another hour of practice, I was reliably hitting the bullseye, blindfolded, most of the time. But more than the improvement to my aim, what I was really excited about was how much easier it was getting for me to either completely block out or tune into my newly enhanced senses. Hopefully, both being and feeling more in control of myself would prevent any future panic episodes like the one I'd had yesterday.

I slipped off the blindfold, turning to face Fenn as I did so. He'd set up a target of his own to practice on, though his was positively minuscule, and he'd tied the little wooden disk to a tree branch. The breeze today wasn't terribly strong, but it was still enough to send the lightweight target flipping around and swaying.

As I watched, Fenn carefully took aim, his eyes closed and head cocked to one side, listening. He swiftly drew back his arm and sent the knife flying with a flick of his wrist. As expected, the knife impaled the bullseye, the tip of the blade emerging from the back of the target.

I began clapping slowly, and Fenn turned to give me that infuriatingly adorable lopsided grin of his.

"Show-off," I accused him teasingly.

"You're not so bad yourself," he retorted, eyeing the knives I'd clustered in the bullseyes of my targets. "Don't worry, you'll be acing this one as well in no time."

Heat warmed my cheeks, and I smiled at him. His faith in me warmed me from the inside out.

"I had a good teacher," I replied, twisting a strand of hair around my finger.

"I still have a little time before my first meeting of the day," Fenn began, his crystalline eyes melting into pools of deep sapphire. "Why don't we—"

Tendrils of inky darkness began writhing inside the shadow of the tree Fenn had tied his target to. My heart went into overdrive, and I reached for the dagger still strapped to my thigh as fear closed my throat. Were we about to be attacked by a Keir assassin, again?

In an instant, Fenn had moved in front of me protectively, one of his throwing knives in hand. I was touched by the gesture, though perhaps a little put out, too, as I wondered if Fenn still thought I couldn't protect myself despite all the training we'd been doing. Then again, I *had* nearly died a few weeks ago... At that thought, any hint of indignation melted away like morning dew beneath the warm rays of the afternoon sun.

The shadows whirled into a mini maelstrom that grew nearly as tall as Fenn. Instinctively, I drew my arm back, aiming past Fenn's shoulder towards what I assumed was head height for the vaguely humanoid shape now visible within the shadows. The little target bobbed in the other-worldy wind, Fenn's knife still embedded in it.

Almost as quickly as it had appeared, the shadows bled away, leaving behind a figure cloaked in a fabric like living shadow. The figure moved, hands reaching up towards—something. A hidden weapon?

Without waiting for the attack to come, I began to throw my knife, aiming for the cloaked figure's head. The reaching hands pulled off the hood—revealing a shiny, bald head.

My eyes widened as I realized my mistake, and just as the knife was about to leave my hand, I used my fingers to shift its direction.

Dorent recoiled as the knife whistled by his ear and embedded itself next to Fenn's knife in the little target. The man brought his hands up defensively, shadows forming into a dagger of his own. He paused, looking between me, Fenn, and the two knives in the little target. A tense moment of silence descended, no one daring to move.

"I've heard of shooting the messenger, but that was just uncalled for," Dorent said, letting his shadow dagger fade into swirls of inky darkness.

Fenn laughed, his deep timbre easing my own tension.

"Baldie, you moron!" I hissed, horrified at what I'd almost done. "Give us some warning before you do that! I nearly beaned that chrome dome of yours!"

"Clients usually find that little trick impressive," he muttered, squinting at me. "I know I'm follicly-challenged, but you don't have to point it out so much," he groused. Dorent paused, eyeing all of the targets we'd set up. "Maybe next time I'll just come in the afternoon so I can avoid becoming a part of target practice altogether."

"That would be advisable," Fenn chuckled, wiping at the corner of his eye.

"Right, well," Dorent blustered, straightening the vest he was wearing and wiping off imaginary lint. "Shall we get down to business?"

Fenn sobered immediately, eyes taking on a hard glint. I walked up beside him, taking his tense hand in mine. Fenn gave my hand a squeeze in silent thanks. Baldie noted the action, but wisely chose not to comment.

"You found something?" Fenn demanded.

"It sure was a hassle, you know, trying to find this girl," he whined. "Lester had quite a reputation, you see, for the things he would do to the people who spilled his secrets. Even after receiving my," he paused, a ruthless gleam in his eye, "undivided attention, a few wouldn't talk until I proved the man was truly deceased."

"What did you find?" Fenn practically growled.

"You wolves are always so single-minded," Dorent pouted.

"Talk," Fenn ground out.

Single syllables were never a good sign when it came to Fenn. I glared at Baldie, raising one eyebrow.

"Fine, fine. You're no fun," Dorent sighed. He leveled his gaze at Fenn, his demeanor hardening. "I can confirm your sister is no longer within Lindora territories, or even in Cyrulia at all. The paper trail was scant, practically non-existent. I did find a record of her being sold to an elderly, wealthy baron in the outskirts of the Lindora Duchy. I'll spare you the details of her time there."

Fenn flinched, going rigid. I squeezed his hand once more.

"Once the old man died, she was sold again, but whomever bought her did so using a fake name. However, the slaver that sold her revealed to me, after much *persuading*, that the woman who bought her was a frequent client of his. And although he didn't know what her real name was, he did divulge that she was an elf."

Dorent let that sink in for a moment. I glanced at Fenn, understanding dawning in my eyes.

"After discreetly doing some digging over in Eldore, I learned a few interesting tidbits. In Eldore, unlike in Cyrulia, slavery is still legal—but the noble elves don't like such a dirty word, so they call them thralls instead. But I couldn't find any records of a female black-furred werewolf enthralled to any of the elven nobles," Dorent continued.

I supposed that if his career as an assassin and information broker ever dried up, Baldie would make a killing as a storyteller. Pun very much intended.

"While I was investigating in the capital, Varennia, I happened to hear some rumors. Apparently there is a popular underground fighting ring, where thralls are forced to battle to the death. Elves pay top coin to watch humans, dwarves, other elves, wild beasts, dragon hatchlings, and...werefolk rip each other's throats out."

Fenn had gone pale, every muscle in his body as taut as a bowstring. He held his breath, not even blinking, as Dorent spoke.

"I overheard a group of elves in a tavern talking about their favorites to win that night's match. One of them was betting on a female werewolf with black fur and blue eyes to win her match against a warrior dwarf," Dorent concluded, his eyes boring into Fenn's.

"Freya's in Eldore?" came the strangled whisper from Fenn's throat.

"I wasn't able to determine for certain that that werewolf is your sister, since they didn't keep any documents with the thrall's original names...but she looked much like you," Dorent confirmed, nodding gravely.

Something pricked the back of my hand, and I looked down to see claws emerging from Fenn's fingertips. His eyes were glowing a vivid blue, and a muscle feathered in his jaw as he fought not to shift. Hope and rage and despair warred on Fenn's features, and his grip on my hand was quickly becoming painful.

Dorent took a wary step back, and I couldn't blame him. I'd never seen Fenn lose control like that before, and I shivered involuntarily. That elven ringleader's days were numbered.

"Fenn," I said softly. "Look at me."

He slowly turned his head towards me, but his eyes went right through me, as if he were seeing something—or someone—who was far away. Slowly, I raised my free hand and gently cupped his face.

"We'll get her back. The important thing is that she's still alive. Fenn, part of your family is still alive! You're not alone anymore. And we can save her, together!" I said softly.

Slowly, Fenn's eyes focused on mine, the pain I saw there reflected in my own.

"We can save her, together. And we will make that elf pay for what she's done," I promised solemnly.

Fenn nodded, his deathgrip on my hand softening. Soon, his eyes were back to their normal, icy hue. He closed them for a moment, leaning into my touch.

When he opened them again, he turned to face Dorent, who was still watching him warily.

"Thank you for the information. Can we count on you to help us get her out of there?" Fenn asked, composed once more.

"The thing is, I'm not exactly...welcome in most parts of Eldore," Dorent said awkwardly, shifting from foot to foot.

I raised an eyebrow at him.

"Aren't you also not welcome in most parts of Cyrulia?" I asked pointedly.

"That's different," he protested weakly. "Anyways, I didn't say no. I can't travel with you, but I can help discreetly when you're getting her out. Though I'll have to charge a little more than my usual fee."

I rolled my eyes.

"Agreed," Fenn said.

"How are we supposed to contact you, though?" I asked curiously.

"Here," Baldie said, handing me a piece of paper with an intricate, circular design on it. "Put a drop of your blood on this, and I'll know to shadow travel to you."

I wrinkled my nose at him, but took the piece of paper anyways.

"Gross."

"That's just how it works, rosie locks. Oh, and here are the herbs he requested for you," Dorent said as he handed over a bundle of pungent herbs.

I looked at him, confused, but it was Fenn who answered.

"Those will help with the pain of your first shift," he explained gruffly.

I tightened my fist unconsciously around the little bundle, trying to squash my sudden discomfort.

"Now that that's settled, how would you like to arrange for payment?" Dorent asked sweetly, rubbing his hands together.

"I'll pay you for your services in my office, plus a down payment for your help with the rescue," Fenn sighed, rubbing the back of his neck.

I barely heard Dorent's response. My mind was too busy with thoughts of my upcoming shift. Fenn hadn't mentioned anything about it being painful before, but then again, how could it not be?

I pushed those thoughts to the back of my mind. I'd deal with figuring that out later. For now, I needed to concentrate on getting ready to go and save Fenn's sister. Now that we knew not only that she was alive, but that she was potentially in Eldore, I'm sure Fenn would want to leave as soon as possible. Which meant we had a great deal of work to do.

"Follow me to my office," Fenn ordered Dorent before turning to me. He sighed when he looked at the herbs still clutched in my hand. "Try not to worry too much. I'll see you later at dinner."

And with that, Fenn pressed a light kiss to my forehead before leading Dorent towards the estate.

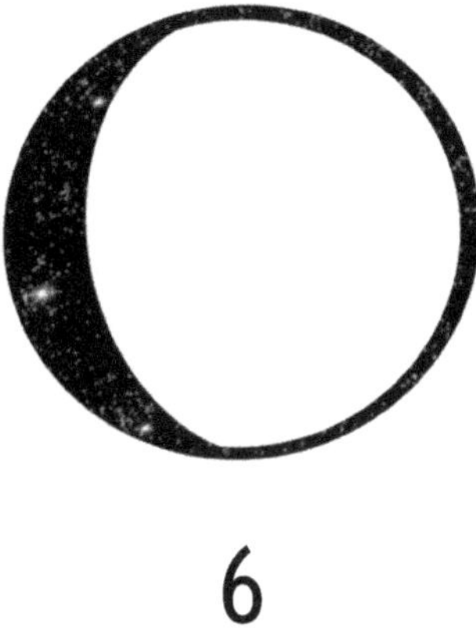

6

My fists pounded into the hay-stuffed bag in front of me in quick succession, the fabric wrapped around my knuckles protecting my skin from the rough bag. Sweat beaded on my forehead, and my breath came in controlled puffs. The rhythmic, mindless motion was the best method I'd found to relieve all of my pent-up stress and anxiety.

Chris had been kind enough to set up this punching bag for me. This way, whenever I had too much free time—which was quite frequently these days—I would have something productive to do. Plus, this technically counted as training too. Of course, I'd also been working on all of the moves Fenn had shown me, and I'd even been continuing to practice with my daggers and throwing knives. I'd also incorporated training my newfound senses into each exercise, and I'd gotten much better at honing in on one sense while blocking out the others so I could concentrate without getting too overwhelmed.

Fenn ended up even busier than he had been before Dorent had shown up. As eager as he and I both were to go after Fenn's sister—Freya, I reminded myself—there were a myriad of small details that had to be taken care of first. Fenn needed to finish organizing and training the staff, writing down any further details for the repair and construction work, going over and signing off on the mountain of paperwork on his desk, including the terms for re-establishing trade routes between Verdania and the crown, plus the other Dukedoms and smaller towns...

The list seemed endless, and that was even before making preparations for an extended trip away. But he couldn't exactly trumpet the fact that he would be leaving his territory and traveling into Eldore. Not only would that risk unwanted attention while Fenn was away and the estate was disorganized, but that could also alert the ringleader of the vengeful beast headed her way.

Therefore, the individuals in the estate we could trust would be spreading the rumor that Fenn and I would be taking some time to ourselves in an undisclosed, but nearby, location, in order to recuperate from the ordeal we had been through.

The other main reason Fenn had decided to wait a couple more weeks before departing was so that I could spend my first full moon in familiar territory.

That thought had me pounding the bag with renewed vigor. I'd been trying to avoid thinking about *that* little detail since Fenn had first told me what he'd had to do to save my life. But the reality that I was no longer human...despite my little episode the other day...still hadn't fully sunk in yet. In my head, I knew that I would still be me...but what kinds of changes would it make in me? It scared me how different and *aggressive* I'd felt after only growing some *claws*. How much would I change after my first full transformation?

And the bundle of herbs Fenn had evidently asked Baldie to acquire for me were burning a hole in my thoughts. How painful would the change be, that special herbs were needed to dull the pain? Or was Fenn just overreacting, or maybe even trying to be considerate of me?

I really wanted to sit down and have a nice long chat about all these important little details, but Fenn had been so busy with everything else that I just couldn't bring myself to ask. Of course, it was possible that knowing these things in advance would only worry me even *more* than I already was...

It would have been a relief to talk with someone about this, but I didn't feel comfortable bringing it up with my assistants or Wendy or Aly. I wasn't even sure if any of them even knew I was a werewolf now. I mean, they didn't seem to have a problem with Fenn being one, but at the same time, none of them really needed to interact with him on a regular basis, either.

And forget trying to bring this up with Bruce or the other werewolves...my face reddened just thinking about their reactions. Although, maybe Tim was someone I could approach for advice. We weren't that far apart in age, and he'd been kind to me since I'd met him. But then again, maybe it would be better not to know these things.

"What did that poor bag ever do to you?" came a teasing voice from behind me.

I whirled, eyes widening, only to find Chris casually leaning against a nearby tree, arms crossed over his chest and his usual, easygoing smile plastered across his face. I scowled at him, surprised he'd managed to sneak up on me. Lately he'd had a much harder time doing that courtesy of my improved hearing.

"Chris! Are you *trying* to give me a heart attack?!" I asked in mock outrage, placing my hand over my heart and fluttering my eyelashes dramatically.

Unfortunately, instead of laughing at my antics like he used to, Chris pushed off from the tree and came closer, his eyes deepening a shade and drinking in my form, the sheen of sweat on my face.

"How long have you been standing there?" I asked quickly, dropping the silly pose and turning to grab the still-swinging bag.

"Long enough," Chris answered noncommittally.

I turned to find him right in front of me. I resisted the urge to take a step back.

"I guess Fenn must not be nearby to give you extra work to do," I chuckled, trying to push down the slight twinge of unease I felt.

Chris grimaced at that. After Fenn had tracked us down during our little trail ride in the forest the other day, he'd made a point of keeping Chris too busy to go on lengthy trail rides with anyone. But on the upside, all the small repairs the stables had needed were now done, and every last piece of tack was now oiled and pristine.

"Don't get me started on that," Chris muttered with a scowl. "I haven't had a chance to have a good nap in days."

Steeling myself, I asked, "Does it...bother you that he's a werewolf?"

Chris looked a little surprised at the question, and took a second to respond. Now I felt nervous for an entirely different reason.

"Well...he seems like a good enough person, considering what he's done not just for my family, but for everyone that was affected by that noble jerk. But that's just it—he's not really a person, is he?" Chris asked.

My heart sank straight down to my toes. *Not a person?* I kept my face carefully blank. Would Chris still say that if he knew I was one too? When I didn't respond in the affirmative, Chris furrowed his brow.

"I mean, what about all those stories we heard about 'the beast of the Forgotten Forest?' How do we know what really goes on in that guy's head when he turns into a monster? For all we know, he could lose all sense of reason and just start attacking people. Doesn't that worry you at all?" Chris questioned.

"That's not true at all!" I said defensively. "Those stories we were told were all lies—have you ever actually met anyone who was 'attacked' by a wolf in the forest?"

"Well...no one that I know," Chris said with a little uncertainty.

"Exactly! Me neither," I continued heatedly. "Besides, Fenn has only ever defended himself from people who were attacking *him*. And I know he doesn't lose his sense of reason because he could always understand what I was saying to him when he was in wolf form, even when he must have been barely conscious from the pain and all the blood he was losing..." I trailed off, as all-too-vivid memories of the night Lester had put Fenn in that cage bubbled to the surface. I stared off into the distance, the blood draining from my face at the memory.

"Rena, do you want to talk about it?" Chris asked tenderly, taking my hands in his and using his old pet nickname for me.

I refocused my eyes, pushing those blood-stained memories back into the depths where they belonged. I must have looked really pale if Chris was dusting off my old nickname. With some effort, I smiled weakly at him.

"I'm fine. I try not to think about that night. I shouldn't have brought it up."

"I probably could have been a little more considerate," Chris admitted reluctantly.

That was probably about as close to an apology as I'd ever gotten out of him. Who knew all I had to do was look a little pale and stare off into the distance for a few seconds? That sure would have come in handy when we were younger and Chris had poked fun at me one too many times.

"Aww, is someone a little grumpy because he hasn't had his afternoon nap today?" I crooned, smiling for real this time.

"Maybe," Chris huffed, his mouth twitching as he tried not to smile.

"I'm sure you'll be able to fit in some more naps soon," I teased light-heartedly.

"You could always join me," Chris said mischievously.

I suddenly became very aware that Chris was still holding my hands.

"At the moment, I think I'm more interested in going for a trail ride," I suggested, slipping my hands out of his so I could unwrap the cloth that still covered my knuckles. I rolled the fabric into a ball and placed it in the back pocket of my breeches.

"That sounds good too," Chris replied easily, putting his hands in his pockets.

"I'll race you there!" I declared, and took off towards the stables without waiting for a response. The word *monster* seemed to echo at my heels.

Fenn watched Serena and Chris through the windows in his office as they headed out for yet *another* trail ride on horseback. Despite the fact that Harold was attempting to inform him of the rest of his schedule for the day, the words washed right through him.

Fenn clenched his jaw in an attempt to quell his rising jealousy. It was clear from the way that hay-smelling blondie looked at her that Chris was interested in her, regardless of his status with her as "childhood friend." *He* should be the one by her side, the one and only recipient of each sweet smile. Then he blinked. *What was wrong with him these days?* She was free to smile at whomever she wanted. It wasn't as if they were engaged, or mates.

But always finding her seat at the tea table empty, her tea long cooled, ate away at him. He hated making her wait, but never seemed to be able to get away from all the work that required his attention. It felt like there was a distance growing between them, a chasm Fenn wanted desperately to bridge.

It had already been a week since he'd last had the time to conduct an early-morning training session with Serena. If only there weren't so many damn things left to do! The first shift was always the hardest, and hers was fast approaching. But he wanted to be on the road right after. Who knew what horrors his little sister was enduring even at this very moment? Worry about both Serena and Freya clouded his mind, making it impossible to focus.

"-Ace? Your Grace!" Harold practically shouted.

Fenn started, swinging his gaze back to his head butler. The older man was frantically dabbing at his balding pate with his eternally present handkerchief. He pinched the bridge of his nose in between his fingers, letting out a heavy sigh.

"I'm sorry, what were you saying, Harold?" Fenn asked wearily.

"Your next meeting with the builders starts in ten minutes, and after that—" Harold began reciting again, a hint of annoyance in his tone.

"Harold, I have a special task for you," Fenn interrupted, ignoring the resulting scowl. "I'd like you to take care of all the minor tasks that don't necessarily require my approval. If there are issues or required approvals, compile them into one list to present to me at the start of the next day. Instruct the Head Housekeeper to begin making preparations for the trip, and to coordinate with the Head Chef and the Stablemaster on preparing the rest. I expect any paperwork that needs to be immediately addressed during the time I will be gone to be on my desk by tonight."

Harold gaped at Fenn, but quickly closed his mouth at Fenn's raised eyebrow. Another habit he'd picked up from a certain redhead.

"As you wish, Your Grace," Harold mumbled.

"That will be all, Harold. Please send Bruce in on your way out," Fenn instructed, dismissing the butler.

Harold bowed and saw himself out. Bruce, who had been standing on the other side of the closed office doors, slunk into the room rather sheepishly. Fenn took his time reading through the day's schedule Harold had given him before deigning to look up.

"I was about 'ter knock," Bruce began, his one good eye lowered submissively.

"I'm sure you've guessed at my intentions," Fenn commented, somewhat enjoying watching the big man squirm.

"Yeh wan' to be ready before th'a full moon," Bruce replied.

"Correct. To that end, I want you to pick a small group to accompany us, while you remain here to keep an eye on things," Fenn ordered. "But let Harold do the talking."

"I'll pick some tha' I know the miss likes," Bruce said with pride.

"Good. Include a couple of your best fighters. And write their names down and have it on my desk in the next two days," Fenn added.

"Understood," Bruce said.

At Fenn's nod, he excused himself to work on the list. Fenn leaned back in his leather chair, glaring balefully at the pile of paperwork already occupying his desk.

He was in for many late nights if he was going to make this work in time. Fenn sighed, but then straightened his spine. For Serena, he could do this.

I chuckled along with Aly, the sound of her warm laughter filling the crack in my heart I didn't know was there. Standing around one of the kitchen counters and decorating cookies with Aly, Wendy, Lily and Sophia had just become my new favorite activity.

"And then she ran straight into the butcher as he was leaving after dropping off some meat. The flour she was carrying spilled all over his shirt!" Aly continued, wiping a tear of mirth from her eye. "But it gets better. She was so surprised that she dropped the bag of flour, and it exploded in this huge mushroom cloud that coated both of them. They looked just like ghosts!"

"An angry butcher ghost!" Wendy chimed in.

"I wouldn't want to be haunted by an angry butcher ghost. Especially not if he had his cleaver with him!" Lily proclaimed, holding her bag of frosting up like a weapon.

"Especially then," Sophia added sagely.

I smiled, popping one of my finished cookies into my mouth. The sweetness of the frosting tantalized my tastebuds, and I closed my eyes in bliss. Cinnamon buns were still my favorite, but I think these sugar cookies might be a close second.

After a moment of comfortable silence, I noticed out of the corner of my eye that Wendy glanced in my direction and none-too-subtly elbowed Aly to get her attention. She raised her eyebrows at Wendy, who ended up making more gestures in my direction. I didn't have to wait long to find out what they wanted to ask me.

"So Serena, how have things been between you and Mr. Tall, Dark, and Handsome?" Aly asked suggestively, her eyebrows raised.

I shifted uncomfortably as every eye turned to me.

"Good…and bad," I said with a sigh.

"Do go on," Wendy urged, taking a bite of one of her own cookies.

"Tell us," Lily cajoled.

Sophia nodded in silent encouragement as her mouth was otherwise occupied with frosted heaven.

"It's just…I love spending time with him, no matter what we're doing. But because there are so many things to do before our little trip, he hasn't even been able to come to our early-morning training sessions. I wish I could help by taking some of his workload, but right now there's nothing I can do. And I know it's selfish of me to want to take up more of his time, but I can't help it. I miss him," I confessed, clasping my hands in my lap.

"That is completely understandable," Wendy said sympathetically.

"At least you'll be able to spend some quality time with him during the trip!" Lily chimed in cheerfully.

"Hopefully some time alone," Sophia commented.

"And it is definitely *not* selfish to want to spend time with someone you care about," Aly added, the sincerity in her voice warming my soul.

"Thanks, girls," I said with a small smile.

"He clearly cares about you too. The look in his eyes when you took that dagger for him…" Wendy recalled. "I'll never forget it. It was like his whole world was ending."

"And the way he held you in his arms was so romantic," Aly sighed, "I hope someone will look at me the way that man looked at you."

I blushed, looking at my hands. Then something occurred to me.

"Wait, I thought all of you ran out of there when the fighting started," I said, looking at them in surprise and confusion.

They all exchanged looks.

"Well, we did take cover when swords were drawn," Lily said slowly.

"But we knew we would be trampled by the panicking nobles if we tried to leave with them, so we found a place to hide, away from the fighting," Sophia continued, looking at Lily.

"It was the same for us," Aly said, glancing at Wendy. "But we were careful, and didn't draw attention to ourselves."

"No one was interested in us, so we weren't in real danger," Wendy agreed.

"I'm sorry I put you all in that position," I said morosely. "I had no idea you were stuck in there with all that chaos. I never would have—"

"Don't you dare say you never would have involved us, Serena," Aly interjected loudly. "If I could go back in time and do it all over, I would choose to help you every time."

"Working in the Lindora household was like living in hell. And you freed us from it," Wendy added, a shadow passing across her features.

Lily and Sophia nodded mutely in agreement.

"We like where we are now so much more. We're getting paid more, and no one will whip us if we make a mistake," Sophia murmured, her eyes misting with phantom pain.

The mystery of the raised scars I'd glimpsed on the backs of Lily's and Sophia's legs suddenly weren't such a mystery anymore. My heart ached for what they must have gone through.

"I'm so glad I met you all, even if I had to go through Lester to do it," I declared emphatically.

Each girl beamed at me. My heart swelled with happiness at the sight of these amazing young women, who had each endured grueling trials, but had pushed through them to a brighter future and greater depths of character. The love and support at this table felt palpable.

"I think I speak for all of us when I say we're glad we met you too," Aly responded warmly.

Before I could talk myself out of it, I blurted out, "None of you are afraid of me, right? Even though you saw what happened?"

Stunned silence met my outburst. My nerves writhed in my stomach, and I bit my lip. Smiles turned into puzzled frowns. Looks were exchanged.

"What do you mean? Why would we be afraid of you?" Wendy asked.

"Because, well...Fenn is a werewolf, and in order to save me, he..." I trailed off, averting my eyes, my voice shaking.

I heard the sound of footsteps, and then Aly was there, placing her hand gently over mine. I looked up at her in surprise, and the understanding I saw in her eyes was nearly my undoing.

"He must have turned you into one, too," Aly said softly, surprise lacing her voice.

I nodded, a lump in my throat.

"To be honest, I never really thought about it that much. I was just so happy you were alive. But *what* you are doesn't change *who* you are. You'll always be the Serena who gave me hope when I was in a dark place," Aly assured me.

She pulled me into a hug, and I closed my eyes. A single tear traced its way down my cheek, and I let out a breath I hadn't known I'd been holding.

"Same here," Wendy added.

"Don't worry about such silly things," Sophia scolded.

"If you turned into a dancing purple sheep with wings, I really wouldn't blink twice," Lily joked.

Everyone laughed, and I laughed with them. It felt like heavy shackles had fallen from my soul, and I could take my first deep breath since I'd woken up after that dagger pierced my chest. Even though Chris thought werewolves were monsters, I at least had a whole group of wonderful friends who didn't see me any differently.

But they haven't seen you sprout claws, a vile voice nagged in the back of my mind.

It wouldn't matter, I thought back fiercely. *I will* always *be me—I won't let this new part of my life change who I am.*

The nagging fear that had been present since I first learned the price of my life finally eased, fading like mist in the morning light, and returning to its native nothingness.

The other three came over and joined the group hug, and I was smiling and laughing again before I knew it.

Later that night, as I was heading back to my room, I noticed that candlelight still spilled from the window of Fenn's study. Every night for the last week, no matter how late it was, I always saw Fenn's shadow in the window, his form bent over his desk. I felt a familiar longing in my chest, and resisted the urge to go to him. I would only be a distraction.

Turning away from Fenn's window, I looked instead at the huge, luminous moon hanging low in the sky as if it was taunting me. I could feel its pull in my bones, and without needing to consult a calendar, I could tell that it would be full tomorrow night.

In less than twenty-four hours, I would be a full-fledged werewolf. I shivered involuntarily. Fenn would be there with me though, to guide me through the process...right?

I slowly made my way back to my room, but I knew I wouldn't be getting much sleep tonight. Though I suppose all the sugar I'd just consumed probably wasn't helping.

I did not light any candles, and instead sat on my bed, staring out the window at the moon. My thoughts raced around my mind, and even though my eyes were tired, I couldn't keep them closed.

I decided then to keep my friends' words in the forefront of my mind, along with the vow I had made to myself to remain true to myself. Even if the changes tomorrow were more than just physical, my values and core memories would serve as my North Star, guiding me home.

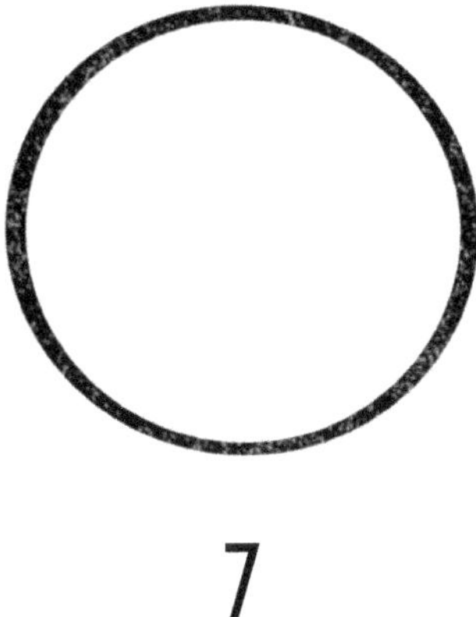

7

As the first rays of dawn touched the sky, coating the scattered clouds in pale pinks and gentle oranges, I sighed, running a hand through my disheveled locks. I couldn't quite recall whether or not I'd managed to doze off for a few hours during the night, but it sure didn't feel like it.

The nearly full moon was still visible in the rapidly lightening sky. Its call tugged at my bones, demanding I submit. I doubted I'd be able to resist once the sun set, and the moon reigned alone over its endless sea of stars.

Butterflies took flight in my stomach, their frantic fluttering setting my nerves alight. I glanced at the bundle of herbs on my bedside table, which I had yet to touch. Fenn had said it was called wolfpaw, after the shape of the leaves. The only other thing he had told me about it was that wolfpaw could dull a werewolf's senses, including pain. *Would I need to consume all of them to dull the pain?* Dread, excitement, and anticipation warred within me, and I bit my lip.

The wait was killing me, and the sun was only just rising! *How would I possibly make it to, and through, tonight, without simply curling into a ball on the floor?*

Just as I was seriously contemplating snuggling into the covers and sleeping the day away, a knock sounded at my door. I sighed.

"You can come in, Sophia," I called.

Maybe I could distract myself by spending some more time with Sophia and Lily. Maybe even Aly and Wendy if they weren't too busy today. After all, I'd felt so much better after our conversation last night.

Silence. I frowned, my hand snaking under the covers towards the dagger still strapped to my thigh.

"Sophia?" I asked a little more uncertainly.

I closed my eyes, focusing on my hearing, which, unsurprisingly, seemed sharper today. I could definitely hear a heartbeat, the shuffle of leather boots on the floor...I snapped my eyes open, knowing who was standing just outside my door.

"Actually, it's me," Fenn called through the door. "Can I come in? Are you...decent?"

I could practically hear him blushing at that last part.

I jumped out of bed, and was about to tell him to come in, when I looked down and realized I was wearing a silky nightgown, with one of the straps falling off my shoulder.

"Um, I might need a minute," I answered, hastily rushing to throw on a robe. "Are you free for a training session this morning?" I asked hopefully.

"I thought we could do something a little different today," Fenn said mysteriously.

I paused, curious.

"What did you have in mind?" I asked.

"It's a surprise," Fenn said, warmth radiating from his voice. "Tell you what, I'll meet you at our usual spot. Dress comfortably, and bring a bag with a change of clothes and a warm cloak. Oh, and would you hand me that bundle of wolfpaw?"

I snatched the herbs and opened the door just wide enough to slip them through. Fenn's warm fingers grazed mine as he took the bundle. He chuckled warmly as I quickly closed the door again.

"Thanks. I'll see you soon," he said through the door.

"I won't be long," I replied, puzzled.

I listened as Fenn walked away, thoughts buzzing through my head. Surprises from Fenn, like Atlas, had always been wonderful, and I was sure today would be no different. Still, I couldn't help but wonder what Fenn had planned for us, and if he could afford to spend so much time away from his work.

Springing into action, I quickly scribbled a note for Lily and Sophia, letting them know I would be out with Fenn and not to worry. That done, I quickly changed into my riding outfit, my soft breeches keeping the morning chill at bay. I slipped on my leather boots and tied my hair back with a simple green ribbon. I glanced in the mirror as I finished with my hair, and grimaced at the dark circles under my eyes.

Shoving some spare clothes and my warmest cloak into my brown satchel, I slung the bag over my shoulder and re-strapped my sheathed dagger to my right thigh over my breeches, the Vulclaria feather fluttering as I moved.

I exited my room, closing the door softly behind me. I hurried down the halls, smiling at the few souls who were up and already seeing to their daily chores. I still found it odd how many people there were in the castle these days, when before it had been so hollow.

A few minutes later, I emerged from the estate, blinking in the early morning light. I jogged over to where Fenn was waiting for me, energy and excitement buzzing in my veins.

"Serena," Fenn greeted me with a smile as I came to a stop in front of him.

I blinked, surprised at how gaunt he looked. His hair was nearly as disheveled as mine had been earlier, and my fingers itched to run through it and smooth it out. There were dark circles under his eyes to rival mine.

Recovering quickly from my surprise, I responded, "Good morning, Fenn," with as much cheer as I could muster.

"I see you've been sleeping about as much as I have," he murmured, reaching out and gently tucking a stray strand of hair behind my ear.

The tips of my ears grew warm, but I smiled at the gesture. For some reason, I had worried things would be terribly awkward between us, since we had been apart for a little while. But maybe I had worried for nothing.

"I've been…a little nervous," I admitted shyly.

"I don't blame you," Fenn said with sympathy. "I think I know how to take your mind off of things."

"How?" I asked, leaning forward.

"Well, I took care of everything that needed doing, so I can spend the whole day with you," Fenn announced proudly. "I thought we could start off with doing something you love—like going for a trail ride."

"That sounds amazing!" I beamed at him. "We haven't had the chance to go riding together before! Well, except for that one time when we were both on Atlas after that fight…but that doesn't really count, does it?"

"It's been a while since I went riding. Care to refresh my memory of how it's done?" Fenn suggested with that mischievous gleam in his eye.

"Of course!" I agreed happily. "Let's go Fenn, we're burning daylight!"

And with that, I took his hand and led him towards the stables. The pull of the moon faded to the background with Fenn's hand in mine, and I could focus on the present.

"I did *not* nearly 'fall off'," Fenn protested, attempting to scowl at me but failing spectacularly. His lips kept twitching upwards.

"Fine, fine," I relented, but couldn't help adding, "You were just leaning over to one side in the saddle to *test* the snugness of the girth. On purpose."

I gave Atlas' coat one final swipe with the brush, satisfied that he was as clean as I could get him. I'm sure he'd end up rolling in the dirt once I turned him out in the pasture to graze, though. It looked like Fenn was also finishing up grooming Clover, the easy-going horse I'd picked out for him.

"Exactly," Fenn sniffed with mock indignation. But then he grinned unabashedly at me. "I can see why you enjoy this so much. I'd forgotten how much fun riding can be."

"I'm glad you see it my way," I replied.

I fished a carrot out of my back pocket and held it out to Atlas. He greedily lipped it up, chewing on his treat contentedly. Fenn did likewise for Clover.

"Are we ready to turn them out?" Fenn asked.

"I think so. Follow me," I instructed as I unclipped Atlas' halter from the cross-ties and began leading him out towards the pasture, which was just a small, fenced-in patch of grass behind the stables.

Fenn followed close behind with Clover, their hoofbeats echoing in the enclosed space of the stables. I opened the pasture gate, walked a few feet in, and slipped the halter off of Atlas' head. He walked forward a few paces before cropping at the grass, Clover quickly joining him.

Fenn and I exited the pasture, making sure to latch the gate securely behind us. Almost right on cue, Atlas found a patch of dirt, lay down and started rolling on his back, scratching his itches and acquiring a nice coating of dirt. When he was done, he stood up and shook like a dog, but only some of the dirt came off.

Now my beautiful stallion had dirt spots all over him. I sighed. Fenn laughed at my expression.

"The work is never-ending with these guys, isn't it?" he laughed.

"You have no idea," I replied with a tired smile.

"Now that it's just about lunchtime, we have somewhere to be," Fenn informed me.

"And where might that be?" I asked, intrigued.

"You'll see," Fenn hedged, but held out his hand to me.

I gladly placed my hand in his, and he led me back through the stables, where we hung up the horses' halters and grabbed our satchels before continuing on toward the forest.

We ended up walking along a sunlight-dappled trail, the wind whispering in the leaves of the trees above us. We walked in comfortable silence, our heartbeats and the songs of the birds sounding loud in quiet.

Before I knew it, the path became achingly familiar, and Fenn tugged me through the curtains of vines in front of us and into the meadow where the Vulclaria spent their days.

"We're here," Fenn announced, his sweeping gesture taking in the field of moonflowers and the fluffy little foxes playing and napping amongst them. Somehow, the huge cherry blossom tree in the center was still in full bloom, and the small pond near its roots was still full of crystal-clear water, despite the fact that autumn was nearly upon us.

"It's as beautiful as I remember," I murmured.

"Still not as beautiful as you," Fenn mumbled shyly.

Delighted, I pecked him on the cheek, and the resulting grin that lit up his face was well worth it. "Thank you, Fenn."

As we slowly made our way over to our spot under the tree, we stopped to occasionally pet some of the little winged foxes that came up to us. They made the cutest little sounds when they laughed, like the tinkling of a bell. We were both extra careful not to step on any paws or tails.

"Fenn, what is all of this?" I asked, noticing for the first time what was laid out beneath the tree.

A plush blue blanket covered the ground, laden with an extensive picnic spread. I saw sandwiches, water skins, fresh bread and berries, and even an assortment of pastries, including croissants, macaron cookies, and of course, cinnamon buns. Clearly Aly and the others had helped set this up without breathing a single word to me!

"Just a little something to eat." Fenn shrugged nonchalantly, but I could see the corners of his mouth twitching upward.

"A little?!" I breathed, touched at the gesture. "Did you put all of this together yourself?"

"I may have had a little help from your friends," Fenn admitted, rubbing the back of his neck rather sheepishly. "But I really wanted to do something to take your mind off of things. And...to apologize. Serena, I'm sorry I haven't exactly been able to spend much time with you lately, even though I'm sure you must be feeling worried."

"I'm just happy you're here now," I replied warmly. "I completely understand. I know there are many things that needed to be done before we go after your sister. I only wish I could be more of a help to you."

"You already are a help," Fenn said, taking my hand and drawing me close. "You keep me grounded. I'd be lost without you."

He closed his eyes and leaned his forehead against mine. My eyelids fluttered closed, and I reveled in this sublime moment. Every other thought and worry fled my mind, until only the two of us existed in this little bubble of tranquility.

I tilted my face imperceptibly upwards, and Fenn captured my lips with his, caressing them sweetly. Just as I was about to wrap my arms around his neck, something small and furry landed on my shoulder and yipped at me.

I stepped back, my surprised eyes meeting another pair of green eyes that sparkled like gemstones. Fenn laughed at the scene we made.

"I know you," I said slowly.

The Vulclaria puffed out its fuzzy little chest and ruffled its feathers, licking my nose. It was the cream colored, green-eyed Vulclaria I'd met the first time I'd come here with Fenn, the one that had given me one of its feathers.

Smiling, I gently lifted it off my shoulder and cradled it in my arms, stroking its downy wings. The little critter made a rumbling, purring sound, and I couldn't help but beam at it.

"I bet being so cute all the time makes you hungry," I crooned.

"By that logic, you should be ravenous," Fenn mumbled. "Why don't you feed it some of the berries we brought? Hopefully the rest of the little beasties haven't gotten into them yet."

"Good idea," I agreed, and the two of us went and sat down on the luxuriously soft blanket.

Fenn handed me a napkin filled with blueberries, raspberries, blackberries, and huckleberries once I'd settled my little friend in my lap. I presented each type of berry one-by-one to the Vulclaria, and it happily gobbled each one up, berry juices staining the fur around its mouth purple. After a little trial and error, I determined that blueberries and huckleberries were its favorites.

Fenn had been quiet while I was feeding my fuzzball, but I looked up at him once the Vulclaria curled up and closed its eyes, clearly intending to take a nap. He was looking at me with such a tender, loving expression that it took my breath away. Trying not to jostle my sleeping guest, I leaned over so I could lace my fingers through his. The smile he gave me warmed my heart.

Soon, however, we were surrounded by hungry little foxes, who were all flapping their wings at us, clamoring to be fed. We laughed and handed out the rest of our stock of berries, while managing to take a few bites of sandwich in between. I noticed that the sandwiches had bits of familiar-smelling herbs in them. I guess now I knew what had happened to that bundle of wolfpaw Fenn had asked for this morning. It made me feel a little better that I wasn't the only one eating them.

The afternoon passed in a warm haze of playing with our fluffy little friends, eating up all the delicious food, trading stories, and simply enjoying each other's company. Before I knew it, the sun was setting, turning the sky into a sea of molten gold.

I felt a twinge of unease as I watched the golden orb slowly sink ever closer to the treeline. I bit my lip, worrying it between my teeth. My soon-to-be elongated teeth.

"There's a reason I brought you here today, you know," Fenn said suddenly, noting the direction of my gaze.

"A reason?" I echoed, my eyes still glued to the ever-darkening sky.

"Yes. Besides this place being home to the Vulclaria, it is also a very important place for my family." The gravity in Fenn's voice surprised me.

I tore my gaze from the changing sky to find Fenn watching me closely. His eyes looked as clear and piercing as I'd ever seen them.

"Your family?" I prompted gently when Fenn remained silent. He nodded.

"This is where my parents brought my siblings and I for our first shifts, under the first full moon after our seventh birthdays. And where my parents' parents brought them, and their parents, and so on. I suppose you could say that this is my family's sacred ground," Fenn revealed slowly.

I blinked, touched that Fenn was sharing such a special place with me.

"What was it like?" I asked, curious.

"Exhilarating. Terrifying. Amazing. The best way that I can describe it is like letting the moon guide you as you take a really big stretch, and then just falling onto all fours as a wolf. It is rather uncomfortable the first time, but it gets easier with practice," he explained as I listened raptly.

"Is it true that all werewolves have to shift during the night of a full moon?" I asked.

"Yes. The rest of the time we're free to choose our forms," Fenn responded.

Twilight had fallen while we were talking, the stars twinkling like diamonds above us. The moonflowers had begun to glow, casting a silver sheen upon everything and every creature their light touched. The Vulclaria began stirring from their afternoon naps, taking flight to play in the warm updrafts rising from the earth.

The cream-colored Vulclaria in my lap lazily blinked its emerald eyes open, stretched like a cat, complete with a little yawn, and gave me a lick before bounding into the air to join its fellows. I looked at the spot it had licked, and was shocked to realize that the glow around me was actually emanating from my skin, and not the copious amount of moonflowers nearby.

I looked over at Fenn, who was grinning like a fox. His skin and eyes were also glowing, though not nearly as strongly as mine. He laughed at my incredulous look.

"It's called moonglow," he informed me. "A werewolf, or any were-human for that matter, exhibits moonglow on full moon nights, though it's strongest on those who are about to transform for the first time."

"It's so magical," I whispered as I slowly waved my hand in front of my face, fascinated by the way the moonglow trailed my hand, leaving luminous wisps behind that quickly dissipated. A nearby fox tracked the movement, the pale silvery-blue glow reflected in its wide, curious eyes.

"It's almost time. Can you feel its pull?" Fenn asked, lifting his eyes to the full moon that had just cleared the treetops.

"Yes," I replied, looking up at the heavens as well. The ache in my bones that I'd somehow managed to ignore throughout the day suddenly came back with a vengeance. I shivered in anticipation.

"I'd recommend taking off your shoes and socks," Fenn advised as he began pulling off his boots.

I nodded and followed suit, neatly arranging them by the picnic basket. After a moment of consideration, I also unstrapped my dagger and placed it in the basket. Fenn placed his boots next to mine, and for some reason, the sight of our boots sitting next to each other made a little bit of happiness bubble up inside me.

Fenn stood and silently held out his hand. I placed my hand in his, and let him pull me to my feet. He led me to the center of the moonflower field while the Vulclaria danced in the air around us.

I squeezed his hand, and he tightened his grip reassuringly. He stopped and turned to face me, the rising moon looming behind him like a great silver halo.

"Remember, don't try to fight the moon's pull, and just allow your instincts to take over. I'll be right here with you the entire time. Close your eyes, and focus on the pull you feel in your bones," Fenn said as he once again touched his forehead to mine, closing his eyes as well.

I took a deep breath and closed my eyes, reassured by Fenn's nearness. I focused on the ache in my bones that I'd been trying so hard to ignore all this time. I felt a tingling warmth spread through my chest, which quickly moved through the rest of my body. The gentle warmth began climbing in temperature until it felt like my blood was boiling.

I cried out, and was only vaguely aware of a soothing hand stroking my back. The fire in my veins was all-consuming.

Just like back in the tea room, I felt claws growing from my fingertips, and my gums began to throb as my canines elongated. A prickling sensation ran across my skin, and the tips of my ears felt pinched. The pressure kept mounting in my chest.

Just when I thought the fire would consume me alive, a shudder wracked my body and my spine bent forward, sending me to all fours. Just like Fenn said, it felt like I was stretching and flexing all of my muscles at once as they shifted and changed shapes.

My ears moved to the top of my head and fur sprouted all over my body, feeling like one big itch that was immediately scratched. I felt my nose elongating into a fuzzy muzzle, and my fingers condensed into paws. My knees made a loud cracking noise and bent backward, shortening.

And then with a final shudder, the fire in my veins cooled, and I could think again. Slowly, I opened my eyes, blinking rapidly to clear my vision. Even though I knew the sun had long set, my eyes could penetrate the darkness, as if there was a perpetual twilight.

I felt something nuzzle the fur on my shoulder, and turned my head to see Fenn in his wolf form, his ebony fur gleaming in the moonlight. A jolt of recognition went through me, accompanied by a strange feeling of warmth, and connection. I shivered, shaking off the odd sensation.

Naturally, even in wolf form, Fenn stood taller and broader than me, and I instinctively pinned my ears back.

Fenn immediately crouched down and nuzzled my face, giving the fur on my forehead a quick lick. My ears came back up, and he nudged my side. I realized he was trying to get me to walk.

I looked down and tried taking a step forward...and immediately collapsed on the ground. Fenn gave me a wolfish grin, and I growled at him in annoyance, but that only made the grin even wider. I'm pretty sure I heard some yipping from the spectating foxes as well. He nudged my side again, so I scrambled to my feet—paws—and tried again. I went to look down at my paws again, but Fenn nudged my snout up so I was looking straight ahead. Taking the hint, I tried to walk forward again, and actually managed to take a few steps forward without another visit with the earth.

Encouraged, I walked a little further, letting my instincts take over and trying not to overthink it. Fenn followed at my shoulder, and nudged me towards the pond. I looked down at the surface of the water, and a huge, red wolf stared back at me. But those were my green eyes peering out of the wolf's face, and they were glowing just like Fenn's. I tilted my head, and the wolf did the same. My fur coat was the same color as my hair, but in wolf form, it seemed to dance like living fire. I had a white belly, and fluffy white fur in my ears, which I could twitch in different directions.

I looked back at Fenn, who was watching me with a strange expression in his icy blue eyes. For some reason, a jolt of recognition shot like lightning through my veins once more when our eyes met, but stronger this time. I tried to turn around and stumbled, but Fenn was right there to hold me up. I snuggled my face in the fur of his shoulder, and made a rumbling noise I can only describe as purring.

Suddenly self-conscious, I gave my fur a couple of quick licks. I saw movement out of the corner of my eye and just barely stopped myself from trying to catch it in my teeth. My little Vulclaria landed on my back and proceeded to inspect me, before giving a happy yip and leaping into the air. It flew in circles around my head before gliding across the field. It hovered and looked back at me, letting out another yip.

For all intents and purposes, it seemed like the fox wanted to race. I glanced at Fenn and took off after it. First I tried trotting after it, but that felt too slow, so I settled into the wolf's mile-eating lope. I suddenly got the urge to run, really run, and so I let my instincts take over and sprinted after the flying fox, nipping at it whenever I got close enough. But it always managed to flit away just in time, so I growled in frustration.

Fenn loped over to me, that wolfish grin firmly in place. Instinctively, I dropped into a crouch and launched myself at him, the look of surprise in his eyes delighting me. I bowled into him, and we tussled in the grass like playful pups. I swatted at him with my still-clumsy paws and he flipped me over easily. I growled at him, baring my teeth, and he growled back.

Instinct took over and I laid my head back, exposing my neck submissively. The growling immediately stopped. Fenn gave me a lick and then let me up. I stood up, my paws itching to run. I looked at the forest and then at Fenn, and tilted my head at the forest, a question in my eyes. Fenn cocked his head to the side, considering. I whined low in my throat.

He nodded.

I gave him a wolfish grin and bounded into the forest, my paws propelling me swiftly across the ground. I was vaguely aware of a black shadow following close behind. Trees blurred past me, and my body knew just what to do in order to avoid every root, bush, and low-hanging branch. The wind rushed past my face, through my fur, and made it feel like I was flying.

My muscles ached, but in a good way. I pushed them harder, faster. I ran faster than I'd ever dreamed was possible. The moon guided me, pulled at me, taunted me, gave me speed and power. It was exhilarating.

Soon I started to tire, my limbs complaining. I stopped, panting, and looked around at my surroundings. I had absolutely no clue where I'd ended up, just that I was far beyond anything familiar. Fenn slowed to a trot as he approached me, and I grinned at him, my tail wagging.

The moon was fully overhead now. I lifted my face into its moonbeams and howled, just for the joy of it. Fenn joined in, and together we wove an achingly beautiful melody that I knew would grace my dreams.

I fell into step beside Fenn as he led the way back toward our meadow. We raced and played among the trees, the moon lighting our way. After what felt like mere minutes wrapped in eternity, we emerged back into the meadow filled with moonflowers. Most of the Vulclaria were curled up, asleep, though a few still flitted among the cherry blossom tree's branches.

Fenn and I found a comfortable, grassy spot, and curled up together, eyelids drooping. He nuzzled my face goodnight, and just as I was drifting off to sleep, my emerald-eyed Vulclaria reappeared and snuggled into my side, yawning and letting out a contented sigh before closing its crystalline eyes.

I had never felt more at peace than I did in that moment, safe with those I cared for under a sea of stars and moonlight.

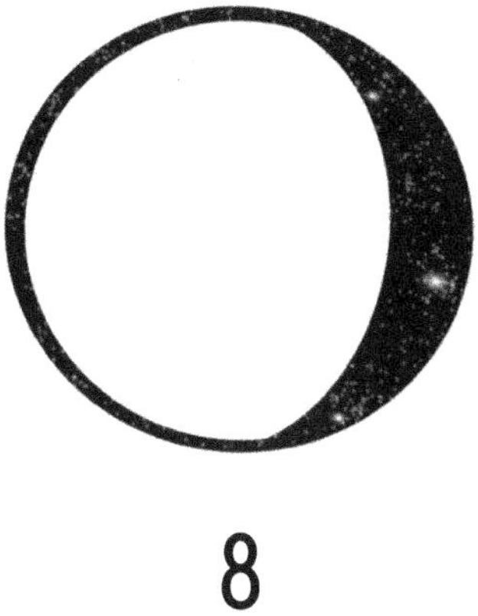

8

A few days later, we were nearly ready to begin our adventurous rescue mission. The entire estate was buzzing with activity from dusk until dawn, as final preparations were being made for our trip. I'd had no idea how complicated it was to plan for an extended trip for even a relatively small group of people.

Even Aly, Wendy, Lily, and Sophia had been commandeered into helping organize everything...which left me with not much to do. I tried to keep busy by relentlessly practicing both the fighting moves and sense-honing exercises Fenn had shown me. After my first shift, I'd found that my senses were even sharper than they were before, so I had to focus intensely if I wanted to block out or hone in on one sense in particular.

I'd also been noticing odd...mood swings. Fenn had been able to resume our morning practices at least, but whenever he was out of my sight I would feel uncharacteristically grumpy and melancholy. I'd even *growled* at Lily yesterday when she'd tugged too hard on my hair while styling it. I'd been horrified, and apologized profusely, but she'd just laughed it off and told me she felt pretty growly sometimes too.

And that was nothing compared to what happened when I was actually near Fenn. I had to keep biting my lip to stop myself from growling and snapping at him. But at the same time, I had to resist the urge to cuddle the way we did while we were wolves. And whenever anyone, especially a female, interrupted us, I'd feel oddly aggressive.

But Fenn and I had bigger fish to fry than my sudden mood swings. I sighed, and went back to packing my bag. I'd already packed most of the essentials, with the help of my assistants. Now I was just adding extras of everything; extra shirts, extra shoes... I'd even packed several fine ball gowns, though for what reason I would possibly need such a fancy dress on a rescue mission was beyond me. But Sophia had insisted I bring some, in addition to their matching shoes and jewelry sets.

After I had finished packing everything I could possibly need, plus backups for my backups, I closed the bag. I'd left out enough clothes to last me for the couple of days or so left until we departed.

Deciding my empty room was not where I wanted to be, I tied my hair up and left, wandering the halls. Seeing everyone else so busy only served to make me feel guilty, so I made my way to the kitchens. Only a couple of maids were there, but they looked like they were taking their lunch break, so I didn't bother them. Instead, I grabbed a few carrots and apples, and popped a leftover macaron into my mouth on my way out.

I took my time walking over to the stables, enjoying the warmth of the sun as it kissed my skin. I stopped by the rose garden and smelled a few of the still-blooming flowers, each sweet scent slightly different than the last.

As expected, the stables weren't all that busy when I arrived. The horses we were taking had already been selected, and the gear packed. Naturally, I would be riding Atlas. I walked up to his stall and called for him softly. He poked his head over his stall door and nickered at me when he spotted the carrot in my hand.

I smiled and gave it to him, letting myself into his stall so I could give him some shoulder scratches. He leaned into my touch, moving around so my hands would be over whatever spot he wanted scratched.

Just spending time with Atlas recharged my soul. I breathed in the comforting scent of hay and horseflesh, reveling in the peaceful quiet broken only by the contented sighs of the horses.

The slightest sound of boots padding over straw met my ears, and I sighed. "Nice try, Chris."

"You sure do look right at home," he commented, sauntering into view. "Thought I'd try and surprise ya. I'm surprised you noticed this time. Usually, sneaking up on you is a piece of cake."

I shifted uneasily. "It's pretty echoey in here. Anyways, what are you doing in the barn? Is there still more gear or feed to pack?"

"No, that's mostly done. You must be excited about going on the trip to visit...what are you visiting again?" Chris asked nonchalantly.

"Just...some hot springs," I hedged, shrugging.

"Ah. Hot springs. Right. Then why did Lily think you were going to go sightseeing?" he questioned.

"Well...probably because we'll be doing a bit of both," I replied, trying to tamp down on the irritation I felt lance through me. "Why were you asking Lily about it?"

"No reason. I just like keeping up with the latest...news," Chris replied.

I snorted. "Don't you mean gossip?"

"Speaking of gossip," Chris said roughly, an edge in his voice, "What's this I hear about you and *His Grace* leaving for a picnic and not returning until the next morning?"

My irritation spiked into defensive anger, and I had to bite back a growl. If I had been in my wolf form, I'm pretty sure my hackles would have been raised.

"Obviously, we went for a picnic and talked. Time got away from us, and instead of wandering through the forest at night, we decided to nap in a safe location," I said tersely.

"Just "napped," did you?" Chris asked suggestively.

I scowled, taken aback. Chris hadn't taken that tone with me since we were little. What right did *he* have to interrogate me about how, or with whom, I spent my time? He was crossing the line.

"What are you implying, Chris?" I asked testily.

"You know what," he shot back. "Just because that guy has more *coin*—"

"Don't talk about things you don't understand, Chris. You have no idea what I, or what Fenn has been through! Forget about me being sold, kidnapped, hunted, and then nearly killed by a noble lunatic! Not only was Fenn *alone* when he found the room where his family was assassinated, without even knowing for sure what had happened to them, but he now has to run this entire place himself *and* find a way to save his sister at the same time!" I raged, the words spewing from my mouth.

I watched with satisfaction as the smugness drained from his face. He stared at me, dumbfounded.

"At least you still have a family," I spat into the tense silence.

"Wait, this trip is to save his sister?" Chris croaked, stunned at my outburst.

I cursed silently. My accursed mood swings had gotten the better of me, and I'd spilled the beans. But there was no use hiding it now. "Yes. But you can't tell anyone."

Chris nodded mutely, his brows pinching together. I could practically hear the gears turning in his head. "If he has to *save* his sister, that means it's going to be dangerous."

I groaned inwardly. I had the sinking feeling I knew where this line of thought was headed.

"That's why we're taking a few guards with us," I said grudgingly.

"Us? You can't go with him! He'll put you in danger!" Chris exclaimed.

"That will make us even," I muttered under my breath. To Chris, I said, "I'm not the same person I used to be, Chris. I'll be fine."

But he was already shaking his head. "If you're going, I'm going," he said firmly. He had that set to his shoulders, the one he always got whenever he got a crazy idea in his head that no one could talk him out of.

"You're not coming with us," I protested. "I put you in danger once, and I won't do it again."

He pursed his lips.

"That's not up to you, is it? Besides, it's my choice to make," he stated, and stalked out of the stables.

I hastily latched Atlas' stall and followed, hustling to catch up. I easily overtook him, catching Chris by surprise.

"Who will watch over the horses?" I tried, grabbing his arm.

"Who will watch over you?" he retorted, arching an eyebrow.

"I can watch out for myself, thank you very much," I said, irritated at what he was implying. *Again.* "And Fenn would never let anything happen to me."

"We'll see about that," he muttered, tearing free from my hold and striding towards the estate.

Towards the direction of Fenn's office.

I paused, trying to wrestle my tumultuous emotions under control before I said something I couldn't take back. I took a few deep breaths—which alerted me to who, exactly, was about to step out of the door ahead, and directly into our line of sight.

When Chris saw Fenn emerge into the sunlight, Bruce at his side, he practically sprinted towards them.

"Chris, wait!" I yelled, frustration seeping into my tone.

Hearing the edge in my voice, Fenn's gaze snapped up from the papers in his hands, his eyes flicking between me and the rapidly approaching stablehand. Chris got to him first, though I was close behind.

Fenn inspected me thoroughly, searching for any sign of injury. Satisfied that I wasn't hurt, he nonetheless stepped forward, angling his body so that he stood just slightly in between me and Chris.

"Mr. Ranger, what seems to be the problem?" Fenn asked smoothly, his tone belying his aggressive stance.

"I know what your little *trip* is actually about," Chris spat. "And I want in."

Fenn stiffened, his eyes cutting to me before returning to a red-faced Chris. "And what would that be?"

"There's no use hiding it! You're going after your sister, and selfishly putting Serena in a dangerous situation!" he ranted, balling his hands into fists. "If she won't listen to reason and stay behind, then she'll need someone to look after her."

"Bold of ye ter antagonize yer employer an' tha one who vouched for ye at tha same time, boy," Bruce growled, his good eye narrowing.

Uncertainty flitted across Chris' features, but it was quickly replaced with stubbornness. He puffed out his chest, glaring back at Bruce.

"That's why I'll be going, too. To watch out for her," Chris fired back.

I bristled, curling my own hands into fists. Bruce noticed the motion, and whether to protect me or Chris, he subtly shifted to my side.

"I can assure you, Serena will be safe with me. Disregarding both your impropriety and how you found out, what makes *you* qualified to "look after her," as you put it?" Fenn asked testily.

"Because I'll actually be around," Chris spat.

Fenn flinched.

Bruce growled.

"Enough of this, both of you! I can look after myself just fine," I shouted. "Chris, you're needed here—"

"He can come," Fenn growled.

I whirled on him. "What? But it's too dangerous for him!"

"That's why he'll have to prove himself first," Fenn said a little too calmly, a challenge in his steely blue eyes.

Chris straightened his shoulders. "And just how d'you propose I do that?"

Fenn smirked. "Find the meadow with a single cherry blossom tree in its center, a pond at its roots. In the forest. Alone. And return with one feather from the creatures there, willingly given."

Chris scoffed. "That's all?"

"Make it back, with the feather, before we leave. If you fail, you stay here, no complaints," Fenn said seriously. "And...you leave to join your family on their trip. Immediately."

I gaped at Fenn, glaring daggers.

"With pay, of course," Fenn added hastily.

"Easy," Chris said haughtily. "I'll be back by sundown."

With that, Chris turned and sauntered towards the forest, a bounce in his step. "And *I* won't make you wait, Serena."

Fenn actually did growl, a deep guttural sound low in his throat. I blinked, shocked by his hostility. Bruce watched Fenn warily.

"This is a horrible idea," I muttered, scowling. "Fenn, why did you goad him into this? What's gotten into you? What if he gets lost in there? And...not that I think he's a bad person, but...you never did say what the Vulclaria would do to someone if...if he didn't pass their soul search."

"Worst case? They would bite him. Best case, they'd just tease him a bit and then run away. He'd never be able to catch one if it didn't want to be caught," he replied with a shrug, though he looked a little uncomfortable.

I visibly relaxed. "That's it? He might just get a bite? Wait, their bite isn't poisonous, right?"

Fenn shifted his weight. "Well, it wouldn't kill him."

"What?!" I cried, horrified.

"The bite of a Vulclaria can have interesting...effects on a person. If they find a dying but pure soul, a bite will take away their pain. Their tears even have healing properties, though the creature would have to be extremely attached to someone for their tears to heal a mortal wound," Fenn explained slowly.

Bruce listened silently, nodding along in agreement.

"And...if the person they bite does not have a pure soul?" I asked nervously. How could such sweet creatures be capable of something like that? Was it simply how they protected themselves?

Fenn and Bruce exchanged glances, Fenn wincing slightly.

"Well," Fenn sighed, scrubbing a hand through his hair, "it can be hard to say. The severity of the bite would depend on the soul being bitten. A soul consumed by hatred, by malice, would likely perish, simply because the light of the fox would purify that corruption. A soul that was somewhere in between, in whatever varying degree, would likely be subjected to some form of trial or torment until whatever was clouding the soul is dealt with."

I put a hand to my mouth. "What kind of...torment?"

"There have been...stories over the years," Fenn said slowly, looking a little uncomfortable. "One tale mentioned that mild bad luck followed the poor man until he managed to get his temper under control, and could handle a bad day without taking it out on others. Another was about a young girl who tried to take from a Vulclaria, was bitten, and had things stolen from her until she learned to share what little she had freely. I'd even heard of a werewolf hunter that took a shot at a Vulclaria kit, wounding it. The mother bit him, trapping him in the form he hated and feared the most: a wolf. Had he repented, accepted his fate, or sacrificed for another, he may well have become human again."

"What happened to him?" I asked when Fenn remained silent.

"Before he could learn from his mistake and change his ways, his fellow hunters spotted him," Fenn said grimly, falling silent.

I felt a twinge of unease as I turned to gaze at the shadows that danced and rippled beneath the towering trees of the forest. Chris wasn't a bad person. He would be fine...right?

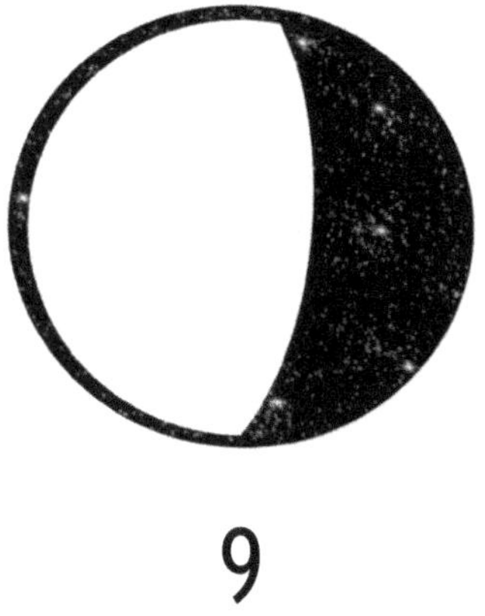

9

"Higher," Fenn barked.

I dutifully angled my kick higher, earning a nod of approval. I repeated the motion tirelessly, my muscles whispering only the barest hint of complaint.

"Now the left," Fenn ordered.

I switched legs, making sure to kick at the same height as I had before. Fenn watched each movement with a critical eye. At his nod, I paused, though I didn't feel the need to catch my breath the way I used to.

"You've really improved," Fenn praised warmly.

"I've had a really good teacher," I complimented. The barest hint of a blush rose in my cheeks. "Though being a werewolf also helps."

Fenn stepped closer, an unreadable expression in his eyes. "That's the first time you've admitted you're a werewolf now."

Flustered, I looked down, fiddling nervously with a lock of hair. "I didn't realize..."

He took my hands in his, and I raised my head, his eyes searching mine. "I understand why you didn't want to say it. Saying the words aloud makes it *real*. And real can be...frightening."

"Just a bit," I murmured, warmth blooming in my chest. Fenn just had this way of making me feel *seen*. He noticed all the little things that no one else ever did.

"I'm glad. For a little while there, I was worried," Fenn admitted.

"Worried that I couldn't handle it?" I asked softly.

"No, never that," Fenn said firmly. "I knew you could handle it. I just...I was worried you might resent me for it."

"I already told you, didn't I?" I pulled my hands from his, only to cup his face, my thumbs smoothing the worry lines at the corners of his eyes. "I'm grateful you saved my life. If I could go back in time and do it all over again, I wouldn't change a single thing. Because even if I wasn't always happy, the decisions I made led me to you. And I wouldn't give that up for anything."

Fenn barely waited until I'd finished speaking before he pressed his lips to mine. In the past, his kisses had been gentle. But now there was an urgency to his kisses, and it was raw and rough and wonderful. His arms wrapped around my waist, pulling me close.

We fit together like two puzzle pieces, each molded to perfectly complement the other. I felt something deep in my chest resonate, and his heart answered, as if the beating of our hearts had become one. I felt warmth pool in my belly, and I deepened the kiss.

Fenn pulled back, and I made a sound of complaint deep in my throat. He cupped my face, the tender way he looked at me sending thoughts of eternity through my mind. Something akin to awe and surprise flickered in the depths of blue eyes, and he searched mine, a question in his expression.

"Did you—" he started.

But before he could finish his question, a loud crash followed by a truly inspired string of curses echoed from within the nearby forest, and we both looked toward the source of the noise.

Fenn and I looked on, unimpressed, as Chris emerged from the forest, covered in smears of dirt. Several leaves and twigs poked out of his sandy blonde hair. I bit back a laugh at the sight, though my lips trembled traitorously.

I glanced at Fenn, noticing he was also attempting valiantly not to laugh, but he made no attempt to tame the smirk on his face.

Chris came to an abrupt halt when he saw us, his face tightening when he saw how Fenn still had his arm wrapped around my waist. He scowled, brushing off some of the forest debris clinging to his clothes.

"I take it you haven't found the meadow yet?" Fenn asked, a hint of satisfaction in his tone.

"What do you think?" Chris muttered darkly. "I'm not out of time yet, though. I *will* find it."

"I'm glad you're unhurt, Chris, and I'm sure you'll find it soon," I said supportively. "Why not grab a sandwich from the kitchens before going out again? I'm sure Aly would be happy to make one for you."

"Yes, *mother*," Chris grumbled.

I frowned, trying not to let his words sting so much. I was only trying to be helpful. But Fenn stiffened at his words, every muscle going taut.

"Don't speak to her like that," Fenn snapped.

"I can say what I want," Chris said defensively, though his tone had softened.

"Apologize," Fenn glowered.

Chris wavered, before finally saying curtly, "Sorry, I must be hungry. Maybe I will go eat something."

And with that, Chris wandered off in the direction of the kitchens, picking leaves from his shirt. Once he was out of earshot, I turned to Fenn.

"I appreciate you defending me. Chris is normally such an easy-going guy. I just don't get why he's been acting like this lately," I said.

But even as the words left my lips, I knew they weren't true. I *did* know why he was acting like that, even if I didn't want to admit it. The way he'd acted just now only confirmed it.

Fenn raised an eyebrow.

"Fine, maybe I do know. But I don't know how to tell him without hurting his feelings and destroying our friendship! I've already lost my mother, I don't want to lose him too," I sighed. "I haven't even mustered up the courage to tell him I'm a werewolf. I don't want him to call me a...a monster."

"You would make a very beautiful monster," Fenn teased. "But I'm pretty sure a monster wouldn't insist on taking care of his entire family despite all of that attitude."

I gave Fenn a trembling smile. "You always know just what to say."

Fenn drew me in for a hug. "This big bad wolf, however, has no qualms about scaring some sense into him."

I laughed, the fear in me easing. How did Fenn always make the world seem brighter? I was very much looking forward to spending more time with Fenn while we traveled.

"I'll try to talk to him before we leave. Maybe then he'll give up this ridiculous challenge," I promised.

"I certainly won't turn down more alone time with you," Fenn purred in my ear.

I blushed, swatting him away, but couldn't help the smile on my face. "Same here. And on the way back, I can get to know your sister, Freya."

Fenn smiled, but worry tightened the expression. "I'm sure the two of you will get along famously."

"If she's anything like you've described, I'm sure we'll be great friends. And who knows, if the two of us team up, we might even be able to beat you in a sparring match."

"You wish," Fenn teased, that mischievous spark returning to his eyes. "Speaking of, I don't believe we've finished our workout routine yet, have we?"

Chris crashed through the undergrowth, cursing at the rotten branches and vines that seemed to reach out to catch in his clothes on purpose. It almost felt like the forest itself was conspiring against him.

Then again, it wasn't as if he'd exactly had much practice traipsing through a forest. He'd only had eyes for the ranch for as long as he could remember. Well, for the ranch and Serena.

The first time he'd seen her, he'd just wanted to tease her for her shockingly red hair. He'd enjoyed watching her reactions. But when he'd tired of that and realized he actually enjoyed spending time with her, he'd pushed his parents to essentially take her on as an apprentice alongside him and his little brother.

Learning how much she enjoyed spending time with him and the horses, especially when her relationship with her mother soured, made him happy he could offer her sanctuary.

If only the noble pig hadn't shown up, then everything would still be perfect. The family ranch wouldn't be a pile of ashes. And she never would have laid eyes on *him*.

The ridiculous challenge Fenrys had laid at his feet had sounded gloriously easy at first. Find some random clearing in the forest and grab a feather from some lil critter. Easy stuff.

But how was it possible that finding one single spot among the trees was proving to be so difficult? At this rate, he was going to run out of time.

After his little run-in this morning with Serena and Fenrys, who had looked *way* too cozy for his liking, he'd grabbed some food in the kitchens and stuffed a satchel full of things to take with him. Chris wouldn't be leaving the forest until he'd succeeded, and shown up his rival.

He had to win Serena back before she moved forward with Fenrys. He had the horrible feeling that he was losing his chance with her, the future he'd always pictured of the two of them taking over the Ranger ranch one day as husband and wife slipping through his fingers like water. Even if it was dangerous, he couldn't afford not to go.

Still getting paid was just a bonus, even if it was Fenrys' coin.

Chris came to a stop in front of a familiar–looking tree and groaned. The faint X he had scratched into the bark with his baling knife stared back at him, confirming his worst fear.

He'd walked in a circle.

Feeling defeated, Chris sat down on a nearby log and pulled out an apple to snack on. He sat staring at it for a little while, trying to come up with a plan to find the meadow he was meant to locate.

Drawing a blank, he pulled out his knife and began slicing the apple, more for something to do with his hands than anything else. Just as he finished cutting the last slice, the rustle of a nearby tree branch caught his eye.

Chris stilled, his eyes searching for any signs of movement. The birds kept regaling the world with their songs, so it likely wasn't a predator. Probably just another bird.

Chris popped an apple slice into his mouth, enjoying the burst of sweet flavor on his tongue. The rustling came again, but this time he caught a glimpse of what had made the sound. It reminded him of a fox. But foxes couldn't climb trees.

Hadn't Serena mentioned something about little winged foxes before? Chris took a slice of apple and set it a few feet away from him on a leaf. Returning to his log, he waited, popping another slice into his mouth.

His patience was soon rewarded when a fuzzy little fox-like creature darted out from its cover like an arrow. It landed, folding its *wings*, and proceeded to devour the apple slice.

Chris tried not to let his jaw drop. He'd never seen a creature like it before. This might be the creature he was supposed to get a feather from.

The fox looked at Chris cautiously as it finished its apple, then cocked its head and took a tentative step towards him. Suddenly, its amber eyes started to glow, and Chris shivered involuntarily. It felt like those eyes could see right through him.

He moved to throw it another bit of apple, breaking the staring contest. But the second he did, the fox growled, turned and bounded into the air, gliding on silent wings.

Chris hastily stuffed everything back into his bag and gave chase. If this thing was headed back to its meadow, he could simply follow it there. He was barely able to keep up with it, only managing to catch glimpses of its tail or wing feathers as he fought through the undergrowth after it.

After what felt like hours, and just as the sun began to set, Chris saw the fox slip through a curtain of vines. He followed after, gasping at what he saw. In front of him lay a pristine meadow filled with flowers that glowed faintly in the gathering twilight. In the middle stood an ethereal cherry blossom tree, its image reflected perfectly in the still pond at its base. And scattered throughout the area was an entire flock of the winged foxes, sleeping, playing, and flitting through the air.

Chris slowly entered the field, annoyed by the fact that there was no cover for him to hide behind. Based on how fast the first fox had moved, he doubted he'd be able to catch one of the little things. Maybe he could trade some food for a feather, or find a discarded one on the ground.

A sharp snap echoed in the air as his foot came down on a dry twig, and Chris froze as every pair of slitted eyes in the area turned towards him. He was locked in another staring contest, and a shudder wracked him as their unnerving gazes bore into him.

After a few moments of tense silence, a portion of the foxes gave what sounded like a warning growl and flew off. The rest went back to what they were doing, practically ignoring him.

Why did it feel like he'd been tested, and found lacking? The feeling made him uneasy. Nevertheless, he walked further into the meadow towards a group of the foxes that seemed to be play-fighting with each other. They were smaller and fluffier than the others, so they must be young kits.

They mostly ignored him as he sat nearby and opened up his bag. He took out the remaining apple slices, placing a handful on the ground in front of him, and ate one himself. The kits started sniffing the air, looking around for the source of the sweet scent.

The bravest one of the bunch, a tan-coated fox with the markings of a barn owl, ventured closer when it spotted the apple slices. After a few tentative licks, it yipped at its fellows and began crunching into the apple pieces. Its friends joined it, and soon Chris had the whole group of them staring at him and licking their little snouts.

Chris chuckled and retrieved the ripe banana he'd brought from his bag, peeling it and holding it out for them to eat. They chirped in delight and made short work of it. The tan fox came closer to Chris, so he held out a hand for it to sniff. Once it was satisfied, it butted his hand with its head, so he gently stroked its soft fur.

Cautiously, he tugged on a downy feather that seemed to be loose on one wing. The fox turned its head and pulled the feather out, dropping it on Chris' foot. He carefully placed the feather in his bag, making sure there was no way it could fall out.

He'd done it! Now he'd be able to go on that trip with Serena, and everything would be right with his world again. But he could afford to stay a few more minutes with the fluff balls before going back.

One of the foxes was nosing at his bag, so he laughed and reached in for the other apple he'd brought. The gray kit tried to snatch it from him, but he pushed it away gently. It whined, a mewling, plaintive sound.

Nearby adult foxes, including a big, dark gray one, turned to look at the kits, watching Chris closely. Uneasy with the attention, he fumbled in his bag, blindly searching for the knife so he could slice the apple.

"Don't worry little ones, I'm just going to make the apple easier for you to share," he murmured reassuringly.

But the impatient gray kit launched itself at the apple just as Chris began to cut into it. The apple, fox, and knife tumbled from Chris' hands, landing in the soft grass.

To his horror, Chris saw a single drop of blood on the knife just as the kit began keening, holding its leg close to its body. The blood drained from his face as every fox in that meadow froze, looking between him and the crying kit. Each one raised its wings and puffed out its fur, growls emanating from deep within their chests.

The fox that had been watching him before, the dark gray, darted forward with teeth bared. The kit's mother sank its teeth into Chris' arm, locking eyes with him for an instant before it pulled back. The fox scurried to its young to inspect its leg, nuzzling its face to calm it down.

Chris abandoned the apple and knife, grabbed his bag and made a run for it, half fearing that the entire flock of the things would be chasing him. He ran through the forest, and didn't stop until he'd made it back to the Verdania castle.

There was hardly anyone about this late in the evening, so Chris hustled to the room he'd been given in the servants quarters, noting along the way that light still shone from the window of Fenrys' study.

Gritting his teeth, Chris quickly disinfected and bandaged the small puncture wound. A small price to pay to win his girl over. But he didn't want to have to explain to either Serena or Fenrys how he'd accidentally injured one of their favorite critters, so he changed into a clean, long-sleeve shirt and slipped into a coat, just for good measure. No one would be the wiser, and the bite would heal in a few days, just like the other scratches he'd gotten while exploring the forest.

Taking the small, downy feather from his bag, he strode straight to Fenrys' study, not bothering to knock before opening the sturdy oaken door. He stopped in surprise when he saw Serena asleep in a plush chair by the fireplace, an open book in her lap. He scowled.

Fenrys looked up at him coolly, but Chris noticed a flash of irritation flit over his sharp features. Serena woke with a start, running a hand through her mussed hair.

"Chris," she said, surprised. "What are you doing here so late? I couldn't find you earlier."

So she'd been looking for him, eh? He smirked, glancing at Fenrys' impassive expression. Then he held out the feather, pinched between his thumb and index finger. "How's that for proving myself?"

Fenrys looked disappointedly at the feather, giving an almost inaudible sigh. "So, you actually managed it."

"I told you, you could do it," Serena said after a moment. She didn't look nearly as happy or excited as she should have.

But it didn't matter. Because Chris would be going on the trip now too. Fenrys couldn't get rid of him that easily.

"Pack your things. We leave the day after tomorrow," Fenn stated, the hint of a growl in his voice.

"I look forward to traveling with you." Chris smiled triumphantly, ignoring the dull throbbing in his arm.

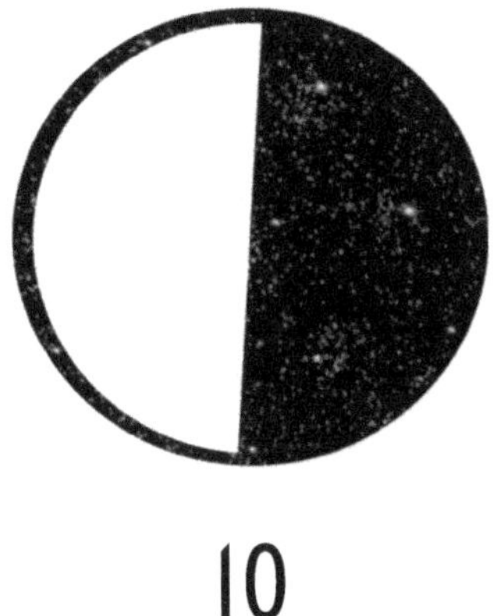

10

As the first rays of dawn gilded the sky and the earth, our entourage set out on our adventure. Aly and the rest of my friends saw us off as we rode away from the estate, waving long after we'd passed out of view. The early morning mist swirled around our horses' hooves, making it feel like we were walking on clouds.

We rode in pairs, creating a column of mysterious travelers. In front rode Tim and his older brother, Danny, as our vanguard. Danny was familiar with the route we would be taking, and would answer any questions directed at our group. He was a few years older than Tim, and he'd started cracking jokes the moment I'd met him. I had a feeling we'd get along famously.

Next came Fenn and I, riding our favorite horses. Atlas, of course, was full of energy, and kept prancing, tossing his head when I pulled him down to a walk again. But as the miles passed beneath his hooves, I knew he would calm down.

Behind us, Chris and another werewolf, Jax, brought up the rear, each leading a packhorse laden with our camping gear and supplies.

Jax was by far the oldest in the group, at thirty-five, and he was charged with watching our backs on the road. He was tall and broad, with dark hair and eyes, and he had a thin scar running through his left eyebrow. I had a feeling that any trouble Danny couldn't joke our way out of, Jax would simply scare off with one scowl.

Tim and Danny conversed quietly in the front, though I could feel Chris' eyes silently boring into my back from behind me. I hadn't had a chance to talk with Chris since our little spat before he went after the Vulclaria feather. Unease stirred in my stomach at the thought of the conversation I would have to have with him. Needing a distraction, I turned to Fenn.

"So Fenn, have you ever traveled to Eldore before?" I asked.

"Not since I was young." Fenn smiled. "My family went on a month-long diplomatic trip to visit the elven monarchs on behalf of Cyrulia. My brother and I were mostly interested in exploring, but Freya really seemed to love all of it. The culture, the architecture, the folklore..."

"It sounds amazing," I breathed, trying to imagine it. "I've never even seen an elf before."

"They're much like humans, just with pointed ears, an aversion to meat, and inflated egos," Fenn said, chuckling.

"Oh. Does that mean werehumans have a hard time getting enough to eat in Eldore?" I asked, slightly concerned.

"It's mostly the highest-ranking members of the royal family, nobles and beast tamers that completely refuse to eat meat these days. Since they opened their borders to trade a few centuries ago, dwarves, humans, and werehumans have all traveled through, with some settling down there. So there are plenty of establishments that do serve meat; just not as many as in Cyrulia," he explained.

"That's good," I said, glancing at Fenn. "Because for some reason, I've been craving meat these days."

Fenn chuckled. "Huh, I wonder why. Must be all that fresh air."

We spent the rest of the day chatting as we passed through the forest, stopping only twice for lunch and to water the horses at swiftly-flowing streams. We'd brought our own waterskins with us, and Danny had assured us we'd be able to refill them with safe drinking water along the way.

As the sun began its final descent, we started passing by some scattered farms. The road widened, and we saw occasional horses and cattle, grazing on the lush grasses in the fields.

Soon the dirt road turned into cobblestones, and we found ourselves moving down the main street of a small village. The houses we passed were simple but sturdy, often boasting flower boxes underneath each window. When we passed the smithy, my jaw nearly dropped at the short, bearded man I saw placing a shortsword in the display window. I tried not to stare, but couldn't quite tear my eyes away.

I heard a low rumble beside me, and I realized Fenn was laughing at me. "Yes, that's what a dwarf looks like. You should probably stop staring before he gets angry," he commented drily.

I blushed, looking at Fenn. "Is it true that dwarves are the best smiths in the land?"

"Generally speaking, yes. Though some of the dark elves' weapons are arguably better suited to combat. But don't let a dwarf hear you say that," he replied.

"Like the dagger you gave me?" I asked, absently stroking the hilt of the dagger strapped to my thigh.

"Exactly. The dark elves use a unique metal alloy of their own invention that's both incredibly light and strong," Fenn explained.

"Why do you keep saying *dark* elves? Are they evil?" I asked.

"No, not at all," Fenn said. "Dark elves are called such because they're a clan that specializes in metalwork, at working with and using the elements found within the earth. In my opinion, calling them earth elves would be more accurate, but I think they wanted to avoid being made fun of as dirt elves."

"Ah," I said with a smile. "I guess that makes sense."

"Look, there's the inn we'll be staying at tonight," Fenn pointed out as a two-story building came into view. It had an attached stable where we could board our horses.

The rest of us waited outside while Danny went in to rent us some rooms for the night. He came back out a short time later with a stableboy at his heels.

"Two doubles and two singles," he announced to the group, sketching a bow in my direction. "The lad here'll take the horses, so we can go straight to dinner. Tonight's dish is beef stew with fresh bread!"

After taking off our saddlebags, we handed the horses over in pairs of two. I gave Atlas' neck a pat and assured him I'd check on him later. I noticed that Chris looked distinctly put out, and quickly offered to stay and help settle the horses. Fenn nodded, so he followed after the stableboy.

The five of us settled down to dinner, with Danny keeping us laughing throughout the meal. Chris slunk in part way through, ate quietly and went to his room before I could get a chance to take him aside for a chat. I felt a twinge of relief, followed by a twinge of guilt for that relief.

But I tried to put it out of my mind and focus on the story Danny was telling about the time Tim had gotten stuck at the top of a tree when he was little, and had to be rescued.

After we'd all finished, I brought Atlas a carrot and checked to make sure he had been properly cared for. Seeing that he had, I retired to my room after saying a quick goodnight to everyone.

The next few days passed in a blur. On our fifth day, we passed the invisible border into Eldore, and I got my first good look at a real elf. The stories, so far, had proven to be fairly accurate. The ones I saw all had delicate, pointed ears, wore flowing robes, and kept their hair long. Most carried daggers, though several also had bows and quivers strapped to their backs.

On the nights when the nearest inn was still too far, we would camp out under the stars. I really enjoyed lying next to Fenn in the darkness, gazing at the array of stars above us, spread across the endless sky like diamonds on a bed of rich velvet. We would tell stories late into the night, and somehow I'd still wake up excited for what new sight, new story, new adventure the day would bring.

After our sixth day of traveling, we stopped at an inn in a sizable town for the night. My head felt like it was on a swivel, I could hardly take everything in fast enough. We'd started wearing the hoods of our cloaks to hide our faces as we moved deeper into Eldore, so I must have made quite the sight, constantly looking this way and that.

Naturally, there were elves everywhere, but somehow these towns reminded me of home. Barefoot children ran laughing through the streets, and the adults bustled about the main street, patronizing the local bakery, butchery, and tailors. The only real differences, other than the distinctive architecture, were the pointed ears and the long, flowing outfits. Most of the buildings incorporated nature in ways I'd never seen before, with potted flowers hanging from every sign post and moss dripping from every roof like a living carpet.

We fell comfortably into our usual routine, with Danny going inside the inn to purchase some rooms for the night, and Chris helping bed down the horses. After the luxury of a hot bath, we all gathered for dinner, which happened to be fileted fish from the local river and a large salad. I think Chris was the only one who actually finished his salad, though.

At first I'd brushed it off as nothing, but I'd been noticing Chris scratching madly at the same spot on his arm for several days in a row. I'd tried to ask him about it, but he'd just brushed me off, saying it was a bug bite. But he'd been awfully scowly and irritable lately, so I wondered if it was really the bug bite that was bothering him. Everytime I broached the subject of our relationship, he'd quickly found an excuse to leave, or some duty to attend to. Honestly, I was starting to get a little worried.

When I brought up my concerns later that night with Fenn, he simply told me not to worry about it, that Chris would open up when he was ready.

"What if he's never ready?" I wondered.

"All you can do is ask. You can't force someone to share if they don't want to," Fenn responded.

I smiled. "When did you get so wise?"

"You haven't seen anything yet," he teased with that lop-sided smile of his.

"Well, I look forward to hearing more of your wisdom, O Great Wolf," I quipped back.

"That's the right attitude," Fenn gloated. "Keep it up, and I might have a surprise for you tomorrow."

"You know I love your surprises," I said with a grin.

"Until then, sleep tight," Fenn murmured, giving me a light peck on the forehead.

"Until tomorrow," I replied.

We both went to our respective rooms, though I was smiling right up until the moment I drifted off to sleep.

The next morning, I was up at first light. I had contemplated trying to sleep in later, but knew I was too excited to fall back asleep. So instead, I took my time getting ready.

I combed out the tangled knots in my hair, and put on a clean summer frock, tucking my coin pouch into one of its many pockets. I threw my cloak over my shoulders to fend off the chill in the early-morning air. Slipping into my softest pair of boots, I quietly left my room and headed down to see if breakfast was ready.

The aromatic smell of fresh bread and fried eggs wafted up the stairs, so I quickly followed my nose to the source of the mouth-watering scent. To my surprise, Fenn, Danny, and Tim were already there, each wolfing down a sizable helping of food.

They waved when they saw me, so I joined them, asking for a plate along the way. Soon I had my own steaming plate piled high with food, and I wasted no time and dug in. After we'd cleaned our plates, we got down to discussing the plan for the day,

"So," I said, raising my eyebrows, "what did you have in mind?"

Fenn smiled at the excitement in my voice. "Well, since we need to restock our food supplies anyways, I was thinking we could make a morning out of it and visit some of the local shops and artisans. I hear there are some great food stalls in this town."

"All right!" Danny exclaimed, giving Tim a high-five.

"That sounds wonderful," I said.

"Great. Let's get going. Jax and Chris will stay to keep an eye on things," Fenn said, getting up from the table.

We followed him outside, and took our time going from store to store until we'd amassed an appropriate amount of foodstuffs for another week of travel.

"Tim, Danny," Fenn called, pulling out his money pouch, "why don't you two take the food back to the inn, and then go exploring until lunch."

Fenn handed each of them a few silver coins, and they grinned at each other. I couldn't help but smile at their reactions.

"You got it, boss," Danny said with a mock bow.

"Thanks," Tim said shyly, before they both headed back to the inn, the bags of food thrown over their shoulders. Passing elves gave the two lanky brothers a wide berth.

Fenn laced his fingers through mine, drawing me close. "Where to?"

"Anywhere with you," I breathed. "Though...maybe we could start with whatever that is." I lifted my chin towards the food cart that was giving off a mouthwatering aroma.

"Good idea," he chuckled. "Your sweet tooth never fails to impress me."

The sweet scent turned out to be a thin pancake filled with fresh cream and strawberries. Even Fenn had to admit they were quite tasty. I marveled at the enchanted stones that heated the metal cooking pans, which seemed to make cooking a much easier and quicker process without having to wait for the flame to become hot enough. When I mentioned it to Fenn, he revealed that he was actually considering acquiring some for not only his estate, but also for the people in his territory, which I thought was a marvelous idea. We wandered around, finding ourselves in what appeared to be a festival market, with stalls lining both sides of the road and ribbons festooning the signs.

"Is there a festival going on today?" I asked the elderly elven vendor of a nearby jewelry shop.

"Why, yes of course! Today marks the beginning of our annual month-long celebration in honor of our goddess, Astraea!" she exclaimed. Then she narrowed her eyes. "Isn't that why you've come?"

"Yes, that's why we're visiting! We just, uh, got the dates mixed up! We're so glad we got here in time after all!" I replied with a smile, nudging Fenn, who nodded absently.

"Ah! I see your fine husband has a good eye!" the elf commented, following the direction of Fenn's gaze.

I blushed crimson, and opened my mouth to correct her, but Fenn cut in first.

"How much for this one?" he asked, pointing to one of the necklaces on display. Was it strange how happy I was that Fenn didn't deny that we were married?

I finally looked to see what had caught Fenn's attention, and nearly gasped when I saw the delicate, golden crescent moon necklace. It reminded me so much of the one left behind by the father I'd never known, that I couldn't tear my eyes away.

"For you, honey, three silvers," she said with a wink. I winced at the price.

"Sold," Fenn said, fishing the coins out and handing them over.

She handed him the necklace and cheerfully tucked the coins into her pocket.

"Fenn, I..." I started, at a loss for words.

"Do you not like it?" he asked, uncertainty flickering across his features.

"No, I love it! Thank you Fenn," I said whole-heartedly.

"I'm glad. It reminded me of the one you used to wear all the time. But since that's not really an option anymore thanks to me, I thought...well I thought you might like to wear this one instead," he admitted hesitantly.

"I think I'll like this one much more than the silver one. At least this one was given to me by someone who cares enough to stick around," I reassured him.

Fenn stiffened. "Was it from a boyfriend?" he asked cautiously. A tiny thrill went through me at the thought that Fenn didn't like the idea of me with someone else.

I laughed. "No, from my father."

Fenn visibly relaxed. I turned my back to him, looking over my shoulder through my hair. "Will you put it on for me?"

Fenn smiled and carefully draped the necklace around my neck, his rough hands tickling my skin as he pushed my curtain of hair aside and fiddled with the tiny clasp.

I looked down when he finished, admiring the way the pendant glittered in the sunlight. I ran a reverent finger over the face of the smooth metal, and looked up to find Fenn watching me closely. Feeling emboldened, I stepped closer and kissed him, the surprise and delight on his face sending warmth through my chest.

"Shoo, you lovebirds, be off with you," crowed the jewelry vendor, though despite the shooing motions she was making, she was grinning from ear to ear.

I laughed and took Fenn by the hand, leading him deeper into the festival. I headed towards the music I could hear, and stumbled across the town square. Men and women were dancing to a lively tune, skirts swishing and hair fluttering with each graceful move.

I stopped to watch them, mesmerized. Every elf seemed so inherently beautiful and graceful that I wanted to capture the moment in a painting forever.

"May I have this dance?" Fenn asked with a tiny bow, lifting our joined hands.

"But of course, my good sir," I replied with a curtsy.

Together we jumped into the square, and were soon swept along by the current of dancers. Guided by the melody, we twirled and pranced and swayed, smiles on our faces and love in our hearts.

II

Another week went by, and despite the looming task ahead of us, I could hardly remember a time when I'd had so much fun. As we moved deeper into Eldore, the architecture and culture became even more pronounced, and I loved trying all kinds of different foods and seeing all kinds of enchanted items. The celebratory air from the festival added an element of wonder and excitement to each place we visited. The only sour spot in all of this was Chris.

He'd become increasingly moody and irritable, and almost every time I saw him he was scratching at his arm. But every time I'd offered to treat the bug bite, Chris would rudely brush me off. I was starting to worry that it was infected.

And for some reason, when we'd heard that a couple of the towns we'd stayed in had lost some livestock to a wild animal attack, he'd seemed a little shaken. Despite my numerous attempts to have that talk with him, he always managed to slip away with some excuse. Now instead of feeling a little relieved at putting off the inevitable, I just felt more anxious.

But I tried not to let Chris' strange behavior ruin the trip for me. Especially since I was finally getting to spend more time with Fenn. And I was enjoying getting to know Danny, Tim, and Jax as well.

All too soon, we drew closer to the capital, and the city where Fenn's sister was supposedly being held in bondage. We stopped in a nearby city a day's ride from the capital, and found an inn to spend the night. This was the biggest inn we'd seen by far, and it had an extensive restaurant and bar on the first floor.

The smell of it made my stomach sour. It didn't help that my sense of smell was now much stronger than it used to be.

Our little pack sat down at one of the empty tables and ordered the chicken and potato dish. At some of the smaller inns we'd stayed at, the only protein option had been eggs, thanks to the elves' general aversion to meat. But the closer we came to the capital, the more meat options there were, which was fortunate for the rest of us, because Fenn could get pretty grumpy when he was hungry.

We ate in mostly companionable silence, though I couldn't help but glance surreptitiously at a group of particularly loud and rowdy elves sitting at the bar. I had always known raised voices and the stench of alcohol to precede a beating at my mother's hand, causing a sense of foreboding to shiver through me.

Fenn noticed where I kept glancing and laced his fingers through mine under the table. I smiled at him, grateful that no words were needed.

"What about you, Serena?" Danny asked, a sly look in his brown eyes.

I jolted in surprise. I realized guiltily that I'd completely tuned out of the story Danny must have been telling. "Sorry, what were you asking?"

The grin Danny gave me told me he knew exactly why I hadn't been paying attention. "I *asked*, Serena, if you've ever seen a sparring match between elves. Because it is absolutely mesmerizing, they're such fluid fighters. I mean, I could still beat them, of course."

"Then prove it!" roared a hoarse voice from across the room.

I flinched as the obviously drunk elf slammed his tankard against the counter. I glanced nervously around the room, noticing that every eye had turned towards us.

Fenn and Jax stiffened as the elf got up and started walking towards our table. He stopped right in front of Danny, and I got my first good look at him. Like most elves, he was clean-shaven, with long brown hair hanging down his back. His mussed robes sported what I suspected to be stains from his food and drink. He was tall, but not as tall as Fenn and Jax.

"We're not looking for trouble, friend," Fenn said evenly.

"You've found it," slurred the elf. "Time to put your money where your mouth is. Unless you're all just a bunch of cowards!"

Danny stood up so quickly his chair fell over, echoing loudly in the silent room. Tim tugged on his brother's sleeve, looking around nervously.

"I think you've had a bit too much to drink tonight. Perhaps another time," Fenn ground out. A muscle feathered in his jaw. I squeezed his hand.

"What, not enough coin for a bet? Or just lacking a spine? I could always take her as payment," the elf leered, raking his eyes over my figure.

I stiffened, memories flashing before my eyes of Lester ogling me with the exact same look in his eyes. My heart began to race, fire replacing the fear in my veins. My gums began to throb, my mouth parting to make room for my growing fangs, and I felt claws push through my fingertips. Fenn's gaze snapped to mine, his eyes widening in alarm before hardening.

I felt my eyes begin to glow, and based on the look the elf was giving me, he'd noticed. Fenn stood and pulled the hood of my cloak over my head, but not before my gaze snagged on Chris', and the shock and horror in his eyes chilled me to the bone. I watched as his lip began to curl in disgust. Fenn put himself between me and the elf, Jax and Danny flanking him.

"She's a flea-bitten werewolf!" he exclaimed, recovering from his surprise. Then he cackled, the sound grating against my ears. Other people in the room started muttering and shifting uncomfortably.

"You're the only flea-bitten bag of garbage here," Fenn snarled, his right fist smashing into the elf's enraged face.

All pandemonium broke loose. Some elves fled for the exit while others crowded around to watch, egging on one side or the other. Jax and Danny glared at anyone who looked like they wanted to join in, leaving Fenn to finish what he'd started.

The elf was reeling from the hit to his face, and was slow to recover. But he came back swinging, landing a few blows to Fenn's blocking arms. I tried to calm down like I had last time, but my ears started to feel pinched and stretched. The noise and the smells started to press in on me, shattering my focus. I was going to shift, and there was nothing I could do to stop it. I stood up, panicking, and Chris recoiled.

"Stay away from me!" he cried, one trembling hand groping for his dinner knife.

I made a run for the door, tears already blurring my vision.

Fenn whipped his head around as I moved, giving the elf a free shot at him. He staggered for a moment before recovering and I heard him really lay into the elf as I burst out of the inn.

I raced back the way we had come earlier in the day, making for the forest. Fortunately, the inn we were staying at was towards the edge of town, so I didn't have too far to go. Still, I could feel my skin ripple, goosebumps emerging.

My heart pounded in my ears as I finally sprinted past the last row of buildings and dove beneath the cover of the trees and the concealing darkness. I went in as deep as I could go before the fire forced me to my knees. Quickly, I ripped off my cloak, my thickening fingers fumbling to remove my dagger and necklace as well.

This time, instead of fighting it, I embraced the change, stretching much less painfully into my new shape. My muscles ached, but in a pleasant way as I rolled my shoulders and shook my fur, settling into my wolf form.

I sighed, looking down at my paws. The look on Chris' face haunted me. I couldn't bear the thought of my friend looking at me in fear like I was some sort of monster.

The pounding of boots on the ground alerted me that someone was running in my direction, and I pricked my ears forward, listening. I tensed, preparing to run deeper into the forest, fearing that an elf was coming after me. I was upwind, so I couldn't pick up a scent.

Just as I was about to run, I heard Fenn call out my name, and I relaxed as he came into view, his eyes going straight to mine. In wolf form, I was nearly eye to eye with him. I whined deep in my throat.

"Are you all right? I came as fast as I could," Fenn huffed, running his hand through his hair anxiously. My sharp eyes snagged on the bruises covering his knuckles. "Jax will sort everything out at the inn, and Danny and Tim will be along shortly. Chris...Chris ran off while I helped that drunken elf off to dreamland."

Fenn came towards me, and I licked his ragged knuckles. He smiled and ran his fingers through my fur. I hummed at the comforting sensation.

"Let's not worry about any of that for tonight. Do you want to try and change back? Remember it's all about slowing your heart rate and remembering what it feels like to be human."

I nodded, but then shook my head. Now that I was a wolf again, I wanted to run, and keep running until I left all my worries behind.

"That's fine by me," Fenn chuckled. "Then I'll join you."

And with that, Fenn removed his cloak, setting it beside mine, and drew his shirt over his head, revealing the well-defined muscles of his abdomen. I turned around quickly, grateful he couldn't see me blush through my thick fur.

He chuckled low in his throat. I growled, but refused to turn around until I heard him shift and he brushed up against my side. I couldn't help the rumbling purr that emerged from my throat.

I bounded into the forest, pausing to look back over my shoulder at Fenn, tilting my head a fraction. He gave me a wolfish grin and followed. I sprang between the trees, my paws flying over the earth. Fenn stayed right at my heels, my very own shadow.

The sound of a low howl brought me to a stop, and I looked at Fenn inquisitively. He flicked his ears towards the sound, so we started loping in that direction.

After only a minute or two, a pair of werewolves came into view. Both were bigger than me, with warm brown coats, and one had his tongue lolling out the side of his mouth. The scents on the air confirmed my suspicions; the smaller of the pair was Tim, and of course the goofy-looking one was Danny. They wagged their tails when they saw us, trotting forward to meet us.

Tim head-butted his brother before playfully pouncing at me. A growl rose in Fenn's throat, but I managed to dodge and pounce back. We tussled on the ground, teeth sliding harmlessly through fur. Tim easily pinned me down, and despite my best wriggling I couldn't get loose.

Then Fenn tackled Tim and I rolled free, only to jump right back in. This time, Danny and I teamed up against Tim and Fenn, and we ended up in one tangled heap of fur. At this point we were more like puppies than anything resembling dangerous beasts.

After we were done play-fighting, we went on a run together, our little pack blitzing through the forest. Small prey animals ran and hid at our approach. I reveled in the feel of my powerful muscles bunching and stretching with each stride, and the blissful awareness that came with running in a pack. The moon overheard was not quite half full, but I could still hear its moonsong in my bones.

A roar suddenly shook the trees around us, reverberating in the very earth beneath our paws. We all went on high alert, hackles raised, ears swiveling to pinpoint the source of the sound.

Whatever it was, it was in the forest.

With us.

And it was big.

With a flick of Fenn's ears, Tim and Danny flanked me, with Fenn taking the lead. As one, we started moving away from the source of that horrendous noise. Moving silently, we headed back towards the clearing where we'd left our cloaks.

All the normal noises of a forest at night had ceased. No birds rustled in the trees, no insects called, no rabbits foraged. It was unsettling. Soon all of my fur was standing on end, my ears straining to detect the slightest sound.

Soon we were approaching the clearing, but something felt...off. Fenn held himself stiffly, as if he sensed it too. We stayed hidden, our sharp eyes piercing the darkness, scanning for even the slightest hint of movement. Seeing none, even after several minutes of waiting, we emerged from cover and into the clearing.

I noticed two things in the same instant; my cloak lay shredded into pieces on the forest floor, and there were huge claw marks on the tree next to it.

The next thing I knew, Fenn was shoving me out of the way as a massive body pounced on the spot I'd just occupied. Belatedly, I connected the dots. It had been *in the tree*. And it had been *waiting* for us.

I struggled to draw in a breath as the sounds of vicious fighting erupted all around me. Snarls and howls of pain rent the air as Fenn and Danny engaged the creature. Tim stood protectively in front of me, though I could see the way his tail quivered, tucked between his legs.

What scared a *werewolf*?

I got my first good look at the creature as the combatants drew apart, circling. It looked as if a man had started to transform into a lion, but gotten stuck halfway through the process. Its thin, golden fur was stained with blood around its muzzle, a single chicken feather stuck there. A large gash ran down its chest, where Fenn's claws had scored it. Its humped back and long, misshapen legs made it even taller than Fenn. There also appeared to be some sort of infected bite wound on one arm, the flesh around it discolored a gruesome shade of purple and black. Black veins spread outward from it in a spiderweb pattern, reaching nearly to the creature's shoulder.

But the most terrifying thing of all was that there was no true spark of intelligence in its eyes. It moved purely on instinct, ignoring the way

Fenn attempted to communicate. Fenn growled a warning deep in his chest when he noted how the creature kept glancing at me.

It roared again, and this time I could hear the pain in its voice. But I pinned my ears back at the cold look in its eyes. It paused, dropping into a crouch. Before it could spring at Fenn, I launched myself towards it, fangs bared and claws at the ready. I scored its shoulder, blood dripping from my sharp claws. I froze, the scent that was flooding my nose and mouth refusing to register in my mind.

I released my hold, stepping back slowly. The lion monster froze, confusion and hurt flashing through its eyes before they went dark with malice again. It let out a guttural growl and fled into the night, leaving a trail of blood in its wake.

I turned on unsteady legs, nuzzling Fenn to check that he was unhurt and getting the same treatment in return. He had a thin scratch along his ribs, but seemed mostly unharmed. I scanned Danny and Tim, noting that Danny had a cut on his back that was already starting to heal.

I whined deep in my throat as my legs started to shake. I collapsed into Fenn, who lowered me gently to the ground. Quickly he grabbed his discarded cloak in his teeth and laid it over me, giving orders to Danny and Tim with a flick of his ears.

Fenn looked deeply into my eyes and growled, the order of an alpha pulling the change out of me before he went and shifted himself, quickly donning his clothes. He gathered my shredded cloak and tossed it to Tim, who had reappeared in his human form alongside Danny. Fenn placed my dagger and necklace in my numb fingers, tucked the cloak around me and swept me into his arms. Without a word, Danny and Tim fell in step just behind him.

"Fenn, was that...? It couldn't...it couldn't have been him, right?" I whispered, unable to speak his name aloud.

Fenn clenched his jaw, icy eyes staring straight ahead. "The scent was...distorted. Twisted. We can't be certain."

"How would that even be possible? He's human," I muttered, my brows drawing together in confusion. "Unless..."

Fenn grimaced. "A Vulclaria bite. That's the only way he could be both human and werelion, neither fully one nor the other. A cursed halfling."

"Is he stuck like that forever?" I whispered, horrified.

Fenn paused, thinking. "I don't think so. Those reports of animal attacks...I think he's switching between forms. He may not even be aware of it himself."

I laughed, the sound falling from my numb lips like stones. Fenn looked down at me, concern knitting his brow. Tim and Danny also glanced at me, before turning their watchful gazes back to our surroundings.

"It's ironic, isn't it? He thinks of werewolves as the monsters. But what does that make him?"

Fenn's arms tightened around me. "That's exactly why. The bite of a Vulclaria forces you to confront the worst part of yourself. You said Chris thought a werewolf was a mindless monster? That's exactly what he's become."

"It's all just some big test?" I asked hoarsely. A single tear traced its way down my cheek. I buried my face in Fenn's strong chest.

"Yes," Fenn answered grimly. "And he's the only one who can pass it."

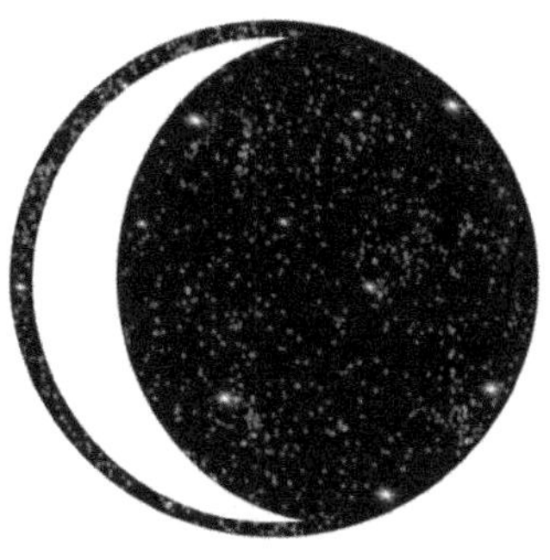

12

I t only took a few hours on horseback to reach the capital city of Eldore, so we arrived around noon. Varennia was a city from a dream. It was as if the forest had merged with the city, or perhaps the other way around. Flowers perfumed the air, and fairy lights twinkled from every vine and branch, visible even in daylight. What appeared to be homes were nestled up high in the branches of the massive redwood trees that towered above us, making me feel small. Shops and community buildings rested on the forest floor, interconnected by a web of boardwalks, which protected the roots below. Crystal clear streams fell from some of the treetops, murmuring softly as they passed beneath the boardwalks to water the flora and fauna.

But the most impressive sight of all was the colossal tree emerging from the very center of the city. The boughs of the tree were riddled with elven structures, and extended nearly to the edge of the city. The mist that pervaded the whole area gave the city an otherworldly feel, and hid the top of the mammoth tree from view.

"That huge tree is where the elven monarchy, their court, and distinguished guests live," Fenn informed me, his eyes roving over the city. "It looks about the same as I remember."

"That's amazing," I breathed. "I've never seen anything like it."

"It does take some getting used to," Fenn chuckled.

I furrowed my brow as I scanned the sea of elves, dwarves, and even humans going about their day. "I don't see any horses."

"Elves mainly ride elk and deer. Horses aren't permitted within the city, but we can stable them in the outer reaches. I know there are several stables that board visitors' horses—for a significant fee, of course," Fenn explained.

I stroked Atlas' neck absently, glancing over my shoulder at Chris. Would he want to stay with the horses? He hadn't spoken to me since the commotion last night, when he'd seen me start to shift. I shivered involuntarily. But if he turned into that monstrosity again, how would we keep him contained, especially since he seemed to have no memory of his time as a beast? What if he upgraded from snacking on chickens to people? There was no doubt in my mind that we'd all be thrown out of the city, or worse, if Chris' secret was discovered. That would make finding and rescuing Fenn's sister rather impossible.

I bit my lip. Maybe it *would* be better if he stayed behind. Especially since we had no idea what would trigger the change in him.

Fenn clenched his jaw as he scanned the city in front of us. Even Danny had gone uncharacteristically silent.

"We'll find her," I soothed, placing a hand on his shoulder.

Fenn's eyes softened when he looked at me. "I know."

"Let's board the horses at the stable up ahead," Danny suggested, pointing to what looked like a clean, well-maintained establishment near the road we were on.

"Agreed. We'll have to leave some of our gear as well," Fenn said, glancing at the bedroll tied to the back of his saddle.

In short order we settled the horses in their temporary home, and I was pleased to see that the horses that were already there looked very well cared for, with gleaming coats and access to fresh water. Fenn paid half the cost up front, the remainder to be paid when we returned. We were able to leave the gear we wouldn't need with our horses' tack.

Chris gave no indication that he would be staying. I wasn't sure how I felt about that, or the sharp glances he kept sending my way.

Having taken care of the horses, we made our way into the city proper, marveling at all the foreign sights and smells. Tim and I practically had our heads on a swivel, there was so much to take in.

We walked deeper into the city, our steps echoing on the well-worn planks beneath our feet. Butterflies with jewel-like wings flitted about from flower to flower, expertly avoiding the pedestrians.

Danny stopped us outside of an inn that looked like it had seen better days. Despite the early hour, however, the tavern appeared to be doing a brisk business. There were elves, dwarves, and humans scattered amongst the tables, all looking a little rough around the edges.

"It may not be the nicest place to stay in Varennia, but this tavern is one of the best when it comes to information. Especially the kind that fancier folks might not want to hear," Danny explained. Then he glanced at Fenn. "No offense."

Fenn scoffed. "I'm offended you just referred to me as 'fancy.' Remind me to hold a special training and sparring session for just the two of us later."

Danny laughed a little nervously. Tim solemnly placed his hand on Danny's shoulder. "It was nice knowing you, brother."

I couldn't help but smile. "Shall we, then?"

Fenn led the way and I followed, Danny somewhat reluctantly following. I did not envy him that special training session. Just thinking about it made my muscles ache with phantom soreness.

Fenn arranged for rooms for us, though he opted for three doubles this time. Eyeing the patrons in the tavern, I wholeheartedly agreed that I'd rather not be alone in a room here. I tried to push any blush-inducing thoughts from my mind.

"Danny, Chris, and Jax, you'll stay here to gather intel. Buy some drinks, make some friends. Any information is good information," Fenn instructed after we'd put some of our things in the rooms, minus anything remotely valuable. "Tim and Serena are with me. If we're not back by dawn, come find us."

A grin split Danny's face, the earlier threat all but forgotten. "Now that's my kind of day."

Jax grunted and made for the bar. Chris followed without a word, his hand scratching his arm absently. I was mildly relieved, knowing that Jax could handle Chris or any fight that may break out, and Danny could sweet-talk his way out of just about anything.

The three of us headed out, and I breathed a sigh of relief. The flowing robes of the elves we passed grew finer and more elaborate the deeper we went into the city, until it seemed like every elf we passed had delicately wrought silver and gold jewelry adorning every limb.

Soon we came upon a huge, elegant cathedral that presided over a vast courtyard. The cathedral itself was made from some sort of stone that shimmered in the light, and stained glass windows added jewel-like tones to it. A detailed stone figure was carved in the center of it, the woman's head haloed by a round stained glass window. She had pointed ears like an elf, and wore a stone diadem that reminded me of a crown. Her feathered wings were raised, as if in flight, and stars fell from her fingertips, forming constellations by her feet. She must be the goddess Astraea that the elves worshiped.

The courtyard laid out before the cathedral was packed with stalls, vendors selling everything from food to weapons and clothing. Thousands of people milled about beneath colorful garlands and wreaths, many with bags or baskets filled to the brim.

"Tim, you take the far side, and find out as much as you can without drawing attention. Remember to act like a visiting tourist," Fenn instructed. "Serena and I will start here. Rendezvous no later than midnight at this spot."

Tim nodded and disappeared into the crowd, his tall form quickly hidden by the equally tall elves. Fenn laced his fingers through mine, pulling me close.

"Are you ready to act like lovesick visitors?" he asked, quirking an eyebrow at me.

I grinned at him. "Absolutely."

We descended into the colorful chaos, hand in hand. True to his word, Fenn gave me a peck on the cheek every chance he got. I'd be lying if I said I didn't enjoy it. My thoughts strayed into dangerous territory, imagining what it would be like going shopping with him all the time like this.

Eating together.

Sparring.

Waking up beside him.

I gave myself a mental shake. I was supposed to be gathering information here, for crying out loud! Most of those around us were elves, either locals or visitors. The visitors all had a similar starry-eyed look on their faces and travel-worn clothes, so it was easier to spot them. Most of the conversations we overheard revolved around the festival itself.

We passed by a vendor displaying a wide range of fine metalwork, from jewelry to knives and small daggers. A flash of icy blue caught my eye. I glanced around, searching for a good excuse. Then I spotted it.

"Hey Fenn," I asked sweetly, batting my eyelashes at him, "would you get us some of those delicious-smelling skewers? I'll be right over there."

"It is well past dinner time, isn't it? I'll be right back then," he said before heading in the direction of the vendor.

I watched him for a moment before turning my gaze to the metalwork on display. I'd purposefully picked a stall with a long line for him to stand in, so I had a little time before Fenn came back. I picked up the dagger that had caught my eye, holding it up to the light. The pale blue crystal embedded in the hilt reminded me of Fenn's eyes. The metal was the same dark variety as the one Fenn had given me, that was both light and sturdy.

"You have a fine eye, miss. That's one of my best pieces, and it has been enchanted to keep its sharpness," the elfin vendor said in a lilting cadence. He appeared a little older, and the calluses on his hands spoke to his work ethic.

"It's very elegant," I complimented, turning the blade over. "I'll give you ten silver for it and the matching brooch."

"Don't insult me. That one alone is worth at least sixty silver," he scoffed.

"Twenty silver then," I countered, trying to feign disinterest.

"Fifty."

"Thirty."

"Forty. Take it or leave it."

"Forty-five for the dagger, the brooch, and some information," I offered, watching him closely.

His eyes narrowed. "What kind of information?"

"I just wanted to know what kind of...after-hours entertainment I might be able to find here," I replied, lowering my voice. "Something along the lines of a performance, or perhaps some sort of sport I could bet on."

The elf watched me warily, thinking. Finally, he said, "Deal. There is a fighting ring that operates underground, if you catch my drift. I haven't been myself, but I have heard tales of it. Seek out the mask seller on the other side of the market. She may tell you the location, if you buy her wares."

"Thank you," I replied, hiding my elation. "You've been most helpful." I handed over the silvers—nearly everything I had—and tucked the sheathed dagger and brooch deep in the bag slung over my shoulder.

Just then, Fenn came up beside me, handing over a mouth-watering meat skewer. We walked beyond the hearing distance of the metalwork stall before I said anything else.

"So, what was that?" Fenn asked after he'd devoured his skewer.

"That," I said with a grin, "was me getting us our first lead."

"Really?" Fenn asked, his gaze sharpening.

"Yes. There *is* a fighting ring here. The vendor didn't know where it was, but he pointed me in the direction of someone who does," I relayed.

"That's great," Fenn said, letting out a relieved breath. "Lead the way."

I took my time wending through the maze of stalls and people, not wanting to attract any undue attention. I kept Fenn's hand firmly gripped in mine, only partially to ensure we didn't become separated in the crowd. We stopped at a few more stalls, and Fenn bought a handful of items to give as gifts to the others.

Eventually we made it to the other side of the market, and I surreptitiously scanned the sea of stalls for the one we needed. After a few more minutes of wandering, my eyes alighted on what had to be the mask seller's stall.

Animal masks of all shapes and sizes adorned the walls and tables of the stall, empty eyes staring out at the crowd. There were full masks and half masks, some encrusted with jewels and some with feathers waving jauntily in the air. Predator animal masks seemed to be the most popular, though I spotted a few rabbit and deer masks as well. A silver wolf mask in particular sent a shiver down my spine. It looked eerily similar to the one Lester had prepared to subdue Fenn.

The vendor was helping another customer as we approached, so I took the opportunity to study her. Unlike most elves, her hair had been shorn nearly to the scalp on one side of her head, with the other side hosting short, unnaturally red hair. Piercings marched up the sides of her delicately pointed ears, and rings crowded every finger. She wore tight black clothes, in high contrast to the loose and colorful robes of most other elves.

"I'm excited for tonight's fight," her customer gushed as he dropped a handful of silver coins into her waiting palm.

"The festival tournaments are always more interesting than the normal matches," she purred, handing him a plain black and white tiger mask.

I noticed that her nails had been filed to a point and dyed black. I swallowed involuntarily. She turned towards us as the male elf left.

"Here for a mask?" she purred, eyes looking us up and down, lingering for a moment on our still-entwined hands.

"You could say that," Fenn replied smoothly, though his gaze was riveted on the silver wolf mask I'd noticed earlier. I gave his hand a gentle squeeze.

"We'd like two masks and the location," I answered.

"First-timers, eh? Interesting choice for a date, but who am I to judge? I have just the thing for you two," she said, turning and scanning the wall of masks. She took two off the wall and turned to hand them to us. "Such stunning eyes require a stunning mask."

I took the white and red wolf mask she offered me, running my fingers over the delicate golden scrollwork. Fenn stiffened, and I saw the other mask she'd picked was the silver wolf one. Fenn was staring at it with a haunted look on his face.

"I think that one might suit him better," I suggested, gesturing towards a black and red wolf mask with some stunning golden filigree. I smirked at Fenn. "Unless you'd like the bunny?"

Fenn forced a laugh, recovering quickly. "I think the black wolf will be just fine."

Mercifully, the elf didn't comment, though I could tell she was curious. Fenn took the offered mask with a tight smile.

"You'll find the entrance inside the abandoned building across from the Jade Dragon Tavern. It starts at sundown. Bring the masks, you'll need to wear them inside," she informed us, holding out a clawed hand for payment.

Fenn dropped the requested silvers in her hand, her fingers curling closed over them. He nodded curtly, though she was already turning her attention to the next set of customers.

We left the market, heading slowly in the direction she'd indicated. We caught up with the man who'd purchased the tiger mask just as he entered a rather run-down section of the city. Here the lights flickered, paint peeled from the buildings, and trash littered the boardwalk. I moved a little closer to Fenn.

The sun had just begun to set when we watched the man slip on his mask as he entered a building with boarded-up windows. I looked across from it and saw a sign that read The Jade Dragon, with a serpentine figurine perched on top, painted a pale shade of green. Light and sound spilled from its open doors, but the stench wafting from it had my curiosity fizzling out instantly.

"Shall we?" Fenn asked, slipping on his mask with only the slightest hesitation.

I nodded, putting on my own.

We entered the building, our steps echoing in the gloomy interior. A fine layer of dust covered everything, except for where others had walked before us. Following the trail through the building, we were led to what looked like an open cellar with a ladder sticking out.

We glanced at each before descending the well-worn rungs, Fenn leading the way. Once we were at the bottom, torches on the walls lit the tunnel before us. A cacophony of sounds reached our ears, along with the scent of sweat, blood, fear, and ecstasy.

As we descended deeper into the earth, the sounds grew to a dull roar, and we emerged into a massive underground room. It was shaped like an amphitheater, with seats surrounding a deep pit that had a domed cage covering it. Torches blazed every few feet, casting dancing shadows across the masked faces of the people who milled about. There must have been several hundred people there. Smartly dressed humans and elegantly dressed elves placed bets with uniformed elf workers, and dwarves purchased tankards of mead from passing waiters.

I winced as a bell rang, silencing the crowd. A suited elf stepped onto a raised platform, surveying the attendees before he spoke.

"Ladies and gentlemen, the night's entertainment is about to begin! Place your final bets for our opening match now. We will begin momentarily," he announced.

There was a frenzy of activity as masked individuals hurried to place their bets before they stopped taking them. The amount of coin that flashed in the firelight in just those few minutes left me in disbelief.

Fenn and I found seats near the top of the amphitheater, as most of the lower levels were already crammed with gaudy spectators. Soon, the flurry of activity died down, and expectant eyes all turned down to the pit below us.

Then the crowd went wild as the first fighter entered the ring.

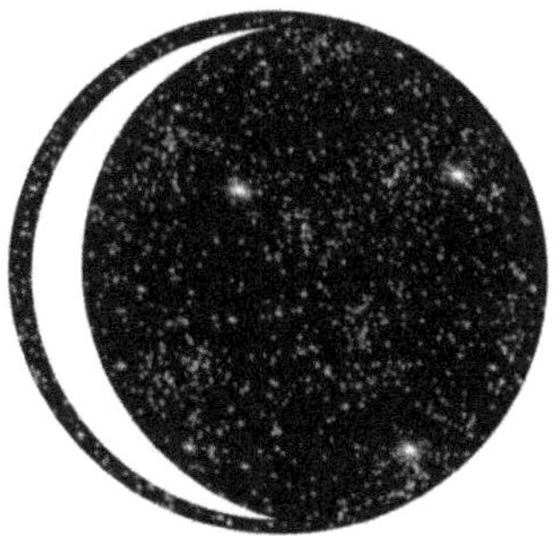

13

The young dwarf who had been shoved into the ring immediately turned around and tried to leave, but the door had already
clanged shut. He pressed his back to it, looking frantically around the
cage, trembling hands clutching a battered short sword. Worn leather
armor was strapped to his chest, though it was partially hidden by his
beard.

The door across from him creaked open, and a confident elf
stepped through, a rapier held loosely in one hand. His long, flaxen
hair was braided, and his chain mail tunic shifted as he moved. The
dwarf shrank into himself when he saw his opponent, who slowly
smiled at him.

"Introducing the first-timer, a dwarf by the name of Gunnor! And
his opponent, the up-and-coming rookie, Alistair, with an unbroken
winning streak since his debut last month! Let the battle begin!" the
announcer boomed, signaling for the bell to ring.

The elf, Alistair, wasted no time, lunging towards Gunnor, his
rapier flashing in the firelight. Gunnor brought his arm up just in time

to block, the leather bracer protecting him from what could have been a fatal blow. Gunnor rolled and tackled Alistair's legs, knocking him off balance. Gunnor raised his short sword in the air, but hesitated, uncertainty flashing across his features.

Alistair took advantage of the opening and expertly swatted the sword out of Gunnor's hands. The short sword fell uselessly out of reach, and as Gunnor sprinted towards it, the elf intercepted him, scoring a deep gash along the dwarf's unprotected thigh.

Gunnor screamed in pain and dropped to the ground, holding his leg. He looked desperately up at the crowd, seeking help, or maybe just a hint of sympathy. He found none. Alistair planted one boot on his chest, leveling his blade at the young dwarf's throat. The motion led my eyes to the obsidian choker around the dwarf's neck, a blood-red gem that glowed with an inner light embedded in it. I looked closer at Alistair, realizing an identical choker rested on his throat as well.

"I yield!" cried the dwarf, his eyes riveted to the blade inches from his face.

Alistair looked to the announcer, who also seemed to serve as referee. The announcer gave a shallow nod, so the elf withdrew his blade, turning and walking to the center of the ring and raising his blade straight into the air in what could only be a victory pose.

"And we have our winner, folks! Alistair's winning streak remains intact! Looks like Gunnor is in for some intensive training, poor fellow! Make sure to collect your winnings and place your bets for the next round, which will begin shortly!" the announcer concluded.

Some of them congratulated each other, standing to go and collect on their winning bets. Others slumped over in defeat. None seemed even the least bit concerned for the young dwarf, who was dragged out of the ring by an emotionless brute.

"This is barbaric," I breathed, just loud enough for Fenn to hear.

He nodded imperceptibly. "I'm not sure if I should even hope that Freya is here, after seeing that. I would rather keep looking for her if it meant she hadn't had to endure something as depraved as this."

I slipped my hand in his just as the next pair of fighters entered the caged ring. This time it was a human versus another human, both men, both battle-scarred and armed with swords and shields. Their fight was much more evenly-matched, and only ended when a blade was pressed to a throat, drawing a thin line of blood. Again, one man yielded, and with a nod from the announcer, the winner was declared, and winnings doled out.

As the cycle repeated itself, I urged Fenn to place a few bets, so we wouldn't stand out. Every time a new match was about to begin, we held our breath, hoping we would see Freya step into the ring, and simultaneously hoping that we wouldn't. We saw a parade of fighters, of slaves, all wearing that distinctive collar.

Some experienced, some green.

Both men and women.

Children.

There were elves, dwarves, and humans. Occasionally, a wild animal would be pitted against the fighter. A tiger whose skin was stretched tight over its skeletal frame was felled by an ax-wielding dwarf. Sometimes the animals would have to fight each other.

Eventually, werehumans began appearing in the matches, some choosing to fight in their animal forms, some choosing to use weapons. More often than not, they won their matches, regardless of the form they chose. We saw a couple of werewolves, but both were gray-furred males. Weretigers and werebears fought wereleopards and even a werelion.

The hours ticked by, until the final match was announced. The promising rookie, Alistair, would be fighting a werepanther, who was apparently a fan favorite. Fenn went and bet on the werepanther, since it seemed not a single person, except those who'd already lost all the money they'd brought, wasn't betting on this final match. We hadn't bought any of the food being offered, however. I don't think either of us could stomach it at this point.

"We've had another magnificent evening folks, but it's time to wrap up tonight's entertainment. For our final match, we have the rising star rookie, Alistair!" the announcer crowed, gesturing to the elf as he entered the ring, waving eagerly to his fans. "Tonight he challenges one of our best fighters and all-around crowd favorite, the She-Demon!"

The crowd stood up and cheered as a tall, platinum blonde with striking features entered the ring. Her piercing violet eyes slid over the crowd to settle on her opponent. Scars criss-crossed her lean but muscular form, and she tossed her braided locks over one shoulder as she unsheathed her sword. Her eyes narrowed, and I noticed she had a thin scar running through her left eyebrow. Unlike many of the others, her gear looked well-cared for, even if it was scratched and worn. Like the others, a collar encircled her throat.

"Let the final match begin!" shouted the announcer, the bell clanging to signal the start of the match.

Alistair lunged forward, his rapier moving like lightning through the air. The She-Demon expertly dodged, delivering a blow of her own that left the elf reeling. Before he could recover, she slashed at his arm, drawing blood. Alistair winced but put his guard up, watching her warily.

They circled each other, searching for openings. For weakness. Alistair moved first, and the pair continued their deadly dance. But after watching them for a while I frowned, leaning into Fenn.

"Is she...?" I whispered, my eyes glued to the fight.

"Yes. She could have won easily, several times over by now. She's an extremely skilled fighter. It almost looks like..." he trailed off, distracted when Alistair managed to wrap his rapier around the She-Demon's sword, flinging it from her hand, before bringing the blade to hover over her heart.

"I yield," she said expressionlessly.

It took me a moment to realize what was bothering me. While Alistair was panting, his brow drenched with sweat, the She-Demon wasn't even remotely out of breath, only the faintest glimmer on her skin.

"She let him win," I breathed.

She had dragged the fight on, toying with Alistair while making it look like she was struggling. I glanced at the announcer, whose lips were twitching upwards, a satisfied gleam in his eyes. I narrowed my eyes. Those who had bet on Alistair would be rolling in coin right about now. I really wouldn't be surprised if a number of these matches were fixed from the start. After all, it was the house that always won the most from the gambling of its patrons.

"What a *shocking* turn of events, folks! The rookie managed to defeat the She-Demon! Who could have seen that one coming?!" the announcer exclaimed with a smirk. "And now, for the moment you've all been waiting for: Who will win a night of pleasure with this fine, young contender? The bidding will start at ten silver!"

I stared numbly at the pit as the elf hooked his thumbs into his belt loops, surveying the women who were bidding on him with a grin on his face. Movement caught my eye, and I realized the She-Demon was slipping out one of the now-open doors, her sword returned to its sheath.

I turned to look at Fenn, noting how his skin had gone pale. A familiar sense of horror and disgust stirred within me, as the meaning of what I was witnessing sunk in. There was no true way for a slave to win in this place.

"Fenn," I whispered, tugging at his sleeve, "now's our chance, while everyone's distracted. Why don't we see what we can find?"

He nodded mutely. We stood as one, wending our way through the crowd to the walls of the underground room. During the last few hours, I'd had plenty of time to locate the entrances the staff used. While most of the uniformed men were busy taking bids and doling out coin to happy and angry drunk patrons, we slipped into a dark tunnel that gaped open like the maw of a beast.

Compared to all the heat and excitement of the main room, the tunnel seemed all the more dark and dreary. A chill went down my spine, and I tried not to think about the packed earth pressing down on us. My nose had been muddled from the moment we'd entered, thanks to the cacophony of clashing scents, so I'd done my best to ignore them. Fenn, on the other hand, scented the air, taking the lead as we crept deeper into the darkness.

We turned a corner to find that blazing torches lined the rest of the tunnel, which opened up into a small, empty room with several branching paths. I realized the tunnel had been left in darkness on purpose, so that guests would not be distracted from the "entertainment" by the light. Or get too curious.

Fenn walked down the rightmost pathway, which had drops of blood splattered along its walls and floor. Some of it was fresh. Most of it wasn't. I saw why after just another minute of walking.

The passageway opened up to reveal rows of cages and cells, most of which were occupied. We walked by the young dwarf, Gunnor, from the first match, lying on a straw pallet, dirty bandages binding his fresh wounds. The further we walked, the more familiar faces I saw. The slaves were caged in nearly the same order they'd appeared in the ring tonight.

Most were either sleeping or licking their wounds. Few bothered to glance up at us. The eyes of those who did were hauntingly empty, devoid of emotion. I resisted the urge to recoil. Soon we passed an empty cage, followed by one that actually had a handful of creature comforts, including a cot with a blanket and a pile of clothes.

Fenn came to a stop, peering between the metal bars. Inside, a beautiful white-furred panther was stretched out on the cot, licking a small cut on its foreleg. A blanket was draped loosely over its back. When it sensed our presence, the great cat looked up, violet eyes finding ours.

"She-Demon," Fenn said, eliciting a low growl from the feline. "We're here for information. I can make it worth your while."

She stretched languidly with a yawn, showing off her sharp fangs. Slowly, she stepped onto the ground, growing taller and thinner until the woman stood before us, the blanket barely concealing her.

"I'm surprised she let you in here," the werepanther murmured. When I shifted uncomfortably, her eyes narrowed. "Unless of course, she didn't. In which case, you must not value your lives all that much."

"Like I said, we're looking for information, and I'll make it worth your time," Fenn said tersely, ignoring her insinuation.

She slowly raked her eyes over his figure. "I'm not interested in spending the night with you, honey."

I bristled, Fenn's ears turning beet-red. "Fenn's not on the table," I spat with more venom than I intended. I felt my eyes begin to glow, but I refused to drop my eyes first.

"This just gets more interesting by the minute," she purred, her eyes not leaving mine. "Then what are you offering me, if not the pleasure of your company?"

"Your freedom," Fenn stated.

She blinked, shifting her gaze to Fenn's. "I've heard such offers before," she drawled, but I saw the faint spark of hope that ignited in her eyes. "You can't afford me."

"Money is no object," Fenn replied in a low tone.

She re-evaluated us, silently considering. Finally, she padded up to the bars, and whispered, "Two days. Meet me at The Jade Dragon at sundown."

Moving back, she said loudly, "Go back down this tunnel and take your first left. And lay off the drinks next time, yeah?"

She glanced towards the other cages before shifting back into her feline form, her violet eyes boring into our backs as we walked back along the passageway. I tried not to peer too closely at the despondent faces in each cage.

We made our way back to the room with the fighting ring. Only a few patrons remained, and most were drunkenly stumbling towards the exit tunnel. Just as we exited the dark tunnel, one of the guards spotted us.

"Hey, what were you two doing back there?" he asked, an edge in his gravelly voice.

I froze, my heart in my throat, before I stumbled into Fenn and started giggling hysterically. Fenn looked at me like I was crazy, but I raised an eyebrow at him, shooting a quick glance towards the suspicious guard.

"Uh-oh, we're in trouble," I sang, adding some high-pitched giggles for good measure. "I don't think we—we were supposed to be in the kissy tunnel."

The guard's shoulders relaxed as he peered down at me. I kicked Fenn lightly in the shins.

"You know how it is with the ladies, man," Fenn groused, pitching his voice higher. "They sure do like their privacy. But whatever makes my girl happy."

Fenn leaned down and gave me a prolonged kiss, and I melted into him. For a moment, I nearly forgot what we were up to. The guard cleared his throat, and we broke apart. I looked up at him through my lashes, adding a few more giggles for good measure.

"Get out of here, you two. Just stay out of the tunnels from now on, ya hear me?" the guard grunted.

We nodded and quickly made our way back to the surface in silence. Once we were finally outside, I let out the breath I hadn't realized I'd been holding. I took Fenn's hand, our fingers intertwining.

We were finally making progress.

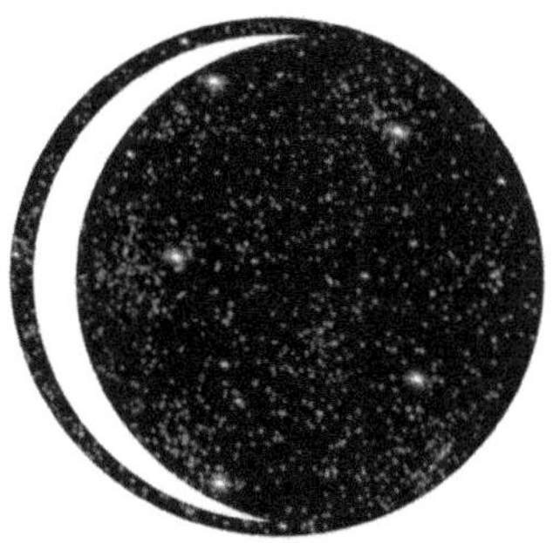

14

Blood splattered onto the dark ground, causing the crowd around us to cheer and scream. Beside me, Chris and Danny cheered with them, grins on their faces and betting tickets clutched in their fists. I caught Danny's eye, raising one disapproving eyebrow.

"What? I love a good fight!" he shouted over the cacophony.

"Would you still like it if you were the one wearing the collar?" I asked flatly.

His smile faltered beneath his gilded tiger mask as he glanced at Fenn, who sat rigidly on my other side, his gaze riveted to the two fighters in the pit. Or, more specifically, the slave collars around their necks.

"Maybe not as much," he admitted sheepishly, glancing down self-consciously.

Chris didn't even acknowledge I had spoken. It was hard to make out his expression under the lion mask he wore. I still had no idea why he'd agreed to come with us to tonight's fight. Maybe he was tired of being cooped up in the inn. Maybe he unconsciously craved the scent of fresh blood.

I banished that thought from my mind, suppressing a shudder. We hadn't heard any more reports of animal attacks, for which I was grateful. But the full moon was a little over two weeks away, and I didn't think I was ready for what that would do to Chris.

Another roar from the crowd drew my eyes back to the match, where Alistair was winning handily against his opponent, a grizzled man. Alistair's rapier struck like lightning, nearly invisible to the naked eye. Metal screeched against metal as the swords clashed, sparks crackling along their edges. The crowd gasped as the two combatants traded blows in a deadly game, neither one revealing an opening.

But after another few minutes, I could tell that the older man was tiring. Sweat dripped from his brow, and his movements were becoming slower. More and more scratches appeared on his weathered skin where Alistair's blade had slipped past his guard.

With a grandiose flourish, Alistair sent the other man's sword flying and brought the tip of his rapier to rest at the older man's throat. A single drop of blood welled at the tip of the blade.

"I yield," gasped the man, his hands hanging limp at his sides.

After a moment, the announcer gave a curt shake of his head. Alistair grinned, a cruel light entering his hazel eyes, and he swiftly slashed his blade across the man's throat.

The roar of the crowd went silent around me as I watched him slump to the ground, the light leaving the man's eyes while his lifeblood soaked into the soil. Fenn went still beside me, but it was Chris' reaction that scared me. He swallowed conpulsively.

"We have our winner of tonight's death match!" crowed the announcer as Alistair gave a bow, basking in the crowd's adoration. "With this victory and his first kill under his belt, Alistair, our rising rookie, has moved up in the ranks and will soon be challenging some of our best fighters! And don't forget to come back tomorrow to witness the brawny weretiger, Tigrain, challenge to a death match our reigning undefeated champion, the Shade! Tomorrow night will be one for the books, folks, and you won't want to miss it!"

Bile rose in my throat, and I had to look away. Danny looked similarly green around the gills, though Chris looked disturbingly unperturbed. Fenn took my hand, his warmth becoming my anchor. I closed my eyes, focusing only on the feel of my hand in his, blocking out everything else.

"Let's go," Fenn said quietly.

We all stood to leave, though we had to wait for a moment while Danny and Chris collected their winnings. I hated that we were supporting this, even if it was to find Fenn's sister.

It was a quiet walk back to the inn. Even Danny wasn't his usual cheerful self. After we filled Jax and Tim in on the night's events, we all went to bed.

I lay awake in the dark late into the night, the only sound Fenn's soft breathing from where he rested beside me, on top of the sheets. But I could tell he wasn't sleeping either.

"Do you want to talk about it?" I asked softly.

Fenn shifted slightly, but didn't reply right away. Eventually he said, "I keep picturing that man, the way he died. But I keep seeing Freya in his place, staring at me as she dies in that pit. The things she must have gone through here...I don't even want to think about it. But Serena, what if...what if we're too late?" His voice broke on the last word.

I turned to face him, meeting his pale blue eyes. "I know I've never met her. But from what you've told me, she sounds like a very strong person. And I don't mean just physically. If she's anything like you, then she found a way to survive even that place. Besides, Dorent said a female, black-furred werewolf is a fighter here. From what I've seen, there aren't that many black-furred werewolves, so it must be her." I moved closer to him.

"You're probably right," he sighed, wrapping his arms around me.

I snuggled into him. "You know I'm right. We'll find her, Fenn. And we'll bring her home."

I stepped through the doors of The Jade Dragon behind Fenn, immediately wrinkling my nose at the putrid scents that assailed my nostrils. Clearly, cleaning was not a priority for the owners. Or staff.

Jax stepped through a few moments later, not so much as glancing at us as he made his way over to a table in the back that had a good view of the rest of the dimly-lit room.

The sun had just begun to set, casting golden rays of light through the fogged windows, and highlighting the dust motes that danced through the air. There were a few dozen people already occupying some of the tables and seats at the bar. I scanned the room, looking for locks of platinum blonde hair.

Fenn spotted her first. We made our way over to the table she had claimed. She watched as we came over from beneath her hood, her violet eyes like twin flames in the shadows.

"I'm surprised you showed," she purred smoothly.

"We're highly motivated," I replied coolly. "As are you."

"Like I said, we need information," Fenn interrupted. "And...just out of curiosity, why did you let that elf win? And how were you able to meet us outside?"

She remained silent, and I almost thought she wouldn't answer. Finally, she said, "Lock-picking comes easily to me, though I can't go out of range of this accursed thing." She fingered the collar around her neck, the faint red glow mostly muffled within her cloak.

"And let's just say I didn't feel like being an escort that night. Besides, there's someone I'd rather not fight, higher up in the rankings. But that's not the information you're really after, is it?"

"You're right. What can you tell us about the ringmaster?" Fenn responded.

"She's a callous elf. Makes herself feel powerful by keeping the men she employs under her boot. No one knows her real name, but she goes by Eris. Average height, black hair. Dark eyes. Carries a whip at her hip," she shrugged. "Before I answer any more questions, I want proof that you can afford me. Eris rarely sells her thralls, but when she does, it's to the highest bidder."

Fenn covertly reached into his cloak, carefully opening the top of his pouch. He tilted it slightly, so the She-Demon could see the copious amount of gold coins in there before returning it to its spot.

Her eyes widened slightly, then flicked around the room nervously. Satisfied no one else had seen, she leaned forward. "Name's Reyna. It's a pleasure doing business with you. What else do you want to know?"

"The layout of the place, the guard's posts and schedules, and how to get a meeting with this Eris," I replied after the introductions were made.

"Did you bring some parchment?" she asked with a small smile.

I handed her several rolls of parchment and a stick of graphite. She got to work right away, drawing a map and noting where the guards were usually posted, as well as the location of Eris' office.

"Anything else?" she queried, nodding her thanks when Fenn placed a drink in front of her.

"We're also looking for someone we believe is one of the fighters," Fenn explained. "A female, black-furred werewolf with dark blue eyes. She'd be eighteen this year."

The She-Demon's eyes narrowed to slits, and she stiffened, leaning forward. "And what would you want with this female werewolf, assuming she is one of us?"

Fenn's eyes were unwavering. "To bring her home."

Reyna leaned back in her chair, her eyes examining Fenn closely. "If you're bringing her "home," then that would make you what? Her lover?"

"Brother," Fenn ground out, stiff as a board.

Reyna blinked in surprise, narrowing her eyes as she scanned Fenn's features closely.

"There is a fighter matching that description here," Reyna admitted slowly. "She's the closest thing I have to a friend in this wretched hell hole. If you're really her brother, then tell me her full name."

"Freya Astrid Verdania," Fenn recited quietly, his eyes drilling into Reyna's.

Reyna's face broke into the first real smile I'd seen on her, a dimple appearing on her right cheek. "Here, she's known as the Shade."

15

Well, I was certainly right on the money about Fenn's sister being strong enough to survive. She was the champion of the place! My mind shied away from everything she must have had to go through to get that title. I felt a sort of kinship with her, despite the fact that I'd never even laid eyes on her.

I brushed my hand over the coin pouch I had hidden in my cloak, just to reassure myself it was still there. Today I was carrying more in gold than I would have made in a lifetime of working on the Rangers' ranch. It was making me more nervous than I already was.

Fenn was carrying an even fuller coin pouch. Hopefully between the two of us, we would be able to buy both Freya and Reyna from Eris. But I had a feeling that Eris might not be willing to let her Shade go so easily.

Jax and Chris walked right behind us, our backup for the evening. Hopefully, everything would go according to plan, and we wouldn't need a distraction or some extra muscle. But we were taking no chances tonight.

Not with lives on the line.

As we descended into the earth, the dull roar of a myriad of voices grew louder. We followed the torchlight, and I was astounded by the sheer number of people that had shown up for tonight's match. Hundreds, if not thousands of people were milling about the floor and the amphitheater, dressed in all kinds of finery.

I saw diamond drops glittering at the ladies' earlobes, and sapphire cufflinks gleamed on the sleeves of silk suits. Most of them held delicate glasses of champagne while gossiping excitedly amongst each other. A line of patrons stretched around the edge of the amphitheater, coins ready to hand over in exchange for a betting slip.

Chris made straight for the end of the line, coins at the ready. I couldn't help the slight curl of my lip at that. Blending in was one thing. But I think Chris was really enjoying all of this.

Our cloaks whispered over the packed soil as we found a place to sit in the middle section of the amphitheater. Reyna had informed us that Eris only ever took guests after the night's "entertainment" had concluded, so we had no choice but to watch and wait through all of the matches. Including the Shade's.

The preceding matches passed in a blur of blood and sweat and cheers. The energy in the room was so thick I could have cut it with my dagger as the audience impatiently awaited the final fight. Tension rolled off of Fenn in waves, his eyes not once leaving the pit.

Finally, *finally*, it was time.

"And now, the event you've all been waiting for! The death match of champions!" the announcer crowed as he twirled his thin mustache. "Entering from the left, the King of the Jungle, the Man with the Iron Claws, Tigrain!"

The crowd went ballistic, many standing to get a better view of the weretiger now entering the pit. He was bare-chested, showing off his arrogance and his many scars simultaneously. He carried twin sabers, his large hands dwarfing their hilts. His shoulder-length, orange hair was wild and untamed, making it easy to imagine him in his tiger form. He raised his twin swords above his head, basking in the adoration of the audience.

"Entering from the right, the Queen of the Night, the Woman with Fangs of Steel, the Shade!" the announcer roared, gesturing to the opposing door as it slowly opened.

Fenn and I stood along with the rest of the audience, craning our necks to see her. Fenn went rigid beside me as a young woman emerged from the shadows, her long black hair pulled up into a high ponytail. Sapphire eyes scanned the crowd disinterestedly before settling on her opponent. High cheekbones accentuated her striking features, and lean muscle rippled over her slight frame as she unsheathed twin daggers, holding them with the grace and confidence of an experienced fighter.

The resemblance to Fenn was unmistakable.

"Freya." The strangled cry broke on his lips. But it was lost in the cacophony of the crowd, like a breath lost to the sky above.

I gripped his hand, trying to give him a modicum of the comfort he'd given me. He squeezed my hand like his life depended on it, his anchor in this storm.

My eyes were drawn to a woman seated across from us, her face shrouded by the viper mask she wore. Blood red lips smiled possessively at the scene below. Cold certainty snaked through my veins.

Eris.

I glanced at Fenn, relieved he hadn't noticed her. I didn't think I'd be able to hold him back if he spotted her looking at his sister like that. But his eyes were glued to the Shade.

"Let the champion death match begin!" howled the announcer, his words barely audible over the roar of the crowd. The starting bell rang, almost as an afterthought.

The two combatants circled each other, each probing for an opening. But I could tell Tigrain was quickly growing impatient. He struck first, his sabers sweeping towards Freya in a wide arc. She dodged, the blades whistling past her torso. I forgot to breathe as I watched their deadly dance, Fenn still as a statue beside me. On my other side, Jax held himself stiffly, while in contrast Chris was cheering with the rest of the audience.

The Shade was quick, far quicker than her opponent. She would slip past his guard, striking shallow gashes into his tough skin and retreating to a safe distance, beyond the man's wider reach. It was like watching a mouse toy with a cat. And it was infuriating Tigrain. He'd only managed to scratch her once, a shallow cut on one leg.

His mounting anger and impatience were making him sloppy, and Freya managed to cut him deeply across the chest, leaving twin gaping wounds. He roared in pain, the sound echoing in the underground cavern.

He dropped his sabers, the weapons clanging against each other as they landed on the ground. And then, he began to shift, his form bending and changing as orange and black fur sprouted from his skin. In moments, a massive tiger had replaced the man, dwarfing the Shade with his sheer size.

Tigrain pounced, maw opening wide as he aimed for Freya's throat. She rolled under him, slicing open his belly with her daggers. He roared again, baring his fangs, but this time, the Shade didn't wait for him. She dropped her own blades, shifting into her wolf form in the blink of an eye. Her fangs gleamed a stark white against the inky black of her fur.

She growled, her hackles raised and fangs bared as they circled each other, blood dripping from the tiger's belly onto the dirt. At some invisible signal, they both leaped at each other, landing in a tangled heap. Growls and roars split the air as claws split skin and fangs sought purchase through thick fur.

The Shade went after Tigrain with a vengeance, aiming for the wounds she'd already inflicted on him. She relied on her speed as she had in human form, doing everything in her power to avoid the more powerful male's claws.

But she was tiring as well, her furred chest heaving for breath. She moved to dodge a swipe of his muscled forearm, but couldn't react fast enough. The force of the blow sent her crashing against the wall, and I saw the breath leave her lungs as she hit the bars and collapsed to the ground, stunned.

Fenn's grip on my hand tightened unbearably, and I looked over to see him trembling, his eyes starting to glow as he desperately fought the urge to jump down there to protect his sister. I dug my nails into his skin, giving him something else to focus on.

"Trust her, Fenn. She's made it this far. She can outsmart him," I said just loud enough for him to hear. I hoped I spoke the truth.

The slight lessening of his grip was the only sign he gave that he'd heard me. A muscle feathered in his jaw as he clenched his teeth, but at least the glow in his eyes began to dim.

I looked across from us, horrified to find that Eris was looking at Fenn, her lips curled in a cruel smile. A chill went down my spine, my guard going up. A terrifying thought occurred to me, but I pushed it away. I would die before I let that woman put a collar around Fenn's neck.

The crowd gasped, and I looked just in time to see Tigrain pin the Shade beneath him, his massive weight making it impossible for her to wriggle free. I watched in horror as the tiger paused, glancing up at the crowd, before leaning down to close his fangs around her exposed throat.

But just before his teeth found purchase, Freya scored her hind legs along the wounds on his belly. He roared in pain, recoiling. That was all the opening the Shade needed to flip herself onto her paws and latch onto his exposed neck.

And just like that, it was all over. Tigrain collapsed onto the ground as the life left his eyes. Absolute silence reigned for a moment as the Shade stood over his body, her chest heaving for air. But instead of looking victorious, she looked...sad. Her head hung low, her tail even lower.

Despite the fact that she had just won, she looked defeated.

"We have our winner!" shouted the announcer as he excitedly stroked his mustache. "The Shade has defended her title as reigning champion once again!"

The crowd came alive then, screaming and cries of jubilation mixed with sobs and boos. My stomach soured at their reactions. Fenn let out a tight breath, some of the tension leaving his shoulders. Jax was stoic as always, but I still noticed how he breathed a sigh of relief. Chris was ecstatic, since he had bet on Fenn's sister to win.

But Freya ignored them all, turning from the prone tiger to pick up her twin daggers in her mouth. She slowly walked to the gate from which she'd entered, limping slightly. She stood there and waited for it to open, not sparing even a single glance behind her as she slipped into the beckoning darkness.

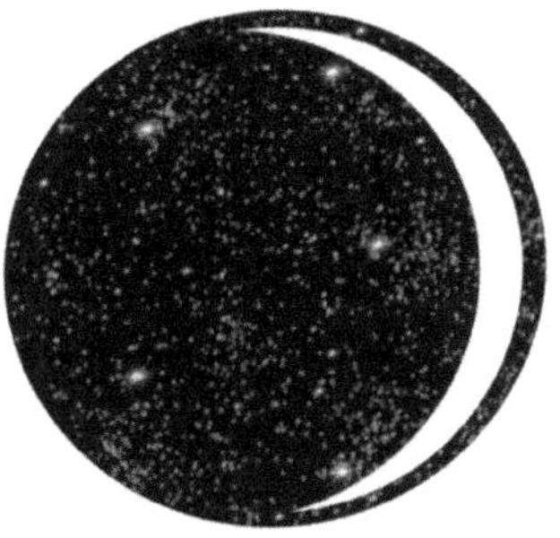

16

"Yes!" Chris crowed, pumping his fist in the air. "I just tripled my coin!"

Fenn rounded on him, grabbing a fistful of his tunic and dragging him forward, fury in his eyes. "Have you no shame?! A man just *died* for your entertainment! My *sister* nearly died!"

Chris scowled and began scratching furiously at his arm. "And? What's wrong with making a little coin while we wait? Don't I deserve to have a little fun every now and again, in between all the life-threatening situations?" he hissed.

"Oh, I'll tell you what you *deserve*," Fenn growled, a dangerous light flickering to life in his eyes. Jax stepped closer, but hesitated when he saw the expression on Fenn's face.

Those nearby were starting to take notice of the commotion, some eagerly anticipating a fight, others shuffling away. I grabbed Fenn's arm, and said loudly, "Calm down, you two. You'll have better luck next time."

Both of them glared at me, but I flicked my eyes at those around us, who were quickly losing interest. Lowering my voice, I whispered, "Save it. Did you both forget why we're here? We can't afford the attention you're drawing, or we risk getting kicked out. Shouldn't we be making our move right about now?"

Fenn looked at me, the fire in his eyes slowly banking into embers. He released Chris roughly, turning away from him without another word. Chris glared at the both of us, muttering "werewolves" under his breath like a curse.

"Why don't you go collect your winnings?" I suggested coldly. "We'll meet you back at the inn."

Chris turned and headed for the group mobbing the uniformed workers without another word. At least his incessant scratching had ceased. I breathed a sigh of relief and followed Fenn, Jax trailing close behind.

"I know he's the alpha, but that doesn't mean you have to let him make foolish decisions, even if he feels justified. Not when there's something—or someone—on the line that's more important," I said to Jax.

He nodded a little sheepishly. I noticed Fenn had turned his head slightly to listen, but he didn't comment. I bit my lip, wondering why other werewolves never seemed to question Fenn. Perhaps there were some werewolf rules that I simply did not know of yet.

I came up just behind Fenn as he stopped in front of the guard that was posted in front of the tunnel that led deeper into the operation. Fortunately, it was a different guard than the one who had stopped us the other night.

"We're here to see Eris," Fenn said gruffly.

The guard looked at him dubiously, saying nothing. He held out his hand expectantly. Just as Fenn was about to repeat himself, I stepped forward, quickly palming a coin from the pouch I carried and depositing it on his open hand.

The large man grunted, moving aside and gesturing for the three of us to enter. We walked through the now familiar tunnel, our wolf vision allowing us to see despite the lack of torchlight. After turning the bend, torches once again lined the walls, and we proceeded until we came upon the door to Eris' room, which unsurprisingly was painted black. I thought that was a fitting color, considering it matched her blackened heart.

We paused, gathering our thoughts, before Fenn knocked, the hollow sound echoing in the enclosed space. After a brief silence, the door swung open on oiled hinges to reveal a plushly decorated room, complete with a desk and several chairs on top of a rich carpet. Bright red sashes adorned the walls, and the viper mask I'd noticed earlier hung on the wall behind the desk.

Eris herself stood before us, dressed in the same black outfit I'd seen her in before, with a coiled whip at her hip. Her black hair was cut in a chin-length bob that accentuated her pointed ears, but it was her wicked black eyes and blood-red lips that really drew the eye.

"I see I have some unexpected guests," she rasped, gesturing with the smoking pipe she held in her free hand.

"I am interested in purchasing two of your slaves," Fenn said coolly, keeping his voice level.

Eris' lips curled in a cruel little smile as she looked at Fenn, and I bristled despite myself.

"Why don't you come in so we can discuss business?" she invited, stepping back from the door. "I'm afraid the third will have to stand, as I only have two chairs for guests."

Fenn and I took a seat each, Jax standing against the wall behind us. I was mildly surprised that no guards were stationed either outside or within her office. Was she just arrogant? No, I doubt she would have lasted so long in her line of work if she was truly that foolhardy.

"So, which one of my darlings has caught your eye?" she asked, settling into her high-backed chair and crossing her legs. She drew on the pipe, breathing out a cloud of smoke. I tried not to gag at the sickly-sweet scent.

"The She-Demon," I supplied, when Fenn hesitated.

"Ah, yes. Quite the beauty that one, if you can get past the surliness. But she is quite skilled, since she's been here for so long," Eris rambled, her calculating eyes watching us closely.

"We're prepared to offer 100 gold for her," I said evenly.

"Don't insult me, child," Eris scoffed. "The She-Demon is worth far more than that—"

"Even if she's not overly inclined to win?" I interrupted. "From what I've heard, she hasn't exactly been drawing in many new customers for quite some time now."

A small thrill of satisfaction went through me as I watched Eris purse her lips. Our research was paying off if that remark had hit home.

"I might consider parting with her for 200 gold," Eris countered, her eyes narrowed.

"One hundred ten."

"One hundred ninety," she offered.

"One hundred twenty."

"One eighty."

"One thirty," I countered.

"One hundred and seventy gold," she rasped. "Final offer."

"One hundred and fifty gold, plus this diamond," I said, lifting the small gemstone I held in my hand up to the candlelight.

Her eyes tracked the precious diamond, a hint of greed flitting across her sharp features. "Deal."

She opened a drawer, rummaging for something. She brought out what looked like a small, flat black stick that had a tiny red crystal embedded in the tip. She pulled on the chain that hung around her neck, revealing a similar-looking black object that had been hidden beneath her dress. She touched the two together, both gems lighting up.

"This is the control device for the She-Demon's collar. All you have to do is flip this switch on it, and it will cause her excruciating pain until your command is obeyed," she explained.

I counted out the one hundred and fifty gold coins, pushing them into the middle of the table in neat stacks. Her eyes watched me greedily, but she looked up as I held out the hand that held the diamond.

"Her ownership contract?" I asked pointedly.

Eris huffed, but pulled out another drawer and sifted through some files until she found the right one. She placed it on the desk, sliding it towards me so I could read it. The name Reyna Ma'Katzya was written on it, along with the details of the sale. I was very glad the She-Demon had told me her name beforehand.

"And how do we know this device is keyed to the She-Demon?" I asked.

Eris smiled cruelly and flipped the switch. Moments later, an agonized scream echoed down the tunnels. That was definitely Reyna's voice. I nodded, satisfied, grateful for the wolf mask that obstructed my features.

I placed the diamond with the gold as Eris switched the controller off and dropped it on top of the ownership contract. I slid both towards me, tucking them away securely. I took a deep breath, glancing at Fenn. He looked at me gratefully. He'd probably never had to haggle once in his life.

Once Eris had scooped her payment into a pouch, she rang a small bell I hadn't noticed before. In moments, one of the guards opened the door to the office.

"What can I do for you, mistress?" he asked.

"Bring the She-Demon here for her new owners," she instructed.

"Right away, mistress," he said as he bowed, closing the door behind him on his way out.

"We'd also like to purchase another one," Fenn started, his posture rigid. "The Shade."

Now that caught Eris' interest, her gaze snapping up from where it had rested on her new pile of gold. Her eyes narrowed, and I could practically see the gears turning in her mind.

"The Shade is one of my best earners. Only for a special kind of client and a vast sum would I even be willing to consider parting with her," Eris commented before taking another pull on her pipe.

"We do understand that, of course," I replied, my words dripping with fake honey. "Naturally, it would only be right to properly compensate you for any loss of business. The diamond you now possess is not the only one we brought today."

"Even so, her price is quite astronomical. One could even say she is priceless. So, what could you possibly offer me in exchange?" she asked, a cruel little smile curving her lips.

"That's—" I faltered.

"Name your price," Fenn interjected.

"You," Eris purred, looking at Fenn. "I saw the way your eyes glowed earlier. You look like a young, strong fighter. Are you willing to take her place?"

"Yes," Fenn answered immediately, refusing to look in my direction.

Behind us, Jax made a noise deep in his throat. Eris looked at the bare skin of Fenn's neck, her split tongue flickering over her lips like a snake's. I was frozen in place, my world tilting around me. A part of me understood that Fenn would go to any lengths to save his sister. But the other part ached at the knowledge that he would abandon me in order to save her.

Recovering from my initial shock and stab of hurt, I stood up and slammed my hands against the hardwood of her desk. "He is *not* on the table. Like we've already said, we can compensate you handsomely for your potential financial losses—with *coin* and gemstones."

Eris threw back her head and laughed, a deep, raspy noise that I knew would feature in my nightmares. The three of us stared at her, dumbfounded, as she wiped tears from her eyes.

"What a chivalrous young man you are," Eris laughed. "I haven't had such a good laugh in ages. Ordinarily I'd be tempted to keep both you and the Shade, but I value my neck too much for that."

"You...you were just joking?" I asked in disbelief.

"Unfortunately yes, little red," she replied, a smile still lingering on her thin cheeks. "Although I would normally consider trading either five thousand gold or even another strong fighter for that trouble-maker, I'm afraid that's no longer a deal I can make."

I remained silent, enraged and confused. "What do you mean by that?"

"I've seen you here the last few nights, so you know how this all works. Didn't you wonder why the Shade's night wasn't auctioned off after her win tonight?" Eris asked with fake sweetness.

My heart sank.

"Don't tell me..." Fenn said, half-standing from his chair.

"She's already been sold," Eris said with a smirk. "Tonight was her final match here. Tomorrow she goes to her new master."

17

F enn sat back down. Hard. The little I could see of his face beneath the mask had gone pale. I'd never seen him look so defeated.

The door opened as the guard from before shoved the She-Demon into the room before closing the door softly behind him. Reyna looked around nervously, her violet eyes taking in the scene in front of her. She remained silent, watching and waiting.

"Who did you sell the Shade to, then?" I asked in as calm a tone as I could manage. "We would like to contact them to inquire about purchasing her."

Violet eyes narrowed as Reyna began to put the puzzle pieces together. She shifted uneasily, the motion going ignored even by Jax.

"Unfortunately, this particular customer cares deeply about his privacy. Paid quite handsomely for my silence, in fact. And since those who cross him are swiftly parted from their heads, I'm afraid I can't say," Eris explained.

"Not even for another diamond?" I tried desperately.

"What good could a diamond possibly do me if I'm dead?" she scoffed. "Darling, these are your new owners," she said, turning towards Reyna. "I would tell you to pack your things, but you don't have any." Eris cackled at her own twisted sense of humor, breathing out another lungful of smoke.

The She-Demon's eyes widened, hope flickering to life before her eyes shuttered once more. She nodded shallowly, clasping her scarred hands behind her back.

"We'll pay double what you were offered for the Shade," I said, desperation leaking into my voice.

Fenn sparked to life at the sound, his eyes ablaze with icy rage. He stood to his full height, his large frame towering over Eris. But she only crossed her legs, unimpressed.

"Like I said, the transaction has already been completed. As tempting as that offer is, betraying my clients is bad for business—and my neck. Now, I believe our business is concluded, so I will have to ask you to leave with your purchase," Eris said in a bored monotone.

Fenn took a threatening step forward.

"Do I need to call my guards?" Eris asked, blowing smoke into Fenn's face.

"That won't be necessary. We'll see ourselves out," I said stiffly.

I looped my arm through Fenn's, tugging him towards the door. After a moment, he relented, allowing me to tow him away from Eris. I gestured with my head for Jax and Reyna to follow, and the four of us left Eris' office, closing the door loudly behind us.

We walked a few paces away back the way we'd come. But instead of taking the tunnel that would lead us out to the amphitheater, I took a left, down the tunnel where we'd found Reyna in her cage.

Once I felt we were far enough out of hearing range, I turned to Reyna and asked in a low voice, "Can you lead us to her cell?"

"Yes," she said after a moment's hesitation. She didn't need to ask to whom I was referring.

Reyna took the lead, her bare feet padding silently along the cold, rough dirt of the floor. Like shades ourselves, we silently passed by cage after cage, the misery of the inhabitants—with a few exceptions—rolling off of them in waves.

The memory of peering out at the world from behind bars rose unbidden in my mind, and I felt a sense of kinship with those we passed. If only there was a way we could bring the law down on Eris and those like her. Since "thralls," as they called them were legal in Eldore, that didn't seem likely. Perhaps after all of this was over, we could come back here, for all the people and creatures we would have to leave behind.

After what felt like a small eternity, Reyna stopped in front of a cell that was much further down than hers had been. Inside the cage, a furry black form lay curled in a ball on top of a filthy, tattered blanket. Iron shackles bound her legs, and a muzzle covered her face. Her eyes were closed, but one of her ears twitched towards us.

Fenn slipped his arm from mine, walking with leaden steps up to the cage. He removed his mask, letting it fall to the floor with a soft *thump*. He gripped the bars, his knuckles turning white.

"Freya," he whispered.

The black head lifted to look at Fenn. The wolf's eyes locked on Fenn's, recognition slowly dawning in the sapphire depths. A whine came from her throat as she stood up and walked on unsteady legs towards the bars, the chains clanking as she moved.

"I'm sorry it took me so long to find you," Fenn said, the words breaking on his lips.

She came right up to the bars, and Fenn took her face in his hands, his thumbs stroking her fur. Tears glistened in her eyes, but refused to fall. She growled softly, as if she was telling Fenn he was late.

Her eyes searched his, before she glanced at the rest of us, her eyes lingering on Reyna.

Noticing the direction of her gaze, Fenn explained, "She helped us find you. We're getting her out of here today, and we're going to find a way to get you out too. That witch, Eris, already sold you to someone, but she wouldn't say who. Some wealthy male who likes privacy." Fury laced his words.

Her eyes widened before narrowing to slits. She wrenched her face from his hands, her gaze dropping to the floor. Fenn looked like he'd been stabbed through the heart.

"We'll find him! We'll find him and buy you or steal you back, whatever it takes! I won't ever leave you again, Freya!" Fenn cried, dropping to his knees.

But Freya was scratching at the dirt with her claws, gouging shallow lines into it. I stepped closer, peering through the bars.

"She's trying to write something, Fenn," I said softly, watching as the letters slowly took shape. "Elf...Ma—"

"I thought the Shade wasn't going to be collected until tomorrow," a deep voice echoed down the hallway.

"The plan's changed. Eris wants her taken care of now. Something about impulsive werewolves," a second voice answered.

We all froze. We'd been so preoccupied with Freya that none of us had noticed the sound of guards approaching. Quickly, I grabbed Fenn's fallen wolf mask and hauled him to his feet.

"Hang in there. You'll be home soon," I whispered softly, sapphire eyes meeting mine for a split second.

She furiously scratched out what she had started to write in the dirt as the four of us fled deeper down the tunnel and around a bend. Out of sight of Freya's cell and the two approaching guards.

"Too bad. I was hoping to have a little fun with her tonight," the first voice commented.

Fenn's head whipped up, his eyes ablaze as he took a step in the direction of the guards. Jax and I held him back, even as my stomach turned at the words. I felt my blood heat up and claws prick through my fingertips in response to the fear and memories the guard's words elicited.

"You know you'd be whipped for damaging the merchandise, right?" the second asked disinterestedly.

I curled my hands into fists, cursing the fact that we had to stay hidden for both our sakes. The pain of my claws poking through the skin of my palms cut through the haze of heat and anger, helping me to focus. I took some deep breaths to slow my heart rate.

"Would it kill you to let me so much as think about having some fun for a change?" grumbled the first voice. "I'm not exactly eager to be whipped. Again."

The second guard sniggered as the sound of jangling keys met my ears. Rusty hinges squealed as the cage door swung open, and a low growl filled the air. It was followed by the thud of a boot meeting flesh, and the growl gave way to a sharp whimper.

"Quit whining and get to your feet already, you flea-bitten dog," grunted the first guard. "Your new owner is eager to see you."

Chains clanked as Freya stood up silently. I wished more than anything that we could just grab her this instant and make a run for it. But we'd never make it to the surface, let alone get the collar off.

"Let's make it snappy, yeah?" the second guard insisted. "I don't want to be out there tonight with whatever creature has been killing the deer mounts around here."

"I heard about that," the other guard replied. "Apparently it's only been eating one animal, but still kills whatever else is nearby."

"If only we could slap one of these collars around its neck. Now that would draw one hell of a crowd," the second guard mused.

"Let's see if the mistress is interested in capturing it," the first suggested. "We could get a bonus."

"You'd go through that bonus in a single night of drinks and women," complained the second as their footsteps carried them away from us, back down the tunnel.

Their echoing voices faded, the faint sound of chains going with them. I silently handed Fenn his mask, and he slowly placed it back over his face, after a moment of hesitation.

"We'll take her while they're traveling, before he can hurt her," Fenn ground out.

"I'll help," Reyna said softly. "It doesn't feel right to leave her behind, after everything we've been through. She's my friend too."

The tiniest of noises had me looking behind me, at the cage in front of which we were standing. Alistair was watching us, a small smile on his lips. But it was the look in his eyes that chilled me to the bone. I was suddenly grateful for the bars that separated us.

"For your silence," I whispered, tossing a silver coin into the cell.

Alistair made no move to pick it up. His smile widened.

"Let's get out of here," I muttered. "We can talk more later."

When I was sure the guards were well and truly gone, I led our little group back the way we had come. We were on high alert for any more guards, but fortunately didn't encounter any on our way back to the main room.

There was still a good number of patrons left, either collecting on their bets or downing one more glass of sweet poison. Reyna drew a few stares, but she held her head high, looking regal despite the dirt covering her form, not deigning to acknowledge a single one of them.

I scanned the attendees for a head of golden hair, before letting out a sigh. I wasn't sure whether or not I should be glad Chris wasn't still here.

If those guards were to be believed, then instead of being tucked safely away at the inn, Chris was likely in that monstrous form of his and rampaging around Varennia.

Right when it was most crucial for us to keep a low profile.

18

"If we wait, we could lose her forever! *I* could lose her forever," Fenn exclaimed, pounding his fist against the inn's wall.

"But we can't go in blind, either," Jax cautioned. "For all we know, this wealthy new owner could have a small army."

"Besides, what good would it do her if you all die in the attempt to save her?" Chris chimed in.

He leaned against a wall, his arms crossed over his chest. Tim and Danny watched silently from the room's sole wooden chairs. Fenn began pacing the confines of the small room, his steps retracing the same path time and again.

"If that happened, she'd never forgive herself," Reyna added softly from where she sat next to me on the bed. She'd had a chance to take a hot bath and eat something since we got back, and I'd given her some of my clothes to wear. Though the sleeves and pant legs were a little short on her tall frame.

"We need more information," I said forcefully. "If we can find out exactly who we're dealing with, and where he might take her, then we can come up with some sort of plan."

Fenn nodded curtly. Since we'd come back from Eris' establishment a couple of hours ago, we hadn't spoken much. It felt like a gap had grown between us, and I didn't know how to bridge it. I was still reeling from how Fenn had been ready to trade himself into the worst kind of slavery to try and save his sister. On the one hand, I admired his love and courage, but on the other, I was hurt. I fully understood and accepted how important family was to Fenn, especially after what had happened because of Lester. But some part of me had thought...had hoped...that perhaps Fenn had started to see me as, well, as a part of his future family.

But I was a commoner, and he was a duke. Was I simply fooling myself? I gave myself a mental shake. We had more important matters to tend to right now.

Turning to Reyna, I asked, "Do you know of anyone in this city who sells information?"

She looked out the room's single window at the star strewn sky, deep in thought. Finally, she turned to face the room. "I don't know if he's still doing business in this city. But a couple of years ago, I did hear about an info broker who ran his own operation not too far from Eris'. If the buyer is wealthy enough to buy Eris' top fighter, then he should know *something*, at the very least."

"Then let's go see him immediately," Fenn said, already striding for the door.

"We might draw too much attention if all of us go," I said quietly, looking around the room. "Besides, we can't risk *someone* strangling the broker—at least before we get the information we need." I looked directly at Fenn for that last part.

He huffed, but paused nonetheless. "You make a good point," Fenn sighed as he ran a hand through his already mussed hair. My fingers itched to run through the inky black strands, but instead I folded my hands in my lap, looking away.

"Why don't you let Reyna and I do the talking?" I suggested. "Chris can come with us to watch out for trouble, while everyone else works on coming up with some ideas on how to counter those damn collars, and making sure we have the weapons we'll need, whether that means coins and gemstones or blades."

Fenn and the others reluctantly agreed, though I could tell Fenn wasn't exactly happy about it. But at the moment, I didn't particularly mind if I left Fenn to stew. I had no clue what to say to him right now, and having some time apart to think things through would prevent me from saying something I would come to regret. Even if that meant spending more time with my former best friend instead.

"So does that mean I will get my freedom once we return from the info broker?" Reyna broke the awkward silence, her gaze darting between Fenn and I.

"Of course!" I reassured her.

"No," Fenn said at the same time.

I looked at him, furrowing my brow in confusion.

"That *is* what we agreed to," I stated slowly.

"We'll need all the help we can get to save Freya," Fenn countered.

"She already said that she would help us bring Freya home," I said angrily.

"How do we know she'll keep her word?" Fenn objected heatedly.

"I am a woman of my word," Reyna stated flatly, drawing herself up to her full height as she stood to face Fenn.

"Then what's the problem with keeping the collar on for a few more days, if you'll be here anyway?" Fenn argued.

Stunned silence met his words. Everyone stared at Fenn, shock written across their features. Even Chris looked surprised at Fenn's outburst. I knew Fenn was stressed and anxious about saving his sister, but he of all people should understand where Reyna was coming from.

"I see how it is, master," Reyna hissed, her violet eyes narrowing to slits.

Fenn winced, but remained silent. Danny and Tim were starting to look uncomfortable now, no doubt recalling how they'd been treated by Lester. How Fenn and I had been treated by Lester.

"Or," I said slowly, letting acid coat my tongue, "we could simply pay her for her help, if you're so worried she will leave."

"Pay her? I just paid one hundred fifty gold and a small diamond for her! Not to mention all the expenses of simply getting here!" Fenn exclaimed.

"Would you still care about the cost if it was Freya standing in this room instead of me, *master*?" Reyna said with quiet venom.

"I..." Fenn started, but looked down.

"We can talk about this with the hypocrite later," Chris said, a note of triumph in his voice. "The ladies and I have a broker to see."

The walk to the broker's operation was a quiet one. Reyna led the way, Chris trailing behind us. The city had long fallen asleep, the glimmering fairy lights above us dancing in the warm breeze.

"Thank you for sticking up for me back there," Reyna murmured, watching me from the corner of her eye.

"I'm sorry about Fenn. He's not normally so…" I trailed off, searching for the right words.

"Uptight? Deceitful?" Reyna supplied readily.

"Hypocritical? Horrible? Irritating?" Chris added helpfully.

I gave them both a tight smile. "Something like that. I understand why he's behaving like this, but that doesn't make it right."

"It's not like I don't understand his perspective. I probably wouldn't trust me either. It's just…I had forgotten how cruel and fickle a mistress hope can be," Reyna admitted quietly.

Surprising even myself, I took Reyna's scarred, calloused hand in mine. "Perhaps not as fickle as you feared," I said with a grin, holding up the control device in my free hand.

Reyna gasped, her eyes riveted to the small device. "Won't you get in trouble for freeing me?"

"I think deep down Fenn knows what the right thing to do is. He'll see that eventually. Besides, I saw the look in your eyes when you heard Freya had been sold, and when you offered to help us save her. I don't think you're the type of person who would abandon someone you care about," I replied.

"Now that's the Serena I know," Chris said, smiling at me for the first time since he'd found out I was a werewolf.

I gave him a tight smile, uncertain whether he had only said what he did to lash out at Fenn. Would he have said the same thing if I had been going against the wishes of anyone else? I'd never stopped being me, despite my new circumstances. Was he only figuring that out *now*?

My eyes skittered away from his, remembering the way he'd looked at me in his beastly form. He might have torn me to shreds without even knowing what he was doing. I shivered and shoved that thought to the back of my mind. I had other things to worry about at the moment.

"Now let's get that thing off of you," I said, turning back to Reyna with a warm smile.

It took a little trial and error, and an accidental zap before we managed to get the collar off. Eris hadn't exactly given us detailed instructions. Or any instructions at all, for that matter.

Reyna fingered the skin on her neck where the collar had been for so many years. It was a much lighter pink than the rest of her skin, as if it had been rubbed raw so many times that it hadn't healed properly.

"You should take this too," I said as I handed over her contract of ownership.

She nodded silently, tucking it securely into her clothes with trembling fingers. When she looked up again, her eyes were rimmed with unshed tears, turning her lashline silver in the dappled moonlight.

"Thank you," she whispered, before pulling me roughly into a hug.

I stroked her back soothingly, holding her as she shook with emotion. I looked up at the hint of moon I could see through the branches above us, determined to keep my own eyes dry.

"This is great and all, but I thought we were in a hurry?" Chris said, clearing his throat.

Reyna laughed, a beautiful, clear sound, and pulled back, swiping at her violet eyes. "He's right. I still have to fulfill my end of the bargain."

Not long after, we found ourselves standing at the threshold of a seedy-looking tavern. I took a deep breath and followed Reyna through the door, my footsteps sounding hollow on the worn wooden floorboards.

Despite the late hour, there were still a handful of patrons inside. A couple of dwarves nursed their drinks at the bar, and a few elves were scattered around at various tables. Some of them watched us closely as we came in, and I was grateful for the hooded cloak that hid my hair from sight. I would be glad when we were back in Verdania and I didn't have to hide my red locks whenever I ventured outside.

Reyna strode confidently up to the bartender, Chris and I flanking her. The older elf, who was absently polishing a glass, hardly even glanced at us.

"I would like to sample your sweetest wine," she said meaningfully.

"Which vineyard?" he challenged, watching us from the corner of his eye.

"The one touched by the stars above," she replied.

The bartender set the glass sharply on the countertop before wordlessly gesturing for us to follow. Not once did his expression change. We trailed close behind as he led us around the bar and through a narrow doorway that hadn't been visible from the entrance or even from the bar itself.

A series of twisted passageways led us to an opulent room with plush couches and chairs taking up the center. Bookcases lined the walls, the wood polished and gleaming, in stark contrast to the bar and tavern we'd just passed through.

"He'll be in to see you shortly," the bartender informed us before heading back the way we'd come.

The three of us sat down facing the door. It didn't take long before the soft padding of leather boots echoed down the hallway.

A well-dressed elf wearing a white deer mask strolled into the room, keen crystalline eyes examining us as he settled into the chair across from us. What was with the fixation on masks? It seemed like just about everyone in Varennia had something to hide.

"Welcome to the Guild of the Winter Wind. You may address me as Winter. You gave the password indicating you'd like to acquire top-tier information. What is it you would like to know?" he asked, clasping his white-gloved hands in front of him.

"We are looking for information on a specific individual—an elf who values his privacy and can afford to buy Eris' top fighter," I replied.

Winter leaned forward, steepling his hands in front of him. "What kind of information about this individual would you like?"

"His name, background, residence and any property he has. A way to contact him. Number of guards in his employ," Chris rattled off.

"Number and location of his thralls," Reyna added.

"I see. We did catch wind of the Shade's purchase. But her new owner is not someone with whom you should risk trifling," Winter warned.

Hope took flight on wings of white in my chest. If we knew who we were dealing with, then one way or another, we could get Freya back.

"This is a matter of life and death. I can assure you, Winter, that we are taking this *very* seriously," I assured him.

Without a word, Winter stood and strode to the bookcase behind him. After a few moments of fiddling, he returned to his seat, a folder in his hands.

"In that case, here is all of the information we have on this particular individual. And it does not come cheap," Winter said as he placed the closed folder on the table between us.

"Payment is not a problem," I replied readily, reaching into my cloak and withdrawing the small pouch I had concealed there. I placed it on top of the folder, the gold clinking as it settled.

In one practiced motion, Winter swept the gold off the table and flipped open the folder, revealing a rough sketch of the elf we were looking for, alongside a plethora of information on him. But what I read made my blood run cold.

Freya's new owner was the second prince of the elven kingdom, Malakin Erebos Eldore.

19

This was bad. This was very bad. And I had the sinking feeling that it was about to get much, much worse.

I paced around the room as Fenn and the others re-examined the file for what must have been the twentieth time. But re-reading the same dismal words over and over again wasn't revealing anything helpful.

I stopped pacing, folding my arms over my chest. If things kept going like this, we'd never find a way to move forward.

"So here's what we know. Prince Malakin is second in line to the throne of Eldore after his older brother, the Crown Prince, who is apparently supported by the elven aristocracy but not the common people. Malakin is highly secretive, but beloved by his subjects thanks to his massive donations to charitable causes. He's always surrounded by many highly-skilled guards, but there have been no known attempts on his life. However, the Guild of the Winter Wind has noted that there has been some suspicious activity in and around his private residence, which is located just beyond the city limits. And that is likely where Freya will be taken. Did I miss anything?"

"That we're screwed," Chris scoffed from where he leaned against the wall of the inn's room.

Reyna shot him a look for that one, but didn't deign to comment.

"That about sums it up," Fenn sighed, running his hands over his face. The dark circles under his eyes no doubt matched my own.

"Now that we know where they're headed, we have the advantage. We can plan a quick surprise attack, grab Freya, and get out. We'll cover our faces so the prince won't be able to come after us," Jax suggested.

"What about the collar?" Reyna asked grimly. "Even if you get her, the prince could just order her to return to him. And trying to remove it without the control device would kill her."

I paled. "You didn't think to mention that earlier?"

"It didn't matter, since you had the controller," Reyna shrugged.

Fenn clenched his jaw, a spark of fury reigniting in his cold eyes. I winced, but refused to back down from his irate stare. Fenn hadn't exactly been happy when he'd found out I'd freed Reyna without his permission. But a bit of yelling was a small price to pay. I knew he'd come around.

Eventually.

"You make a good point, Reyna," he ground out, looking away first. "Before we make our move, we'll need to locate the device and snatch it before it can be used against us."

"I can locate it," Tim volunteered. "I'm fairly skilled at reading people. If I can watch him and either see or figure out where the controller is, then Danny could try approaching him."

"How would Danny going up to him help? Wouldn't that ruin the element of surprise?" I asked, confused.

"I, uh...well, you could say I have a talent for lightening someone's pockets. Without their permission. Or knowledge," Danny admitted sheepishly.

"You're a pickpocket?" Reyna asked, arching an eyebrow.

"I've found that people rarely expect the smiling, friendly guy to liberate their belongings from them. They're always watching out for sullen, intimidating guys, like Jax. That's why they never see me coming," Danny explained.

Jax grunted, but I could see the corners of his lips twitching.

"I knew I liked you for a reason," Chris commented with a wry smile.

Danny nodded at him, though I could see from the way that he shifted how uncomfortable that comment made him. But his smile never faltered.

"So you can talk your way past his guards, snag the controller, and casually stroll back to us with the prince none the wiser?" Reyna clarified.

"Yes," Danny replied simply.

"And then we can distract the guards and grab Freya. If we have the horses nearby, then we could make a quick getaway out of the city and back to Verdania," I concluded. "Chris can be in charge of having the horses ready."

"Now we just need to figure out what route they'll take through the city. Reyna, what pathway do you think the prince is most likely to take?" Fenn asked stiffly, gesturing at the map of Varennia that he'd laid on the low table.

Reyna stalked forward, but began to dutifully examine the map, tracing the various pathways that spanned out from the central tree like a delicate spider web.

"Here, here, and here," she pointed out. "And this would be the best spot to make our move."

"Gather your weapons," Fenn growled. "We move out immediately."

I forgot to breathe as Danny strolled amicably up to the armed group, his hands in his pockets and his friendly grin securely in place. The prince and his entourage had just left the sheltering canopy of Varennia and were passing through the outlying farms. Two cloaked figures were huddled in the middle of two dozen armed guards, their faces obscured by their hoods.

My heart froze for a moment as the eyes of one of the guards slid over the dense bush Tim and I crouched behind. I let out a breath when the guard's gaze slid over me, continuing to sweep the area, looking for threats.

Chris had tied the horses to some trees just inside of the forest, tacked up and ready for a quick getaway. Fenn and the others were scattered around the area, waiting for their moment to strike.

It had been surprisingly easy to locate the large party, and we'd stayed out of sight as we followed them through the city. Tim had had plenty of time to pinpoint where the taller cloaked figure had tucked away the controller. Now it was our turn.

The first rays of dawn were just beginning to lighten the sky, covering the stars with a blanket of light. Two guards detached from the group to intercept Danny, but not before he made it to within a few yards of the prince and Freya.

I strained to hear what he was saying, but his words were lost to the wind. But I watched as the prince gestured to his guards, allowing Danny to come closer to speak with him. Obviously taking advantage of their assumption that Danny had no clue he was addressing royalty, he draped his arm over the prince's shoulders, laughing and holding his hands up when the guards rounded on him, weapons drawn.

I scanned the faces of the guards, noting the looks of either anticipation or irritation on most of their faces. My eyes returned to the face of one male elf in particular who looked vaguely familiar. I furrowed my brow, attempting to place him in my memories. A feeling of unease stirred in the pit of my stomach.

I fingered my throwing knives, easing the first one out of its sheath. I shifted position, angling for a better view.

I returned my gaze to Danny, watching as he looked down, the smile slipping from his face. My blood froze in my veins as I followed his gaze to the tip of the blade now protruding from his side.

As the thin rapier blade ripped through him, Danny staggered, falling to his knees. Behind him stood the blonde elven guard I'd noticed before, a cruel smile on his face as he looked down at Danny.

The look on his face sent a shiver down my spine, and the memory clicked into place. That guard was Alistair, the fighter we'd watched win every one of his matches. Except now, his ragged clothes had been replaced with gleaming armor, his wild hair slicked back.

The fighter who had heard us talking about rescuing Freya.

Who had smiled at me through the bars.

They'd known we were coming.

This was a trap.

And we'd walked right into it.

I felt my blood begin to heat as fear and adrenaline coursed through me. Before I could even blink, Tim had shifted into his wolf form and burst into the open. He arrowed straight for his brother, roughly tossing aside the elves who tried to stop him.

As Fenn also appeared, his massive black form roaring at the unsurprised guards, I threw my first knife, embedding it in the back of a guard that had turned to attack Fenn. He went down with a cry, but I felt a twinge of relief at the fact that he was only injured.

Malakin began gesturing at the cloaked Freya, and I caught a glimpse of the black control device in his hand. I watched in horror as Freya shifted, the cloak ripping to shreds as her form swelled and changed.

"Kill them!" Malakin's shrill command echoed in the air.

Freya balked, refusing to turn on her would-be rescuers. The prince flipped the switch, sending pain lancing through her. She growled and shook her head, trying to fight him. She began to tremble, her growl turning into a howl of anguish as the pressure mounted.

Regardless of whether Freya or Fenn won the fight, neither would ever recover from it. I looked around, desperately trying to think of a way out of this waking nightmare.

"Chris!" I called out to him. He was still in his hiding spot not too far from me. "We have to retreat! Now!"

"What are we supposed to do? Join the fight so they can escape?" he asked fearfully as he scratched at his arm.

Freya took a halting step towards Fenn and the others, who were fighting tooth and claw against the guards. Then another.

"I don't know, but we have to do it now!" I cried, throwing my second knife, and watching another elf stagger. "You just grab Danny and get him to the horses. I'll distract them."

"No! No, I'll be the distraction," Chris objected forcefully. "You work on getting them all out—they'll listen to you."

Before I could say anything else, Chris bolted into the fray, his borrowed sword raised over his head. My heart lifted at Chris' sudden display of selflessness. Perhaps restoring our friendship wasn't so far-fetched after all.

I jumped into motion, hurling another knife at a guard, wounding him in the shoulder. Dodging flailing limbs and weapons, I somehow made it to where Danny lay, his hands pressed against his side. Blood still poured from the wound, and I could tell that even his enhanced healing was struggling to knit the wound back together. He was barely hanging onto consciousness.

"Reyna, help me get everyone to retreat!" I called to the flash of pale fur in the corner of my eye.

She yowled and began freeing Jax from his opponents. I tore two strips of cloth from my tunic, pressing them against Danny's wound.

"Let's get you out of here," I told Danny, as I hastily wrapped a make-shift bandage over the wound.

"Run," he rasped, his eyes focusing on something behind me.

"You're not going anywhere," a cruel voice said from behind me.

I looked up into the wicked face of Alistair, his bloodied rapier held loosely at his side. I drew my dagger and stood, the dark metal whispering as it emerged from its sheath.

"We'll see about that," I growled.

Just as Alistair raised his rapier to run me through, Chris bowled him over, scratched but very much alive. Alistair slashed Chris' arm, and he roared in pain. The cut sleeve of Chris' tunic hung on by a thread, revealing what he'd kept hidden for so long.

Darkened veins raced up his arm from the rancid bite wound. But what I hadn't noticed before was that the wound almost resembled a tattoo of a lion, its massive mane radiating outwards like the rays of a dark sun.

Fear and hope warred within me as Chris' form began to stretch and change, his golden hair growing into a golden mane. The guards, the prince, and even Freya stopped to look as Chris took on his half-shifted lion form. "Now's our chance! Run!" I hollered, sheathing my blade and running as fast as I could with Danny leaning on me.

Reyna, Fenn, Jax and Tim raced towards me, their four-legged forms surrounding me like a furry shield. Tim supported Danny on his other side, and we were nearly at the tree line before even one guard was able to break away from Chris.

"Come on, Chris, you too!" I called, hoping against hope that he would understand me, or at least follow us.

I risked a glance back and saw Chris hurling elves left and right, his powerful form a force to be reckoned with. Soon the trees obstructed my view, but I swore I could still feel the malevolent eyes of the prince boring into my back.

The others shifted back, and we quickly tied Danny to his horse and mounted, and began spurring our horses into motion. But I pulled back, searching desperately for movement in the foliage, for golden strands of hair.

"Hurry up, Chris!" I called, my eyes trained back the way we'd come.

"Serena, we have to go, now!" Fenn barked, his anguish and frustration bleeding into his voice.

"But Chris, he—" I started to protest.

"If we go back, we'll all be captured, and then we won't be able to help either one of them," Fenn interrupted. "It would probably be more dangerous for us if he returned like that. But we'll come back for them both."

I nodded mutely and grabbed the reins of Chris' horse before digging my heels into Atlas, sending us shooting past Fenn. Tears blurred my vision, but I refused to let them fall.

I tried to block out the forlorn way Freya had held herself as we disappeared from view. I hated that I was leaving Chris behind, because despite everything that had gone wrong between us, I didn't want to picture a future without my oldest friend.

I made a mental vow to save them both.

No matter the cost.

20

“**W**ell well well, look who needs my help,” Dorent preened, flicking an imaginary piece of lint off of his shadowy cloak.

“Can you do it or not, Baldie?” I snapped.

“This is *me* you’re talking to,” he sniffed. “Of course I can dig up some information on the elven princes. Wake up on the wrong side of the dog bed today, did we?”

“How quickly can you put together a report?” I asked, trying to soften my tone. I knew I shouldn’t be taking out my frustration on our friendly shadow assassin, of all people. Clearly I needed to work on redirecting my pent-up anger towards something a little more productive.

“With any significant level of detail? I’ll need at least a few days. But I can give you what I already know right now, so you can start planning,” Dorent replied.

“That would be helpful. Thank you,” I said with feeling.

"You are very welcome, little red. I am happy to see you appreciate my greatness. Here, you can start with this," he gloated as he handed me a few pieces of parchment.

I glanced through them, reminding myself to read more thoroughly about the princes later. What really caught my eye were the two sketched portraits of the princes. Both had the same coloring and high cheekbones, but that was where the similarities ended. The second prince, Malakin, had long blonde hair and pale gray eyes, but despite his bland expression, something about him left me feeling unsettled.

The first prince, Arryn Kaelon Eldore, also sported long blonde hair, but he had emerald eyes and a strong jawline. I skimmed over his basic information, noting that Arryn was supported by the elven aristocracy, while his younger brother was supported by the commoners. His favorite sport was mounted archery, and his subjects generally held a less-than-stellar opinion of him. Rumors were circulating that their crown prince engaged in debauchery on the royal coin. In stark contrast, the second prince was viewed as generous and amicable, no doubt thanks to the many events he attended in Varennia, during which he was very free with the royal coin.

But based on the fact that Malakin had just secretly purchased a thrall, I had a feeling that the common perception of the two royal princes was far from the truth.

And saving our friends would depend on whether or not we could separate truth from fiction.

"This is incredibly helpful, Baldie," I said with a smile. "Why don't you take partial payment in advance, to help things along?"

"That would be amenable," Dorent huffed, the look he gave me telling me how he felt about the nickname. "Oh, and here's the thing you asked for, for the rancher, or Ranger, or whatever his name is."

He dropped a pendant into my hand, the clear crystal glittering when it caught the light. I smiled grimly, not bothering to correct him. "Thanks. And I look forward to seeing you as soon as possible," I hinted.

"No stone will go unturned," he vowed as shadows obscured his form.

And just like that, he was gone.

I turned on my heel and made for our room in the inn, the parchment clutched close to my chest. Rushing to free Freya had been reckless, and it had cost us. But this time, we would be prepared.

"This is taking forever," Reyna growled.

"I know," I sighed. "But we need more information, and this seemed like the best way to get it."

I winced as I shifted my weight, the tingling feeling of pins and needles racing down the leg that had fallen asleep. The elves' wooden benches were elegant. But comfortable? Not so much.

We'd been sitting on this bench just across from a tavern the second prince was known to frequent every Wednesday, pretending to read our books. The prince had never been known to miss this particular appointment, but we'd been waiting for quite some time.

I certainly hoped that Fenn and Jax were having better luck with investigating Arryn. Tim was tending to Danny back at the inn, since he was still recovering from that nasty wound. I was just grateful it hadn't been fatal.

Normally, I would have preferred to be by Fenn's side. But I doubted either of us knew what to say to the other. For now, it seemed focusing on recovering Freya and Chris was the best thing for us.

Suddenly, Reyna nudged me, her gaze locked on an elf passing by. My heart jumped, and I squinted at the male. My shoulders slumped when I saw emerald eyes instead of gray ones beneath the brim of his hat.

But then I sat up straighter, a light coming on in my mind. That wasn't the second prince we were looking for. But it was his brother.

We waited in silence until he had passed, then put our books in our bags and stood. We followed him from a safe distance, occasionally stopping to admire the goods in a stall or shop window. I was surprised to see the first prince out and about, considering his lack of support among the common folk, and without so much as a single guard. I was even more surprised that no one even looked twice at him, despite his sorry excuse for a disguise. Apparently his subjects couldn't recognize their own future king.

Instead of pausing at the shops he passed, Arryn walked with purpose, without appearing hurried. Soon the shop fronts gave way to personal residences as we moved further from the central tree.

We stayed farther back, relying more on our hearing and sense of smell to keep track of him. Eventually, Arryn came to a stop in front of a large manor and knocked on the door. A portly elf answered, her face lighting up when she saw him.

She quickly ushered him inside. I looked more closely at the sign that stood just in front of the large residence.

It read: Ryn's Home for Children.

I pulled Reyna around a corner, out of sight of the windows of the obviously beloved and well-maintained home. The connection was easy to make, though it was the opposite of what I expected.

"It would seem this one is rather philanthropic," Reyna comment-ed, though she seemed troubled for some reason.

"It would seem so," I said absently.

"These brothers are more different than night and day," Reyna added, looking pensive. "If only Arryn had been her owner, we could have negotiated her freedom already."

"But that's just it, isn't it? An elf like that wouldn't have purchased a thrall to begin with," I sighed.

"I suppose you're right," Reyna grumbled. "Should we stay and wait for him?"

"How long he stays will indicate what kind of person he is, but I think we should see if we can meet with him. If Fenn and Jax had been onto him, we would have seen them by now. I think it would be better to keep him in our sights, considering how elusive he is. We may not get another chance."

Reyna nodded, then cocked her head to the side. "What if we go inside in order to donate to the orphanage? Then we may be able to speak with him, or at least observe how he treats the children."

"Good idea. I want to gauge if he has even the faintest inkling of what his little brother has been up to," I said darkly.

After making a quick stop at a nearby shop, we made our way to the orphanage's door and knocked sharply. After a minute, footsteps sounded on the other side, and the same woman from before opened the door.

"Can I help you?" she inquired politely, looking us over, her eyes lingering on our rounded ears. Her matronly hair was pulled back in a tight bun, and a frock covered her robes. Faint lines around her mouth and at the corners of her eyes told of her experience, despite the air of youth innate to all elves.

"Yes, we were hoping to make a donation today. And we brought some sweets to give to the children," I said politely.

"Oh my, how thoughtful. Please, come in," she said as she stepped back, opening the door wide. A soft smile graced her mouth, lighting up her eyes. It wasn't hard to imagine this woman taking meticulous care of the little ones.

Reyna followed me inside, her footfalls light on the well-worn floorboards. I glanced around curiously, wondering at how much love radiated from each meticulously maintained item and piece of furniture. There wasn't a cobweb or speck of dust to be found.

"Right this way," she said as she led us down the hallway.

As we passed the next room, I nudged Reyna, my eyes glued to the prince as he played with a group of young elven children. His back was to us, but he laughed warmly as he helped them construct a miniature fort out of painted wooden blocks. They looked at him with eyes full of adoration, telling me that his undivided attention was not remotely out of the ordinary.

I glanced at Reyna as moved past the open door, following our hostess further down the hallway. She looked just as surprised as I felt. The two princes were practically night and day, making me question the source of the rumors about them.

Soon we entered what was clearly a receiving room for visitors, an office of sorts. Plush chairs and couches were arranged around a central, low table, with a desk pushed back against one wall, and what must have been drawings by the children themselves lining the walls in lieu of oil paintings.

"I hope we weren't interrupting you," I said as my eyes swept across the room, taking in every little detail. So far, this place had displayed a perfect harmony between function and comfort, without any of the useless frills that I would have expected a noble to add.

"Oh, not at all, dears," she said as she blustered around the room, setting out two more teacups. "Ryn and I were just catching up."

I took the proffered tea cup and sank gratefully into a soft chair, Reyna doing the same. I sipped cautiously, pleasantly surprised by the light and fragrant taste of the sweet, berry-flavored tea, which was devoid of the bitter aftertaste I'd grown accustomed to at Lester's.

"Ryn? Like the name on the sign?" I asked casually, trying not to appear overly interested.

"Why yes! It's only thanks to him that this place was created, and is still around," she said warmly, directing a fond smile in the direction of the hallway.

I blinked, hiding my surprise. Before I could respond, a light knock sounded on the doorframe, and the elf himself poked his head in.

"I don't mean to interrupt, I just wanted to let you know that I'll be on my way now," he said quietly. "I wish I could stay, but I have some things to—"

"Oh, Ryn, wonderful timing! These two ladies are here to donate to the orphanage!" the matron cut him off, causing him to appear a little flustered. "Come, sit down with us for just a moment dear."

He shifted uncomfortably, but took a seat across from us and accepted the cup of tea our hostess handed him with a quiet murmur of thanks. I was surprised he obeyed so readily, considering it seemed he had somewhere to be.

His eyes met mine for the briefest of moments before they moved over Reyna, a polite smile stretched across his lips. I felt her stiffen beside me, as she breathed in sharply. I glanced at her curiously, surprised to see her still staring at the prince, her brow pinched in confusion. I thought I saw a flash of recognition in her eyes, but I blinked and it was gone.

The prince missed her odd reaction, since he had almost immediately looked down at the teacup in his hands. He seemed fidgety. Nervous. Stiff, even. Which I found exceedingly odd, considering unlike his frail younger brother, this prince looked like he was no stranger to training, and training hard. Even the loose robes the elves favored could not fully disguise his well-developed muscles. But he seemed to lack confidence in himself when interacting with others, despite his easy interactions with the children just moments ago.

"How wonderful of you to have created such a happy home for the children!" I exclaimed, addressing the prince. "You must be a very kind person."

"I just do what I can," he deflected, looking uncomfortable at the attention.

Did he have something to hide, or was he just unused to conversing with strangers? I would have thought that being a prince meant he'd be accustomed to interacting with others.

"What did you say your names were?" the matron queried. "Everyone here calls me Thea."

I was about to answer her with false names when Reyna beat me to it.

"My friend's name is Serena," she said as she gestured to me, before standing and turning her full attention to the prince. "And my name is Reyna."

He looked up then, his emerald eyes finding hers. He finally looked at her, really looked at her. His lips parted, the color draining from his face. He stood abruptly, his tea cup tumbling from trembling fingers and shattering on the floor.

He looked like he'd seen a ghost.

"Oh dear! Do you two know each other? What in the name of Astraea is the matter?" Thea exclaimed, worry lining her brow.

It felt like time stood still as Reyna stood, and looked deeply into Arryn's eyes. A single tear traced down his cheek.

"I think we need a moment," I murmured to Thea, handing her the bag of sweets I'd purchased earlier. "Would you mind passing these out to the children?"

"Ah...I suppose," she said uncertainly, concern furrowing her brow. With one more glance between the two, she quietly exited the room, closing the door behind her.

"Reyna? Is it truly you?" Arryn asked hoarsely. He stood frozen, as if moving would break the spell and she'd disappear right before his eyes.

"I never thought I would see you again, Ryn," Reyna said unevenly. A storm brewed behind her violet eyes, a whirlwind of emotions and memories.

"I've been looking for you ever since that day," he stammered, his hands clenched into fists. "I wasn't sure if...if you were even...if you were still alive. Where have you been this whole time? What...what happened after...?"

Reyna's eyes shuttered. She went rigid and took a step back, clasping her hands in front of her. Arryn's eyes dropped, noticing for the first time the scars that covered her hands and disappeared beneath the sleeves of her blouse.

"I was sold to the thrall fighting pit in Varennia, Your Highness," Reyna said flatly.

The prince looked stricken.

"How do you know...wait, you've been here...in this city...the whole time?" he asked faintly. He glanced again at the scars on her hands, the scar that split her eyebrow in two.

Reyna nodded mutely, her lips pressed in a thin line.

"Who did this to you?" he asked, clenching his jaw. He took a step forward, reaching out as if to touch her face. When she flinched, he dropped his hand like he'd been burned. Rage and sorrow warred across his features, his earlier awkwardness all but forgotten.

"The same woman who just sold her friend to your brother," I said slowly, watching as my words hit home.

His eyes widened in shock before narrowing on me. "You knew who I was when you walked in here. What is this? Are you trying to blackmail me with her?" A dangerous light entered his red-rimmed eyes, and his hand drifted to his waist, where I had no doubt a weapon was concealed.

It seemed that where Malakin relied on guards, Arryn felt confident in his ability to defend himself, with weapons if not with words.

"I may have known who *you* were, but I had no idea you knew Reyna. And I don't think Reyna expected you to be one of the princes," I said as I looked at Reyna. She nodded shallowly in confirmation.

He glanced at her, his eyes darting between us. Satisfied with whatever he found in our faces, he relaxed a fraction.

"Your accusation against my brother constitutes treason," he said solemnly, and formally. "Which makes me curious as to why you would risk making it."

I held his emerald eyes with my own. "For the same reason you founded this orphanage. To save someone who cannot save herself."

He looked taken aback by my bold statement. "Be that as it may, why would I believe you over my own kin?"

"Would you believe me?" Reyna asked quietly, but forcefully. "Would you believe me if I told you what goes on in this city right under your nose? That your subjects bet on who will live and who will die, and curse the dying for their own financial losses?"

She stared at him with haunted eyes. "Or what fate awaits the victor?"

He curled his hands into fists, his brow furrowing with rage, whether at the truth she spoke or the expression on her face, I couldn't say.

"I had no idea—" he started, his voice rough.

"What about Alistair?" I interrupted. "One of Malakin's guards? Ask any of the patrons of the fighting ring, and they will attest to the fact that they watched him spill blood in that pit. All to ensure that Malakin's prize wouldn't get away or be killed before he could purchase her."

I saw the spark of recognition in his eyes when I said the cruel guard's name.

"There is no love lost between myself and Alistair," he admitted. "But that doesn't prove—"

"Have you never known Malakin to keep a thrall? Has he never unsettled you, never given you the slightest hint that he could be capable of something less than honorable?" I pressed.

Arryn shifted uncomfortably, some emotion I couldn't name flitting across his chiseled features. But I blinked and it was gone.

After a moment of tense silence, the prince finally spoke. "There have been...incidents. I'm not saying I either do or do not believe you. But I would be interested in hearing more."

He glanced at Reyna as he finished speaking, the double meaning of his words clear. She was keeping her face carefully blank, the mask of ice she had worn when I first saw her fighting in the pit firmly in place.

"At the very least, I could surely help you free your friend," he continued, clearing his throat. "It's the least I could do."

"Yes, it is," Reyna whispered hoarsely, with a quiet anger that I'd never heard from her before.

I was surprised to see the mist in her eyes. She always seemed so strong that it was jarring to see her look so vulnerable. I took her hand in mine, silently offering her reassurance.

She gave me a weak smile before looking away. I didn't know her story, but I realized that I hoped she would share it with me one day. Even if that day was far in the future.

I turned to look at Arryn again, noting how his eyes were glued to our hands. I saw a flash of jealousy in his eyes, and stifled a smile. I had a feeling I would be seeing much more of this elf before all was said and done.

"Welcome to the team," I told him with a secretive little smile.

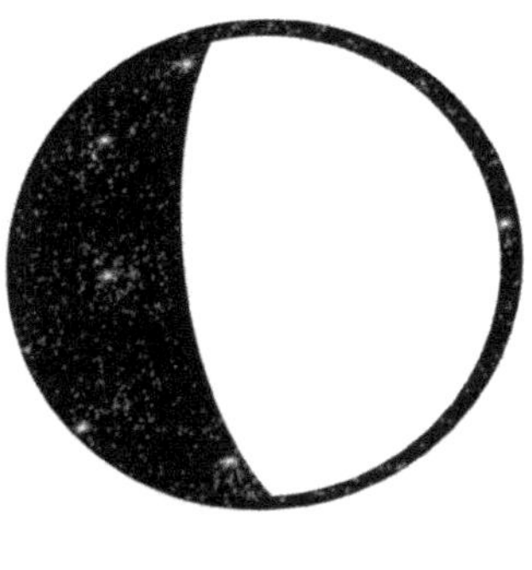

21

"I knew he was up to something, but never in my wildest nightmares..." Arryn trailed off.

His eyes scanned the detailed report we'd just received from our shadow assassin for the fifth time. The grim look on his face when he'd handed it to me had spoken volumes. I myself had read the report at least ten times, as had Fenn and Reyna.

The report was damning. Dorent had earned his gold thrice over with this one. Freya was only the most recent in a string of hundreds of purchases of thralls—many of them female. Many of them strong and capable fighters.

And this had been going on in secret for at least the past five years.

"What could he possibly need that many slaves for?" I mused, aghast.

Arryn flinched at the word, glancing at Reyna. She remained looking stoically ahead, out the room's small window.

"I could not begin to guess," the prince sighed.

"Malakin started his thrall shopping spree about five years ago. Was there any specific event that happened around that time?" Fenn asked.

"Five years ago?" Arryn furrowed his brow.

"Any family feuds? Broken friendships? A lovers' quarrel?" Danny suggested from where he lay on the bed. He wiggled his eyebrows at that last suggestion. If his sense of humor was still intact, then I had no doubt he would be making a full recovery any day now.

I saw the moment a memory sparked behind the prince's eyes. He looked down for a moment, setting the report onto the table. Steepling his fingers, he paused, as if recalling the details of some insignificant memory.

"About five years ago now, there was...an incident," he said slowly. "At the time, my brother had been seeing someone. The daughter of one of the most distinguished noble families in Eldore. They were inseparable, completely enamored with each other. He proposed, and she gladly accepted. I remember my brother had been particularly ec-static about her well-respected pedigree, since he believed that securing a match with her would earn him the approval of the nobles, and therefore solidify his support for his bid for the crown."

"Let me guess; the girl felt used," Reyna commented drily.

"Something like that," Arryn grimaced. "Needless to say, things did not end well. She broke off the engagement, and the status of her family prevented Malakin from seeking any sort of revenge. The annulment came as a complete shock to my brother. It shattered him. I think he really did love her, and felt betrayed by her sudden—well, sudden to him—change of heart."

"Relationships can be difficult," Fenn muttered.

I stiffened.

"Yes, they can be," Arryn replied, glancing once again at Reyna. "He changed after that. I'd always known he coveted the throne. But that was when he stopped hiding it."

"And...the king and queen...did nothing?" Fenn asked.

"My father has been...ill for some time now. And my mother could not bring herself to punish her grieving baby, no matter how much he lashed out. Instead, I later learned that she sent the girl and her family a large payment in lieu of a public apology or reprimand," the prince explained, a surprising edge of bitterness in his tone.

"I have come to learn that greater wealth and status often result in more problems, instead of fewer," I said softly.

Arryn gave me a small smile. I noticed Reyna had turned to face him as he talked. Her eyes had softened, if only a little.

"You say that he stopped hiding his ambition for the throne," Fenn said slowly. "Could that be part of the reason why he is gathering a small army of obedient slaves?"

Arryn looked troubled, but not terribly surprised at the suggestion. As if he himself had been thinking along the same lines.

"If it's not," he paused, glancing surreptitiously at Reyna, "for the purpose of pleasure, then...I can only think of one reason."

"And that is?" Jax prompted when the prince remained silent.

"To take the throne by force," he answered grimly.

He closed his eyes, his pain written plainly on his refined features.

Reyna hesitated before she went over to sit beside him. She offered no words, but when Arryn looked over at her, the tiniest spark of hope ignited in his eyes.

"It looks like putting a stop to Malakin's plans are in all of our best interests. Including those of the people of this kingdom," Fenn said slowly.

The weight on Fenn's shoulders had doubled in the time it took him to say those two sentences. I yearned to comfort him, but the rift between us felt far too wide.

"I had hoped this day would never come," Arryn said heavily. "But I will not run from it."

"Can we count on you to help us put an end to this?" Fenn asked solemnly as he held out his hand.

The room held its breath, every eye turning to the prince. He met every pair of eyes, his gaze assessing. Satisfied with what he found, he stood and stepped up to Fenn.

"Yes," he said simply as he grasped Fenn's outstretched hand firmly. "Besides, a friend of Reyna is a friend of mine."

Reyna looked down, but not before I saw the slight bit of color in her cheeks.

"Glad that's settled, then. Quite the, ah…interesting assortment of folks you got here," Dorent commented drily from behind us, eyeing the prince warily.

He stood leaning against the doorframe, popping small sweets into his mouth. I hadn't even heard him enter.

"This is Dorent, our…information gatherer," I said to Reyna and Arryn. "But you can call him Baldie."

Arryn nearly laughed aloud, but pretended to cough instead. He stared into the shadowy recesses of Dorent's hood, no doubt checking to see if he could spot even a single lock of hair. Reyna gave the shadow assassin an appraising look, her sharp eyes taking in the slight movement of the shadows around him.

"Information gatherer, eh?" she asked as she raised an eyebrow at him.

"Something like that," Dorent replied as he shifted uncomfortably, as if he was trying to decide whether to be more offended or nervous.

"So, can you provide us with a map of the castle where Malakin is keeping his thralls?" I asked.

The look he shot me was equal parts irritation and gratitude. "Of course—acquiring a map is child's play for me. You'll be happy to know I also pinpointed the exact locations where Freya and Chris are being held."

He pulled out a rolled-up piece of parchment from within his cloak. He swaggered into the room and spread the map on the table. Once everyone had gathered around, he began pointing out different spots on the map and explaining what each symbol meant.

"And the timing of the guards' patrols?" Fenn asked.

"I've got it down to the minute," Dorent said. "The fact that Malakin likes his castle running like clockwork will work in our favor."

"Our?" I questioned.

"Well, I can't exactly allow you to have all the fun, now can I?" he said with his usual pluck. "I can't let the dark guilds of Eldore catch on to my presence here, but so long as no one actually sees me..."

"You can help us from the shadows," I finished.

"Aren't you clever," Danny quipped.

Dorent practically beamed at him. If he were a bird, he surely would have been preening his feathers.

"Yes, I am, aren't I?" he gloated.

"In that case, we can come up with a much better plan of attack," I said, trying to steer the conversation back on topic. "And this time, we should assume we will be expected."

"Based on Baldie's report, I do not think it would be wise for me to advertise the fact that I will be involved in this," Arryn said, his lips twitching when he said the nickname. "As I do not know who is on my brother's side, including those within the court he has bribed. Therefore, I will only include my most trusted guards."

Fenn and the others nodded in agreement.

"I think that is wise. Numbers are practically meaningless in the face of betrayal," Fenn commented darkly.

"Will we be going with a frontal assault or a silent infiltration? I am ready for either," Reyna declared, showing her canines in a snarl.

"If we can pull it off, a silent infiltration would be best," Fenn said. "We have the same problem as before—we need to get the control devices first, or else Malakin will just order his thralls to kill us again. And I don't have it in me to fight my little sister. Not after everything she's been through."

I leaned a little closer to Fenn, tapping the back of my hand against his. After a moment, he hooked his pinky finger around mine. I felt the knot in my chest loosen, and it felt like I could breathe a little easier.

Arryn looked at Reyna. "My friend, his sister," she explained, answering the silent question in his eyes.

He nodded.

"I'm something of an expert when it comes to sneaking into and out of places. My claws won't click on the floor the way yours will, and I could open a door for the rest of you to come in," Reyna offered, glancing at the werewolves in the room. I noted that Arryn showed no surprise at her mention of claws, so he must have already known what she was.

"We'll take you up on that," Fenn said.

I looked down, biting my lip. Would I be able to shift on command? Reyna had taken me to a shop where I got some of my clothes and items enchanted so that they would either melt into my fur or change sizes as I did, but despite my numerous attempts, I had yet to successfully shift in either direction unassisted.

I couldn't use the full moon as a crutch, since fingers would definitely be necessary for this. And I had a feeling that this time, Fenn wouldn't be around to help me through it.

"This time, let's have multiple plans. Just in case," I suggested.

"Good idea," Arryn said. "If Astraea's willing, then we won't have to use them. But just in case, I would prefer to be prepared."

"Then let's work out a few different approaches and go through them until everyone has them down. Arryn can explain them to his men when he gets back," Fenn said.

"And don't count me out," Danny chimed in. "I'll be right as rain in time to help out."

Fenn nodded a little grudgingly.

"Just make sure you stick close to me or Jax," Tim added.

"This time, there will be no injuries. No losses," Fenn said gruffly. "We do this quickly and cleanly. Our first priority is to detain Malakin and get the master control device. We can get the thralls out safely so long as the collars are out of the picture."

"So," I asked with a mischievous smile, "who claims the first right to 'detain' Malakin?"

22

I signaled to Tim that we were in position, and he slunk off to relay the message. Fenn crouched beside me, his eyes constantly scanning for guards, or anyone who might raise the alarm when they spotted us. We should still have another ten minutes before the next patrol came by, but it never hurt to be careful.

The night air was still, as if the very stars above were holding their breaths, the nearly full moon watching over us from afar. An owl hooted in the distance, its cry sounding lonely to my ears. The subtle whisper of the wind through the leaves and the quiet crackling of torches were the only other sounds.

I shifted my weight impatiently, the rough-hewn stone at my back scratching against my thick cloak. I glanced up at the window above my head, hoping to see a familiar face peering back at me.

But it remained dark and empty, the slight glow of a single candle illuminating only the crates stacked nearby. I sincerely hoped no one would need to visit this supply room so late in the night.

The slightest scraping noise had Fenn and I peering up at the window, watching as Reyna slowly opened it all the way. I smiled grimly as I boosted myself over the windowsill and into the room, my booted feet landing softly on the rug. Fenn was right behind me, and once he was through, Reyna closed the window, just in case someone came to investigate the draft.

As we crept out of the storage room and into a dimly lit hallway, I whispered softly to Reyna, "Are the others inside already?"

She nodded, and I let out a breath of relief. We both looked at Fenn, waiting as he closed his eyes and inhaled, sorting through the scents of the castle. Reyna and I did the same, attempting to pinpoint the scents of Freya, Chris, and Malakin. After a minute, the familiar scents of hay and horses, with a new bitter undercurrent that was uniquely Chris', teased my nose, telling me he was located deeper in the castle, likely in the dungeon. A sense of deja vu hit me, and I hoped this would be the last time I had to sneak around some noble's castle.

I opened my eyes, giving up on tracing either Malakin or Freya's scents—I simply wasn't familiar enough with them. I could tell Fenn had located both of them by the look in his eyes as he gestured for Reyna and I to follow him deeper into the belly of the beast.

Thanks to all of the information on the layout and patrol schedule that Baldie had gotten for us, we practically breezed through the castle. We did have to hide around corners and inside unoccupied rooms whenever a patrol came by, but thanks to our sensitive hearing, we always had plenty of time to hide.

Once, after a pair of guards had passed us, I peeked around the corner to get a good look at them. They were both male elves, relatively well outfitted with leather armor and well-cared for weapons at their sides. But what sent a chill through me were the slim black collars that encircled each of their necks, a faint red glow emanating from the gem that even the torchlight couldn't disguise.

This prince appeared to have serious trust issues.

I hadn't noticed a collar on Alistair, though perhaps that was simply because someone like him did not need to be forced to kill. But if I assumed that every single person in the castle was collared...then we had better avoid detection until we had that master controller in hand.

I doubted any of us could bring ourselves to hurt so many innocent people. And based on what we'd seen so far, I would not be surprised if Malakin used them as living shields.

After what felt like hours, but was probably only minutes, we closed in on Malakin's personal chambers. A pair of collared guards were posted in front of the doors, their posture rigid. Unfortunately, these two were very much alert, despite the late hour.

I looked between Fenn and Reyna, a silent question in my eyes. Fenn pulled out the small timepiece he'd brought, glancing at it before returning it to his pocket. He shook his head, a worried crease between his brows. Tim and the others should have been here by now.

I felt a touch of unease, but shook it off. If I was going to be a help instead of a hindrance tonight, then I needed to be in full control of my emotions.

We waited with bated breath as the minutes ticked by. Finally, we saw Tim peek his head around the opposite corner, which was just out of sight of the guards. Fenn gave him the signal, and he nodded.

At the same moment, Fenn and Tim slunk towards the guards, launching themselves at them when they got close. One startled guard let out a strangled cry that Fenn quickly muffled. Tim and Fenn used the hilts of their daggers to strike each guard in the temple, easing them to the floor as they fell unconscious.

We all froze for a moment, listening intently to see if the noise had attracted any unwanted attention. When no alarms were raised, we relaxed a fraction. Fenn and Jax, who'd waited around the corner, quickly lifted the guards and locked them in a nearby room with the help of Reyna and her lockpicks.

Hopefully, the pair would be out for the rest of the night.

Reyna quickly turned her attention to the gilded door that led to Malakin's rooms, her scarred fingers moving the metal wires deftly and confidently.

If it hadn't been for the collar, I had a feeling Reyna would have escaped the fighting pit on her own long ago.

A sharp click echoed in the air, and Reyna turned the golden handle slowly, opening the door a crack. She peered inside, her free hand hovering above the sword at her hip.

After a tense moment, she opened the door wider and waved us in. Tim closed the door softly behind us. We padded silently through the receiving room and made for the open doorway that clearly led to the bedchamber.

I hardly spared a glance at our opulent surroundings, other than to double-check for movement. Every surface that could be gilded had been, and oil paintings were framed in gold on every wall. I noted with a faint hint of amusement that the sole bookcase in the room was almost entirely empty.

The deep breathing of two sleeping individuals met my ears, and I peered around Fenn to see Malakin asleep in a massive four-poster bed, surrounded by what I considered to be a ridiculous number of pillows.

And on the floor at the foot of the bed, curled up in a ball, slept a massive black wolf. Her chest rose and fell rhythmically, her head resting on her paws. Fenn went rigid when he saw her, so I placed a hand on his back, reminding him what we were here to do.

As I moved past Fenn towards the bed, he caught my hand, his conflicted blue eyes finding mine. I smiled at him reassuringly, a part of me happy that he was worried about me despite our recent...disagreement. He slowly released my hand after giving it a tender squeeze.

I crept forward on silent feet, the others staying back. My softer, smaller hands were better suited to this task. I approached the bed, hardly daring to breathe as I got close. Malakin looked deceptively innocent, the hard planes of his face softened by sleep. He was certainly handsome, but I knew his lovely features hid a rotten core.

Slowly, so slowly, I leaned over his prone form, searching for the master control device. Dorent had determined that the prince always kept it on him, even while bathing and sleeping. Now I just needed to locate it and take it off of him without waking either him or Freya.

Simple.

I started to panic when I didn't see it right away. I closed my eyes and took a deep breath. If I had a small, precious object, where would I keep it? Suddenly, I remembered the weight of the crescent moon necklace resting on my collarbone. When I opened them, I looked more closely at his neck.

There!

I reached for the glimmer I'd seen, my fingers lifting the delicate golden chain into the air, revealing the black control device. Luckily for me, the prince had chosen a golden chain instead of a silver one.

Slowly, I rotated the golden chain, pulling the clasp closer to my fingers. Danny had given me a few pointers, but I still wished he was here to do this part instead. After another deep breath, I cradled the device in one hand and began to open the clasp with the other.

And then someone sneezed.

I froze as a low growl emanated from my left. I slowly turned my head, meeting the gaze of a very much awake Freya. I was shocked to see that her normally blue eyes had turned blood red, the same color as the gem in the collar around her neck.

Without warning she lunged forward, and I instinctively stumbled back, my hand dropping the device and fumbling for my dagger. A second furry black body slammed into her an instant before her claws would have reached me, and she and Fenn rolled across the bed in a whirlwind of fangs and snarling.

Malakin's eyes flew open, and he scrambled upright, widened eyes quickly taking in the chaos in his bedchamber. His gaze settled on the two werewolves locked in combat, and his surprised expression melted into one of cruel delight.

"I knew you animals would try again!" he exclaimed, his voice still raspy with sleep. "I'm going to have to punish whoever let you get this far, though."

He'd noticed what I did—that while Fenn kept hesitating to attack, Freya did not. Tufts of fur went flying as claws found purchase, and a cacophony of growling and snarling filled the air.

"Kill him, Freya darling," he crooned, the red gem pulsing at her neck.

While he was distracted, I darted forward, my eyes locked on the controller. I could hear the others engaging the thrall guards that had burst into the room. My instincts were telling me that our only chance was about to slip through our fingers.

Unless I could do something about it.

My fingers hooked around the delicate chain, and just as I was about to snap it, Malakin backhanded me across the face. Stars burst across my vision and I staggered, momentarily stunned. My instincts roared at me to shift and shake the life out of the surprisingly strong elf, and I felt my fingernails growing into claws.

"Nice try," Malakin laughed, the sound cold and hollow.

"I don't give up that easily," I ground out, curling my hands into fists. How I wished I could wipe that smile off of his handsome face!

I resisted the urge, knowing that I needed fingers to grab and operate the controller. I glanced around, noting that Reyna and the others were fighting fiercely to keep the thralls at bay long enough for me to get the device. Fenn and Freya were still locked in combat, blood dripping from their wounds.

I was on my own.

Or was I?

I unsheathed my dagger, the dark blade gleaming. The Vulclaria feather fluttered from the movement, dancing like a flower in a hurricane.

A howl of pain drew my attention back to the battling wolves, and my heart constricted when I saw the gaping wound in Fenn's shoulder. Before he could recover, Freya lunged, her fangs poised to sink into Fenn's neck.

In an instant I'd grabbed the downy feather and made my wish. A blinding white light filled the room, dazing everyone in it. The sounds of battle ceased as every eye turned towards me. I shielded my eyes, straining to make out the shape I knew I would see.

As the light began to fade, my sweet little Vulclaria darted through the air. Before anyone had time to react, the fox had gripped the device gently in its jaws and launched off of Malakin's chest, snapping the chain in the process.

"No! Stop!" Malakin screamed. He tried to grab the winged fox, but it expertly avoided his clumsily grasping arms.

I just smiled at him.

The moment that the small black device was no longer in Malakin's possession, Freya and the guards went still, the red glow leaving their eyes. They looked around, confused, and lowered their weapons.

Freya suddenly seemed to realize what she had nearly done, a low whine rising deep in her throat as she released Fenn's neck. She flattened her ears against her skull and tucked her tail between her legs, remorse written in every line of her body. Fenn gave her head a couple of licks before nuzzling his face against hers. I bit back a growl, tamping down on the sudden spike of possessiveness I felt and telling myself not to be so ridiculous.

The Vulclaria flew right into my open arms, and I caught it gently against my chest. I held out one hand, and the fox opened its maw, allowing the controller to drop. I curled my fingers around the accursed object, which felt cool and smooth to the touch, a smile lighting up my face.

For the first time since we'd set out on this wild adventure, we finally had the upper hand.

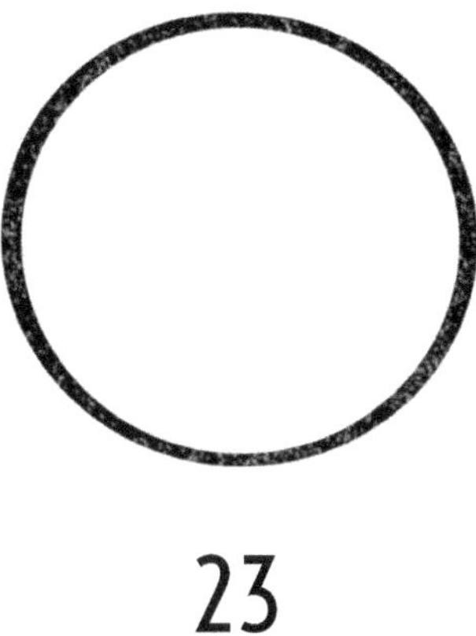

23

"Give that back, you filthy human peasant!" Malakin shrieked as he lunged towards me.

Fenn was there in an instant, an icy rage burning in his eyes. He tackled the prince, pinning him to the ground with his massive weight. He placed one paw on the elf's chest, his claws pricking the skin of his throat. He bared his fangs, a growl rumbling from deep in his chest.

Suddenly a burning rage filled me, so intense that I gasped. A surge of protectiveness and raw pain hit me, nearly driving me to my knees. The little fox that was still in my arms licked my face, the sensation a rope I used to come back to my senses, and distance myself from the intense emotions. It took me a moment to understand what had just happened.

I knew what he was about to do the instant the thought formed.

"Fenn, stop!" I screamed, trying to break through the haze of red that clouded his vision. "Killing him won't undo what he's already done! It will only land you in hot water! Are you going to abandon your sister already? Abandon me?"

I could feel it when my words pierced the fog of animalistic fury in his mind. I had no idea how or why, but I was feeling all of Fenn's emotions, almost as if they were my own.

Fenn withdrew his fangs from where they rested on the prone prince's neck. A single bead of blood formed, like a ruby in a field of snow. He looked at me then, as if he was seeing me for the first time. Then he glanced at his sister, a whisper of remorse in his heart. He shook his head, as if dislodging his dark thoughts from his mind.

And then all of a sudden, his well of emotions just...disappeared. I probed the space in my mind where they'd just been, realizing there was now a wall there, and I could barely sense only the faintest echo of emotion on the other side.

Fenn looked away from the silent question in my eyes, his glare returning to the elf under his paws, who had apparently wet himself, judging by the unpleasant smell coming from him. I realized the others were staring at us, and I tried to pull myself together.

We weren't done yet.

I stroked the Vulclaria absently, its purr a comforting rumble. After taking a moment to compose myself, I turned towards Reyna.

"Would you restrain him, please?" I asked, jerking my head towards the prince.

"Which one?" she asked with a mischievous twinkle in her violet eyes.

"Whichever one gives you the most trouble," I muttered, returning her smile.

She winked at me as she walked past, pulling out the rope she'd brought with her. It was the work of a moment for her to tie the prince's hands roughly behind his back after searching him—carefully--for weapons. His shoes were taken, and his ankles tied loosely together, so that he could only shuffle slowly forward.

"Freya, can you lead us to where he's keeping Chris and the other thralls?" I asked gently. "I think it would be best if we could take the collars off all at once."

She nodded her head and padded towards the door, looking back to wait for me.

"Reyna, Fenn, let's bring him with us in case we run into any uncollared guards," I suggested.

"You all will be executed for high treason," the prince spat as Reyna roughly hauled him to his feet.

"Will we now?" I asked sweetly, throwing him off. "Then what will happen to you when the king, queen, and crown prince learn of what you've been up to?"

He scowled sullenly at me, but hissed, "They've never cared about me before. Why should they start now?"

"Well, enslaving the daughter of a neighboring country's duke, and therefore risking a war between the human and elf kingdoms might just do it," I commented drily. "Not to mention your plans to use your thrall army to overthrow the king and claim the throne of Eldore before your brother could be crowned."

Malakin went pale, his gaze darting to Freya, and then to Fenn, putting the pieces together.

"A duke's daughter...?" he mumbled. "You have no proof!"

"Not even your parents can protect you from the maelstrom that's coming for you," Fenn promised darkly as he reattached his cloak after shifting back to his human form.

"We'll make sure of it," Reyna hissed, her eyes narrowed to slits as she shoved him forward, forcing the prince to either hop or faceplant into the ground.

"You're going to tell us where each and every one of your thralls are," Tim ordered, his normally kind eyes hardened with hatred.

"And you'll order your guards to stand down," Jax added.

"Unless you want to lose a few fingers," Danny ground out, more serious than I'd ever seen him.

Malakin's face darkened with rage, but he held his tongue. Instead, he spat at Danny's feet. "Should have killed you when I had the chance."

"I suppose you should have," Danny agreed coldly.

The prince looked taken aback.

Apparently the prince had never had the chance to learn that it was often the kindest people that snapped the hardest when they were hurt too badly. I made a mental note to shower Danny with treats when we got home.

"Thanks for your confession, little brother," Arryn said as he emerged from the shadows.

"I see Dorent has been giving you some tips," I greeted him. "Especially on making those grand entrances."

"Arryn?" Malakin exclaimed, going paler than before. "You heard...?"

"I heard everything," he sighed as he looked at his brother sadly, his arms crossed over his chest. "Malakin, just because you were hurt by that girl doesn't give you license to hurt others. I can't tell you how disappointed I am in you. And yes, Baldie has been quite helpful when it comes to moving around silently and quickly."

"The front guards?" Fenn asked.

"My men have taken care of them. They'll be questioned once we get them back to the palace," Arryn informed us. "And I've set up a perimeter so no one can escape."

"Nice of you to show up after someone else has done all the hard work," Reyna muttered.

Arryn stiffened, his emerald eyes going hard as they cut to her before returning to his brother. "Answer me this: Were you purposefully trying to get me killed that day in the forest, when we were boys?"

"Don't tell me you're just figuring that out now, dear brother?" Malakin cackled, a cruel smile on his face despite his dire situation.

Arryn stalked forward and forcefully punched his brother in the face in a rare display of pent-up frustration and anger, sending the other elf reeling. If someone hadn't been holding him up, Malakin surely would have collapsed. "I have half a mind to run you through here and now for what you've done."

"Do it then," Malakin spat as he wiped at the blood trickling from his nose.

"Don't tempt me," Arryn muttered darkly. "But I'm not the only one who seeks retribution from you, and I won't deny them their satisfaction." He glanced around at the rest of us, his gaze lingering on Reyna.

Stunned silence descended, but before it became any more uncomfortable, I interjected, "Freya was just about to lead us to where some of the slaves have been imprisoned."

He nodded gratefully to me before collecting himself and turning to the black wolf. He inclined his head to her, and said, "Nice to meet you, Freya. Please, lead the way."

We followed Freya down to the prince's dungeons, the stench of the place making bile rise in my throat. There were many thralls locked away, not just Chris. My Vulclaria climbed from my arms to settle around my shoulders, making a soft keening noise as it surveyed the poor souls in each cell. I followed my nose and stopped in front of one of the cells.

"Fancy seeing you here," I quipped, though my heart ached at the fact that Chris had wound up behind bars for a second time because of me.

"Took you long enough," he said with a lopsided smile, despite the fact that the rags he wore couldn't disguise the bruises and welts all over his body. Even the bite mark on his arm, which had started to look like a tattoo of a lion, was plainly visible. From the look in his eyes, I could tell he was now fully aware of his new monstrous form.

"Sorry about that," I replied, apologizing for more than just my tardiness.

"Get me some food and a hot bath, and we'll call it even," he said wearily. "Oh, and a coin bonus wouldn't hurt."

"Let's start with this," I said softly as I handed him the crystal necklace. "It will keep you from shifting."

Chris hesitated a moment before he put it on. But I knew it would bring everyone some peace of mind. The fact he didn't question me only confirmed my suspicions of his new self-awareness.

Reyna handed her prisoner off to Fenn and unlocked the cell with the key she'd taken off of Malakin earlier. She wrinkled her nose at him, whether in laughter or because of the smell, I wasn't quite sure. I noticed that the Vulclaria would pin its ears back whenever Chris came close. I wondered what exactly had happened for the sweet creature to react that way.

"Nice to officially meet the reason I nearly died. Again," Chris said wryly to Freya, though he still curled his lip at her four-legged form. He eyed the winged fox, keeping his distance from it.

She growled softly at him in response, but I saw her tail give a tiny wag. I was looking forward to when Freya could give him a piece of her mind.

Prince Arryn watched quietly as we went around freeing all those who had been imprisoned, an unreadable look on his face. He followed us quietly back up to the front of the castle, seemingly deep in thought.

Once we had assembled everyone in the courtyard, the moon hanging low overhead, I flicked a switch on the device, ordering every thrall to come to the courtyard if they weren't already. After a while my little friend grew bored, and leaped into the air. The Vulclaria circled above my head a few times before disappearing in a shower of light, presumably returning to its forest home. The back of my neck felt a little cold without its warm presence.

We stood aghast as hordes of elves, humans, and dwarves began pouring out of the castle. Some were dressed in fine clothes, some in simple tunics. A large number were armed and outfitted as guards. Many wore thin sleeping shifts, and shivered in the cool night air. All looked afraid and confused, and only became more so when they spotted our ragtag group. I did notice a spark of hope igniting in some eyes as they spotted the bound prince.

Once it seemed like all of the thralls had assembled in the courtyard, I stepped forward, Fenn, Reyna, and Arryn flanking me. I think we were all surprised by the sheer number of them—Arryn especially. It was one thing to see numbers on a piece of parchment, but quite another to see hundreds of thralls in person.

"Hello, everyone!" I called, and waited for their attention to shift to me. "As you can see, the second prince, Malakin, has been apprehended for planning to usurp the throne of Eldore—by using all of you. Although keeping thralls is not illegal in this country," I paused, glancing pointedly at Arryn, "treason is."

Excited murmuring broke out, quieting only when Arryn stepped forward, albeit a tad nervously.

"As the crown prince of Eldore, I would like to apologize on behalf of the king and queen. What happened here shall never happen again. This I swear to you in the name of our goddess, Astraea," the prince vowed solemnly. He bowed to the crowd, a show of humility that shocked everyone, including myself and Reyna, who I noticed smiled approvingly at him.

"Today you will be freed from your collars. Those who have families here they wish to return to may leave at any time. The Dukedom of Verdania in the neighboring kingdom of Cyrulia, where thralldom—slavery—is illegal, is willing to offer sanctuary and a fresh start to any who want it," Fenn announced, his deep voice carrying through the crisp night air.

"And I will personally provide aid to any and all who require it, should you wish to settle here in Varennia or in another city or town in Eldore," Arryn added. I noticed that although he clasped his trembling hands behind his back, his voice remained steady.

"How do we know we won't be enslaved again?" cried a voice from within the mass of people.

"You have my word as the next King of Eldore that I will do all in my power to pass a law banning all forms of thralldom henceforth and forevermore," Prince Arryn declared with a confidence that echoed in the heavens.

Stunned silence met his declaration. Then, one person began to clap, and the whole crowd of thralls began to cheer, their cries of joy reaching the stars.

I felt my eyes begin to mist, and a quick glance at Reyna showed me a similar glimmer in her eyes. Her smile was absolutely radiant as she watched the people rejoice. Arryn was also watching her, the tenderest of expressions on his face, his hands now hanging loosely at his sides.

I raised the master control device above my head and flicked the switch. The sound of the collars hitting the ground was like music to my ears, a ringing symphony of freedom.

I smiled as I watched a black blur tackle Fenn, the discarded collar all but forgotten on the ground, the red gem dull and lifeless. Freya shifted back to her human form to wrap Fenn in a hug, and he quickly draped his cloak around her.

I turned away to give them some privacy, just in time to watch Chris throw his collar to the ground and stomp on it, muttering, "Good riddance."

I sidled up to him, a mischievous grin on my face and laughter in my heart. "Want to be in charge of destroying all the collars?"

"Absolutely," he replied, a wicked gleam in his eye.

"Maybe Arryn will even give you a bonus for services rendered to the crown," I hinted.

"If he survives," Chris laughed, watching as the prince was swarmed by newly-freed thralls, each wanting to shake his hand and thank him personally. Some also wanted to tell him their tales, while others simply wanted to know how he would help them find a new home. He looked surprised and a little nervous at first, but I soon saw him relax as the genuine sincerity of the people reached him.

Some of Arryn's men came forward, medicine bags in hand, to help treat those who were injured. Most of the thralls appeared unharmed, though I had a feeling their invisible injuries would take time to heal.

"Would you make sure someone sees to Freya's injuries?" I asked Chris.

He followed my gaze to the drops of blood on the ground from her open wounds. He hesitated a moment before he nodded silently and headed towards one of the elven guards. There were still some things I needed to talk about with him, but that could wait. It felt like something had changed in our relationship. I just hoped it was in a positive direction.

I turned towards a sudden commotion, my heart spiking in fear before I identified the cause. My gaze snagged on a bound and gagged Alistair, and a spike of relief shot through me despite the hatred in his gaze. But surprisingly, the cruel guard wasn't the source of the noise. Some of Arryn's men were shackling Malakin's wrists and ankles with iron bands. He kept making odd gestures, and almost looked like he was mouthing something. But the guards were too busy trying to restrain him properly to take notice.

I followed his gaze to a shadowy corner of the courtyard. I squinted, relying on my enhanced vision to pick out the details. I could barely make out the ghost of a shadowy form, as wisps of inky darkness coiled like mist around him, his hair waving as if underwater.

Wait, *hair?*

A spike of alarm shot through me like a lightning bolt as the figure melted into the shadows before shooting like a spear across the courtyard. In an instant I pieced together the tragedy that was about to unfold.

It would be too late if I shouted for help or tried to get there in time.

That is, if I was human.

Time slowed down as my heartbeat sped up, the weight of this moment pressing down on my chest. The last few times I'd tried to shift on my own, I hadn't been able to do it. But this time, I wasn't asking. I was *demanding*. I recalled the feeling of the full moon's call, and *willed* my body to change its shape.

All my senses sharpened as claws shot from my fingers and fur covered my form. Faster than ever before I sprinted towards the three unaware figures, drawing out every ounce of strength and speed from my screaming muscles.

Heads started to turn, cries of alarm sounding as I raced the wind, the shadow on the ground inches from my reaching claws. We were nearly upon them now.

The mass of shadow leaped into the air, rapidly expanding into the form of a deadly assassin, his dagger raised and poised to plunge down into Arryn's chest, a second dagger aiming for Freya's exposed throat.

I gathered my legs beneath me and launched myself at him, fangs bared and claws extended. I barreled into him, my open jaw closing around his wrist, and sent us both tumbling to the ground.

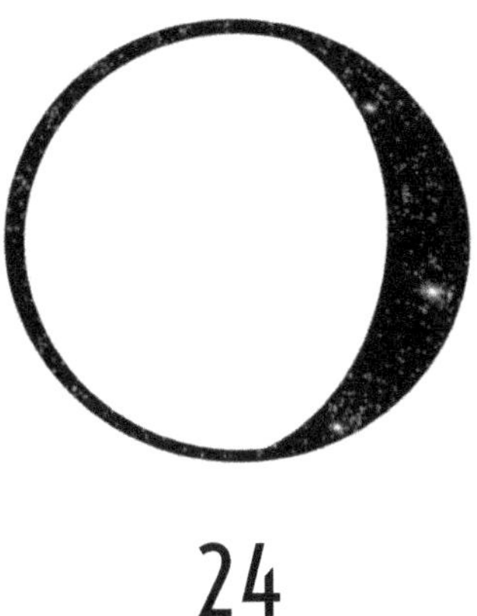

24

I bit down hard, the snap of bone echoing in the courtyard. The shadow assassin only gritted his teeth in silence, glaring at me with unrestrained malice.

I growled at him, the warning clear in my eyes. But he grinned back at me, his body dissipating into slippery shadows once more. I clambered to my paws, putting my back to Arryn, Chris, and Freya protectively. I growled at the empty air, my eyes darting this way and that as I dared the assassin to try again, so I could finish what I'd started.

I felt attuned to my wolf form like I never had before, even on a full moon night. I let my instincts take over, my senses on high alert. Fenn's fur brushed against mine as he joined me, and I rejoiced that my pair was by my side.

Reyna growled softly, her pale feline form appearing on my other side as we formed a circle around our three loved ones. I glanced at Malakin, feeling relieved that his excited expression had turned into one of irritation. If he didn't seem assured of victory, then this must be the final trick he had up his sleeve.

Movement caught the corner of my eye, and I whirled, my claws digging into flesh before it melted back into the shadows. Fenn flicked an ear at me, silently scolding me for being too impatient. I huffed at him, but resumed my vigil.

"As if building a thrall army wasn't enough already, now he's contracted with a shadow assassin?!" Arryn muttered darkly, his sword drawn in steady hands. "I'm getting a little tired of my brother trying to kill me, and getting other people caught up in the attempt!"

"Quite the brother you've got there," Chris commented.

Arryn grunted at him.

Freya was focused on the shadows beneath us, her twin daggers at the ready.

This time when I saw a wisp of shadow moving, I held still, feigning ignorance. I flicked an ear at Arryn, Fenn and Reyna, discreetly catching their attention. This time, I was going to catch my prey.

The pool of shadow hesitated, waiting to see if we'd noticed the movement. The shadows slithered directly underneath Arryn like a snake, coiled and poised to strike. I tried not to tense, keeping myself fluid and ready. I could tell Reyna was struggling to do the same, her hackles raised and fangs bared in a silent threat. Arryn changed his grip on his sword, readying himself for the next attempt.

We were ready when the assassin materialized beside Arryn, his dagger already slashing at his neck. Arryn blocked the killing blow with his own sword, the clash of steel ringing in my ears. The force of the ricochet knocked the surprised assassin off balance, giving us all the opening we needed.

Reyna pounced first, her claws raking across his chest, the leather armor there parting like warm butter. Fenn and I attacked as one in a blur of black and red, our quick claws and fangs not leaving the man time to gather himself enough to fade back into the shadows.

He desperately lunged at me, the blade in his uninjured hand scoring my side, leaving a burning trail behind. I roared in pain, whirling and snapping at him. Fenn went ballistic as he came to my defense, his eyes narrowed to slits. I tried to push through the fog of pain, to not give in to the instincts that demanded blood.

I failed.

As a pair we fought the skilled assassin, dodging his thrusts and inflicting wounds of our own. Reyna watched from her position next to Arryn, her sharp eyes watching for any stray movement or attack directed at our three friends. Soon the man began to pant, sweat beading on his brow as his wounds began to take their toll. The shadows flickered, clearly not strong enough for him to escape, but forming a needle-like dagger was a different story. My instincts screamed at me as his eyes and hand shifted towards Fenn, commanding the shadows to pierce his heart, but before the blow could land, I had my fangs around his throat.

Just like that, the fight was over.

The shadow assassin's lifeless body slumped to the ground, his daggers clattering onto the cobblestones. I stared at him, my chest heaving, as the fog cleared from my mind, and I realized what I had done.

I began to shake, a whine rising involuntarily from my chest. I backed away from the prone form, but before I could turn tail and run, Fenn was there, his comforting presence a balm to my raw and ragged soul.

I shifted back to my human form, grateful for the enchantment that made my clothes and items reappear on me, and flung my arms around Fenn's neck, burying my face in his soft fur. But the tears that pricked my eyes refused to fall. He rested his head on my shoulder, and I focused on simply breathing in the scent of him, like dappled sunlight on green pine boughs.

My safe haven from the storm.

My sanctuary.

My mate.

That thought cut through the pain in my heart, my side. When had I started thinking of Fenn as my pair? My mate? I wasn't even entirely sure what those words meant. They'd just...appeared, in my mind, as if it was the most natural thing in the world. As if those words had always been there, just waiting for me to notice them.

The sound of metal clattering against metal pulled me from my thoughts, and I looked up in time to see Arryn's elves escorting a shackled Malakin out of the courtyard. His protests fell on deaf ears, his former thralls letting out a wild cheer as he disappeared from sight.

I felt strong arms close around me, and I looked back to see that Fenn had shifted back while I was distracted. I buried my head against his chest, and he stroked the top of my head.

"Looks like I owe you my life once again," he murmured into my hair, his breath sending warmth through me.

"Just returning the favor." The space that had yawned between us had all but disappeared. "Fenn, what does it mean that you're my m—"

"Well, I don't know about you two lovebirds, but I am about ready to get this show on the road," Danny interrupted as he slung an arm around our shoulders.

"I'm glad to see you're all healed up now," I told him with a smile.

He winked at me, ignoring the death glare Fenn directed at him for the interruption. But I could tell from the slight twitch of his lips that he was trying to suppress a smile at the man's antics.

"What do you say we leave sorting out all the thralls to His Highness over there and go get something to eat?" Chris suggested as he and Freya joined us.

"*Former* thralls," Freya and Reyna snapped in unison, their scowls turning into smiles as they glanced at each other.

"Attempting to deposit the workload on me before escaping, are you?" Arryn teased good-naturedly as he approached. "I propose a deal; we take everyone to the palace and sort out all the little details after some sustenance and rest."

"Deal accepted," Fenn said, nodding his head in thanks to the prince.

"Thanks." I smiled wearily at Arryn. "That would be wonderful."

"I'll make the announcement and arrange for transportation then," Arryn exclaimed, clapping his hands together before walking towards his men.

A short time later, after Fenn had bandaged the wound in my side, which was already starting to heal, we were rattling along in a gilded carriage bearing the crest of the royal family. Freya and Reyna sat across from us, though Chris had opted to sit up front beside the coachman, allegedly so he could see how the elves used their large deer in lieu of horses.

To my surprise, silence lay over the four of us like a blanket, the very air thick with words left unsaid. Now that the adrenaline of the fight had worn off, no one knew what to say. I understood, in my own way. It was almost easier to bottle up your thoughts and emotions, to leave them for another day. But if that day was pushed further and further down the road, eventually that bottle would shatter from the pressure.

We did not just risk our lives to let that happen.

"So, how did you two become friends?" I asked to break the silence. Hopefully, we could ease into the more serious questions.

Reyna looked to Freya, speaking without uttering a word. "Eris allowed us to train during the day, so we would put on better displays at night. I watched Freya for a while after she was brought in. She reminded me of myself, so my friend and I decided to teach her."

Freya snorted. "Teach? More like beat up."

"It worked, didn't it? You started winning more fights after a while," Reyna smirked.

"Is your friend still with Eris?" I asked, happy they were talking so lightheartedly. "We could—"

"She's dead," Freya cut me off, grief and another emotion I couldn't name clouding her face.

I mentally kicked myself. Clearing my throat, I tried again. "I'm so sorry to hear that."

Freya gave me a tentative smile, but sadness still tinged her features. "She would have been so happy that we helped free those thralls."

Reyna nodded. "She always was soft, despite her best efforts not to show it."

Silence descended again, so I nudged Fenn. He tensed, so I laced my fingers through his. He gave my hand a light squeeze. Now I wasn't sure who was reassuring whom. Freya noted the movement, her gaze turning curious.

"Freya, what happened that night, when Lester made his move?" Fenn asked abruptly.

I winced at his sledgehammer approach to such a loaded question. Subtlety was not his strong suit.

But Freya didn't look particularly taken aback, as if she had expected the blunt question. She looked down, as if she were gathering her thoughts, before meeting Fenn's solemn gaze.

"Someone must have let them in, because they descended on us with no warning. It was the night of the new moon, so we had all retired early. I awoke to the dying screams of the guards posted outside my room. The men weren't at all surprised to see me when they broke down the door, as if they'd been coming for me. As if they knew where to look. I killed two of them, but more kept pouring through the door. They hid their faces. They bore no emblems. But they were all armed with silver," Freya told us slowly, the words halting at first.

She closed her eyes, as if the memories were too painful to bear. Reyna leaned against her, a silent pillar of support. I noticed the murmur of voices in the coachman's seat had quieted, as if they were listening too.

"Eventually, the men overcame me with sheer numbers. Just before I was knocked out, I scented our parent's blood. When I came to, I was chained to Lester Lindora's bed," she continued, her voice cracking.

Fenn stiffened beside me, and I closed my eyes as well. I had the sinking feeling that I knew where this was headed.

"He dressed me up like a doll. Played with me. Hurt me. But he didn't like that I didn't play along. So he said that if I did not obey, he'd kill our little brother. So I played along, just like he wanted. But then he became bored with his pliant, obedient doll. So after a while, he sold me off to a slaver, and I ended up in Eris' ring. A different kind of doll," she relayed, the words pouring from her like water from a fountain.

Rage radiated from Fenn, a tic feathering in his clenched jaw. Her story echoed mine, a familiar ache in her voice. It seemed this same story had played out many times, long before Lester had first set foot in my mother's home by the woods.

"We buried all three of them at home," Fenn said haltingly.

Fenn slipped his hand from mine to take Freya's hand in both of his. Scars marred both of them, lines etching hardship into the skin like a tattoo. Freya stared at their hands without seeing them, her misty eyes looking at something none of us could see.

She took a shuddering breath before she continued. "Even then some part of me knew he'd never keep his word. But I still hoped someone would come for me. That you'd come for me when my letters stopped coming. To take me out of this nightmare. But at the same time, I feared Lester had sent someone after you as well. That only your ghost would find me." she shivered, and Fenn rubbed her hand soothingly.

I put my hand on her knee, feeling kinship with this stranger who'd suffered because of Lester far longer than I. My throat constricted at the thought of everything she'd gone through. Alone.

"Lester can never hurt anyone else, ever again," I whispered hoarsely past the lump in my throat.

Freya slowly looked at me, a hint of relief and understanding in her sapphire eyes. "He hurt you too?"

I nodded.

"Did you make him pay?" she asked.

"We took away what he treasured most, something he could never get back," I said solemnly. "His reputation. In front of the Imperial Family, and every important noble of Cyrulia. Right before he met his end."

"Good," she said firmly, a little bit of light coming back to her eyes.

I could see the brilliance of her fighting spirit had been dimmed by her time as a thrall. But I could also tell that it was a resilient flame, one that was already starting to rekindle.

"Freya," Fenn whispered roughly, "I'm sorry I took so long."

She met his blue eyes with her own, the sapphire depths devoid of resentment, and filled with love and gratitude instead.

"You made it just in time."

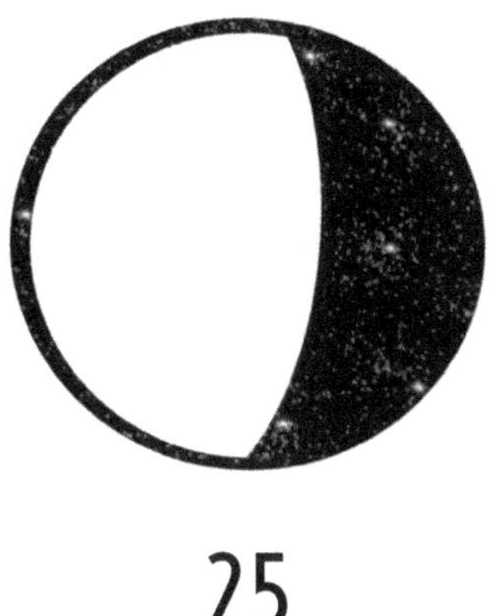

25

I was so exhausted and mentally worn out from the events of the last twenty four hours that I didn't even have it in me to feel awkward about the fact that Fenn and I were sharing a room in the palace. I simply pulled my boots off, flopped onto the silky soft bed, and mumbled a 'good night' to Fenn. I was asleep before my head even touched the pillow.

I slowly surfaced from a deep, dreamless sleep, the quiet sounds of someone walking around the luxurious guest room pulling me from the comfortable depths. I blinked my eyes open but closed them immediately, convinced I must be dreaming.

When I opened them again, Fenn was still walking around the room in nothing but a towel, his black hair still damp from his bath. Heat rose in my cheeks at the sight of the chiseled muscles on Fenn's abdomen, a few errant droplets still beaded like pearls on his taut skin. His biceps flexed as he used a second cloth to towel his hair dry, his scars undulating like waves on the sea.

As if he could feel me staring, he turned his head to meet my gaze, his glacial blue eyes softening. I could get used to seeing Fenn every morning when I woke up.

"Good morning, Serena," he said warmly, with his signature lopsided smile.

"Morning," I mumbled sleepily as I sat up, rubbing my eyes.

"Like the view?" he asked mischievously, quirking an eyebrow at me.

My blush intensified, but I refused to look away. "You could say that."

Fenn looked downright delighted, his grin widening. He stalked over to me, his eyes deepening into pools of sapphire, and braced his arms against the bed around me, trapping me.

Heat unspooled in my belly as I met his gaze. I leaned forward slightly, closing the distance between us.

"You know, you're the only one besides my family who never looks away," he murmured.

I blinked, surprised. "Why would I look away?"

"Direct eye contact is considered a challenge among wolves," he answered.

"You need someone around to push you," I replied. "How else are you supposed to learn and grow?"

"I didn't think I needed to until you crashed through the forest and into my life," he said huskily.

My eyes dropped to his lips. "I suppose you've met your match."

"No."

I looked at him, confused. A sliver of hurt pricked me. "No?"

"I've met my alpha mate."

"Is that why—?" I started, my mind swirling with questions, my heart lifting.

"Yes. A werewolf only has one destined mate, like the human concept of a soulmate. And they—we—can share our thoughts and feelings without needing words. Like what happened yesterday. I've been holding back, because I didn't want to overwhelm you right after your first shift," Fenn explained, his eyes dropping to my lips.

"You've known that long? You had to know that I—that I—" I looked away, unsure how to feel about all of this. Excited? Angry? It felt like Fenn was putting into words things I already knew, but couldn't name.

Fenn gently lifted my chin with calloused fingers. "That you weren't sure if I felt the same?"

I nodded mutely, the understanding and love in his eyes cutting me to the bone.

"I'm sorry I haven't said the words yet. I—I was scared. That if I said them aloud, it would be too real, that I could lose you like I lost my parents and my brother," he whispered hoarsely.

"I'm not going anywhere," I said with sincerity. "Now or ever. I want to stay by your side."

His eyes searched mine, looking for any hint of deception, but finding none. I reached for him, my hands tangling behind his head, his damp onyx hair cool against my skin.

"I love you," I whispered.

"I love you too, Serena LaRoux," he breathed, before capturing my lips with his own.

A knock sounded at the door just as I finished braiding my long red hair, which was still slightly damp from my own bath. Fenn had shown me where the baths were located, on the lowest floor of the tree palace, in between some massive roots. Then he'd gone off to attend some formal meetings with Prince Arryn, to work out the details of what came next.

I felt a little dismayed that I couldn't go with him, but I was still looking forward to today's plans. I grabbed my bag, the motion pulling at the freshly-healed skin on my side. Now I was healing nearly as fast as Fenn.

The knocks came again, more insistent this time.

"I'm coming!" I called, glancing around the room one last time to make sure I hadn't forgotten anything. When my eyes landed on the mussed bed, I unconsciously brought my hands to my lips, a smile tugging at the corners of my mouth as I recalled the sweet sensation of Fenn's lips pressed against mine.

More knocking pulled me out of my reverie, and I yanked open the door, startling Reyna, whose fist was still raised. She smiled at me, raising an eyebrow when she spotted some of Fenn's things on the table.

"It's not what it looks like," I blustered, warmth tinting my ears pink as I realized what Reyna must be thinking. I closed the door quickly behind me, hoping Freya hadn't noticed from where she was standing a little behind Reyna.

"Good morning to you, too, sunshine," Reyna purred, giving me a wink.

I rolled my eyes at her, but smiled just the same. I waved at Freya, still a little uncertain how to behave around her. "Good morning."

"Morning, Serena," Freya returned the greeting with a fleeting smile.

"Who's ready for a day full of sun and shopping?" Reyna asked, a devilish twinkle in her eye.

"If we must," Freya muttered, looking none too excited at the prospect.

"That's the spirit!" Reyna said cheerfully. "I do believe our guard is waiting for us at the entrance."

I grimaced at the thought of having some aloof elf silently watching the three of us wandering around Varennia. We would draw enough attention as it was, despite the elven robes we were all wearing, without a royal guard shadowing us.

Nonetheless, I followed along as Reyna towed Freya towards the entrance. It would be nice to simply get to know these two better, without some huge threat or worry hanging over our heads for a change.

I was both relieved and nervous when I spotted our "guard" for the morning. Chris turned when he heard us coming, an easy grin lightening up his demeanor, though it still seemed a little strained to me. Freya stiffened slightly when she saw him, but Reyna and I returned Chris' smile.

Perhaps today I would finally have a chance to clear the air between us. Though I wasn't exactly looking forward to some of the questions I was going to have to ask. A slight feeling of unease twisted my stomach, but I pushed it aside.

"Took you three long enough," Chris said with his usual sass.

"Well, you know us ladies. We had to take our time getting ready to impress you," Reyna quipped back at him with a sly little wink.

I had to suppress a laugh at Chris' baffled expression. He had no clue how to handle her, and I was going to enjoy every minute of it.

Taking in the warmth of the dappled sunlight, the sound of murmuring voices and bell-like laughter was a treat after the events of the last few days. The sense of peace felt like a balm soothing the rough parts of my heart.

We fluttered from shop to shop, looking at all of the fascinating things the elves had created. Apparently, an elf could enchant just about anything. Naturally, we all ended up purchasing something—or in Reyna's case, several somethings. I could hardly blame her, seeing as she hadn't been able to buy anything since she was a child.

I ended up buying small hair accessories that would always return to their owner if lost or stolen for my friends back home, as well as some brooches for the men. I made sure Chris was at the other end of the shop when I got his. Freya purchased some new clothes, and a simple but elegant crystal necklace. Reyna bought a little bit of everything, and was soon laden with bags and boxes.

Chris ended up getting small trinkets to give to his family, but I could tell he was far more interested in the food stalls. Our little group of carnivores made a point of following our noses to whatever smelled the best, from meat skewers to fish filets. Unsurprisingly, it was either a human or a dwarf running those businesses.

The elves, on the other hand, were geniuses when it came to sweets. They had varieties of hard sweets and mini pastries that I'd never seen before, but each delivered a uniquely wonderful taste and texture. I made a mental note to see if I could find a pastry cookbook before we left.

We told jokes and stories as we went along, unaware of the sun rising and beginning to fall all the while. Chris was a little uncertain at first, his barbed comments towards us and especially Freya stinging a bit, but soon his wry sense of humor had even Freya offering a tentative smile, once he'd moved past the somewhat expected dog jokes. Freya's tongue was surprisingly sharp, and thanks to her friendship with Reyna, she'd amassed quite the arsenal of cat jokes to counter Chris'.

I also noticed Chris and Freya covertly glancing at each other when they thought the other wasn't looking. Sometimes Reyna would nudge me, flicking her eyes subtly in the direction of one or the other. We'd grin at each other knowingly, a simple little secret for the two of us to share.

When Reyna pulled Freya into another dress shop, I volunteered to wait outside with Chris. Reyna winked at me cheekily as she went inside, mouthing 'good luck.' I took a deep breath in the silence that followed, trying to find the right words for the questions that had been lingering in the back of my mind all day.

"What is it?" Chris asked, his bluntness startling me. "I've known you for years, and I can tell when you're mulling something over, remember?"

"You know me too well," I sighed, a rueful smile tugging at my lips. "Chris, I wanted to apologize."

"For what?" he asked warily, his eyes narrowing.

"For dragging you into all this? For getting you thrown into some aristocrat's dungeons not once, but twice? And we're not even—" I broke off, biting my lip.

Chris sighed, running a hand through his sun-kissed locks. "It worked out all right in the end. My family is far better off than they were before, or would have been otherwise. The first time I'll lay at your feet. The second? That was entirely thanks to my own bull-headedness. And you're not interested in being anything more than friends, are you?"

I shook my head and dropped my eyes, afraid of the hurt I'd see on his face. My stomach twisted, and I fingered my necklace, searching for a feather that was no longer there.

"I think I've known for a while. I just...I wasn't ready to accept it."

I looked up in surprise. Chris was looking through the window of the shop, his warm brown eyes fixed on our two friends, who were preoccupied with examining a lilac-colored dress. After a moment, I realized it was Freya who held his attention, as a shy smile lit up her face.

"And now?" I watched as Chris watched Freya, his arms crossed over his chest.

"Now I think I can finally accept that you only have eyes for that broody duke," Chris admitted with a rueful smile. He turned back to me, a sheepish look on his face. "And I owe you an apology too."

"You do?"

"I essentially called you a monster. I didn't handle it well when I found out what you were. I know I hurt you. And I'm sorry for that," he said haltingly.

"Thank you, Chris," I murmured, before I furrowed my brow. "I take it you're still having trouble with the idea that werewolves aren't mindless monsters?"

He shrugged, looking a little uncomfortable. "I'm working on that."

"I struggled with it too, you know," I whispered, a lump rising in my throat.

Chris looked at me in surprise. "You did?"

"Of course," I said, leveling my gaze at him, hoping the sincerity in my tone would reach him. "How could I not? All the stories we heard growing up, the rumors, and the way those mercenaries acted at first? You think I wasn't scared?"

"So what changed?" he asked quietly.

"I decided to measure them, and eventually myself, by actions instead of words. A mindless monster wouldn't lay down his life for mine," I said quietly, turning my gaze back to Freya. "He was ready to take her place, you know."

Chris followed my gaze, his expression unreadable. "Rather ironic, then, what I turn into." He absently scratched at his arm, where I knew the bite mark still festered.

"It was rather...unexpected," I said delicately. "From what Fenn told me, a Vulclaria bite's effects will fade when the person changes their thoughts and behavior."

Chris grimaced. "Great. Somehow that makes me feel worse. Maybe Fenrys should just lock me back up in his dungeon."

"We could always see if the elves have some sort of potion or enchantment that could help," I rushed to say.

Chris sighed. "It might be worth looking into." After a few moments of silence, suddenly Chris abruptly said, "You owe me a thank you, not an apology, by the way."

I paused, running through the events of the last few days before I realized what he meant. I smiled at him whole-heartedly and said, "Thanks for rushing in to save me. Without you, we might not have been able to get Danny away from Alistair in time to save him."

"You're welcome, Serena," Chris replied, a shadow lifting from his face.

That night at dinner, Prince Arryn gave the rest of our small group a summary of how the day's meetings had gone. Apparently, most of the elven nobility had hardly contained their pleasure at the fact that Malakin's actions had all but shattered any chance he'd had at ascending the throne.

"But enough about politics. Please, eat to your hearts' content," Arryn requested as the main course was served by liveried elves.

I took a tentative bite of a succulent pork dish, then set down my golden fork, trying and failing to convince myself to use the luxurious silk napkin in my lap for its intended purpose. I still couldn't help but calculate how many coins such a high-quality item would cost, and how many days I could have lived off of it. And that was just the napkin! As far as I could tell, every utensil and goblet was made of pure gold, and the feast arrayed on the table could have fed a small town for a month. I noted that Arryn had made sure there were several meat dishes, which I doubted was normal fare for a royal elf.

"I also wish to extend an invitation to you to the audience I have requested of the King and Queen tomorrow afternoon," Arryn said formally.

"We would be honored to accept," Fenn replied, just as formally. He slipped my hand into his under the table, banishing the nervousness that had taken root in me with the prince's invitation. With Fenn by my side, I had no reason to be scared.

Arryn smiled, his air of seriousness dissipating like mist in the morning sun. "Now that the formalities are out of the way, we can relax a little."

Most of the group was able to talk and eat without much tension after that. Naturally, Danny's charisma and jokes had everyone laughing along, including the normally reserved crown prince.

But it didn't escape my notice that Reyna had a stiff set to her shoulders, and although she laughed along with everyone else, she was avoiding looking at Arryn. From his posture, I could tell that the prince had noticed. Again, I wondered exactly what had happened between the two of them.

As the plates were cleared away and dessert was served, conversations slowly quieted. I took my time enjoying the cold, sweet cream that lay in front of me, savoring the creamy texture and hint of vanilla.

Fenn gave me a look as I polished off the last bite. "I'll ask the chefs for the recipe."

I beamed at him, warmth filling my heart. "I would appreciate that."

"Will he be punished?" Reyna's quiet question cut through the room, but Arryn only sighed.

"Leave us." Arryn commanded the servers who lined the walls. Once they'd all shuffled out, he answered. "Punished? Yes. Executed?" Arryn steepled his fingers in front of him as a shadow passed across his sharp features. "I'm not sure."

"You said it yourself that he committed treason," Freya commented quietly. "Among other things."

Fenn stiffened beside me, the unspoken meaning of her words hitting home. Everyone looked uncomfortable, but ready for an answer.

"As the crown prince, growing up I was," here he glanced at Reyna before continuing, "largely untouchable by those who coveted power. To trifle with me was to invite war with Eldore. But the same cannot be said of my brother."

"What do you mean?" Danny asked.

"There were a number of incidents that have never been made public. When he was five, his nanny tried to drown him. Some scheme to weaken the royal family's power. When he was eleven, it was discovered that his personal maids were stealing from him. And then the lady he fell in love with fell out of love with him—if she had ever truly loved him to begin with," he explained, his voice heavy.

"While that is unfortunate, it still doesn't justify his actions," Fenn stated. "His was not the only rough childhood."

"Of course, you're correct," Arryn sighed. "The problem lies with Malakin. He became so paranoid and distrustful of the people around him that he ended up isolated. And while I can understand that, having gone through my own tribulations with others, I still can hard-ly comprehend how his solution to his trust issues was to surround himself with thralls to guarantee he would not be betrayed again."

"His pain does not justify what he has done to us," Freya said with feeling.

Arryn looked her in the eye as he said, "No, it does not."

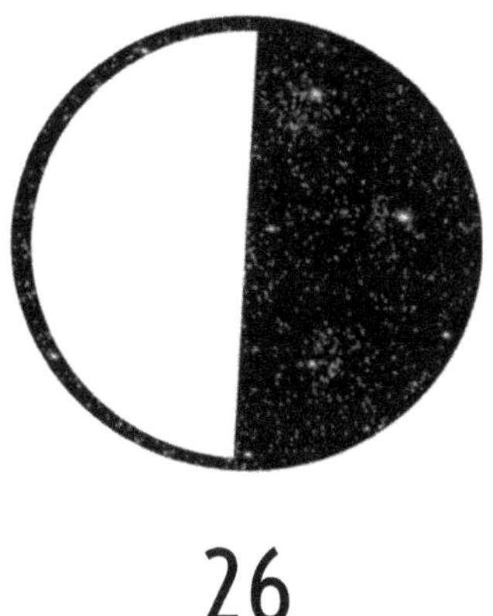

26

I tried not to fidget with my borrowed dress as we followed Arryn down the long corridor. In keeping with the style of the elves, the hem of the light-weight dress brushed the floor. A soft, beaded belt wrapped around my waist, which provided an elegant and flattering silhouette. Long sleeves fluttered as I moved, making the golden embroidery glimmer with every window we passed.

The interior of the elven palace was a fascinating combination of the natural wood of the tree and the additions of the elves. As children, Chris and I had made a treehouse not far from his home in a sturdy oak tree. It was a small, one-room hideaway nestled between two of the largest branches, cobbled together with bark walls over supporting sticks we'd fastened together. The palace reminded me of our old treehouse, but on a far grander scale.

A special kind of moss glowed in the lamps that lined the walls, casting a cool blue tint over everything within. I peeked inside some of the rooms we passed, amazed at the furniture that seemed to grow out of the walls and floors. Each piece was smooth and elegant, but

I wondered if the elves were able to rearrange the room at all, given the way the furniture was shaped. Perhaps this was a glimpse into why the elves seemed so steeped in the old traditions, even those customs which no longer served them.

The simple but elegant shoes I wore hardly made a sound on the thick moss carpet. Beside me, Fenn was dressed in similar formal attire, the dark blue fabric of his tunic accentuating the color of his eyes. And despite Reyna's protests about wearing traditional elven clothes, she looked breathtaking in her violet gown. Freya walked a step behind, her long dark hair brushing against the soft, navy fabric of her dress.

Chris and the werewolves had stayed behind, opting for some light sparring with the elven guards over what promised to be an extended audience with the rulers of Eldore. I almost wished I could join them.

After some time, we came to a stop in front of two massive doors that were covered in symbols and elven runes, with the crest of the royal family emblazoned in the center. Two guards stood in front of the doors, spears with dark metal tips held at their sides.

When Arryn came to a stop in front of them, the guards bowed in unison before opening the two great doors.

"Thank you," the prince said quietly, before gesturing for us to follow him.

The five of us strode into the vast throne room, and I stared in awe at the colorful stained glass windows that lined either side of the great hall, casting a rainbow of warm colors onto the mosaic tiles of the floor and the gathering of court elves that were arrayed like jewels in a crown. Two grand thrones stood at the opposite side of the room, and full racks of a deer's antlers adorned the top of each gilded throne.

As we approached the raised dais on which the thrones sat, I got my first good look at the king and queen of Eldore. The queen was a radiant creature, her long, wavy light blonde hair falling past her waist, an elegant diadem circling her high forehead. Delicate features framed kind green eyes, and her pointed ears were partially hidden by her flaxen hair. Her deep emerald dress matched the king's robes, and I noticed her fine-boned hand rested lightly on top of her husband's, faint worry lines marking her brow.

My keen sense of smell picked up on the musty scent of sickness that wafted from the frail-looking king. His blue eyes hovered over dark circles and sunken cheeks, his skin a few shades paler than it should have been. I felt a slight twinge of sympathy for these two over-taxed parents, but suppressed it when the memory of Malakin's dungeons surfaced in my mind's eye.

"Your Highnesses," Prince Arryn greeted them with a bow. The rest of us followed suit.

"Prince Arryn," the king rasped, "What is this I hear about you imprisoning your brother? And who are these *humans*?"

He said the word humans like it left a bitter taste in his mouth. I suppressed a smirk at the thought that there wasn't actually a single human in the room. But it was always nice to hear someone's true thoughts, to know how best to proceed.

"Father," Arryn rebuked sharply, "this is Duke Verdania of Cyrulia, his younger sister Freya, and their companions, Serena LaRoux and Reyna Ma'Katzya."

As we were each introduced, we gave a curt bow or curtsy. When he introduced her, Reyna stiffened, but didn't glance at Arryn.

"Verdania, you say?" the king said pensively. "I do recall meeting you some years ago, when you came to discuss trade. How have you been?"

"I believe you are thinking of my father, the previous duke, Your Highness," Fenn said smoothly. "He spoke quite highly of you and Eldore."

"Is that so? I am glad to hear that. But what brings his son here so suddenly?" the king asked.

"That brings us to the reason for today's audience," Arryn jumped in smoothly. "Duke Verdania aided in bringing Malakin's crimes to light."

"Crimes? What crimes?" the king blustered, coughing into his fist. Whispers broke out amongst the gathered elves.

"Malakin has certainly been rather...distant, as of late, but surely he's done no wrong," the queen spoke for the first time, her voice carrying an almost lyrical quality to it.

Arryn sighed through his nose, glancing down as if to gather his thoughts. After a moment, he looked up, and with a heavy heart began to inform his parents of his younger brother's misdeeds. "Malakin has been amassing an army of thralls, from both the legal and black market. Among them was Duke Verdania's own sister, a member of Cyrulia's nobility. Owning thralls is no crime in Eldore; but assembling an army of them in order to usurp the throne is high treason."

A deadly silence descended over the room as the crown prince's words sank in. All eyes turned to the king and queen, and I watched as the color drained from their faces.

"My Malakin would never—" the queen started, but was cut off by her husband.

"What proof do you have of these allegations?" the king asked heavily, resignation in his even tone.

"I intend to present all of the evidence at his formal trial, including hundreds of thrall collars, along with their sale contracts containing Malakin's signature and seal," Arryn elaborated. "Along with the testimonies of my personal high guard."

"We have received reports of an unusually high number of missing persons as of late," the king said slowly. "I would like to compare the two lists of names."

"Of course. Some of those individuals may still be held in bondage, in the illegal thrall fighting pits operating here in Varennia, as well as across the land," Arryn added, his sharp eyes noting which of the court elves in attendance shifted uncomfortably at the mention of the ring.

"It would seem you have quite the story to tell, Crown Prince," the king said heavily, his free hand now gently stroking his wife's trembling hand.

"Indeed," Arryn said gravely, and proceeded to relay the details of everything that had happened up to that point. To my surprise, Arryn pulled no punches, readily admitting to his own naivete when it came to his brother. He did, however, skirt around Reyna's part in the story, simply mentioning that she had assisted in Malakin's capture.

An uncomfortable silence descended like a heavy fog as those in attendance slowly digested the vivid tale the prince had told. All of us paid careful attention, noting which lords and ladies looked unsurprised or uncomfortable at such shocking revelations. I had a feeling we'd be helping Arryn ferret out some rats from the court in the near future.

Fenn stepped forward, breaking the silence. "Your Highnesses, I would like to request permission to bring those operating these illegal fighting rings to justice."

The king considered Fenn closely, recognizing the fury in Fenn's eyes and the steel in his spine. After glancing at the queen, he nodded. "You may conduct yourself freely with Prince Arryn's authority. However, I would ask that you take care of this matter discreetly."

Fenn paused, then bowed to hide the twitch of his lips. When he spoke, it was with deadly certainty. "Thank you, Your Highness. I have no intention of revealing my title, at least not until I have the sinners on their knees."

The king's eyes widened a fraction, before they narrowed in an appraising manner. A look of respect crossed his face, a look mirrored on Prince Arryn's features. The ruler's request puzzled me for a moment before I realized what he meant. Although suppressing news of such an egregious crime would prevent widespread outrage among his subjects, I suspected his main purpose was to avoid conflict with Cyrulia.

"Your assistance in this matter is greatly appreciated," the king replied warmly. "Prince Arryn will see to it that you have everything you should require in order to carry out this mission."

"That would be greatly appreciated, Your Highness," Fenn replied. "And do I have your assurance that the...thralls I will free, and have already liberated, will remain so, and will not be sold to new masters?" An edge of steel lined his voice, and a whisper of Fenn's determination touched my mind.

The king glanced at his queen once more, and I could practically see the thoughts churning through his mind. Despite such an action not stemming from a change in the law, it would certainly set a precedent. The kind of precedent that could one day lead to the eradication of legal thralldom in Eldore.

But after what had been done to an aristocrat of a powerful neighboring nation, he could not afford to simply do nothing.

And I had a feeling that when a golden crown rested firmly upon Arryn's golden head, thralls would become a thing of the past.

"You have my word. I will have documents drawn up for each of the freed thralls," the king finally said.

Gasps went through the spectating elves, sounding like the whispering of leaves in the wind. However, I did notice that a handful of those in attendance looked pleased. I had a feeling that Arryn was watching just as closely, picking out who among them might make the staunchest allies going forward.

"The queen and I would also like to extend our deepest apologies to you, Duke Verdania, and to Lady Verdania as well. A reward is in order, for bringing this grave matter to our attention," the king added.

Instead of causing a war between Cyrulia and Eldore. The unspoken words hung in my mind, as I'm sure they did in Fenn's. I also found it rather gratifying that the king was suddenly being so respectful of the "humans."

I glanced at Freya, wondering if she felt the apology was sincere. But her face was a carefully constructed mask. Only the barest hint of emotion flickered in the depths of her sapphire eyes.

"Thank you for your assurances, and for your most gracious apology and offer. I would be honored to arrange the details at a later date," Fenn said smoothly.

"Now that that has been settled, prepare for a grand feast in honor of our guests and the great service they have rendered us!" the king announced, lifting one thin hand into the air.

After a moment, applause filled the audience chamber, and the court elves bowed and curtsied to their monarchs before slowly filing out. After doing the same, Arryn turned towards us and ushered us out of the room, back the way we had come.

"I'm pleased that worked out. Especially keeping the thralls free going forward," the prince murmured quietly, careful not to be overhead. Fortunately, most of the elves had left before we did, and the few stragglers seemed more interested in preparing for the feast than eavesdropping.

He glanced at Reyna as he said that last part. She held his gaze before looking away, her normally open expression hidden behind a mask. The prince's shoulders drooped a bit before he straightened his spine.

"We are too," I replied, glad that Fenn finally seemed a little less tense. "You both did a good job in there."

The two males flashed me quick smiles, relief plain in both of their eyes. I stepped closer to Fenn so that our shoulders were brushing as we walked.

"Well, I will leave you to it. I know the ladies would like some time to prepare before the feast and dance this evening," Arryn said rather cheekily. He gave us a nod before he left, striding confidently down the corridor.

That night passed in a blur of warm laughter and colorful fairy lights, an unending stream of delicious elven food passing beneath our noses. Fenn and I twirled around the dance floor, the sights and sounds melting together into a symphony of joy. Even timid Tim joined in, expertly leading some fine elven ladies in a lively dance. I hid a smile when I spotted Reyna and Arryn dancing together, Freya and Chris a step behind them.

Warmth filled me every time Fenn looked at me with that tender expression in his eyes. I saw my future there, a lifetime of morning kisses and moonlit runs. The stirring music uplifted my soul, lending wings to my steps as my mate held me close. I followed where he led, trusting him to guide my feet the way he'd led my heart.

27

The next week passed quickly. As a group, we met with Prince Arryn every day, planning out the raid on Eris' underground fighting ring. Each meeting took hours, but there was never a dull moment among them.

Even Dorent pitched in, albeit a tad reluctantly at first. Standing within Eldore's palace made him more than a little jumpy. I took every chance I got to sneak up behind him and place a hand on his shoulder, and every time, he would jump and disappear in a shadowy mist, before reappearing to scold me once he realized I was simply teasing him.

But the fat purse of coin that Arryn had dangled in front of his hooked nose like a carrot had done wonders in terms of motivation. I'd never seen the man so enthusiastic.

In between meetings, we would often explore the palace and the city in small groups. These outings served as both information gathering sessions and a chance to relax and get to know one another better, outside of life-threatening situations.

What I was most excited about, however, was my upcoming outing with Fenn. For one of the first times since I had met him, we actually had a chance to spend some time together outside of problem-solving, training, or some werewolf-related business.

I was finally going on a normal *date!*

I spent a little longer than I had anticipated getting ready, choosing to wear a casual sundress with comfortable but stylish shoes. I made sure my golden crescent moon pendant was visible, though I caught my fingers absently searching for my Vulclaria feather. I smiled sadly, missing the soft feather, but using up my one request had certainly been worth it.

I brushed out my long crimson hair, wishing for a moment that Lily and Sophia were there to help me style it. I was looking forward to seeing them again, and giving them the small presents I'd picked out over the last few days.

After glancing at the clock and doing a final check in the room's mirror, I headed out, closing the door softly behind me. Fenn was waiting for me just where he said he'd be, right outside the palace. He looked incredibly handsome, his dark blue tunic bringing out the color of his eyes.

I stood looking at him for a moment, marveling at how far we'd come. I smiled to myself, remembering how dark and brooding he'd seemed when I first met him. I supposed he was still rather broody, but not nearly as dark.

As if he felt my eyes on him, he looked up, those icy blue eyes finding mine. A smile lit up his face, his expression mirrored by my own.

I hurried over to him, my steps as light as air.

"You look exceedingly beautiful today," Fenn greeted me as he took my hand in his, lifting it to his lips and brushing a kiss on the back of my hand.

I blushed, telling him, "You don't look too bad yourself." I laced my fingers through his, running my fingers lightly across the thin scars that wrapped around his hand from a lifetime of training and fighting.

"Shall we?" he asked.

"Lead the way," I answered.

We walked hand-in-hand through Varennia, wandering this way and that. Had we been human, we would have become lost in an instant, but with our keen senses of smell, I knew we could always find our way back. We revisited the sprawling market where we'd found the mask-seller, purely for the fun of it this time.

Fenn bought some sweets for me to try, and laughed when I started trying to guess the ingredients. Since we'd both already purchased a number of gifts for all of our friends, we didn't buy much else besides a couple of artistic trinkets. Though Fenn did end up purchasing a nice silk neck tie for his butler.

At the mention of that disagreeable man, a thought tickled the back of my mind, but I couldn't quite grasp it. A feeling of unease stirred in my stomach, but I pushed it down, determined to enjoy my date with Fenn.

I pointed us in the direction of a sweet aroma, and we tried a new dessert that was a thin layer of fluffy cake, topped with fresh strawberries and a light, fluffy cream. The wonderful taste flooded my mouth, and I was suddenly grateful that for some reason, werewolves could eat much more than humans without any negative consequences.

Fenn flicked my nose, showing me the bit of cream that now rested on his fingertip. My ears grew warm as he licked the cream from his finger, a mischievous gleam in his eye.

Inspiration struck, and I let the happiness inside me bubble to the surface, pushing through the wall in my mind behind which I faintly sensed Fenn's emotions. He stilled, looking at me in surprise, before a big grin split his face.

"You took me by surprise!" he laughed. "Should I return the favor?"

A moment later, the wall between us lowered a fraction, allowing a sense of peace and contentment to flow across my mind like a snow-fed stream, clear and bright.

"I suppose I could get used to this," I said softly.

Fenn leaned forward, closing the distance between us. "You'd better," he murmured, his breath tickling my ear.

I tilted my face up, the rest of my treat forgotten, and brushed my lips over his. Fenn's hand gently slid up the back of my neck to the back of my head, his touch leaving a trail of warmth in its wake. He kissed me again, more insistently this time, and I slid my arms around his neck, my fingers tangling in his black hair. His lips tasted like sweet strawberries, the kind I could enjoy forever.

We became lost in each other, heedless of the stares of those around us. The wall lowered further, and love and joy swirled in the invisible space between us.

The wind rushed through my thick fur as my paws flew over the uneven ground, the gray tones of a wolf's vision revealing the path before me. Fenn's dark fur brushed against mine as he kept pace beside me, and I reveled in the feeling.

A howl rose in the distance, and I howled back, alerting Jax of our position. Tim and Danny chimed in, their low tones carrying through the air and forming a mental map of where each of us was located.

We'd formed a semi-circle around the entrance of the seemingly abandoned building, but the scents of blood and fear and metal coins seeped from the hole in the earth, alongside the faint roar of an excited crowd. Tonight was a death match, so we knew there was plenty of prey caught in our meticulously-laid trap.

Fenn howled, a low, angry note that signaled the start of our raid. Moments later, I heard the distinctive thuds of bodies hitting the floor from three buildings nearby.

Eris' lookouts were now out of commission.

It had been inevitable that word of our planned initiative would reach her ears. She'd hired some guards and stationed lookouts nearby to appease her uneasy guests. But she had no real reason to worry; after all, the elves had done nothing about the thralls' misfortunes for centuries, not to mention the high status of a number of her patrons.

So why should *she* be concerned?

The slight creaking of leather armor met my ears as elven royal guards moved into position on either side of us, filling in the gaps in our net. Archers scaled buildings to attain a better vantage point, their quivers filled with specialized arrows.

Once everyone was in position, Prince Arryn approached the open doorway of the building, his best fighters around him. In another moment, their silhouettes disappeared into the gloomy interior. Leather boots tapped against the metal rungs of the ladder as they descended, a strangled cry testifying that a patron had waited a little too long to make his exit. From the sounds of it, he was swiftly knocked out and shackled. The clank of the shackles shifting as his unconscious body was laid roughly on the floor of the tunnel set my teeth on edge, and a soft growl escaped my throat.

Fenn bumped my shoulder with his, sending a hint of calm and courage through our mental bond. I sighed through my nose before rubbing my face against his. I was still having a little trouble when it came to reining in my instincts, especially when in wolf form. But at least it was slowly becoming easier.

A few minutes of silence ensued as Arryn and his team made their way to the main room with the fighting pit. He'd assured us that we'd done more than enough fighting already, and that it was his turn to clean up this rot that had been allowed to fester in Eldore for so long. I'd almost argued with him before thinking better of it. Besides, they already knew what we looked like, and ladders weren't exactly designed for a wolf to climb, anyways.

Suddenly a cacophony of screams and the clash of steel reached our ears as the underground battle began. It didn't take long before the pounding of panicked feet reached the ladder, and the first group of masked patrons emerged into the dark of the night.

The *twang* of the archers' bows thrummed through the air as patrons began dropping to the ground. I marveled at the pinpoint accuracy of the elves, suddenly grateful that Malakin had relied on close-combat for his security.

Tonight the elves were using thin, dart-like arrows, the tips of which were coated in a strong sleeping potion. Unlike a regular arrow, these were designed to pierce only an inch or two into the target, just enough to deliver the swift-acting potion.

Those on the receiving end would be unconscious for at least eight hours, providing more than enough time to restrain them and transport them to the palace. Since, naturally, the elves had a vast dungeon within the maze of roots beneath the great tree.

I shook my head. The nobility and their dungeons. Though I supposed we would have been in a tight spot without them this time around.

A handful of Eris' guards broke from beneath the cover of the building, terrified patrons held in front of them. They were using them as living shields. One went down, followed by another. But the rest made it past the archers' line of sight. And right into our paws.

Fenn and I surged forward, fangs bared and claws ready. I leaped at one of the guards, knocking him to the ground and loosening his grip on the elf he was using as his shield.

The patron took his chance to crawl away, and without a moment of hesitation, I scored my claws along the guard's exposed arm. The elf yelled in pain, reaching for his weapon. But I pinned his arm down, growling deep in my throat. After a few more moments, his eyes rolled back in his head, his body going limp.

I bounded after the escaping patron, lightly scratching his leg. He, too, slumped to the ground after a few moments. I huffed in satisfaction, glancing down at the gel-like substance coating my claws. Using the sleeping potion this way was a little riskier than using an arrow, and took longer to take effect, but was incredibly helpful nonetheless.

The fact that I had taken my first life the other day still didn't sit right with me, so I'd jumped at the chance to put these people to sleep instead of having to make that sort of choice. I knew what I'd had to do had been right, and worth it to save my friends. I knew that in my head, but I still saw the crazed eyes of that shadow assassin in my nightmares.

Fenn pulled me from my grim thoughts when he trotted over to me and gave me a wolfish grin. He'd swiftly taken care of his own targets, and from what I could hear, it sounded like Jax and the others had done the same.

We only had to knock out a few more guards that made it past the elven archers. Though at one point, a drunken elf had stumbled down our street, took one look at our massive wolf forms, and ran away screaming about some monsters. Fenn had looked at me, concern in his blue eyes, but I'd reassured him with a quick nuzzle.

His words might have hurt me before, but I'd come to the realization that I didn't need to let the opinions of someone else bother me. I'd never thought of Fenn as a monster, not when I knew of his kind heart. So I had no reason to think of myself as one, either.

Once it seemed like no one else would be coming, Fenn howled, alerting the others, and he and I loped through the streets to where the rest of our number were stationed.

It had come as no surprise that Eris had a secret exit from her underground operation, one that let out in the backroom of a nearby shop. But to our delight, Reyna knew exactly where to find it.

The door to the shop hung ajar, one of the hinges detached courtesy of the force the elves had used to break it open. Inside, a welcome sight met our eyes. Reyna, Freya, and Prince Arryn stood over Eris and her personal guards, who had been disarmed and tied up.

"How dare you break into my shop in the middle of the night and tie me up?" Eris was shrieking at the prince, while he perused what looked like the shop's ledger.

"I must say, your accounting is incredibly creative. If I hadn't visited this shop myself, I might have been impressed by the high quality and sheer quantity of products you were selling," Arryn stated calmly, snapping the leather-bound book shut. He glanced at Reyna. "Though I suppose the high-quality part is accurate."

Eris glared at Reyna and Freya, hatred pouring off of her thin frame. "Prince Malakin won't stand for—"

"My brother has been detained," Arryn cut her off abruptly, her face paling when she realized who she was yelling at, as we padded silently into the room. "Ah, there you two are."

All eyes turned towards us as Eris went pale at the realization that she was speaking to the crown prince, and after a moment, understanding dawned in Eris' eyes. "You! You were the werewolves that came to see me. This is all because of you!" she snarled, struggling against the ties that bound her.

Fenn stepped forward and growled, his threatening tone halting Eris' attempt to come closer. Changing tactics, she spat on the ground instead.

As if an insult from a slaver could be anything but a compliment to us.

Freya and Reyna bristled, but the cold look on Arryn's face felt both comforting and a little unsettling at the same time. "Control yourself, woman! There is only one animal in this room, and it's not those two."

Reyna glanced at him then, a spark of surprise and gratitude igniting in her violet eyes. A small smile graced her mouth, and I was happy to see that Arryn noticed the expression before it faded.

"The controller," Reyna reminded him.

"Search her," Arryn ordered the guards that lined the room and hovered near the prisoners.

Two guards hauled Eris to her feet, holding her still while a third swiftly searched her for the master control device. For her own safety, whenever she'd purchased a new thrall, she'd touch their control device to her main one, transferring its control. That was why when we purchased Reyna, she'd had to transfer that authority back to a single controller.

The guard frowned, then shook his head as he turned to his prince. The device wasn't on her person.

"Where. Is. Your. Controller," Arryn said slowly, enunciating each word.

Eris smirked. "Wouldn't you like to know?"

I snarled, my instincts demanding I extinguish this threat. Fenn growled lightly, and I reined in my anger.

"Did you hide it in this shop?" Arryn asked, his calm tone belying the emotion that simmered in his eyes. Fenn pricked his ears forward, his gaze riveted on Eris.

She glanced at him, her red lips parting in a smile. "Nice try. You think I don't know that werehumans can sniff out a lie?"

Now it was Fenn growling in frustration. Reyna in particular looked ready to shift and tear her to pieces. But Eris held the leverage here.

And she knew it.

28

A couple days later, we were still searching for the master control device. The guards had combed through every inch of the tunnels and the surrounding area above ground, all to no avail. All of us had even covered the same area with our noses, using the scent of Reyna's old control device as a guide.

Nothing.

We hadn't even been able to move the collared thralls to the palace, because taking them beyond the invisible boundary Eris had set would send pain shooting through the thrall until they made it back within the boundary. The most we'd been able to do was provide thick blankets and regular, warm meals to the thralls.

The news that Eris had been raided and her operation shut down spread quickly, the rumors becoming grander and more fantastic as the hours passed. At least we'd been able to capture a handful of masked patrons, who hadn't yet heard the news and had come to the abandoned building for an evening of sport and betting.

Eris had been confined in one of the more secure cells in the dungeon, far separated from any of her guards. The elves had as of yet been unable to get her to reveal the location of her control device, much to the frustration of Freya, Reyna, and Arryn.

Freya had been especially distraught, and even talking at length with Fenn hadn't seemed to help. She had seemed to be in slightly better spirits after she'd returned to the palace with Chris one afternoon, though. I began to notice that the look in his eyes that had once been reserved for me I sometimes caught when he looked at Freya.

It made me happy to consider that Chris might be moving on, and looking to a future with Freya instead of the past with me. Though if I was being honest with myself, I'm not sure how happy I was that he had grown so attached to Fenn's sister, of all people. I found it odd that he was so drawn to her, considering his aversion to werewolves. Perhaps Freya would be able to help him past his prejudice in a way I couldn't.

That evening after dinner, another meeting was called. The guards Arryn had assigned to search for the controller gave their report—another day of fruitless searching. Everyone's faces fell at the announcement, another sliver of hope shattered. It felt like the more time that passed, the less likely we were to find the device.

After a few minutes of planning the next day's search, the meeting ended, with Freya leaving first and Chris slipping out soon after.

Fenn and I decided to go for a walk around the extensive gardens the elves had cultivated. Fairy lights sparkled in the trees, and the soothing sound of fountains permeated the air, alongside the sweet and delicate fragrance of many varieties of flowers, including plenty I'd never seen before, alongside a few that I was familiar with.

"Moonflowers," I murmured, pointing them out to Fenn.

"They grow well in forests like the ones that cover much of Eldore," Fenn commented, gazing at the glowing petals.

"What about those?" I asked, gesturing towards clusters of smaller flowers surrounding them. Where the moonflowers glowed, these ones glimmered.

"Starflowers," Fenn answered. "They're similar to moonflowers, but they mostly grow in open grasslands."

I gazed at them appreciatively. They came from different worlds, but complemented each other so well, as if they'd always been destined to shine, side-by-side. I slipped my hand into Fenn's, and we continued along the stone path.

We walked in companionable silence, soft moonlight guiding our steps. I could feel the tug of the nearly-full moon, but resisted the urge to shift into wolf form. Soon it would be full, and its call would become a demand. But that night didn't frighten me the way it once did.

I looked at Fenn, the moonlight accentuating the sharp planes of his face, turning them to silver. I etched the image into my mind and onto my heart, savoring the peace of this moment. His eyes cut to mine, his blue eyes reflecting the moon back at me like luminous pools. He smiled, the corners of his eyes crinkling. I leaned my head on his shoulder, inhaling his fresh pine scent.

The soft murmurings of voices met my ears, faint over the sound of the nearest fountain. I raised my eyebrows at Fenn, and he nodded, an answering spark of mischief in his eyes.

We crept towards the voices, our footfalls imperceptible on the smooth stone beneath our feet. Ahead of us was a large fountain that had elegant benches facing it in a circle, an abundance of floral trees and bushes surrounding each one.

I was surprised when I recognized Chris and Freya occupying one of the benches, only a few inches of space between them. Fortunately, we were downwind, and they were so focused on their conversation that we were able to get close enough to hear them without being detected.

Fenn stiffened when he realized who the pair were, as did I. Of course, I'd noticed the two of them spending more time together lately, but based on Chris' constant rude comments and jokes about werewolves, I had not expected Freya to be eager to spend any more time around him than was necessary, regardless of his unexpected interest. And after the way Fenn and Chris had nearly come to blows on several occasions, I couldn't imagine Fenn was particularly excited about this new development either. Chris was probably the last person Fenn wanted around his sister.

"What if we can never free them?" Freya asked, her voice tinged with fear and worry.

"The prince has his best people on it," Chris replied. "Not to mention the dog— I mean, werewolves. I'm sure it's just a matter of time until the controller is found, one way or another."

"You're probably right," she sighed. "I just can't help but picture myself in their shoes." She'd glared at him when he started to refer to our friends as dogs, but I was surprised Chris had actually changed what he was going to say because of it.

"Of course. I mean, you were in their place just a few days ago, after all. It's only natural that someone like *you* can empathize with them. And in the end, they got the collars off of Malakin's thralls, didn't they?" Chris asked.

I scowled at Chris' rudeness, but Freya hardly seemed to care. I supposed she'd grown used to being insulted since she was first captured, but that thought only made Chris' rudeness seem worse. Beside me, Fenn was practically grinding his teeth at this point.

"Only because Serena used her Vulclaria wish," Freya said sadly, before suddenly brightening. "Oh, Chris, that's it! Maybe I or someone else could travel back to Verdania in order to get a Vulclaria feather! It could take a while, but surely a Vulclaria could find the controller where we couldn't!"

I saw Chris stiffen at the mention of the little foxes, his hand absently scratching at his arm.

Freya didn't seem to notice. She leaned over and tentatively placed her hand over his for a moment, before jumping up. "I have to go tell my brother—he'll love this idea! Thanks for listening, Chris!"

Freya raced off through the gardens, without even a glance in our direction. Fenn made as if to follow her, but I tugged him back. He looked at me with a scowl, but didn't argue. I doubted Freya would be happy that we'd eavesdropped, even if it was by accident.

Chris just sat on the bench, staring at the fountain as if lost in thought. Fenn and I were about to quietly leave when Chris pulled something out of his pocket. I paused, curious.

I squinted, trying to make it out, and nearly gasped in surprise when I put the pieces together. Chris was running his fingers over the Vulclaria feather he'd gotten. I had yet to puzzle out how he'd befriended one Vulclaria but still gotten bitten by one at the same time.

But based on what we'd just heard, it looked like Chris was considering using up the Vulclaria feather that had cost him so dearly, for Freya, in spite of his disdain for werewolves. I could hardly believe it.

I glanced at Fenn, seeing my surprise reflected in his startled expression as he came to the same conclusion. I practically wanted to kick myself for not thinking of that solution myself! Though whether it was Chris or someone else who made the wish, it seemed we had a surefire way to free Eris' slaves.

Just as I was thinking Chris might contemplate this a while longer, he mumbled something that even my sharp hearing couldn't quite make out. A bubble of light appeared in front of him, growing brighter and brighter until with a flash, a young Vulclaria appeared. It pounced on Chris, giving him an affectionate lick before leaping back into the air and flying in the direction of Eris' underground operation.

A huge grin spread across my face, and Fenn and I quietly retreated from the gardens, racing straight for Prince Arryn's personal study.

No one got a wink of sleep that night. We'd been too joyously busy, thanks to Chris. Right after we left the gardens, Fenn and I had managed to rouse Arryn from where he'd fallen asleep at the desk in his study, just in time for Freya and then Chris to barge in with their happy news.

Freya burst into the room, hope shining brightly in her sapphire eyes. She bobbed a quick curtsy to Arryn before turning to Fenn. "Why don't we use a Vulclaria feather to find this controller too?"

Fenn smiled, playing along. "I think that's a great idea, Freya. Do you know anyone who currently has a feather, or should we make a trip back home?"

"I know it might take some time, but—" she started.

The door to the study, which Freya had left ajar, creaked open, the guards there stepping aside to permit Chris entry. His steps seemed heavy, but his eyes looked clearer than I'd seen them in some time.

"That won't be necessary. I've already used mine," Chris said as he locked eyes with Freya. He held out his hand, uncurling his fingers to reveal Eris' controller lying on his calloused palm.

Freya's sapphire eyes widened in shock. A heartbeat later, she threw her arms around Chris in a hug. I tightened my grip on Fenn's hand, but fortunately he had the common sense not to interfere, despite the whisper of irritation and anger I could feel through our bond.

After a moment, Arryn cleared his throat. "That certainly makes things easier. Now we'll be able to free the thralls before any of the court can make a move to prevent it. You have my thanks."

Freya finally released Chris from her arms, allowing a dazed but undeniably content Chris to respond to the prince. "You're welcome, uh, Your Highness." Clearly, Chris thought his wish had been well spent.

Freya swatted his arm at his awkward response, but smiled all the same. I think even Fenn had to admit the look on her face was price-less, a very positive change from the gloom that had lingered on her expression since she'd been rescued.

"As thanks, I would like to bestow upon you a reward for your aid. In addition to a purse of coin, I would also like to offer my personal assistance in your search for a cure, or antidote," Arryn stated formally, glancing at Chris' arm.

Chris stiffened a bit, looking at Fenn and I with an accusation in his gaze. Freya cocked her head, confused, but I just smiled.

"I would be honored, Your Highness," Chris said more formally this time.

"Good. Now that's settled, I do believe we have quite a few thralls to free," Arryn announced with a tired smile.

Then he called for the guards out front, instructing them to assemble the royal guards immediately, and to ensure that enough rooms had been prepared. The pair quickly left the room to see to their duties, their eyes alert despite the late hour.

After that, the night passed in a blur of activity. A team of maids and guards began preparing to receive the thralls, while a second team went with the prince to deactivate their collars.

Naturally, we went with Arryn's group, eager to finish what we'd started. But I think Reyna and Freya were the biggest help of all. Once we reached the tunnels where all the thralls were kept, Reyna and Freya went and talked with each one, calling them by name and explaining what was going to happen.

After that, even the thralls that had been the most distrustful of the elven royal guards began to follow their instructions. A few of the younger ones wept as their collars fell to the ground. Others brought their hands to their necks, shock and disbelief giving way to a spark of hope when their fingers met only skin instead of cold metal.

To prevent any fighting or other issues between the thralls while the collars were still on, Arryn had decided to leave them in their individual cages. But now he and his guards went around, unlocking the doors one by one. And Reyna and Freya were there to welcome every one of them to take their first steps as free individuals.

Arryn watched Reyna when he thought no one was looking, an expression of soft wonder on his face. But his princely mask would fall back in place anytime she glanced his way. For the first time, I wondered if Reyna would be coming back to Verdania with us, or if she would choose to stay here, in Varennia.

With him.

I didn't have much time to dwell on that thought, though. Once each thrall was freed, Fenn and I would go up to him or her, laying out what would happen next and offering sanctuary and employment within the Dukedom of Verdania. The offer was the same for elf, human, dwarf, and werehuman alike.

Many took us up on the offer, though some declined, saying they had families they wanted to return to. For those cases, they were reassured that the prince would personally see to it that they received what assistance they would need in order to find their families. A handful asked for time to think about it, so we simply told them to come to us if they had any questions we could answer.

We made quite the parade that night, the finely-dressed elven royal guards escorting dozens of newly freed thralls in rags, their bare feet padding softly along the wooden boardwalks. Most of the subjects of Varennia were fast asleep, though I did spot a few pairs of curious eyes and fluttering curtains from the windows that faced our procession.

Freya finished the conversation she was having with one of the dwarves and came over to walk beside Fenn. The light that filled her eyes reflected the stars above, though traces of shadow still lurked in their sapphire depths.

"Thank you, Fenn. And…and you too, Serena," she said, the sincerity in her voice touching my heart. "Not just for saving me, but for saving them, too."

Fenn put a hand on her shoulder, pride in his eyes. "Thank you for holding on until we could get here."

"If you and Father hadn't taught me so well, I might not have," she said, a trace of sorrow in her tone. She looked around at all those around us with light scars around their necks, scars that matched her own. "There are more like us, throughout Cyrulia and Eldore, aren't there?"

Fenn sighed, turning his gaze on them too. I had a feeling he was seeing his sister in each bowed head.

"Most likely," I murmured, as Fenn nodded silently.

"Sometimes, when I watched the light fade from my opponent's eyes in the pit, I wondered if my life was worth them losing theirs," Freya murmured, her eyes distant as memories played in her mind's eye. Fenn tensed, and my own heart ached at the words.

Her gaze landed on Chris before it returned to us. "But now, I think I've found the answer. I want to help the people who have been enslaved. And stop people like Eris, before they turn more little girls into killers. Like me."

She took a great, shuddering breath as I pulled her into my arms. "It wasn't your fault, what that woman made you do. But you can live for those who died too. Live enough for all of them, and find meaning in saving those who don't have a brother to come for them."

Fenn put a hand on each of our shoulders. "We find meaning in voluntarily taking on responsibility, however heavy it may be, and making progress towards our goals. I'm happy you've found yours, Freya."

Freya nodded, and I knew that eventually the sorrow and guilt that filled her heart would be replaced with light and purpose.

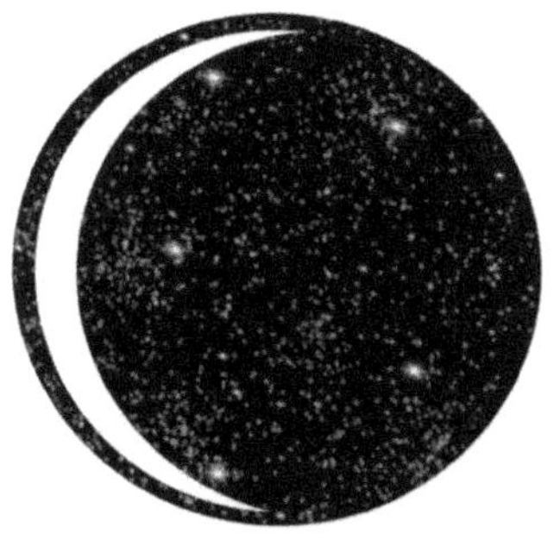

29

"I feel silly," Freya protested. She turned slowly in front of the floor-length mirror, the soft silks of her deep indigo dress fluttering with the motion. Matching jewels glittered at her throat and her wrists, partially covering her scars.

"But you look gorgeous, darling," Reyna reassured her from where she was putting the finishing touch-ups on her face paint. Her floor-length gown brushed the floor as she moved.

"I'm sure you're just not used to it yet," I chimed in, glancing at my own reflection. "I'm certainly not." My deep emerald gown shimmered in the candlelight, my hair like cascading fire against it. Gold stitching embellished the bodice, matching the gold and emerald jewelry that dripped from my wrists and neck.

"There was a time when I *was* used to it," Freya said sadly.

"Don't you worry, you're still a mighty warrior under all those frills," Reyna teased lightly, pushing aside the shadow that flashed in her eyes. As far as I knew, Reyna had never been to such a grand function before, but she seemed as relaxed and comfortable as she always was. Well, at least when Arryn wasn't around.

"Just think of this as your battle armor, but for high society," I said with a smile. "That's how I've come to look at it, anyways."

That got a smile out of both of them. "I like the way you think," Freya complimented me.

I gave her a dainty little curtsy, fluttering my eyelashes like I'd seen some of the court ladies do. Reyna joined in, and soon all three of us were laughing, palpable warmth filling the room.

A knock sounded at the door. I went to open it, revealing a very handsome Fenn standing on the other side. He looked regal in the formal embroidered suit of the Duke of Verdania, the golden stitching standing out against the black fabric. I noted with a small smile that he wore an emerald brooch that matched my own accessories.

"You look...exquisite," Fenn said warmly, his eyes drinking me in.

Color rose in my cheeks. "You look quite dashing yourself," I replied.

When we just stood there, staring at each other, Reyna noisily cleared her throat. I started, then smiled sheepishly.

"Your escorts have arrived," Fenn announced a little belatedly, with a grin on his face. "Are you ladies all ready?"

"Ready as we'll ever be," I replied, smiling warmly at Freya. Fenn followed the direction of my gaze, and proceeded to compliment his sister and Reyna.

"So, are they ready yet?" asked a familiar voice. I looked over Fenn's shoulder, noticing that Chris and Arryn stood in the hallway as well.

"Ready for battle," Freya replied with a touch of humor.

Fenn offered me his arm and I placed my hand on the dark fabric of his sleeve. We walked out of the room, pausing to wait while Chris clumsily offered his arm to Freya, who took it quite graciously, and

Arryn did the same for Reyna. She hesitated a moment before taking it, but instead of Arryn looking dismayed at her uncertainty, he looked triumphant in the fact that she had taken his arm, despite the scrutiny it was bound to bring her tonight.

Prince Arryn led the way with Reyna on his arm. We fell into line behind him, royal guards bringing up the rear. I could understand why Arryn had been going around town in disguise if his every move was shadowed by silent guards every moment he was within the palace.

We paused outside the great doors to the banquet hall, and the elf at the door announced our arrival to the room as we descended the stairs in pairs.

I'd never seen a more magnificent room. Interlocking branches and vines formed the walls and ceiling, with stained glass filling the gaps on the walls and clear glass in the sizable gaps in the roof. Moonlight bathed the floor in its silvery light, the stars above arrayed like an infinite number of fairy lights.

A long banquet table took up one entire side of the room, with the other half reserved for dancing. Musicians played a soft melody in a specially-designed alcove that amplified the sounds of the instruments. The finely-dressed elves began to whisper as we descended, looking like jewels scattered across the ground.

Unsurprisingly, many of the elves in attendance flocked to Arryn once he reached the floor. Most of the ladies hardly even attempted to conceal the curious glances or outright glares they were sending Reyna's way.

But fortunately after just a few minutes, the arrival of the king and queen was announced. They took their seats at the head of the table, and the other elves took the cue to find their own seats. Our group made straight for the head of the table, with Arryn and his partner seated on the monarchs' right hand side, and Fenn and I seated to their left. Chris and Freya sat beside us, and both were doing an admirable job of hiding their nerves.

Once everyone was seated, the king stood with some difficulty. "Welcome. This banquet is held in honor of our guests, and as thanks for the great service they have provided Eldore, by ridding our great nation of not one, but two malfeasants. After the feast, several important announcements shall be made," he announced, before raising his glass. "But first, let us toast, to Duke Verdania!"

"To Duke Verdania!" echoed the cry along the table, glasses raised. A few of the attendees looked less than thrilled to be toasting to a "human," especially a meddling one.

But I ignored them and raised my glass with the rest, enjoying the fruity liquid. I glanced at Fenn as I set my glass down, noticing that despite the smile on his face, his eyes were hard. I had a feeling that Fenn would have phrased the king's summary of what had happened over the last couple of weeks a tad differently.

Servers appeared at our sides, placing the first course in front of us. To no one's shock, it was a lush salad topped with pine nuts and fresh berries. I was immensely grateful for the pointers Freya had given me on elven etiquette, so I wouldn't embarrass myself or Fenn.

The second course was a light tomato basil soup, followed by a savory pie filled with roasted vegetables and mushrooms. Dessert was my favorite course by far, since each plate was filled with an assortment of pastries, including small cakes, tarts, and macaron cookies. I vaguely recalled Aly mentioning that the recipe for macarons had first come from Eldore, which would certainly account for the amazing flavors I tasted for the first time.

I made a mental note to ask Arryn for some dessert recipes before we left. Aly would be beside herself if I managed to bring some new ones back.

Throughout the meal, we all made small talk with the king and queen, though I could tell from the look in the queen's eyes that we would always be the people who had shattered her perception of her youngest son. Even if it was a parental lack of guidance that had led him down his destructive path. I just hoped she'd come to realize that what we'd done had prevented many deaths, including, potentially, her own.

Finally, the dishes were cleared away, and the king rose once more. I gave an inward sigh of relief that the dinner ordeal was over. And from the looks on Chris and Freya's faces, I wasn't the only one.

We all stood up and followed the elven monarchs towards the other side of the room, where a raised dais with four thrones was located against the wall. Arryn joined his parents, his regal but carefully expressionless features like a mask concealing his true thoughts and feelings.

Once the king and queen were seated, Arryn stepped forward. "His Highness the King of Eldore has granted me permission to make the following declarations, as the Crown Prince and future King of Eldore." He paused, his gaze sweeping over the assembly, daring anyone to object. When none did, he continued. "My younger brother, Prince Malakin, has been forthwith stripped of his birthright and imprisoned for high treason."

Shocked gasps and whispers came from the nobility. Many were obviously pleased at this turn of events, though most simply seemed dumbstruck. I did notice one older elf looked particularly pleased, and suddenly realized he may be the father of the elf maiden the second prince had courted. It seemed Malakin would find no sympathy among the nobility.

"Silence!" roared the king. The elves immediately quieted, and I couldn't help but admire the king's commanding presence, despite his weakened state due to his illness.

"A formal trial will be held once the full investigation has concluded. Now, onto the main purpose of tonight's celebration," Arryn continued. He gestured for Fenn and I to join him on the dais.

I gave his arm a gentle squeeze, and he smiled warmly at me before we made our way next to Prince Arryn. For a moment, the gazes of the aristocratic elves rooted me to the spot, making me feel like an impostor in a noble's dress. I quickly snuffed that thought out, focusing on what Prince Arryn was saying.

"To thank them for their tremendous assistance to the crown, Duke Verdania, Serena La Roux, and those in their party are hereby awarded the title, Friends of the Elves, and may pass freely through Eldore as they see fit. They are to be treated with the utmost respect. Should I hear otherwise, the offending party will be punished severely."

I plastered a smile on my face, trying not to look too stiff. After a moment of hesitation, applause filled the room, along with some cheers from the more vocal elves. I suspected that what they were really happy about was the fact that Malakin had lost his right to challenge Arryn for the throne.

Prince Arryn gently placed a golden medal around both of our necks. The crest of Eldore was stamped on the front, with the words "Friend of the Elves" on the back.

As he gave Fenn his medal, he whispered softly, "I'll give you the rest of the medals for everyone else afterwards."

Fenn nodded imperceptibly.

After a little more fanfare and grandstanding, we returned to stand beside our friends. I was honestly relieved to rejoin the crowd and escape the curious eyes of the elves. But I was also grateful for the aid of my glittering "battle armor."

"Good job," Freya breathed, giving me a shy smile.

"Thanks," I whispered back. "Are you ready?"

"Ready as I'll ever be." There was a hint of nervousness in the way she held her shoulders, but I could also see the excitement in her eyes.

"We have one more special announcement this evening," Prince Arryn declared as he gestured in the direction of our group. "Lady Verdania, if you would."

Freya straightened her shoulders before joining Arryn on the dais, her back as straight-edged as the finest sword. My sharp ears caught more than one admiring comment from some of the male elves in attendance, which had Chris glaring at them shamelessly.

"The House of Verdania and the Kingdom of Cyrulia will be entering into diplomatic relations with Eldore, with the intent to establish a mutually beneficial exchange of goods in the future. Although this is a departure from Eldore's long-standing refusal to engage with other countries, after much consideration, we have determined that it is time to lay aside old grievances, and prejudices. Lady Verdania has kindly agreed to serve as a diplomatic emissary between Eldore and Verdania," Arryn said with a flourish.

"It will be my greatest pleasure to learn more about the wonderful residents of Eldore, and to explore the rich culture of her people. I still recall the sense of awe I felt the first time my father brought my brothers and I to visit your lush forests and stunning cities, and I hope to extend that awe to the people of my own territory," Freya stated eloquently.

"With all due respect, will we truly be expected to cater to a meat-eating *werewolf?*" an older elven female asked pointedly. Murmuring broke out among the crowd, and I gritted my teeth at the way disdain dripped from her tone.

Arryn narrowed his eyes, but allowed Freya to defend herself. "As you surely must have noticed tonight, *werewolves* such as myself are perfectly capable of enjoying exclusively non-meat dishes. I must say, the feast tonight was truly magnificent, and I shall be enquiring with the chef if I may use his or her recipes in my own estate. I am confident many of my people would also glady partake of such delectable, *meatless* fare," Freya replied smoothly.

I admired how she'd complimented the hosting royal family, addressed the elf's concern, *and* added another reason for establishing diplomatic relations all in one answer. It was clear the elves would be happy if humans switched from eating meat-based to plant-based food because of their influence, so this solution even played to their pride.

I could see why Fenn had suggested his sister for the role of diplomat. Clearly, the previous duke and duchess had taught her well.

The elf pursed her lips, however, and I could tell that her real objective was to discredit Freya, for whatever reason. And sure enough, her next question bordered more on the accusatory side.

"How do we know our children will be safe on the night of the full moon, when all werehumans are forced to assume their *beastly* forms?" she asked, a light of challenge in her eyes.

"The werehumans already within this city seem to manage just fine. I see no reason why that should pose any more of a challenge to me than it does to them," Freya stated readily. "Besides, werehumans retain their sense of reason even on full moon nights."

I could tell the elf was growing more and more frustrated at the smooth and unruffled Freya. Addressing valid concerns was certainly important, especially since the rumors of the Verdania's nature had already started circulating. But I had the sneaking suspicion that the questions wouldn't remain civil for long.

"Hmph. And what possible qualifications do you have to be an emissary? No *thrall* has ever held a position of any sort in this court!" the noble spat, venom on her tongue and a look of triumph in her dark eyes.

Freya stilled, her pupils narrowing to slits. Her careful smile was frozen in place as silence descended. Before the building wave of tension could thunder through the room, Prince Arryn cleared his throat.

"It would seem, Lady Bryar, that you have not been listening." She flushed scarlet, her ears turning a bright pink. "Lady Verdania has been extensively educated by the former duke and duchess of Verdania. And clearly, Lady Verdania is no thrall. Such unseemly accusations are unbefitting of this court, and your rudeness violates the edict of respect given to an Elf Friend."

"But Your Highness, surely you can't mean that we are forbidden to question someone simply because of a title—" Lady Bryar started.

"Genuine questions are welcomed. Thinly-veiled efforts to discredit and malign, however, are not. Or are our esteemed guests meant to inform the rest of Cyrulia that the elves of Eldore are uncivilized and closed-minded?" Arryn asked slowly and coldly, emphasizing each word.

"N-no, of course not, Your Highness," Lady Bryar stammered as she bowed her head.

But I had a feeling her tongue would loosen when the crown prince wasn't around. Though if she were smart, she wouldn't open her mouth while any of us were around, either.

But that was what worried me.

I glanced at Reyna. She was biting her lip, worry clear in her eyes as she watched Freya's tight face. When she caught me looking, she nodded. We would be spending the rest of the night sticking close to Freya. After such a rough start to her diplomatic dreams, I didn't want to leave her alone.

Our final night in Varennia wasn't going to be as joyous as I'd hoped, but I knew that in time, such opposition would fade into the background. And Freya would go on to make a difference in the lives of many.

30

"Welcome home!" Aly exclaimed as she wrapped her arms around me. I smiled happily, grateful to be back in Verdania once more with everyone I cared about, including some new friends, like Reyna and Freya.

"It's good to be home," I replied. Only a few months ago, I'd never even known this place existed. But now, I couldn't imagine my life anywhere else.

"I want to hear everything! Leave nothing out," Aly said with a saucy wink.

I proceeded to tell her just about every juicy detail of the trip, though I glossed over a few of the more sensitive secrets. She was a little put out that I hadn't told her the real reason for the expedition before, but decided she'd forgive me in exchange for a very, very detailed description of Prince Arryn.

"He sounds positively dreamy," she sighed. I chuckled to myself.

"I hate to burst your bubble, but he only has eyes for Reyna," I reminded her..

"Oh, just let me daydream for a minute," she retorted.

"I *did* bring back more than just a story," I taunted, a wicked little grin curling my lips.

"Is it...something edible?" Aly asked.

"No, but it's the next best thing." I revealed a small book I'd kept in my bag, handing it to her with a flourish.

"What is this?" she gasped as she read the golden letters on the cover before reverently flipping it open and thumbing through the pages. She ran her fingers over the smooth parchment before looking up at me. "I can't believe you managed to get your hands on the cookbook of the elven royal family's pastry chef!"

"I do recall a certain *someone* helping me out of a rough spot in the Lindora castle who mentioned she would like it if trade and cultural exchanges with Eldore resumed," I stated. "You would have loved it, Aly. They had pastries and macaron flavors I'd never even heard of before!"

"Thank you so much, Serena!" Aly exclaimed, the corners of her eyes glistening. "Thank you for remembering."

"Now, this wasn't an entirely selfless gift. I am very much looking forward to tasting some of these desserts again!" I teased.

Aly laughed, the sound rich and full. "That can be arranged."

"Great, because I was thinking Freya could ask for a dinner cookbook next time. What do you think, should we swap recipes with our northern neighbors?" I suggested.

Her eyes lit up. "What are we sitting around for, then? I'd better get to work! I want to send over some of our best pastry recipes."

"Including one for cinnamon rolls?"

"Naturally."

With a smile and a wave, I left Aly to it and went to see how all of our new additions were settling in. Those who'd chosen to work in the Verdanian estate were given rooms in the old servants' quarters, and those who had just been looking for a new place to call home had been placed in Verdain. The coin to cover their first year of rent was coming from part of the reward the king had granted Fenn, as thanks for his help. I'd also insisted that the little house by the woods that I'd grown up in be used for the same purpose. It made me happy to think that someone else could make the place into a cozy little home, rather than leaving the building to sit empty and abandoned.

The place, no, the people here that held my heart had been such a welcome sight for sore eyes, especially after all of the new, harrowing experiences that had already started featuring in my nightmares. As soon as Bruce had laid eyes on our little caravan, he'd had everyone assembled, ready to help right away.

Though of course, that hadn't spared us from a tongue-lashing. I'd just accepted it as Bruce's way of telling us he'd been worried, and maybe missed us every now and then.

But that was nothing compared to when Aly, Wendy, Lily and Sophia had gotten their hands on me. Our sweet reunion had abruptly given way to a bombardment of questions and frantic scrambling over the state of my hair. But every nagging word had sounded like music to my ears.

Chris, Reyna and the others had gone off to help get everyone settled, as well as get some much-needed rest. Freya had been overcome with emotion at seeing her home once more, so her introduction to everyone had been put off until dinner. She and Fenn had gone off for a quick run through the forest, though they'd likely be returning soon.

As if he'd been summoned by my thoughts, Fenn appeared from around the corner, Freya by his side. Both had damp hair, as if they'd just finished washing up after their run. I faltered for a moment, wondering if I should give them some privacy, but when Fenn's gaze met mine, the warmth there left no doubt in my mind.

"How was your run?" I asked as I drew near.

"Much needed," Fenn replied.

"It's nice to be home," Freya said with a sad smile.

"It sure is," I agreed.

"There's something I wanted to show both of you," Fenn stated, offering an arm to each of us.

I took one arm and Freya took the other. Fenn led us through the rose garden and towards our training spot, but veered slightly closer to the building. Curiosity filled me, and I glanced at Freya, raising my eyebrows. She shrugged, just as clueless as I was.

My steps slowed when I noticed a huge, dusty sheet covering the space where the statue had been before The Incident. Fenn smiled mischievously at me, tugging me forward. Sure enough, Fenn walked right up to the hidden statue, which looked taller and wider than I remembered.

"I think you've tortured us long enough, dear brother," Freya said drily after we'd been standing silently in front of the veiled statue for a few minutes.

"Don't tell me it couldn't be repaired," I said a little nervously.

"I suppose Freya's right. And no, nothing like that. Never fear, I did not have them sculpt a monument to *The Incident*," Fenn teased.

"Don't ask," I muttered at the look Freya sent my way. The tips of my ears grew warm.

"I had something else in mind when I commissioned this." With one sharp tug, Fenn pulled the sheet off the statue, sending the fabric billowing to the ground.

By the time the stone figures were completely uncovered, tears were streaming down Freya's face. I felt my own eyes start to mist.

"Oh Fenn," I murmured, gently placing my hand on his arm. He smiled, but no words made it past the lump in his throat.

In place of the generic sculpture I'd accidentally destroyed during training stood a magnificent monument, a tribute to Fenn's lost family. One massive wolf stood tall, his head lifted proudly and defiantly. His mate sat beside him, her loving stone gaze trained on the wolf pup that played in the space between them. They were exquisitely carved, every tuft of fur in place. A single line of text was carved into the base of the statue.

The Light of Love Will Never Fade.

"It's perfect," Freya whispered, her voice choked with emotion.

"It's a beautiful tribute," I added.

Fenn nodded, his eyes riveted to the three wolves. I leaned against Fenn, offering my silent support. I could sense the melancholy and grief that filled his heart, and sent him my love and understanding through our bond. He took my hand, a wave of gratitude washing through him and into me.

Movement caught the corner of my eye, and I spotted Fenn's family butler, Harold, standing off to one side, his gaze also pinned to the statue. I narrowed my eyes in suspicion when I saw the expression on his face, a memory tickling the back of my mind, like an itch I couldn't quite reach.

But then everything clicked into place, memories connecting with stark clarity. The words Freya had spoken echoed in my mind, my own experiences with the man lending their support. Another suspicion took root, reminding me of how Prince Malakin had purchased Freya right before we'd gotten there, a fighter he'd shown no interest in previously. Or the crest in the broken wax seal on the letter that had been on his bedside table... Had it all truly been a coincidence?

How had I not realized it sooner? Then again, I'd been rather preoccupied lately. But how could I possibly tell Fenn and Freya? The wounds in their hearts that were just starting to heal would be ripped open once more.

I bit my lip, and Fenn glanced at me, sensing the dramatic change in my emotions. He followed my gaze, his muscles tensing when he saw what I did. The absolute loathing that twisted Harold's face as he glared daggers at the sculpture of the three wolves. Heedless of the tears streaking the grief-stricken faces of the two orphaned youths who were supposedly his masters.

I spoke the words with trembling lips, hoping I was wrong, but knowing that I wasn't. "Freya, what did you say about someone letting the assassins in that night? The traitor?"

Freya frowned, but answered anyway. "I do remember Lester bragging about the person he'd bribed to open the gates and distract the guards. I'd nearly forgotten—I buried all my memories of Lester and what he did to me, but...he did say that...that his inside man was...the werewolf-hating butler."

No sooner had the words left her lips than Fenn had closed the distance in an instant, his glowing blue eyes radiating fury and his fist tangling in the butler's tunic. The color had drained from Freya's face as the full implications of those words hit her, and after a moment we both hurried after him.

"Y-your Grace?" Harold stammered nervously, his hands waving in the air as if they were trying to use an invisible handkerchief to pat his perspiring forehead. The hatred I'd so clearly seen on his face had melted into a mask of mild concern and indignation.

"They trusted you!" Fenn growled, his livid face inches from the butler's. "*I* trusted you!"

"W-what is this about, Your Grace?" he tried again, his gaze darting between the three of us.

"Did you or did you not betray my parents by conspiring with Lester Lindora and allowing entry to the monsters that murdered them?" he ground out.

"That's preposterous! I would never do such a thing. Has that red-headed peasant filled your mind with lies?" Harold rushed to say, pointing an accusing finger at me.

Fenn went still, his eyes narrowing. He'd heard what we all had. Harold's heart rate had stuttered, increasing as the lies left his traitorous lips. Freya put a hand to her mouth, horror in her eyes.

"You should know better than to lie to a werewolf," I said quietly.

Harold's eyes widened a fraction before he dropped the act, his mask of careful concern melting away. In one swift motion he drew a hidden dagger from his sleeve, plunging it straight towards Fenn's heart. The silver blade glinted wickedly in the sunlight as it descended.

"Die, you monster!" he shrieked, a crazed look in his eyes.

Fenn easily caught the butler's wrist and tightened his grip. I heard a sharp crack as the man's wrist bone fractured, the dagger falling harmlessly to the ground. Fenn released his grip as Harold fell backwards, his wrist clutched protectively to his chest. Before the man could try to make a run for it, Fenn planted his boot on Harold's chest, pinning him down.

"Why?" Freya asked softly, before her brow furrowed in anger. "Why would you do this? We thought of you like family!"

"Monsters like you don't deserve to have a family! You don't deserve to even live!" Harold spat. "Not after what you've done."

"And what, exactly, did the big bad werewolves do?" I asked pointedly.

"They killed my daughter! What kind of monster would kill such a sweet, innocent little girl? She was my whole world," he sobbed.

"Fenn's parents killed your daughter?" I asked skeptically, glancing at Fenn. From what I'd heard of them, the former duke and duchess had been strict, but they didn't exactly sound like the kind of people that would go around killing humans. Their entire lives were dedicated to properly taking care of the people within their territory.

"No. But werewolves can't be trusted, not around regular humans. That's why the Hunters exist, to protect those foolish enough to trust such dangerous beasts!" he replied vehemently.

"What are the Hunters?" I asked, looking between Fenn and Freya. I vaguely recalled one of the tales Fenn had told me about the werewolf hunter being bitten by a Vulclaria. But were they still around in the present day?

"Hunters are humans that have organized around the common goal of eradicating werewolves from the face of the world," Fenn replied grimly. "Though my family hasn't encountered one in decades. They're fanatics that don't distinguish between the truly dangerous and the innocent."

"Lies! Our cause is noble! Since I was but a boy, I've saved countless lives from the claws of monsters, and prevented others from going down the same horrible path."

"So you were a Hunter before your daughter was killed?" Fenn asked quietly.

"My family have been Hunters for generations. My daughter would have made the finest Hunter, if only that damn wolf had just died quietly like all the others!" he proclaimed.

"Don't tell me...you brought your daughter with you when you went around killing people?" Freya gasped.

"Monsters. Not *people*. How else would she have learned the trade? The silver just didn't work fast enough," he spat.

"If a silver blade or arrowhead is embedded too deeply to be removed, the pain of the silver poison will drive a werewolf mad as he or she dies," Fenn said slowly. Then he started. "Don't tell me you missed the wolf's heart and watched him thrash around in pain until he got too close to your daughter!"

"He bit her. I had no choice!" Harold cried desperately. "I couldn't let her turn into a monster!"

I staggered, horror lancing through me. I met Fenn's eyes, the terrible truth of it all leaving me feeling numb and cold.

"You killed your own daughter so she wouldn't live on as a werewolf?" I whispered, stunned. His reaction to me, the way he'd been treating me since he got here suddenly made perfect sense. I reminded him of his daughter, a human girl who had been turned into a werewolf.

"What other choice did I have? I-I'm sure she understood," he stammered, though I could see the doubt in his own eyes.

"So killing your own child wasn't enough for you? You had to go and kill someone else's, too?" Freya asked coldly, her face filled with condemnation.

"The only monster in this scenario is you," Fenn growled, echoing the words I'd spoken to Lester.

"The only person you have to blame for your daughter's death is yourself, you murderer. That truth will never change, no matter who you point your finger at," I stated harshly.

"No! No, you're wrong." Harold denied it, hatred contorting his features.

I looked at Fenn as Harold continued his mumbling and ranting, denying what I think even he knew to be true. "What are you going to do with him?"

Fenn and Freya exchanged glances, and I could see the conflicted feelings there. On the one hand, Harold should face justice for what he'd done. On the other, they didn't want to risk what it would mean if they showed mercy to a man who would likely try to finish what he'd started.

Sudden inspiration struck me. "What if you leave his judgment and punishment up to the Vulclaria?"

"That's not a bad idea," Freya murmured. "They'd be able to tell better than us if he'll try to harm us or someone else again. Fenn?"

After a few moments of tense consideration, Fenn finally nodded. "We'll leave it to them."

We headed out for the Vulclaria's clearing immediately after checking Harold for more weapons, gagging him, and tying his wrists and ankles loosely together so he couldn't try anything else. The normally peaceful hike through the forest was tense and quiet.

When we finally arrived, Fenn shoved the Hunter to his knees in the middle of the clearing and we stepped back, leaving him to face his judgment alone. Every fox head turned towards us, crystalline eyes passing over the three of us and settling on the former butler. Silence descended, not even the birds daring to interrupt this ethereal soul searching.

After only a few moments, the winged foxes began to keen, their hackles raised and teeth bared. The young kits hid behind their mothers, while the males took to the sky and began circling above our prisoner. His eyes darted from fox to fox, sweat beading on his wide forehead.

Muffled screams rang out as the flock of Vulclaria descended, each one delivering a swift bite. Before the last one had flown away, Harold's body began convulsing, shudders running through him as his limbs contorted. His legs bent backwards, his arms shortening as claws ripped through his fingernails and gray fur sprouted from his rippling skin.

He grew a long, pink tail as his body rapidly shrank, his two front teeth growing longer and protruding from his shrinking mouth. His eyes bulged, pupils dilating until only beady black eyes remained in his pointed face. Whiskers grew from his cheeks, and his ears grew more rounded, moving up the sides of his head. Soon he disappeared inside his clothes, which slowly deflated.

And out he crawled, his character reflected in his new form.

"He makes one ugly rat," Fenn commented.

"It's kind of fitting how the hunter has become the hunted," I added drily. I felt a little shaken, seeing the Vulclaria like that. I much preferred their cute and cuddly behavior.

"I think it's past time we get a trustworthy butler," Freya said.

"Couldn't agree more. And I think I have the perfect person in mind," Fenn replied.

"What do you think of my choice?" Fenn asked me later that evening as we strolled through the forest, hand-in-hand.

"I think it will be good for Tim. Help him come out of his shell a little more." I smiled as I recalled the look on Tim's face when he'd learned of his appointment to the position.

"I'm glad you approve. He'll have much to learn, though, so I've been considering hiring a mentor for him, since we accidentally turned the only suitable teacher into a rat." He grimaced.

"We're better off without him. I can't say I ever cared for the man, but I'm sorry you lost someone you cared about," I said sympathetically.

Fenn sighed, looking off into the trees. A gentle breeze kissed my skin, bringing with it the pine and earthen scent that was unique to this forest. When he spoke, I could both hear and sense his frustration. "I feel like a fool for not seeing it."

"You couldn't have known, Fenn. He was so skilled at hiding his true thoughts that not even your parents realized. If Lester hadn't liked to monologue so much, we might never have found out his true intentions." Now it was my turn to sigh. I'd never thought that I'd feel even the slightest hint of gratitude for that man, but here we were.

"You always know just what to say," Fenn murmured as he pulled me into him. He wrapped his arms around me and pressed a kiss to the top of my head.

I rested my cheek on his chest, smiling even though he couldn't see it. "Right back at you."

We stayed like that for a while, simply enjoying each other's soothing presence, back in the place where we belonged. Eventually Fenn pulled away, cool air filling the space where his warmth had been. Summer was giving way to fall, and soon the leaves would regale us with their red, orange and yellow majesty. As we continued our walk, I found myself picturing a future where I could watch the seasons pass by his side.

"Fenn, I've been thinking," I started slowly, peeking at him from the corner of my eye.

"A dangerous pastime," he teased.

I bumped him with my shoulder, and was rewarded with his quiet chuckle. "I found it inspiring how the king and queen of Eldore work together to manage the kingdom, even if they're each responsible for very different things. So I was wondering if…if maybe while you're hiring someone to teach Tim, you could also hire a tutor…for me."

Fenn looked at me, an unreadable expression in his blue eyes. When he didn't say anything right away, I rushed to explain. "That way, if we could divide your workload between the two of us, you wouldn't end up exhausted and working through the night. It might take some time for me to learn everything, since I don't really know much when it comes to running an estate, but…but I'm positive I can learn. That is…if you don't mind me sticking around."

I looked down at my feet, biting my lip. The doubt that had been eating at me for weeks returned in a rush. I knew that Fenn cared about me, knew that my instincts had determined him my mate. But I was just a commoner. And worse, a fatherless commoner who'd taken her mother's maiden name. Could I truly stand by his side proudly?

Fenn tugged me to a stop, and I looked up in surprise to realize that while I'd been lost in my thoughts we'd arrived at Moonglen. The tranquil little pond was just as I remembered it, with the crescent moon reflected in the still, luminous water with moonflowers growing all around it. The only difference was that a handful of Vulclaria were chasing fireflies in the deepening darkness.

Fenn gently cupped my face with his hand, such a tender expression on his face that I could hardly stand it. "If you left, I would go with you. I have no intention of letting you go. I will follow you to the ends of the earth. And forget about hiring a tutor."

My heart, which had swelled with love at his words, deflated a little. "I know I didn't get much in the way of an education, Fenn, but I can still help you!" I frowned, shrugging out of his touch. Was he going to insist that he handle everything alone? Things would just go back to the way they were before, leaving us both frustrated.

Fenn laughed, and my scowl deepened. "You didn't let me finish! I was about to say that you should forget about getting some tutor because *I* will teach you!"

"You will?" I breathed, pink coloring my cheeks. I felt a little silly for misunderstanding and not letting him finish, but also happy that Fenn would be teaching me himself. That meant I'd be spending practically every waking moment with him!

He nodded, a look of excitement in his eyes. I beamed, already picturing the two of us working side by side. "Thank you, Fenn. I cannot wait!"

"Isn't that my line? I'm the one getting the help here," he teased.

"I suppose it is." I gave him a quick peck on the cheek, and was rewarded by the sight of the tips of Fenn's ears turning red.

Fenn took my hand and led me into the middle of the moonflowers, their glow painting us in a soft, silvery-blue light. The Vulclaria took notice and abandoned their game, flying over to investigate us. I was delighted to see that one of them was the little fox that had given me one of its feathers.

I giggled as it landed on my shoulder, and gently stroked its delicate head. It began to purr, the soft vibrations putting me at ease.

"Do you remember when we first met?" Fenn asked suddenly.

"I don't think I could ever forget." I chuckled, remembering that night. "Of course, I had no idea for a while that the wolf I saw here was actually you. I remember, you were watching me from right over there." I used my free hand to point across the pond to where I had seen his icy blue eyes peering at me from the darkness.

"That turned out to be quite the exciting night," Fenn added, a smile tugging at the corners of his mouth.

"That's one way of putting it." I laughed at Fenn's dry sense of humor. When we first met, I could have never guessed he had this hidden side to him. "But even if I could go back in time, I wouldn't change a single thing."

"Nothing?" Fenn asked, a hint of surprise coloring his voice. "Not even...what happened at Lester's?"

"Not even that. Because if it hadn't been for him I never would have met you. You made it all worth it." My honesty left me feeling a little exposed, but I didn't regret saying it. Not when Fenn was looking at me like I was the most precious thing in the world to him.

"I feel the same. Which is why...Serena, I have something to ask you." Fenn turned to face me fully, his dark hair falling across his forehead in a way that made my fingers itch to brush it aside.

Just then, my little fox gave a chirp and leaped into the air, the tips of its wings brushing my cheek. I watched it for a moment before turning back towards Fenn when I heard him move.

My heart froze in my chest when I saw Fenn on one knee in the moonflowers, a little black box held up in his calloused hands. A golden ring was nestled inside, a shimmering moonstone set as the center of the golden moonflower that bloomed from the band. I put a hand over my mouth as tears pricked my eyes.

"Serena LaRoux, would you do me the honor of becoming my wife?" Fenn asked, his icy blue eyes shining with love.

For a moment, time itself stood still, and not even the wind dared to interrupt us. Fenn had banished all my doubts with a single question, a question I'd been both fearing and dreaming of for a while now.

"Yes! Yes, a thousand times, yes!" I said around the lump in my throat.

Fenn rose and took my hand, slipping the gorgeous ring onto my ring finger. I stared at it in awe and disbelief, my heart so full and warm.

I couldn't put into words the joy I felt. Instead, I shared them through our bond.

I threw my arms around him, my fingers tangling in his dark hair. His strong arms wrapped around me, holding me close. His lips met mine, the broken pieces of our hearts fitting together like a puzzle, their jagged edges smoothed away by relentless waves of love.

And when I looked into his icy blue eyes, I saw a future filled with light and love. And I was going to treasure every moment.

Epilogue

This time, when I slipped into my elegant white wedding dress, it was with a smile on my face and love in my heart. A warm spring breeze wafted from the open window, lifting my lace veil, and setting my gauzy skirts aflutter.

"You look like an angel," Sophia said with a smile.

"No, I think she looks more like a princess," Lily argued. "Especially with all those jewels." She gestured to the iridescent emeralds that sparkled at my neck and wrists, in addition to the pearls that were stitched into the bodice of the dress.

"Thanks in no small part to all your hard work. I still can't fathom how you always manage to get it so soft and wavy." I ran my fingers through my red locks for emphasis, marveling at how it framed my face so well.

"Many hours of practice," Sophia replied, as she wove a handful of moonflowers through the veil and into my hair, connecting the two.

"I'm glad that this time, Wendy isn't still frantically making last minute adjustments. I'm excited to see which of her designs she's picked out for herself and the other bridesmaids, plus the maid of honor." I smiled to myself, picturing what state the other dressing rooms must be in by this point. I reminded myself to save some pastries for whomever would be tidying up afterwards.

"Very true. Though I have a feeling she's still doing some last minute adjusting on her own dress," Lily said with a chuckle.

"You make a very good point," I replied.

"It's nearly time, My Lady. Are you ready?" Sophia asked.

So much had happened since I first met Fenn that fateful night. We'd both been in danger too many times to count, and somehow come out the other side intact—for the most part. But I'd been ready for this moment longer than I was willing to admit, even to myself.

I took a deep breath, letting it out slowly. Lily handed me my bouquet, the familiar weight of my dagger hidden within the starflowers and moonflowers bringing me a sense of comfort. Unlike last time, I had no intention of using the blade.

But it just felt right to have Fenn's gift with me today. My very own good luck charm.

"I'm ready," I declared firmly, my spine straight and my head held high.

Freya, Reyna, Wendy, Chloe and Aly were waiting for me in the next room, each looking absolutely stunning.

"You have outdone yourself, Wendy," I complimented as I admired her dress.

I'd chosen emerald green and pale blue as the official colors of the wedding, and Wendy had done a marvelous job of weaving the two together. Each of my friends wore elegant, pale blue dresses with emerald embroidery in a floral pattern, with simple, matching emerald necklaces. Moonflowers glimmered, a small bunch tucked behind each girls' ear.

I could almost imagine that these were nymphs of the forest, come to wish me well on my special day. I already felt like I was floating on air, despite the slight hum of excitement and nerves in my core.

"All in a day's work," Wendy replied, but I could tell how happy she was at the compliment. I had a feeling she would be flooded with orders from the attending nobles by this evening.

Only Freya's dress was slightly different, the style sleeker than the others'. I had chosen her as my maid of honor, not only because I knew it would make Fenn happy, but also because we'd grown so close over the last few months. Freya had spent so much time helping me learn the ins and outs of managing a ducal estate, not to mention all of the manners and social etiquette I needed to know.

Of course, I'd also spent many happy days learning the paperwork side of things from Fenn. But there were some things only another lady could teach me.

"You look stunning, of course," Reyna purred, giving me an approving look.

"Beyond lovely," Chloe commented. She was the only noble from my time at Lester's that I'd grown close to, and I was happy we'd kept in touch, writing to each other frequently. I was glad that she'd accepted my invitation to be one of my bridesmaids again, even though the last time hadn't gone so well.

"My brother will practically swoon when he sees you," Freya added in a playful tone.

"Thank you," I said with a slight blush. "I think it's finally starting to sink in that I'm about to marry the love of my life."

"I love that for you," Aly said warmly, taking both of my hands in hers and leaning closer to whisper in my ear. "And I want all the juicy details later."

My cheeks burned a bright shade of scarlet that rivaled my hair. Aly winked at me, while Reyna wiggled her eyebrows and Freya looked distinctly uncomfortable. There was no such thing as whispering when it came to werehumans.

A fact Aly knew all too well.

Sophia cleared her throat. "As...entertaining as this is, I believe it is nearly time for the ceremony to begin."

"Let's get into position, ladies," Freya suggested. "We'll see you soon, Serena!"

And with that, my friends filed out of the room, heading for the altar. The guests should have all arrived by now. I fingered the golden crescent moon necklace that I'd kept hidden under the neckline of my dress, running my fingers along its smooth surface. My fingers itched to run along my soft Vulclaria feather, and it took me a moment to remember it was gone. But thanks to my sweet little fox, all of our living loved ones would be able to attend our wedding.

What greater gift could I possibly ask for? I tucked my special necklace away, nodding to Sophia and Lily. As I walked through the halls of the Verdania home for the last time as a LaRoux, I found myself pausing in front of Fenn's family portrait painting. When I first saw the boy in that picture, I never could have imagined I would soon come to know and love him as my mate. I reached out a hand to gently touch his painted cheek, his piercing blue eyes holding my gaze even now.

It saddened me that I'd never have the chance to know Fenn's parents or little brother. From what he'd told me of them, they sounded like kind and wonderful people, even if they'd been rather strict with their high expectations of him. I hoped they were watching over us today, so that they could see their living children reunited, and their son happily married to his mate.

I swept my gaze over the painting one last time before I moved on, the other paintings and suits of armor that lined the hallway now dust-free and shining. The repairs and renovations had gone smoothly, for the most part, so the estate had been returned to its former glory—just with new furniture and decorations.

When I stepped into the sunlight, Atlas was tacked up and waiting for me. His dark coat shone, and moonflowers festooned his silky mane and tail. His specially made ornamental bridle and saddle seemed a little ridiculous to me, but I still had to admit that he looked stunning.

Mr. Ranger was holding the high-spirited horse steady, his calming presence able to tame even the wildest equine. I'd never seen him wearing anything other than his work boots and trousers, but he looked quite respectable in his new formal attire.

"You look beautiful, Serena," he said warmly as he opened his arms.

"Thank you, Mr. Ranger," I replied as I gave him a hug. I'd never known my real father, but whenever I tried to picture his face, this man was the one that came to mind. "And thank you for giving me away today, even after everything I've put you and your family through."

"Oh sweetheart, none of that was your fault. I'm just glad we all made it out the other side of that storm in one piece. Besides, that old barn needed to be renovated anyway." His smile crinkled the corners of his chocolate brown eyes, filling them with a familiar kindness.

"Thank you for saying that." Then I smiled mischievously. "The next wedding you attend might well be Chris'."

"I can only hope," he chuckled good-naturedly.

Sophia and Lily helped me carefully settle into the saddle, so as not to tear my dress. I gave Atlas' neck a few gentle pats, and he tossed his head as if to say he was ready to go.

Atlas had brought me to Fenn that night, so it seemed only fitting that he should carry me to him now.

Mr. Ranger walked beside me as I directed Atlas across the grounds and towards the ceremony. With my sharp hearing, I could tell that all the guests had assembled, and the musicians were softly playing, the peaceful notes lingering in the warm air.

Fenn and I had decided to hold the wedding outdoors instead of inside of a grand church or cathedral. Neither of us had particularly fond memories of weddings in churches—after all, we'd both nearly died at Lester's hand that day.

It was a break from tradition, but we both wanted only happy memories of today, ones not tinged by the darkness of the past. And as the altar came into view, I had to admit everyone had done a fabulous job putting it all together.

Rows of cushioned seats were parted by a carpet of rose petals, leading to an archway covered in flowering vines, with moonflowers and starflowers interwoven throughout. A partial gazebo had been constructed behind the archway, reminiscent of the gazebo in the rose garden where Fenn and I had first met—in human form, anyway.

The royal families of both Cyrulia and Eldore were in attendance at the front, Arryn looking the part of the dashing prince, with the rest of the Rangers and some of our friends seated directly behind them. A few newer, but no less precious, faces were also present, those of the thralls we'd rescued who had chosen to stay, and who had become our friends. Mrs. Thompson sat among them, and I'd been so happy when she'd agreed to supply her largest ever batch of cinnamon buns for the reception. My mother sat next to her, her form still gaunt from the illness from which she'd slowly been recovering.

I'd made her promise to remain silent if she wanted to attend. Her betrayal still stung, but for some reason, I had the feeling that the love of those around me would lend me the strength I needed to forgive her someday, even if I never quite forgot.

My heart soared, seeing all of those precious to me present today. My gaze swept across each one, committing this scene to memory, one I knew I would cherish always.

My bridesmaids and maid of honor stood in a line on the left side of the archway, with the groomsmen and best man on the other. Tim, Danny, Jax and Chris seemed a little fidgety because of all the attention, but they cleaned up well. I noted that Chris could hardly take his eyes off of my maid of honor, a fact that surely hadn't escaped Mr. Ranger. And I hadn't seen Arryn look away from Reyna since I first spotted him.

But it was the person waiting for me at the end of the path of petals that really took my breath away. Fenn stood tall and proud, looking unbearably handsome in his decorated suit. His dark hair had been neatly combed, and pinned to his jacket was the blue brooch I had given him.

As if he could feel my eyes on him, he turned, his eyes meeting mine. The world around me went silent, my focus narrowing to two icy blue pools of love. He smiled, just for me, and I shyly returned it, sending my love ahead of me through the invisible thread that stretched between us. His smile widened, and I felt his joy flutter into my heart on the wings of a butterfly.

Movement caught my eye, and I nearly laughed aloud when I noticed that my little Vulclaria had hidden itself among the flowers, with only its sweet little face and emerald green eyes visible. I made a mental note to save it one of Mrs. Thompson's cinnamon buns.

The guests began to turn around in their seats as they followed Fenn's gaze, the music changing to a slower, sweeter tempo as I gently pulled Atlas to a stop at the edge of the path of petals. Mr. Ranger passed the reins off to another and offered me his hand. I took it, dismounting lightly onto the soft green grass.

As we walked down the aisle, in step with the slow beat of the music, it felt like my vision tunneled, the faces on either side of me blurring into a single tapestry of smiles and bright colors. It felt like that walk lasted both an eternity and the blink of an eye. Before I knew it, I was walking under the archway, the heavenly scent of the flowers infusing the space with an ethereal sweetness.

Mr. Ranger stepped aside as I took the last few steps to stand beside Fenn. For a moment, a flicker of the old doubt returned, making me question whether I should really be the one standing here, next to him. But the love in his eyes when he looked at me washed those thoughts away, leaving not a single wisp behind.

We turned as one towards the wedding officiant, whose white and black robes nearly touched the ground. The music quieted as the man cleared his throat and began to speak.

"We are gathered here today to witness and celebrate the joining of these two hands in sacred matrimony. Through great trials and tribulations they have persevered, and now look forward to cloudless skies and golden fields. Now, please face each other and join hands."

Fenn and I turned to face each other, calloused hand meeting calloused hand. I knew it wouldn't always be easy, but we were no strangers to hard work. I had faith that whatever storms came our way, we would weather them, together.

"Do you, Fenrys Verdania, take this woman to be your lawfully wedded wife, to live together in matrimony, to love her, comfort her, honor and keep her, in sickness and in health, in sorrow and in joy, to have and to hold, from this day forward, as long as you both shall live?"

His eyes were steady, unwavering. "I do."

"And do you, Serena La Roux, take this man to be your lawfully wedded husband, to live together in matrimony, to love him, comfort him, honor and keep him, in sickness and in health, in sorrow and in joy, to have and to hold, from this day forward, as long as you both shall live?"

My voice was firm, unfaltering. "I do."

"And now, for the exchange of rings and promises." Tim stepped forward, handing the rings to the officiant, who handed the first golden band to Fenn with a nod.

"With this ring I, Fenrys, take you, Serena, to be no other than yourself. I vow to always be your protector, your confidant, the partner of your soul. Loving what I know of you, and trusting what I do not yet know, I will respect your integrity and have faith in your abiding love for me, through all our years, and in all that life may bring us."

He slipped the smooth metal onto my ring finger, beside the moonstone one he had placed there that starry night, as he spoke the words. His love echoed through our bond with every word, an unspoken melody, a promise for my soul alone to cherish.

The officiant handed me the ring's partner, its mate. I ran my fingers over its smooth surface as I took my turn.

"With this ring I, Serena, take you, Fenrys, to be no other than yourself. I vow to be the guardian of your spirit, the challenger of your mind, and the safe haven of your heart. My soul will forevermore be your other half, bound by a love no weapon can break apart. My heart is yours, from this day forward, through every sorrow and success, for the rest of my days. You are my home, and I see my forever in your eyes."

I slid the golden band onto his finger as I spoke the words, my eyes never leaving his through my veil. I sent him my love, my secret vow, the kind that can only be made between two fated werewolves.

"By the power vested in me by the crown of Cyrulia, and with the blessing of Eldore, I now pronounce you husband and wife, and the new Duke and Duchess of Verdania. You may now kiss the bride." And with that, the officiant stepped back, his role fulfilled.

Fenn reverently lifted the veil from my face before his hand gently brushed my cheek. I leaned into his touch as we drew closer, closing my eyes as his lips found mine.

The future was uncertain, but I had the strangest, reassuring feeling that it would be filled with light and laughter, surrounded by our loved ones. Fenn and I still had so many things to experience together. I was looking forward to going on a real vacation with him. Going on more adventures with him. Fighting with him, loving him. Starting a family with him.

I would endure the pain that had brought me here a thousand times over so long as it led me to this single moment, when it felt as if our love had been written in the stars.

Because he was worth it.

And he was mine.

Thank you for reading Daughter of Wind and Moonlight! I hoped you enjoyed reading it as much as I enjoyed writing it. You can purchase Son of Fang and Fury, the whole story from Fenn's perspective, here: https://amzn.to/423SsiL

To be alerted when it is released, subscribe to my newsletter here: https://k-s-gerlt.ck.page/c4b596cf47

If you would like to read an exclusive, cut chapter of Daughter of Wind and Moonlight, order merch, see character art, and receive updates and release notifications for the next book, please sign up here: https://k-s-gerlt.ck.page/c4b596cf47

Also by K. S. Gerlt

The Werewolf's Mask Series

The Werewolf's Mask

Daughter of Wind and Moonlight

Son of Fang and Fury

Daughter of Steel and Strife

Son of Prejudice and Pride

The Werewolf's Mask Series Coloring Book

The Kingdom of the Stars Series

To Crush a Star

To Forge a Constellation

About the Author

K.S. Gerlt is an award-winning artist and the author of The Werewolf's Mask series. An avid reader herself, she has always loved diving into the magical worlds within books, from the classics to modern fantasy and adventure. She grew up in Southern California, where her pastimes include horseback riding, ice skating, and painting.